T0367888

MARS 2112

JOHN ASHCROFT-JONES

ARCHWAY
PUBLISHING

Archway Publishing books may be ordered
through booksellers or by contacting:

Archway Publishing
1663 Liberty Drive
Bloomington, IN 47403
www.archwaypublishing.com
1 (888) 242-5904

ISBN: 978-1-4808-4737-8 (sc)
ISBN: 978-1-4808-4738-5 (e)

Library of Congress Control Number: 2017907733

Print information available on the last page.

Archway Publishing rev. date: 05/24/2017

CHAPTER

1

JANUARY 6, 2112

THE STRAITS OF HORMUZ

The early morning sea soon would reach high tide. Max squinted into the seven o'clock sun, which was beginning its climb up through a hazy sky to reach its azimuth when the midday temperature was expected to be around 52 degrees Celsius.

The lethargic wavelets slapped against the flanks of the concrete breakwater, looking like a jumble of huge toy jacks protecting the dike that stretched into the hazy distance in either direction. From the top of the dike, Max gazed through dark-tinted, polarized sunglasses from under the rim of a cream linen Fedora, scanning the Gulf of Oman to the horizon. Nothing. They had not arrived. His eyes swept up and down, inspecting the water close to the breakwater. No sign of them.

He looked out over the Gulf of Arabia, its surface a

good five meters lower than the Gulf of Oman behind him. A flotilla of empty ships from several countries had formed in an orderly queue, each waiting its turn to enter the locks and to be floated up to sea level in the Gulf of Oman. Returning to their home ports to be refilled with all manner of merchandise for the gulf states, they went by sea. Fleet owners regarded them as the most fuel-efficient mode of transport. The ships' sails were rolled into their masts or yardarms, depending on the configuration of each ship's rigging.

It had been only fifty years since global warming had gone far past its tipping point. Then sea levels had risen rapidly and had been rising ever since. The battle against rising tides was not yet won, but he and his work were part of that battle. He had seen from space where the North Pole ice field once had been and which now served as one of the world's busiest shipping sea lanes.

A movement in the corner of his eye brought him back to the moment as he saw the shuttle train that ran along the dike coming into view through the heat haze a kilometer away. He made his way back to the station to catch it. He would ride it back to Ras Al-Khaimah.

The thought of space reminded him that he had only a few more days of vacation to enjoy on Earth before he went back to his job. He sighed and boarded the shuttle, which almost silently sped up to three hundred kilometers per hour on its superconductive maglev track.

Ann met him at his favorite local restaurant

near a place called Khasab that evening. Arabesque reception rooms led to indoor dining areas. A timber deck canopied with old Felucca sails looked out over the beach and the incoming surf of the Arabian Gulf. The tail of a recent shamal left the gulf's waters choppy under a steady, dry breeze. They arrived an hour before sunset with the intention of dining on some of the excellent local seafood.

"What do you fancy?" asked Ann when they were settled at a table.

"I'd like the barbecue menu so I can get into the holiday mood," replied Max. "Those huge prawns to start with, with grilled hamour, rice, and salad for the main. We can choose a sweet or cheese later."

The hamour, also known as reef cod, was a local variety of fish that had the curious life cycle of growing as female with the ability to change sex at maturity. A shortage of one sex could trigger this mechanism to work either way, ensuring that stocks could be replenished.

Ann agreed on the prawns to start. "Screw the cholesterol," she noted. Max smiled, and she settled for a red snapper with rice and trimmings for the main course. They ordered an ice bucket with a white wine from a new vineyard in Tierra del Fuego. A wine buff had even given Max the nod about his choice. Having ordered, they settled into martini aperitifs and chatted easily about their impending return to work in space.

They were sitting in a secluded part of the beach restaurant, which Max had carefully chosen for its proximity to the sea. They enjoyed the pleasant breeze, the end of last week's shamal, coming off the water and cooling them. The sound of the surf discreetly masked their conversation. Max had chosen a seat that afforded him a visual command of anyone who approached. He had good reason to be cautious.

Eight years before, his company, Aqua4, with its major project, Luna2, had won the contract with his seawater purification technology. There was no real competition, as his system was so radical that no earthbound technologies could compete. His victory had earned him a few enemies who were jealous of his success. Keen to learn the details of his system, they were constantly attempting to eavesdrop on his affairs, electronic communications, and employees in order to try to get any information on his business. This state of affairs was now a fact of life. Max suspected that if they discovered enough of his technology, his very existence might be superfluous to their requirements.

"So back to Luna2 in just four days," said Ann.

"Yes, we have a new consignment of piping to connect to the Vac-riser, more PolyAl and four Sun-pumps to install."

"Wow, that will make, say, another twenty-five thousand cubic meters a day." Ann furrowed her brow as she ran the numbers in her head. "That will mean another 9,125,000 cubic meters a year on top of our current production!" She smiled and then gazed into the distance. "And ...that makes a sphere with a radius of ..." She paused as she made some curious moves with her thumbs and fingers, which Max knew she called her hand abacus. "That's 129.6 meters!" she said and grinned happily.

Max, accustomed to her mental mathematical prowess, could only shake his head in amusement. He noted that Ann had mentally done the multiplication in a heartbeat yet again. God, he was so lucky to have her as his soul mate, lover, and partner in business and life. Brains and beauty, heart and soul, all wrapped in a treasured parcel full of wit and surprises. After six years with her, he was still smitten.

"Yes, dear, I'm sure you're right. Thank you," he said. "That is a good amount of water, but we've got to install the equipment first."

"And once the installation is complete, there is only the maintenance, which is minimal. And thanks to your technology, the energy is free!" Ann said, glowing. "All thanks to the Sun, the glorious Sun," she said. "I think the Egyptians had something when they worshipped Ra." She laughed.

"Ah, it's also thanks to the graphene tubing and the vacuum of space aided by my peristalsis-assisted tubes."

"The solar pumps will speed up the whole process," said Ann.

"Increased production can't come too soon. The Moon bases want more water sent up to them. They contacted me yesterday."

"How's their terraforming base getting along up there?"

"Dunno. They are pretty tight-lipped about that."

"Not surprised, with the Americans and Russians already established and the Chinese, Indians, and now the South Americans all entering the land-grab market." She shrugged.

"They all need our pure water," Max replied. "The Moon's reserves are limited, and until we can tap the stuff floating around our solar system, Mother Earth is the major source, our watering hole. On top of that, the solar water-cracking technology that gets lovely hydrogen and oxygen separated economically on a large scale is booming—all of which will boost demand for our pure water."

"Yes," Ann agreed, "water, pure water, is the key to everything."

They paused in their conversation while they split open the grilled barbecue prawns the size of small lobsters and inhaled their smoky, garlic-tinged, and spicy tang.

"Yummy," Ann said.

"Mmmm, the best in the area. Old Saddiq gets 'em daily from the fishermen who keep their boats in the next bay."

One of the few welcome effects of rising seas was a resurgence of marine fish populations. The fish, with the newfound flooded lowlands, now enjoyed vast new areas of relatively shallow waters, which the warmth and increased sunlight had turned into rich feeding and spawning grounds for many species.

The global fish population, therefore, had recovered

from its sadly depleted state of the 2020s, when numbers had reached critical levels all over the world as a result of overfishing, mismanagement, and pollution. Whole tracts of the world's oceans had become dead zones with no life at all, either animal or vegetable. The Great Barrier Reef, the marine equivalent of the Amazon rainforest, was now an underwater desert. Mercifully, the fish population had bounced back elsewhere and had returned to the menu.

"I was out on the dike today."

"Oh, yes? Did you see them?"

"No, I may go out again tomorrow and have another look," Max said. "Have you finished your research? Want to join me?"

"Yes, and oh, yes!" Ann said, enthused. "Shall we take the rib and our scuba gear?"

"Yes, that would be great. We only have four days left before takeoff, so why don't we spend the day on the water, camp overnight on one of the islands, and maybe spend our last days on the water too. If we are out on the water all day, our chances of seeing them would be much better. The breakwater with its overgrown jacks are home to some really good fish. Maybe we could catch something for lunch and supper. Pack some salads in the icebox, bread, water, and wine, and we will be well set up."

"Lovely idea," Ann said, glowing. "It seems like ages since we roughed it like we used to."

"Yes, work seems to have taken over our lives," Max agreed. "It's settled then. The only thing I have to do is switch on the compressor for the tanks before bed, and we can grab the rest in the morning."

With tomorrow's plans decided, they tucked into the main dishes with keen appetites, finished up with a trio of cheeses—Roquefort, Brie, and Camembert— with fruit accompanied by the excellent wine. They finished with coffee, chocolate mints, and Arabian sweets.

"Wow, I'm tight as a tick," Ann said and smiled as she settled into the autopiloted, electric runabout they used for the rough, off-road terrain of the northern United Arab Emirates.

"Yes, Saddiq did us proud," Max agreed while flipping on the autopilot and letting the four-by-four take them home. Home was one of the few places Max owned scattered around the globe, usually chosen for either their outstanding location or proximity to a launch pads to take him to his work. This particular home was a modest two-bedroom villa on one floor with a pool and four-car garage sitting on a hectare of land perched on the cliffs overlooking the Arabian Gulf.

Presently, the car came to a halt in its allocated garage and switched off. The charging plate under the car switched on, lighting an indicator in the car. The villa, meanwhile, having been alerted by the car's arrival at the security gate, was now at its preset temperature, and the lights were on inside and out. Intruder defenses all over the premises were aware of its owner's presence. The couple entered the main living space, which looked over the sea from a height of 240 meters.

"Zon, shower," said Max to the house computer, whose voice recognition knew Max and obligingly slid open the bedroom and shower doors and set the water temperature. "Zon, breakfast at 0530 and pump the scuba tanks."

"Copy," confirmed Zon.

Ann was in the kitchen area.

"Want a nightcap?"

"Okay, what do you fancy?"

"Cocoa, with a shot of Crème de Cacoa for me please, and you?"

"Same here," replied Max, grinning with pleasure.

Ann knew that grin and said, "You bring the nightcaps. I'll jump into the shower before you."

"Okay see you in a minute."

Max busied himself with the nightcaps and brought them into the bedroom on a platter with some dark chocolate mints.

Goddess Ann emerged from the shower with skin glowing, bobbed hair slightly mussed, and eyes sparkling. The effect on Max was immediate.

Sometime later they fell asleep, nightcaps hardly touched.

JANUARY 7

Before dawn the next morning, they were awakened by the smell of coffee and hot pain-au-chocolats made by Zon.

After they dressed for a day on the water, they ate breakfast and hitched the "Rib" to the four-by-four, having packed the boat's freezer. Max included a case of his favorite beer and wine along with five seventeen-liter flagons of mineral water to join the fruit and salads and some fresh baguettes. There was permanently a range of condiments, herbs, spices, sauces, and relishes with the cooking equipment aboard. The Rib was always kept in a state of constant preparedness, as both Max and Ann were keen on water sports.

They were on the road by 0615, heading for the Oman Gulf side of the dike. Twenty-five minutes later they were on a beach about ten kilometers south of the dike.

Max unhitched the rib, and cranking a handle, the two carbon fiber hulls spread apart to give a catamaran with a beam of four meters. Being eight meters long, the two pontoons were indeed *"Ribs"* inasmuch as they had rigid hulls, but the skipper could draw on large buoyancy tubes at the throw of a lever, one that came out of slots, airbag fashion, just below the gunnels. This gave massive extra emergency flotation, but it was not normally deployed, leaving two sleek hulls with a trampoline net between for normal use.

When towed, the Rib ran on its own rear wheels. When unhitched, steerable front wheels made a functioning vehicle. Max easily winched up the light eight-meter-high aerofoil carbon mast, which housed a Kevlar sail that unrolled when the mainsheet was hauled in, making for a single high-performance sail five meters wide at the foot. There were additional sails, a storm jib, and a gennaker for added safety and performance if needed.

Ann had sent the four-by-four back to the villa so there was nothing more to do but get aboard and winch in the mainsheet. The Rib quickly picked up speed and was soon shooting along the beach toward the dike. The beach started to get rocky, so Max steered for the sea and skimmed onto the water at fifty knots, which slowed to eight knots until Max, leaning down, threw a lever that released the two front wheels, which sprung up into the hulls, and a counterbalanced dagger boards dropped down. Throwing another lever, the rear wheels also came up into the hulls, and counterbalanced rudders engaged the water. Thus, the sand yacht effortlessly became a sailing catamaran.

"All I have to do now is complete my design and make this baby fly as well," joked Max.

"You will." Ann grinned.

"Not sure I want to," he replied. "What with the solar panel decks and all the built-in gizmos, this old gal has been a good test bed, but if I start chopping her around any more, she might start to complain. Anyway, the hulls were never designed for flight. Having said that, I like the idea. Give the sucker submarine capability while I'm at it."

"See." Ann smiled knowingly. "Remember that jet motorcycle you made that could fly?"

Max winced at the memory. "Damn near killed myself too."

The only problem with such a devoted and adoring partner was she was utterly convinced he could design anything he wanted, he mused.

"Will you keep an eye out for them?" he asked.

"Yes, but I think it may be too early."

"Yes, maybe. Do you want to get kitted up? We will be at the dike in a few minutes."

"Okay." She dropped into the port hull and soon popped out in a new yellow bikini with her diving kit. Max sighed at the sight.

"Take the helm while I go below." He also dropped into the hull and then came back on deck, ready to dive.

"See where the breakwater sweeps out into the gulf to house the locks? We will stay away from there and drop anchor about a hundred meters off the breakwater."

The catamaran was now "hull up" with one hull airborne in the stiffening breeze, and skimming along on a broad reach soon covered the eight kilometers to the dike.

Dropping anchor, the boat settled to the easy swell as they slipped into the water and dived to two meters, where they could see the pre-inundation shore level below them. Small fishing huts, a wharf and jetty, a few abandoned vehicles, and several old fishing boats gave a surreal tableau when seen through a veil of dappled sunshine. Schools of fish of all shapes, colors, and sizes swirled back and forth. Beds of seaweed and soft coral covered the seabed, which had been barren desert

before. It now had a green lushness it had hitherto
never enjoyed.

They swam along the breakwater, the concrete
fingers of the giant concrete Jacks now barely
recognizable being so covered in weed and coral. It
was plain to see the attraction for the fish. The whole
food chain was there, all thriving and eating each other.
Such was nature.

Max reflected that when *they* came, all this would
be thrown into turmoil.

Ann was poking around the Jacks with the trident
of her harpoon gun. Doubtless she was thinking of
lunch, just another foreign element in the food chain.
As long as there was no grumpy moray in there! They
grew to four meters, thick as her slender thigh, with
an evil maw of razor teeth. They were to be avoided.
Normally shy but ill-tempered and territorial, many a
diver can attest to their ferocity, and many of those
who had ventured to hand-feed them had lost fingers.
Their rear-curving teeth making it difficult to free
oneself once the beast had latched on.

Max felt a protective pang. He stifled the thought
but could not help thinking what he would do if he lost
her. God, he loved her!

He swam over, pretending to himself he was not
afraid for her. She was a tough little thing and was a
strong and experienced diver. She knew the dangers
and had come through her fair share of scrapes. But
the sea is an unforgiving mistress, whether in it or on it.

A low throbbing came to them. Ann looked at

him. He gave the diver okay sign, having identified the throbbing as the sound of a ship's auxiliary propeller. One of the locks must have opened to deliver a ship into the Gulf of Oman. Doubtless, there would be two or three more following from the huge locks. This may be a good sign because fish were often frightened away from the gates, and they could expect some good catch to come their way.

Max checked his air gauge. *A quarter used*, he noted. *Plenty at this depth.* There was no fear of decompression (the bends), as they were too shallow to be affected. No, he was not worried on that score. What was it then? Why had this nagging unease come over him, this worrying about Ann, and this intangible sense of foreboding?

All was well, he convinced himself. He tapped his tank to attract Ann's attention as they had an old-school minimalist kit and motioned to the surface. She nodded and swam upward. They met in the sunshine, and Max checked their position relative to the boat, which bobbed peacefully seventy-five meters away. All was okay. Half a kilometer away, they could see the ship they had heard slowly moving away from the dike and unfurling her sails. Soon she would be under sail, and her throbbing would stop. Max could see no other ships in the locks. Reassured, he was ready to continue and bag some lunch.

"Honey, we forgot to put down the lobster pots!" cried Ann.

Max laughed with growing good humor, his apprehensions evaporating with the morning haze. The day was now bright, and his head could feel the growing heat of the day. It was good in the cool of underwater, but the thought of lobster rekindled his intention to get something for lunch … and dinner for that matter. With the morning's exercise, he could feel he was working up an appetite.

"Let's get some live bait and set them now," he said. "With any luck, we will get something for dinner. I don't see lunch as a being a problem. We could spear any number of these snapper or hamour."

"That's what we had last night."

"True, we are spoiled for choice. How would milady fancy a sea bass, kingfish, or even a ray?"

"Great." she said, and they dived down and made their way back to the boat, having speared a small fish, which, whilst not qualifying as *live* bait, having been impaled by all three barbed prongs of Ann's spear, was nonetheless suitably bloody and gutsy to attract any passing lobster. The pots baited and set, they went down again to finish their diving.

They spent the rest of the morning following the wall of the breakwater and only took one fish, a monkfish, which was all they needed. Indeed it was more than enough for two, so they went back to the boat. It was now 12-30, and having been in the water so long, they had a hearty appetite.

An island lay about five kilometers to the south, so they upped anchor and empty lobster pots and sailed over while Max cleaned the monkfish. It was he who had spotted and speared the fearsome fish.

"Ugly brutes, aren't they?" observed Ann, who had eaten them in the past but was unaware what the whole fish looked like.

"Sure are," Max said and smiled. "But damn good to eat. Cooks love 'em. A good chef can dice up one of these brutes and serve it up as scampi. The flesh texture and taste is similar, and with a good sauce, it is a commonly used substitute."

"I seem to remember something like that. I am sure I had some of this *scampi* before when my equally poor flatmate miraculously produced it. Along with Thousand Island dressing, which I knew was a tomato sauce and mayo mix. I knew there was a catch. She gleefully confided she got the recipe from her sous chef ex-boyfriend."

"It is a lot of fish for surprisingly little meat. The brutes are all head as you can see, with a mouth that could swallow a football. Once that grotesque head is gone you are in business, and the meat is so good." He laughed. "If any of those girls who adore scampi saw the fish they were eating, they would probably faint."

"Bet you would be the first to show them." She laughed.

Max just smiled. He baited the pots with chunks of the monkfish head. When they reached the island, they sailed around, and finding a suitable cove with a beach in the lee of the island, they dropped the pots alongside some rocks. Having beached the craft on the sand, they put on some protection from the sun. Max rigged up an awning onshore and donned a dish-dasha and Keffiyeh. Ann wore a long white flowing muslin dress with a broad-brimmed floppy hat. Both took sunglasses kicked on sabots and went ashore to eat.

Max foraged for firewood and soon had a bed of charcoal for the skewered fish to be grilled. Ann spotted some samphire among the waterside rocks, destined to be blanched and drizzled with some ghee and served with the skewered monkfish. Ann made a piquant sauce for the fish. With the samphire, baguette, olives, salads, and cold beers, she made up lunch under the gennaker canopy Max had rigged up. They ate and drank leisurely, rested an hour, and went to explore.

Toting his camera, which doubled as a powerful telescope, Max guided them up the side of the hill that made up the south side of the island. Climbing the boulder-strewn slopes, they came upon an oddly shaped tree.

"That's a very strange tree, but quite beautiful," said Ann, who had been squinting at it for a few moments. "It's kinda alien, weird. What is it? Do you know?"

"It's a dragon's blood tree. I thought they only grew on Socotra," observed Max, somewhat puzzled. "Mind you, this island is pretty similar. They are prehistoric, a throwback. As I say, I thought they we unique to Socotra. Their sap is blood red. Hence the name, its claimed in folklore to have all sorts of medicinal properties."

Socotra, which is at the western end of the Arabian Sea off the horn of Africa, is an island that has been isolated for thousands if not millions of years and could be mistaken for another planet. Like Madagascar, its isolation from mainland Africa had produced some unique flora and fauna.

The summit gave a panorama of the Omani shore, the dike, and the Gulf of Oman. More ships had appeared out of the horizon. Their sails were full and masts tilting slightly, a sight that would be familiar to seamen of three centuries before. Until, of course, the ships pulled closer where the fact they carried sails was one of the few similarities to the old square riggers.

These modern marvels were four hundred meters long with displacement to match. Their hulls were aluminum with towering masts of carbon. Their rigging was a rope derived from synthetic spider's silk. The sails themselves were made up from fabric derived from fossil oil, which was now deemed too valuable a resource to simply burn (not to mention the practice's bad press as one of the contributing factors to high sea levels). Their decks had solar panels that, together with wind generators, charged batteries that ran the electric impellor jets in and around the harbor plus all the power systems.

The couple scanned the horizon.

"Still no sign of them," Ann noted. "May I borrow the camera?"

"Sure." Max passed it to her, and she squatted and extended the monopod to steady the image at maximum zoom. She proceeded to study the sweep of horizon, flipping between the various filters to correct for UV, haze, and glare. "Mmmm, no sign."

"Maybe tonight or tomorrow," Max ventured. "Hard to tell with them. They could appear anytime."

They spent an hour at their vantage point and then returned to the boat and went for another dive. The air tanks were topped up from the boat's compressor. The water, although warm, felt refreshingly cool compared to the burning heat of the afternoon. The beach shelved down to about four meters deep, and then there was a steep drop-off to unseen depths. They followed the edge of the drop-off.

The underwater seascape was completely different to the man-made environment of the dike and the sunken fishing village. This was all natural. After all, this was already an island before the sea rise. They engrossed themselves in the new undersea abundance. Max's thoughts drifted as they hung immobile in the water.

Two meters above the seabed at the edge of the abyss to their left, they let themselves be carried along by a steady two-knot current over the ever-changing undersea panorama.

Max's mind, while aware of the tableau passing below him, was preoccupied. This morning's sense of foreboding had returned, and he could not isolate the cause. Something was nagging at his subconscious. All seemed normal, idyllic even, which made it all the more strange. He could not ignore it, however, but he put it aside for the moment. He would discuss it with Ann this evening.

Then he motioned to Anne to check her air. They were down to a quarter of a tank each and agreed to return to base. The current had taken them in an eddy almost around the island as Max had mentally calculated. So they surfaced, checked their position, and carried on around the island under their own power for the first time during the dive.

Presently, they rounded their cove, and passing where they had dropped their pots, they were pleased to find just one huge lobster in one of the pots, feeding on the monkfish head. They bagged it and took back to the beach, leaving their pots to sit overnight.

That evening came at around 1730, and nightfall swiftly followed. They rinsed off the salt water in the shower on the boat and changed into casual evening wear of shorts and T-shirts.

Ann busied herself with the cooking on Max's charcoals. They often reversed roles, but they agreed that Ann's way with lobster was the best.

She put on a pan of water and rinsed the salads while the covered pan of three parts water and one of basmati heated. Next, she put about five centimeters of water in another pan and put it on the coals. She wandered down to the water's edge and chose a large smooth and flat stone and a smaller pebble the size of a golf ball. She rinsed them in the sea and came back with them and the lobster. It had been kept alive inside the net in the water. She put the stones by the coals to dry and picked up the lid. She reached into the net and grabbed the lobster behind the head and popped the victim's head first into the pot, swiftly followed by the lid.

She held down the lid and paused. One or two seconds later, the lobster complained bitterly, exploding into action. It thrashed furiously and *screamed*. The pot clattered noisily for a few moments, and then all was quiet. She let go of the lid, stood up, ran a few steps on the spot, wiggled her bum, squeaked, giggled, flapped her hands, and gave Max a mischievous sidelong grin.

Max had been observing this pantomime.

"You're evil," he said and smiled.

"Not," she said, still grinning. "Most humane way to do it."

"Ask the lobster," he replied "Oops, too late!"

In twelve minutes she rescued the lobster and pulled out one of its tentacle to test it was cooked. It was now bright red, so she put it on a plate to cool. She now went about getting the salad ready. That done, she tackled the lobster.

She cracked all the parts open using her two stones. She used the lobster water to cook some fresh samphire for a few minutes and used the remaining stock to make a bisque. She then broke the beast in two, separating the head from the tail. Next came the claws, and finally, the legs were broken down to component parts. She now cracked the claws and legs with her two trusty stones and separated the meat into a bowl. She was then left with a heap of dismembered parts, more or less cleaned of their meat. These parts went into the bisque, and she added dried herbs and seasoning.

She cut the lobster tail lengthwise and then deveined it. Fresh samphire was drizzled with lightly salted ghee. She separated two eggs and whisked the whites into the bisque. In a bowl she beat the yolks with a fork, slowly adding her best virgin olive oil, drop by drop at first until she had about one and a half cups worth of mayonnaise, to which she had added a clove of crushed garlic.

The basmati had been cooked in three parts water, and so it did not need draining. She served everything on one large platter.

"*Et voila!*" she announced. "*Tout est prêt.*"

"Wonderful," said Max, who had been watching her in anticipation of the treat.

They stacked wood on the fire which being tinder dry, leapt into flame.

They took a quick shower together on the boat's trampoline, donned silk kimonos, and settled down to eat with a bottle of cold white wine. Max felt so at peace that his unease earlier that day was forgotten. Indeed, he wondered why he ever had such misgivings.

Later that night the stars came down to meet them as they lay together on a futon on the webbing between the two hulls of the rib moored fifty meters offshore.

Given the circumstances, loving came naturally, leaving them gloriously sleepy. Both drifted wordlessly into peaceful sleep, lulled by the gentle movement of the boat, the slap of wavelets, and the song of the cicadas from the shore.

JANUARY 8

The lovers slept, limbs entwined under the mosquito net strung from the rigging. Although on the sea there were few insects, the netting made a personal, cozy boudoir. While they slept, there were subtle changes taking place during the dark hours.

The cool of the night together with the high humidity condensed the water vapor, creating a sea fog that clung to the surface of the water and stole toward the island, and created an impenetrable veil, deadening sound and cutting visibility to a few meters. The breeze had stopped. The water, seemingly flattened by the weight of the fog, became smooth and undulated to a slow pulse. The sea monster was sleeping.

Later into the night, Max stirred. His subconscious recorded the changing movement of the boat. He slowly opened his eyes and saw nothing. Noting the total darkness and the absence of starlight, he lifted the hem of the mosquito net and peered out. The moisture of the fog on his face, he recognized immediately and explained the absence of light. He thought for a moment. Weighing the situation and deciding there was no threat, he shrugged and rolled back on the futon. Anne stirred and murmured.

"Mmmm, wazzup?"

"Nothing love, just a bit of fog. The sun will burn it off in the morning."

"Nnnnnn, yes." She snuggled and went back to sleep.

They slept till dawn when a pink milky glow awoke them. The fog was still thick around the boat, but all was quiet, so they decided to make breakfast aboard. Max volunteered and got up. Still naked, he gave a loud whoop, took six bounds along the rib's net, and plunged into the sea. He stayed underwater, doubled back to the boat, swam under the starboard pontoon, and exploded out of the water under where the futon was unrolled on the net. With both hands, he shoved hard vertically. The futon with Ann languishing on it shot skyward. She shrieked and fell back onto the futon with peals of laughter.

"You're bat-shit crazy," she said and gasped. "a bloody certifiable loon." Then she succumbed to more fits of laughter.

Grinning, Max hauled himself out, toweled himself down, and got busy with breakfast.

He raided the boat's larder. He found oats, powdered milk, raisins, dates, nuts, and a block of dark chocolate. He made up a liter of the milk powder and put one cup of oats and two of milk on a low heat on a gas ring. Stirring as it gently bubbled, he added the nuts and dried fruit. He had put water on to boil on the other ring while chopping a banana and shaving flakes of chocolate. The boiling water went onto java coffee grounds in a cafétière, and he served up the porridge while it steeped.

The shower, which hung over the trampoline net from the rigging, was a thirty-liter black plastic bag with a tap and a screw-on sprinkler rose. Ann used it before she went below to tidy up and dress in a fresh white bikini.

He gave her a call, and she emerged, glowing and bright said-eyed.

"Coffee smells good. I caught a whiff below."

He pushed down the strainer plunger of the cafétière. They sat on deck to eat breakfast and drink their coffee.

"These dates are lovely."

"So they should be. They're the Emirate's finest" said Max.

"What about this fog?"

"Should disperse in about half an hour. I've noticed it is thinner already," said Max "I suggest we motor south on the batteries till its clearer and find the morning breeze to sail."

"Great! I was hoping you would not suggest diving just yet after just taking my shower."

"Yes, we will explore a bit first and dive when it gets hot. Okay by you?"

"Perfect. Thanks, love."

Weighing anchor half an hour later and running on the near silent electric impellors, they soon saw the fog burned off by the sun. Away from the lee of the island, they soon found wind too. Max cut the motors, hauled the mainsheet, and they were soon rushing along at eight knots. The boat relaxed under the sail, moving with the gently rising swell. The only sound now was the lapping and gurgling of the water as it passed under the hulls.

Max rounded to a bearing of 190 degrees to take them SSW along the Omani coast. The north of the Emirates is shared with, and borders Oman. Fujairah is the only Emirate on the east coast facing the Arabian Sea. The two countries have relaxed and friendly relations, and borders are a formality among locals. Many cross them on their daily commute.

They were soon sailing at ten knots, and at 1030, they were off Leema Rock and anchored on the north coast in thirty meters of water. They were close by the rock, and as the wind was steady from the south, the boat quietly bobbed on the gentle swell.

They dived for ninety minutes and explored the submarine wall of the rock. The whole area is renowned for its fish, and they were surrounded by all varieties with an abundance of seaweed and coral. Max kept them to a maximum of five meters deep to avoid the need for decompression. In any case, the sunlight and colors glowed at their best at this depth.

He turned on his small underwater video camera and filmed Ann as well as the fish. She was naturally photogenic, and she knew it. Playing to the camera, she took off her bikini, and unashamedly natural, she swam around with the large fish. A *real water nymph*, Max thought.

Returning to the boat, they fished with hand lines

for fun and hooked a few fish, keeping just one sea bass for lunch. Ann cooked the fish by wrapping it in seaweed, steaming it with herbs, and serving it with cucumber, tomatoes, shallots, Ann's vinaigrette recipe, pitta bread, and hummus. They ate under a sail canopy and drank ice-cold beer.

The electric freezer Max considered an essential piece of equipment aboard in this climate (if only for his beer), allowing food to be kept cool or frozen. It ran off the batteries, which in turn were charged by the solar panel decks and a wind turbine. It had a large insulated portable plastic box that could be removed from the freezer unit for picnics away from the boat. It was one of Max's designs as he couldn't find anything suitable on the market.

They pulled up the anchor at about 1400 and set off back toward their island, leisurely exploring the rugged coast and coves on the way. Running before the wind, they felt no breeze, and movement through the water was nearly silent.

Ann stared at the water from where she was lying on the bow as Max took the helm of the boat. She suddenly sat up and pointed.

"There, there, *there*, Max. Look! Look! They're here!" she pointed off the starboard bow.

Max looked in that direction, shielding his eyes.

"Yes, I believe you are right," he said after a moment scrutiny. "Well spotted."

All that could be seen was the ruffled surface of the water as though there were upwelling currents.

A flying fish hit the sail and then dropped, flapping helplessly onto the net. Two more closely followed by two more.

"That's dinner," Max said, eyeing the delicious fish.

Yes, Max was sure they were here. All the signs were there. They had awaited the arrival of the sardine run for days. The spectacle was well worth experiencing.

The rising seas and temperatures with the reshaping of the world map had meant a resurgence and redistribution of fish types. Schools of dolphins moved up the coasts of India, Pakistan, and Iran, chasing shoals of sardines, corralling them into huge underwater balls of frightened fish and then rushing in and devouring them by the ton. It was a frenzied food fest that also attracted predatory fish and sharks.

What Ann had spotted, Max knew, was the sardines swimming for their lives with the dolphin following. The fish were being driven up to the barrier formed by the dike where the Gulf of Oman narrowed and the Strait of Hormuz was blocked. This was now a cul-de-sac. The sardines were trapped in a killing ground.

Scores of seabirds flew overhead. Gannets and pelicans were attracted by the signs of the approaching schools of sardines, and were diving to pick off unwary fish, all adding to the mounting frenzy. They joined the bonanza, also feasting on injured fish and detritus left over by the dolphin's orgy of killing.

Ann was excited. She jumped around the trampoline net, squealing in delight, picking up flying fish and throwing them back in the water. Avoiding getting a painful hit from the flying projectiles, she bounced around from fish to fish, laughing and giggling as she grabbed the flapping fishes. Still a little girl at heart, her mood was soaring in anticipation of the spectacle to come.

Max sailed north on a bearing of 10 degrees to bring them back to their island, accompanied by the sardines on the flight to their doom.

They were approaching the island as the sun was about to set. The water was now thick with sardines. Ann was now in a high state of excitement. Many birds were wheeling and screaming overhead in anticipation. Flying fish hit the sail and flapped around on the net, and Ann was laughing in delight.

Sailing the last few kilometers to the island, the sun dropped into the sea, and for a second the red glow of evening sunset was suddenly replaced by a lurid green light, everything turning green in a phenomenon known to sailors for centuries and traditionally surrounded by folklore.

Surprised, Ann suddenly stopped her antics and stared at Max.

"Wazzat?" she said and trembled "What's that, honey?" She looked fearful, eyes and mouth open wide, her face a ghoulish green, high excitement suddenly changing to fear.

"What. Is. That?"

"That's Neptune rising from his lair," Max answered matter-of-factly, suppressing a slight smile. "He always announces his arrival like that."

Ann squinted at him for a moment in the green glow, and then a grin slowly spread across her face.

"You rotter," she said, wrinkling her nose. "You had me going there ... but only for a moment."

He explained the phenomenon, which had now faded, lasting only a few seconds.

"Oooooh! That's wild. I *like* said green flash, that optical phen ... om ... non."

"Phenomenon," Max helped her out. She was still jittery.

"Yes, I really like that," she said, her sudden fear passing.

"We are privileged to see it. It is rare to see it so pronounced." Max marveled at the wonders of Mother Nature, though not for the first time.

"When we have a quiet evening aboard, I'll tell you about Saint Elmo's Fire. That really used to spook out the old sailors in the seventeenth and eighteenth centuries."

"I like spooky." She grinned.

Max smiled and imagined a fireside night while a storm raged outside their cottage, telling stories of old sailing lore.

Night had fallen, but they easily found their cove in the dark by GPS and anchored at 1930.

The water was busy with undersea activity. The agitation was palpable. They decided to go have a look. They equipped themselves with powerful torches. Max had his underwater camera, and Ann had her harpoon gun. Then they slipped into the water.

They were not disappointed. The party had started. There were schools of local fish everywhere, skitting nervously around, clearly aware of the imminent danger. In the powerful flood of light from the torches, they appeared and disappeared in and out of the gloom. The couple looked around at the even denser schools of sardines, which had became more numerous and ever more excited as their masses grew. They saw not a single dolphin. Having been down for an hour, they surfaced and went back to the boat.

"What do you think is happening?" asked Ann.

"I think the dolphin will just swim back and forth during the night, slowly herding the sardines up against the dike. Although dolphins have echolocation, I think the feeding frenzy will start in the morning as soon as the light is right."

They set the lobster pots baited with the head of a flying fish in each trap and set about to cook dinner aboard. Having had a long day, they simply filleted the flying fish and fried them in a ribbed cast-iron skillet with sliced courgettes in a little ghee. They were eaten with garlic and chili nan bread made on a flat iron pan while the fish was cooking. The meal was completed with a light salad and a twist of lemon. Max found a chilled bottle of white wine.

They turned in at 2000 and were soon in deep sleep.

JANUARY 9

They were woken by slithering and bumping against the hulls of the boat in the night, witness to the turmoil below. They slumbered on till dawn when the commotion became so frenzied they were unable to ignore it. In fact, Max was listening intently, building a mental picture of the aquatic developments. It was clear the carnage was going to start before long. There was a sea fog, not as thick as yesterday but restricting visibility to about a hundred meters. Excited shouts in Arabic from the gloom told Max they were not alone on the water. The local fisherman's grapevine was obviously fully aware of the bounty on their fishing grounds.

It started at 0514 precisely. Some tactic by the dolphin had started the water boiling with sardines desperately trying to flee the onslaught.

"Okay, let's go and dive." said Max.

Ann looked at him quizzically. "You sure?"

"Yes, I don't want to miss this spectacle of nature in the raw."

"What about the dolphin and sharks?"

"Don't worry about them. They will be totally focused on the game. Our only worry is that any sharks getting a smell of fish blood in the water may stir up their own frenzy and start snapping at anything and may accidentally bite us."

Ann shivered and paled. "Not sure I like that idea," she said, doubtful.

"Don't worry, honey," Max encouraged. "The plan is this. We move the boat over to the dike and moor hard up next to it. That way we will have the Jacks behind us, and so we won't have anything surprising us from the rear. If things get nasty, we can retreat onto the crannies or climb onto the dike. Besides, you know we have the shark prods. They're damn effective."

"Oh, yes, good idea, yes. I'm happy with that," she said. "I'd forgotten the prods. They're good. I was imagining little me with just my harpoon gun."

"And me, my love. And me. We'll watch each other's backs."

And so they sailed over to the dike and anchored a matter of meters from the breakwater Jacks. They kitted up and dropped over the side to witness the spectacle. Both had a shark prod on a two meter long pole, and Max had his underwater video camera on a headband.

Pandemonium was the scene that greeted them as they slipped underwater. Panic-stricken fish were darting everywhere. Gone were the ordered schools moving in swirling unison. They were replaced by fish in a free-for-all searching for a sense of security, but without the protection of thousands of others moving as a unit, they were now a confused mass of frightened fish darting to and fro.

There wasn't room for all to hide in the crannies offered by the dike's Jacks, so most ended up as a mass of frenzied individuals chasing around in disorder. The dolphins, which they saw for the first time, were taking full advantage of the confusion by flashing through the sardines and gorging themselves on the bounty. As species, they were one of the fastest fishes in the sea.

Capable of swimming at sixty kilometers per hour, they could easily catch and feed as they wanted.

The water became stained with fish blood and bits of sardines, what game fishermen called *chum*. This, as Max had warned, brought in the sharks. Their sensitive sense of smell and vibration meant they could hone in on food from kilometers away with unerring accuracy.

These apex predators were quick to take advantage, their sleek heads suddenly coming through the swirling fish, mouths agape, slashing their heads from side to side. The sardines were small, and the sharks swallowed them by the dozen. The sharks were also after the dolphins, which sometimes fell prey themselves, slowed by their full bellies and intent on their own prey.

The sharks were now in a feeding frenzy and slashed at anything that moved. More than once they had to resort to poking a maddened beast that passed too close. They didn't have to discharge the explosive tip of the prods, which would have been fatal for the shark. The sharks weren't interested in human flesh. They were just blundering around in the confusion, and their gaping jaws sometimes came too close.

They were glad of the breakwater close behind them. It was one less direction to worry about. As the carnage progressed, the water became cloudy with blood, and visibility was dangerously diminished. They decided to get out before it got too ugly, and one of them got a bite from the rows of razor teeth flashing past faster and faster.

"Wow, that was *crazy!*" Ann said and gasped as they quickly boarded the boat.

The din above the water was in sharp contrast to the quiet fury below. The gruesome play underwater had been enacted in silence. Up here the screaming gannets wheeled and swooped into the water only to then frantically flap skyward again with some chunk of fish. They greedily gulped the bits down before the birds wheeled and dived again. The pelicans gulped fish whole.

"I think we left at the right time. I'm sure that last big brute was eyeing you with intent." Max observed as they boarded the boat and stripped naked.

"Don't!" She shivered and smiled grimly. "That was getting a tad too hairy as you would say."

"I would never have forgiven myself if you were hurt."

They showered the blood and fish offal from their hair and bodies, pulled up the anchor said, and sailed back to the island.

The waters around the island, which were ten kilometers from the epicenter of the carnage, had settled down. Most of the fish were gone, hiding or eaten, but the water was untainted by blood or chum. They checked the lobster pots, but unsurprisingly, they found them empty.

"No lobster, no fish! We'll starve tonight!" joked Max.

"Not sure if I could face fish for lunch said ... or tonight ... or for a few days," Ann said.

"Don't be silly. Once you have blown the fishy smell away, you'll be back for your seafood."

"Give me a day or two."

"Madame, that you shall have. Tomorrow we fly to the moon, our moon, far away from fresh fish."

"Yes, I'll miss my fresh fish then."

Max offered to cook a late lunch, and as they both quelled a modest hunger, they sat down to a simple vinaigrette salad with avocado halves filled with halved hard-boiled eggs and topped with different cheeses, all carefully seasoned with a dash of Tabasco.

Having eaten, Ann perked up. While she had marveled at the morning's fish fest, it had left her feeling slightly queasy. Max was right. She didn't like the look of that last shark either. It had given her a fright when it had come much too close. He was right to call a halt to the dive when he had. He seemed able to instinctively read the situation and the mood of the sharks.

They took a siesta during the afternoon under the sail awning and rose an hour before sundown to have a leisurely swim, reasonably sure that any sharks were probably lazing around the breakwater with full bellies.

They swam and dived with just snorkeling gear and explored the cove. Ann found some oysters and mussels. They collected a bagful for the evening meal. It would be their last on vacation since they were due to return the next morning.

Finishing their swim, they returned to the boat and put out some fishing lines with multiple small hooks baited with small bits of fish. They had noticed while snorkeling that the only signs of fish after the carnage of the last hours were some very confused and frightened sardines. They had somewhat settled now, but they were hungry after expending so much energy in avoiding the snapping jaws of the dolphin, so they were easy to catch. Only five sardines were tempted, but two red snapper took the bait.

They packed up the cool box and went to the beach for a barbeque. It was Max's turn to do the cooking.

While Ann prepared a salad and quartered some small lemons, Max dug a pit in the sand and lined it with hot rocks from the barbeque fire and covered them with a layer of sand. The sand oven prepared, they opened the oysters and selected a bottle of champagne.

They toasted their last evening of vacation and ate some of the oysters raw with a squeeze of lemon. Having finished the entrée, they put the sardines and snapper in the sand oven prepared by Max. The fish were wrapped in foil, stuffed with herbs with a drizzle of olive oil. More of the oysters and the mussels also in foil with oil joined the fish. The whole was covered in more sand and simply left to cook for twenty minutes. Ann prepared some wholemeal brown flatbread that she baked on a skillet.

While they waited, Max opened a bottle of a Chilean white wine to accompany the second course. Presently, they brushed away the sand and ate the cooked shellfish with the flatbread. Next came the fish. Their eyes had popped out, which meant they were cooked. They enjoyed these with Ann's excellent salad and honey vinaigrette with mayonnaise. The chilled wine complemented the fish being light and dry, with a fruity bouquet.

For dessert Anne found some chocolate chip ice cream. Then they indulged a variety of cheeses and some vintage port to finish things up. Max made some coffee, and they relaxed while the sun set.

"Not bad for a beach barbeque," Max observed.

"Perfect. I'm stuffed." murmured Ann, her head on his lap.

They relaxed by the fire, which threw flickering shadows across their faces, the boat, and the beach around them.

"We need to call the four-by-four to pick us up in the morning. Or do you want to go back to the house tonight?"

"The morning will be fine. Let's make our little break last. It would be a shame to rush back tonight."

"Agreed. Much better here. It's so peaceful."

"Even better would be to have the hopper collect us here in the morning and let the four-by-four take the boat back."

"Excellent," agreed Ann. "I'm happy to stay here for our last night. No worries."

So they relaxed on the beach until they were ready for bed and returned to the boat to sleep on deck under the mosquito net canopy.

The next morning Max called the four-by-four, which set off from the house to rendezvous on the beach of the mainland. They breakfasted on muesli, fruit, and coffee after a dawn swim. They then sailed back to the mainland to meet the four-by-four. As they rounded the point, they could see the four-by-four waiting at the GPS location Max had given.

Running up the beach, they packed up the boat and hitched it to the four-by-four, and when they heard the hopper arrive overhead, they sent it back to the house with the boat in tow.

The hopper was so named because it had the ability to fly as an airplane and hover as a helicopter. It hovered for a moment and then came to rest twenty meters away.

"Well, my love, good-bye to our little holiday on the sea." Max grinned and kissed her forehead. She sighed.

"It was great. Just what we needed. I now feel ready for Luna2."

"Me too, we have a busy time ahead."

CHAPTER

2

The hopper sped over the desert flying at 950 meters on a 200 degree bearing over the hinterland between Abu Dhabi, the capital of the Emirates and Al Ain. They could see the predawn glow behind them to port. Keeping to a steady 420 kilometers per hour and maintaining their bearing, they were making for Abu Dhabi's empty quarter.

This quarter, the Rub' al Khali, has historically only been occupied by scattered groups of Bedouin nomads. Few still kept to the rigors of the old life. With the coming of the oil bonanza at the beginning of the twenty-first century many had migrated to towns and cities with their schools, hospitals, and all the benefits of a more comfortable urban life. The Rub' is the true desert of romantic tales, with rolling sand dunes and very little vegetation. This romantic notion belies the fact that it is one of the most inhospitable places on the planet. Few people realize how vast the area is, running as it does into Saudi Arabia and the Yemen.

For seemingly endless vistas, the huge dunes roll away to every horizon, offering nothing but heat and dehydration.

The sheer size of some of these dunes, which can reach hundreds of meters high, is also sometimes misunderstood. Some can be stable, and others can be loose. They are usually formed by the winds into ranks like waves, making travel across them extremely difficult.

The Bedouin caravans, with ancient knowledge of their routes, naturally avoided crossing the dunes, preferring to travel from oasis to oasis by night in the valleys between them, resting and sleeping during the heat of the day under the shade of their black tents.

The high temperatures, lack of water, and the difficult terrain have discouraged habitation. Hence, the name "Empty Quarter." This suited Max's purposes. His launch site was buried in this wilderness. Buried is the literal description. In a natural bowl in the topography, surrounded by vast dunes was the launch area. If one flew over the site, he or she would need keen eyes at a low altitude to see any trace of anything manmade.

Max, guided by GPS, found the natural bowl marking their destination and lined the hopper up on one of the dunes. Touching a button on the instrument panel, a shutter door in the side of the dune opened. The opening, a mere fifteen meters wide by ten high, allowed entry to the inside of the dune. The hopper hovered for a moment and then disappeared into the side of the dune. The doors, perfectly camouflaged, rolled closed behind them.

Commander Jackson was there to greet them. He saluted Max and Ann.

"Welcome back, Mr. Max, sir." He was grinning and shaking hands.

"Welcome, Miss Ann. Delighted to see you." He nodded at her, smiling and taking her two hands. Everyone loved Ann. She smiled back.

"Thank you, Commander. Delighted to be here. And regards to your wife."

He led them away from the hopper pad into the operational areas, chatting easily with Max. "Happy New Year! Had a restful break? We missed you. All is ready for you, sir."

"Yes, thanks. We had a great time. Did some diving and sailing, managed to resist using my ComPad the whole time, went kinda native. That's why I've not left any vidmail. I assumed you would bleep me if there was anything major."

"No, all's good. Ready for you to check over."

"The tubes, pumps, and stuff get away okay?"

"Yes, no problem. They went from Pacstation. I've had notification from Luna2 that they have arrived, and they are being unpacked and checked right now. Want to speak with them?"

"No, let them carry on. Alsa will call if there is any hitch."

Alsa was a Kenyan who was about two meters tall and came from the Masai tribe. Max had implicit faith in him, and his second-in-command, Anthony Sanderson, a Brit. Both were skilled engineers and superb spacemen.

The launch station was a master of camouflage. Max had taken an existing dune with all its natural form and placement among the millions of others and made it his base. First, it was injected with a liquid polymer that set, stabilizing the sand. The dune was then excavated in secrecy from the inside, the spoils being removed at night and spread over the floor of the natural bowl to avoid altering the appearance of the natural topography.

These spoils also covered a tube that stretched across thirty kilometers in the floor of the bowl. This track then swept up inside the dune at an 80 degree angle exiting through a door at the crest, similar to the one by which they entered. The size of the dune was such that the inside could be enlarged at will. The launch site, however, was a simple arrangement and really only consisted of the operations center and the ramp. Because they were underground, the temperature inside was a stable and comparatively cool 20 degrees Celsius.

Thus, the base inside the dune was there just to serve the ramp and the needs of the operators. The air inside the whole tube, prior to launch, would be pumped out to form a partial vacuum so the spaceship's acceleration met little resistance on its thirty-kilometer run up to launch.

The sonic boom of the Mach-5 projectile exiting the

dune, while terrific, was so far away from anywhere that it could not be differentiated from the many other sonic booms from aircrafts that were permitted to fly supersonic over the desert. In seconds the spacecraft would be at low orbital height and on its way, largely unnoticed. Once exiting the tube and at a height of a thousand meters, the main engines fired up to achieve escape velocity.

"Everything is ready for launch. Do you want to inspect it all?" offered Commander Jackson.

"Not yet. If you say all is ready, that's all I need to hear," replied Max. "Her ladyship and I will freshen up and see you after lunch. Blastoff at 1505?"

"Yes, you have plenty of time."

Max led Ann to their quarters, which, being subterranean, were windowless but had a screen on one wall that could give them any view they desired. With her head still on vacation, Ann chose an underwater scene, and the room became an aquarium. She dialed in soft music.

They showered and rested on the waterbed, and after an hour's sleep, duly refreshed, they put on lightweight, close-fitting jumpsuits. Ann chose a subtle cream that matched her blonde hair, and Max opted for black.

They made their way to the dining room and ordered omelets. Ann chose chicken, and Max chose a Serrano ham. They ate both with avocado and salad. They followed with some brie on crispbread, fruit, and coffee.

Thus rested and fed, they joined the Commander in the control center where he was directing operations prior to launch.

"All okay?" Max asked.

"Fine. Give us a few minutes, and we will have you on your way. We are just pumping air out of the launch tube now. Should take another twenty minutes."

"Good. We had a nap and some food, so we are ready when you are."

"Blastoff should be on schedule unless, of course, we have unexpected air traffic."

"Good. Tell me when to go."

"Will do, sir." Max noted that on duty in front of other staff, he always addressed his CO formally. That was his services training.

The spaceship underwent all of its preflight checks and was sent backward down the tube from the maintenance bay on the basin floor to the end of the ramp thirty kilometers across the basin. There was a low throb from the evacuation pumps, which were reducing pressure in the launch tube. Max watched the proceedings while technicians monitored their consoles. Flight operators were building a map of air traffic over the desert to avoid any conflict with civilian or military air traffic.

There was a huge screen showing the Luna2 station in geostationary orbit above the Pacific.

The commander brought Max from his contemplation to announce that they should take the pod to the ship across the bowl. Max nodded, and taking Ann's hand, he led her to the shuttle pod's airlock. The pod was shot down to the boarding point across the basin down the tube, which was now an almost compete vacuum. The lack of air in the tube meant the pod simply dropped two hundred meters and coasted along the horizontal section to the boarding bay. They were met by technicians who cheerfully ushered them into the launch preparation room, where the doctor asked if they had any problems. This was more a formality because the couple was under close health monitoring when on Luna2. This was merely an opportunity to discuss any ailments incurred on their vacation.

"I'm okay. Thanks," replied Max. "Ann, you fine too?"

"Yes, couldn't be better."

"Great," said the doctor. He did some basic checks, took a blood sample from each of them, and wished them a pleasant flight.

"Thanks. See you when we get back."

With that last formality, Max and Ann boarded their spacecraft and settled into pilot and copilot seats and strapped on harnesses while the technicians closed the ports and disengaged the airlocks. Flipping a few switches and studying the large touch-screen control panel, Max made preflight checks to the craft while chatting with the commander. All systems were normal for takeoff, and Max gave the word for a ten-second countdown. The superconductive rails were already charged at this point, and with all lights green, they rapidly accelerated across the basin, pulling four gravities. Ann gripped the armrests, bracing herself against the g-force. The lights in the tube flashed by in a blur, and in seconds they shot into sunlight. The main engines fired, and their acceleration continued until they reached the escape velocity of 28,200 kilometers per hour. They watched the sky turn rapidly from blue to black as they left daytime Arabia for space.

Now weightless, they turned to each other.

"Okay?"

"Okay."

"Did the Earth move for you, honey?" Ann giggled. She loved the rush of takeoffs and derived a positively sensual pleasure from the experience.

"Like being born again out of that tube," replied Max.

"Wow, strange notion," replied Ann "I bet you made your mom's eyes water."

"I believe I did. She was a tiny thing. Wish you could have met her."

Ann was silent. Max's mother had passed away just before they met, and Max hadn't talked about her much. His dad was also long deceased.

Max reported back to the commander that the takeoff was event-free and confirmed all systems were normal. They then busied themselves, checking their trajectory, and they called Luna2 to confirm they were on schedule. Luna2 had been notified of their takeoff from launch base.

All flight controls had been checked, and Max

flipped on the autopilot. They looked out of the large windows to enjoy the view.

Max had checked their bearing as 194 degrees, which took them on the shortest route, directly to Luna2. Their flight took them across the eastern Saudi Rub', over Yemen, and then over the Gulf of Aden.

Looking starboard, Max pointed at the end of the Gulf of Aden.

"See the Aden Dike? It's not as impressive as Hormuz, but it is as vital as the Gibraltar Dike." From their altitude it was just visible and seemed insignificant enough. The five-meter change in sea level was undetectable at that distance. Where the Red Sea opened into the Gulf of Aden, the sea narrowed to what in Arabic was known as the Bab-El-Mandeb or the Gate of Tears.

Being only twenty-one kilometers, this Red Sea dike, with extra land barriers at each end where the old land level was only meters above sea level, was small compared to the fifty-five-kilometer Hormuz barrier, but it had to contend with deeper water.

Numerous countries had implemented their own sea defense programs with varying degrees of success.

The Gibraltar barrier was only sixteen kilometers but considerably deeper at between three and nine hundred meters, so it presented a more demanding engineering solution. When the Straits of Gibraltar were projected to be closed to preserve the Mediterranean Sea levels, it was imperative to close off the Red Sea as well. This could have been done at Suez, but it was decided to construct the Red Sea barrier. The Saudis, which had the low-lying Jeddah, the Red Sea port serving Mecca, funded that project entirely having also had a substantial stake in the Hormuz project.

The Aral Sea was reinstated through water management when it was realized how valuable an asset it was. So was the Dead Sea by using a siphon from the Red Sea.

The Baltic Sea was protected by a barrier from the top of Denmark at Grenen to Kladesholmen via the Paternoster archipelago in Norway.

Also important for North America were the Canadian barriers, which were the key to retaining the Hudson Bay. This barrier joined Killiniq, Knight, Goodwin, and Maccoll islands with the Resolution and the Lower Savage Islands, leading to the mainland again. While this was the longest barrier at seventy kilometers, it preserved the water levels of Ungava Bay, Foxe Basin, and the Hudson Strait and Bay. These waters formed a considerable sea that was subject to inflows of freshwater and progressively became less saline. Fortunately, the Great Lakes were landlocked and more easily retained.

There were also plans for the Gulf of Boothia, the Beaufort Sea, Bering, Okhotsz, and Sea of Japan. Time, however, was not on the side of the larger, long term and more ambitious plans.

Thus, these relatively short sea defense walls had protected the waters of the Arabian Gulf, the Mediterranean, the Black Sea, the Hudson Bay and the Baltic, saving the coasts of many nations from inundation. These projects were the most cost-effective in history. Dollar for dollar, they were arguably more cost-effective than the Panama and Suez canals combined. Economists and historians were still debating the case. Only time would tell the full long-term benefits.

The rapid sea rise of the 2030s, 40s, and 50s had thoroughly shaken those nations with vulnerable coastlines. As water was one of the primary early means of exploration and trade, those countries which for millennia had logically sited their capitals and major cities on their coasts and river estuaries were dramatically affected.

Cities that had benefitted from trade across the world's oceans down the ages, from ancient Venice to London, Rotterdam, New York, and Boston, now faced inundation. Many of the world's most important cities therefore, now had the most serious problem since their foundation.

The sudden sea rise had very effectively united the world's nations to come up with solutions. It was metaphorically and often literally "All hands to the pumps." The damage by methane gas emissions to the atmosphere from the arctic tundra regions had created a domino effect. Once the Arctic ice cap had started to diminish, the land-based ice fields of Canada and Russia, the world's biggest countries, were going too. This land-based water raised sea levels and also released the locked methane, which together with the soaring CO2 emissions caused a spiraling meltdown.

Suffice to say that for now there was an uneasy standoff resulting from the change in sea levels. It would have been idealistic to think the global calamity united mankind into a concerted effort to save the planet. Not so. Self-interest among those nations not timmediately affected by sea rise meant those nations ignored the issue and did little. Those who were poor or underdeveloped were incapable of doing anything. That meant some nations did not keep to the internationally agreed pollution emission limits.

Rapidly emerging and populous third-world countries were understandably reluctant to restrain their newfound industrialization, blaming excess pollution on the richer, industrialized nations. Monitoring the situation was almost impossible. Those nations who were least threatened by water levels were reluctant to do anything.

Undeveloped nations, preoccupied with their local affairs, were powerless and merely intent on survival with little foreign aid from first-world countries. Some countries literally ceased to exist, their citizens becoming refugees.

Russia and Canada were affected dramatically, but sea levels were of little concern to them. Newly thawed arctic tundra opened up vast tracts of habitable, arable farming, and minerals lands were now accessible rather than being buried in snow, ice, and permafrost.

Meanwhile, the global weather had rapidly

deteriorated. El Nino and his cooler sister, El Nina, seemed to appear in force every year. Storms, typhoons, and hurricanes were common with consequent flooding and damage. There were signs of shifting Oceanic sea currents with as yet unknown consequences.

Then there was the global pandemic of 2026.

The repeated reemergence of the Ebola virus together with various mutations had gotten out of control. The virus, through being treated with only partially effective vaccines, evolved into a particularly virulent strain. Furthermore, it had now evolved to become an airborne contagion. Hitherto, the virus was only transmitted by contact with body fluids. Now it became a monster, virtually uncontrollable.

To make matters worse, it was found the virus was able to live on corpses for an unknown number of years. This was discovered when cadavers, exhumed by floodwaters, were found to be highly infectious. Mass graves were therefore no longer an option. Nor was interment of any kind. Cremation was the only sure and simple solution, particularly in poor countries. In third world countries, this produced a hellish landscape reminiscent of a Hieronymus Bosch painting or a dream by Dante as innumerable pyres smoldered for twenty-four hours a day. This added to deforestation, air pollution, and toxic greenhouse emissions.

Mainly, via global air transport, the virus moved in huge leaps around the planet before it could be contained. The pandemic was swift to take root in all major cities of the planet. It was not finally brought under control until 2034. Estimates of deaths were difficult to establish. The closest estimate was set at 42 percent of the world population. Some countries were badly affected. Africa, particularly West Africa, as the origin and epicenter of the disease, was virtually depopulated. Cities with densely packed inhabitants were exceptionally vulnerable and consequently suffered most, incurring an 85 percent mortality rate.

By 2040, the pandemic was over, but humanity was badly wounded by the global events that had overwhelmed any traditional disaster response mechanisms. Moreover, the warmed planet had given rise to many other new diseases spreading mainly from the tropical regions. Zika had ravaged North and South America before spreading globally. Malaria, West Nile, dengue, and other mosquito-borne diseases proliferated. Dysentery, typhus, polio, and bubonic plague ravaged poorer countries. The loss of life was staggering.

It took modern medical practice twenty years to achieve some semblance of normality. Governmental health ministries as well as the pharmaceutical and medical industries had taken a beating, being found complacent, lacking in investment and foresight. Little progress had been made in the development of a new generation of antibiotics to replace the first generation originating with penicillin, which through overprescription and poor supervision had become ineffective.

Here was one benefit the succession of scourges had wrought on mankind had brought about. It resolved the ongoing debate about genetic editing. In 2015, a technique for editing any genetic sequence, animal or vegetable, was developed. Once the sequence had been mapped and the target section to be edited was established, the process could be easily, quickly, and very accurately carried out. The process known as CRISPR promised a disease-free future. Furthermore, it promised the possibility of correcting genetically transmitted diseases. The most contentious was its application to humans. The global events of past years had brought about fresh thinking.

By 2084, there was a new world order. Avenues had been closed, but new possibilities opened. The whole geopolitical structure of the world had shifted. There was now a global pioneering spirit that rose to meet the new opportunities offered by thawing lands and opening seas.

The lost lands, cities, and traditional routes had to be forgotten, and a whole new global framework was created. Dutch engineers, past masters in the battle against the sea, were in high demand for their knowledge, expertise, and technology. They were to be found in all corners of the globe, directing elaborate schemes for sea defenses and land reclamation where possible.

There was a state of flux, whereby nations took stock of their ravaged territories and coastlines and attempted huge damage limitation programs. The reduced global population brought benefits. Firstly it reduced the growing problems of imminent global starvation and overconsumption, and secondly, there was a reduction of CO_2 emissions and pollution. The new world order, as advocated by some at the turn of the twenty-first century, was now a reality, although it was far from what they had imagined.

The reality was a wakeup call. Mother Earth could wreak havoc if the activities of mankind were continued unrestrained and without planning at a global level. The realization that mankind's existence on the planet was as yet very short and could swiftly end if it did not treat the environment with due respect shifted people's attitudes. The awareness of the age of the planet was reborn, and her anticipated lifespan brought the reality of man's existence into sharp focus.

In effect, Mother Earth did not care for humanity. Man could either care for her or suffer the consequences. She could erase all traces of human existence in a few million years and continue in her ordained position in the solar system and galaxy for eons to come.

Humanity would merely be a miniscule footnote in Earth's history.

CHAPTER 3

As they flew over the Gulf of Aden their path took them over the waters between the Horn of Africa and the island of Socotra, which lay off the portside.

"Remember that dragon's blood tree we saw on our island?" asked Max.

"Yes, what a funny tree. So beautifully symmetrical in its organic way."

"I wonder about that tree. I was sure it was only found in Socotra, that island down there. I must look it up on the Web sometime." He pointed to port.

Anne returned from her examination of the Red Sea dike and peered past Max to the island far below

"Why not now?" said Ann, tapping her wrist keypad. A couple of seconds later, she had a few webpages up on the main screen and began surfing.

"Mmmm, there's lots about the island and its long history of being abused by man. It's rated along with the Galapagos Islands for its unique flora and fauna. Can't see anything specific about the dragon's blood tree not being found elsewhere."

"Well, we saw what we saw," Max replied and shrugged.

By now the panorama was unfolding beneath them, the horn giving way to Kenya on the starboard with Madagascar on the portside ahead in the distance.

Kenya and its Rift Valley, Lake Victoria, and Mt. Kenya could all be seen interspersed by the vast grasslands.

"While you're on the Web, you could look up Madagascar. It also has some pretty strange stuff—baobabs, lemurs, and whatnot."

Ann stared down at the island.

"It's pretty big," she observed.

"It's bigger than Italy, bigger than the United Kingdom. It also evolved separately from Africa for millennia," added Max.

"Yes, those baobabs are weird, kinda upside down," said Ann staring at the screen where she had found pictures of them.

"And the lemurs are so cute."

"Really smelly little things I've heard," Max replied nonchalantly, fearing what might be coming.

"Spoilsport. I still think they're cute. Those big eyes get me."

Max shrugged. "Just don't ask to bring one home. They're a protected species."

"Okay. Oh, well, good."

Max was relieved.

Madagascar's history was also a tale of destruction by man. Several species of lemur were even extinct.

With Madagascar still coming up to port, there was Tanzania to starboard with Mt. Kilimanjaro's extinct volcanic peak, now devoid of snow, poking through clouds surrounding its flanks.

Their flight continued down the east coast of Africa past Mozambique and Madagascar. Keeping their heading, it took them out over the South Indian Ocean and over the Southern Ocean.

Their trajectory took them over the old, and now with the partial closure of the Mediterranean Sea, the new sea route rounded the Cape of Good Hope as it used to be called. The partial closure of the Red Sea and Gibraltar Strait meant that while the use of the Suez Canal as a shipping route was still viable, there were economic and time penalties to using the Mediterranean as a shipping route. Cargoes that had their destinations on that sea would be obliged to use the locks either on the Red Sea or at Gibraltar. Those with longer routes or those that were of such a massive size they would not pass through the locks now reverted to rounding the cape as the preferred route. The use of wind meant the cost of fuel was no longer a factor in the choice of route. Time was the only penalty, and that was offset by ships being larger and more numerous.

"The show is over till we get to Antarctica," Max announced.

Ann nodded, engrossed in her Web crawl for information on all the places they had flown over.

The Norwegian Claim of Antarctica was in the distance some minutes later. The view as it unfolded was that of barren rock tundra.

What was once the ice sheet that covered the entire continent and spilled into the sea of the Southern Ocean was now restricted to the center of the continent. For more than three hundred kilometers inland, there was an almost complete lack of ice and snow except for in the lee of scattered mountains.

The Weddell Sea was clear of permanent ice. Apart from isolated icebergs that had calved from the glaciers that snaked their way over the tundra from the central ice mass, the sea was now navigable right up to the landmass.

This vast tract was claimed by Norway, the first nation to reach the South Pole, a country that knew snow and ice, and it was one of the few countries to have respected the frozen continent. Its reputation for ecological awareness had made them the forerunners of dealing with the events that had overcome Earth's last virgin continent. The extreme climate and some fragile international agreements were the sole obstacle deterring man's desecration of that continent. The problem, however, did not come from activity on Antarctica.

The meltdown of Antarctica was a process that began as a result of the breakup and melting of Western Ice Sheet, which is made up of the Weddell

Ice Shelf and the Ross Shelf. It is where the Antarctic ice partially extends out from the land to form a floating mass of ice. The key to the integrity of this ice mass was the Ross Shelf, which acted as a sort of dam that slowed the progress of the natural glacial flow by a process called buttressing.

Once this critical dam was gone, it paved the way for the breakup of the Weddell Sea Ice Shelf. As the melting continued, large portions of sea ice the size of cities or islands would break loose and be taken away by currents and wind. They would be broken up and melted by the warmer Southern Ocean. The loss of the Western Ice Sheet, which was partially land-based ice, together with the loss of other land-based Antarctic ice sheets was responsible for a one meter sea rise on its own.

The snow and ice loss in Canada and Russia, the two largest countries of the world, together with Greenland, the world's largest island, accounted for a further four meters. This loss also affected the albedo, a measure of reflectivity. The whiteness of the snow normally covered the land and polar ice cap and reflected much of the Sun's short-wave radiation back into space. With the snow covering the land and sea ice cap gone, the Sun's heat was fully absorbed, which speeded warming. The Greenland ice fields were land-based, which meant that any loss from the glaciers directly created an immediate sea rise.

The net result of the ice lost in these regions together with the ice loss in the rest of Antarctica and the shrinking of glaciers from the continental mountain ranges added up to a total rise in sea levels of seven meters between 2030 and 2090.

Furthermore, the loss of the frozen areas of Russia and Canada had released vast quantities methane, one of the most aggressive greenhouse gasses, which added to the greenhouse effect originally brought about by rising atmospheric carbon dioxide through burning of coal and fossil fuels.

These multiple accumulative factors were generally known as the feedback effect.

The result was a self-fueling, runaway global warming, a self-feeding cycle, nothing short of an epoch ending and catastrophic situation.

There was little to be done here in Antarctica. The damage was done, a grim reality that could only be solved elsewhere by a concerted international effort to rectify the atmospheric imbalance. Nowhere on Earth was the effect of man's activities more glaringly evident than here.

In the early twenty-first century, man realized they had brought about such dramatic and possibly irreversible changes to the planet that the epoch of Earth's geologic chronologic history had passed from the Holocene. The next epoch, man's epoch, was to become termed the Anthropocene. These epochs, periods, and eras were normally measured in millennia. It was yet to be seen how long the Anthropocene would last.

Max's part in this unfolding drama was the

formation of his company, Aqua4, and his main creation, the Luna2 project. These were his contribution to save the planet and an attempt to tackle the problem of rising oceans. Luna2 was the repository of excess water, the fact it was purified gave it added value in a world where fresh, pure water was increasingly scarce.

CHAPTER

4

The space capsule was now aligning itself for its trajectory. The rockets fired to make corrections to their course so that they would arrive at Luna2 in geostationary orbit on the equator in the middle of the Pacific Ocean.

There was a very good reason for the selection of this location. Max's calculations had identified the optimal location for a small moon in close proximity to Earth. Any tidal heave from the gravitational pull of such a mass in fact helped minimize the effect of high sea levels, merely creating a bulge in the surface of the Pacific where it had little effect on occupied landmasses.

Luna2 was an ice moon, the headquarters of Max's company, Aqua4.

Luna2 also had a moon nicknamed Luna3. Luna3 was more of a tethered satellite, and without it, the much larger Luna2 would not be possible. The purpose of Luna3 was to act as a centrifugal anchor for the outer end of space elevator (sometimes just known as the spacelift), and it kept the cable taut

Luna2—or L2 as many referred to it—was barely visible. They were approaching during the night, and it was in the shadow cast by the Earth and could only be seen by a faint black patch where the stars were blotted out by its bulk. However, because of its small size in the vastness of space, this was not appreciable until one was within about six hundred kilometers.

The odd lights used by the various maintenance and working parties on L2 appeared as stars across its face and helped to camouflage its presence from Max and Ann who had been eagerly looking for its first appearance. The homing beacon had been located by the avionics some time before there was any visual sign of Earth's new satellite.

The headquarters of Luna2 was in the core. It was selected to be in the center of the mass of the ice because the water provided excellent protection from solar and galactic radiation. The dynamics of creating a moon were such that the base was protected from meteorites and the Sun's radiation. Being in the center, it also meant the station was not disrupted by the ever-changing surface as more ice was continually added. The lift cables ran straight through the center. There were also various tunnels to the core for service, access, and maintenance.

The heads-up display on their craft's screen showed L2 clearly before it was visually discernible and showed all the flight data for manual navigation. It was, however, unnecessary for Max or Ann to touch anything as the craft would automatically dock itself. Manual override was for unusual maneuvers or emergency.

"There. I see it," whispered Ann, who had sharper eyes.

Max shook his head. While the heads-up display had drawn a circle around L2, he could not truthfully say he could see it yet.

"You win again. I can't," he admitted.

"Only 'cause you're too proud to have eye laser correction. You know how good it is, and it's really quick."

"Just another thing to go wrong, and it's not vital yet. Besides, I've a beautiful pair of extra eyes."

"Flattery won't fix your eyes." Ann grinned.

Max shrugged.

"It can wait. I've got too much to do to take time off just now. Ah! I see it now. There are some new lights I took for stars. That confused me. Must be some crews out on a new sector."

"The PolyAI film must have arrived, and they are covering sector six," suggested Ann.

"Could be. Although I haven't heard anything from Alsa." He flipped a switch in the intercom to the station.

"Alsa? You there?" There was a brief pause, and the commander's deep voice came over.

"Mbwana, welcome back. We see your approach. All systems fine, sir?"

"Yes, fine, thanks. Can we have a chat when I dock?"

"At your service. We expect you in sixty-five minutes. All clear for docking."

"Thanks. See you in sixty-five. Out." Max turned to Ann and touched her hand.

"Well, honey, this really is the end of our little break. We have some hard work ahead now."

Ann smiled ruefully.

"Yes, it was really good while it lasted. But I feel rested, and I'm keen to get going again."

"Great, I hope we can take another visit to Earth soon, but there is urgent business to attend to up here with all the new equipment to install and commission."

The shuttle's guidance system had now locked onto one of the entrance tunnels on Luna2's surface and slowed to 250 kilometers per hour to comply with speed restrictions. Even the boss respected his own rules. The craft dived into the tunnel and cruised along toward the center, some 125 kilometers to the core. On the way various craft passed on their way to the surface and in passing blinked a blue salute light to *Space Shuttle One*, as Max's craft was known. SS1 blinked a polite reply. No need to break radio silence.

"All seems normal," Max observed.

"Any reason why it shouldn't be?" asked Ann.

"Mmmm ... no. But then you never can tell in space. I'm still a bit puzzled by the lights on the surface. Maybe it's just a new sector being worked on like I said before. I will discuss it with Alsa presently."

"I'll be glad to get to our quarters and have a

shower and a bite to eat," Ann suggested "We haven't had anything since breakfast."

"Yes, good idea. I'll just have a quick chat with Alsa, and if he can explain the lights, we can retire and wash and eat. Just to put my mind at rest."

"Okay, sweetie, you'll excuse me while you boys talk business if you are in for a session."

"Of course. I don't think it is anything important. Otherwise, Alsa would have mentioned it."

A few minutes later, the craft passed marker lights on the walls of the tunnel and automatically slowed to twenty kilometers per hour as they approached the docking area. The tunnel opened out to a vast chamber some two kilometers long by five hundred meters wide, and the shuttle slowed to a stop next to an airlock. A concertina access way moved out from the wall and clamped onto SS1's hatch door, and with a soft hiss, the air pressure equalization with the shuttle was established.

The couple unclipped the harnesses they had put on for approach and docking, and Max gave the control panel a final check, opened the hatch, and ushered Ann through.

Their magnetic boots stuck them to whatever flat surface they wished, or they could simply float along the corridors using the handrails. While Luna2 had a slight gravity by virtue of its mass, this was only noticeable on the surface. In the core there was no gravitational effect.

Alsa was there to greet them, and they said their

hellos and chatted on their way to the operations room. Max broached the question of the surface lights, and Alsa was able to explain that the PolyAl film had arrived and that they were in the process of covering sector K.

The PolyAl served two purposes. By virtue of its aluminum content, it acted to reflect the Sun's rays to minimize the heating of the icy surface. Secondly, it formed a vapor seal, which slowed sublimation of the ice when sunlight was present.

As the bulk of the artificial moon grew, the problem of vapor loss diminished in some respects and worsened in others as the dynamics of space played on the physical body. As L2 maintained its geosynchronous position over the Earth, it passed from sunlight into night as it moved in and out of Earth's shadow. L2 was subject to the same daily cycle of day and night as it would experience at the equator—a twelve-hour day and a twelve-hour night. Because of its tidally locked position with no rotation of its own like the Moon, it presented the same face to the Earth.

Naturally, the point of entry of the spacelift came to be known as ground zero. This meant that it corresponded with its relative position with Earth. L2 was therefore subject to the same sunrise and sunset. Based on Greenwich Mean Time or GMT, it was the same time zone as Hawaii. The longitude was 160 degrees west on Earth and over the equator.

The elevator cable was originally created by a static space fabrication station (or *statite*) and fed down toward Earth and directly out into space with a counterweight thatwas added to as needed to retain tension. Because of the properties of the carbon nanotube composition, the cable structurally only needed to be 150 millimeters wide and three millimeters thick. For practical reasons, however, the cable was a constant six hundred millimeters wide by three millimeter to allow the cars sufficient purchase for their drive wheels. For redundancy three such cables were used. The tubes used for moving superheated seawater into orbit acted in structural unison with the original cables.

The Earth end of the cable was tethered to a floating station in the Pacific at the equator. This station was the Earth Terminus for the space elevator. On the Sun side of Luna2, there were the goods and passenger facilities used to transfer space bound travelers and cargo. There was also a storage base and manufacturing area.

The Earth Terminus was also the launching point for the seawater extraction to space. An equatorial solar furnace superheated seawater to extreme temperature and pressure, which sent the water into low orbit. Most of the salts were removed in what was effectively a distillation process. There were pumping stations at intervals whereby the steam was sent on to Luna2. There it was distributed over sectors of Luna2 to evenly form the pure water ice satellite. The pure water ice found a ready market in space to supply the new settlement on the Moon, and it was sent back to Earth to form rainfall in more arid regions.

Luna2 now stood at a diameter of about 520 kilometers and contained 65.5 million cubic kilometers of pure water ice, and it was growing daily until such time as rising seas no longer threatened.

The spinoff from this seawater extraction meant that rising seas were partially controlled. An equilibrium point had not yet been achieved, but the worst ravages of flooding and land loss had been avoided. Meanwhile, the gravitational pull of Luna2 also resulted in a stationary tidal *hump* in the middle of the Pacific, where the extra water depth was largely unnoticed. This *reservoir* of water would otherwise add to the flooding over the world.

The nature of its geostationary position and conditions of space were such that Luna2 was daily exposed to direct sunlight, unprotected by an atmosphere. This meant the water would sublimate (i.e., boil and vaporize on a daily basis) where it was not shaded by photoelectric solar arrays and/or PolyAl film. This had caused problems initially and meant the ice had to be shielded by aluminum foil, but as the mass of the satellite grew, its own micro-gravitational field kept the vaporized water on the surface to re-condense and freeze when out of the sunlight.

In the early days of the space elevator when there was only one cable, seawater had to be sent into space by one tube, now multiple pipes also acting as car traction cables enabled people and goods to shuttle to and from space.

Water from the Pacific was now sent up in a cluster

of six pipes each of sixty-centimeter diameter. The pressure of the superheated seawater made them stiff and rigid. Internal repair *moles* ran inside the pipes to constantly monitor and maintain the inner surface while external crawlers did the same for the exterior. There were now six clusters of six pipes so that at any one time there were up to seventy-two cars moving up and down the cables. Capacity was growing all the time, and there were plans for another twelve such clusters.

The pipes were bonded to each other. Thus, they derived greater strength and rigidity. They formed the main core of the cable structure that the goods and passengers cars used for traction. This was achieved at ever-increasing speeds as the technology and system developed. Elevator speeds were unrestricted by air resistance, and higher speeds were attainable for the same energy input.

One of the advantages of carbon as a tube material was that it was also an excellent electrical conductor. Electricity was sent from space during the day when solar arrays shielding Luna2 were used to power the Luna2 station and elevator cars. The Earth Terminus used its solar furnace to superheat the seawater, and they also called on a fusion reactor to meet any solar power shortfall because of a lack of sunshine.

Micrometeoroids were a constant maintenance issue, while larger objects traveling at thousands of kilometers an hour, natural and man-made, were an ever-present hazard. The key was to have built-in redundancies. Hence, the constant demand for pipes.

The technology to produce long chains of carbon nanotubes had been in its infancy until the 2020s. Since then, it had rapidly advanced to the extent that it could be produced by compact mobile machines. Also the advances in the production of synthetic silk copied from spider's thread was another new technological breakthrough that produced materials many times stronger, lighter, and more elastic than steel and were not subject to corrosion.

These two key technologies were the means to the practical deployment of a space elevator and therefore led to a renewed interest in space exploration, mining, and settlement on the Moon. Other moons in our solar system were also attracting attention. Conditions on all the other seven planets of the solar system were considered too extreme for practical human habitation, except Mars, which had a very small resident group of pioneers.

The space elevator was the means to an easy and cheap method to escape Earth's gravity with the bonus of having an environmentally low impact. It was the key to space exploration.

The Earth Terminus directly below Luna2 was a position in the Pacific Ocean about forty kilometers due north of the former Jarvis Island, also known as Bunker Island, which was a low-lying, uninhabited island only known for guano mining two hundred years before it was submerged by rising sea levels in 2025. The island now formed a base for a complex of installations that served the early establishment of the Earth Terminus, built on pylons over the now seven-meter-deep water submerging the island. Because of Luna2's gravitational pull, this was some nine meters higher than the level before sea rise.

The next nearest island was Kiribati or Christmas Island 340 kilometers to the northeast, also part of the group known as the Line Islands. It had suffered the same fate and was now submerged beneath the Pacific.

The Micronesian inhabitants of the island group had been relocated wherever they wished, mostly to the United Kingdom and United States. Others chose one of the other Pacific islands, as was the case of most of the older inhabitants who could not or did not wish to change their lifestyles.

Many of the young islanders found work in a new industry on the sea. This took the form of plastic recovery engineering. During the twentieth century in the north and to a lesser extent the South Pacific, there had developed a huge floating mass of plastic garbage, a severe environmental problem. The winds and currents created a gyre of oceanic proportions that served to collect vast amounts of floating plastic garbage that wasn't biodegradable. The size of the problem was hard to imagine. Plastic flotsam and jetsam had accumulated in a vast area of the ocean. A similar floating plastic mass had also developed in all of the major oceans and seas, now including the new North Pole Sea.

As a result, one could sail for days surrounded by this scourge. The impact on marine life was immeasurable. The plastics, some toxic, breaking down into minute particles, were ingested by phytoplankton and krill. They plastic found its way into the very bottom of the food chain, and so it traveled on up. Fishing nets trapped all forms of fauna. This mass of floating plastic had earned itself the name "the Plastic Sargasso."

Max had an interest in this new reclamation industry, which served the dual purpose of harvesting the seemingly inexhaustible supply of plastic and provided the raw material for PolyAl film and the more basic raw material Pacific Sargasso Plastic or PSP. PolyAl film was a specific grade of plastic sheet with an aluminized content to provide a relatively vapor-proof and reflective sheet needed on Luna2. PSP was an unprocessed plastic used for plastic components.

The plastic trawlers were factory ships designed to reclaim this ready-made plastic and to sort and process it into pellets that were then taken away by barges to make PolyAl and PSP. The pioneering Max had set up the first of these ships and a PolyAl film plant at Bunker Island. The business had grown too large for the facility, which had to be built on pylons on the sunken island and was now in production in Chile.

CHAPTER 5

H aving finished chatting with Alsa, they made their way to their quarters to wash before a much-awaited meal. They glided through the passage to the penthouse suite reserved for Max's use. They entered and were welcomed by the room's management system, which recognized its owner and adjusted all the controls.

The floors and ceilings, inasmuch as there were such things in zero G, were screens that by default showed colored walls so that one did not confuse which was up and down. In the lack of gravity, one could easily become disoriented and lost in the complex of rooms and passages that made up the L2 station.

Many surfaces were screens which could display anything desired on voice command. Max could study works on the surface of L2, various Moon stations, Earth cities and landscapes, celestial and planetary views. All could give a complete 360 degree projection of a scene with surround audio to give a sense of total immersion of the viewed scene. Whatever was visible by CCTV cameras both in Max's organization and augmented by a database of images and videos could be instantly viewed. Alternatively, all this was available on the VR headsets or on the standard spacesuit helmets.

"Welcome back, sir. I sense Miss Ann with you," Jeeves, the room management system's greeted them.

"Yes, thank you, Jeeves," said Max.

The AI was jokingly named Jeeves to acknowledge Reginald Jeeves, the fictional valet, a character created by P G Woodhouse, an author of humorous stories in the early twentieth century. The computer was programmed to interact with his master and mistress in a like fashion, pedantically formal after the style of the Edwardian era.

"Welcome back, Miss Ann," continued Jeeves.

"Thank you, Jeeves. Jeeves, we will shower and dine later. Please alert Chef Gaston. Give our compliments and request he surprise us with whatever he chooses to serve. Also invite the commander, the captain, and their wives. Informal dress."

"Very good, Miss Ann."

They could have ordered automated food, but as there was no hurry, they preferred the quality of hand-cooked food. No machine could replicate a good chef's skill, intuition, judgment, and taste buds.

Some quiet music started and the luminescent walls glowed and pulsed in sympathy. They stripped off their tunics and undergarments, putting the soiled clothes into a trapdoor which shot them via a vacuum tube to a central laundry where they were cleaned and in three minutes automatically returned folded inside the same trapdoor.

Moving to another panel, they floated into the shower cubicle.

The zero-gravity cubicle used compressed air to manage the shower. It used a stream of air instead of gravity to control and direct the flow of water. Apart from the fact they were weightless, the shower was as normal. Shampoo and soap were dispensed from ceiling units. Once cleaned and rinsed, they called for pulse jets to massage them and remove the stiffness of their flight to the station. Once clean and massaged, they were blow-dried by a mini tornado that also removed all traces of water from the cubicle.

"Water please." The voice recognition knew Max liked a cool shower, and so the AI shot jets of cool water into the cubicle. Ann squealed and gasped at the onslaught of water.

"Too cold for you, Miss Ann? Would you like it warmer?" asked Jeeves. Ann nodded, covered in goosebumps.

"Yes please, Jeeves."

The water immediately came through five degrees warmer.

"Aaaah … okay now. Thanks, Jeeves."

"My pleasure, Miss Ann."

Refreshed, they dressed for dinner in casual attire—anything comfortable that allowed free movement to perform the contortions sometimes needed in zero gravity. Ann chose a black Japanese floral silk pajama suit, and Max opted for a black monosuit. Shoes were unnecessary and not worn.

They floated across to the dining room where they were joined by Commander Alsa and his wife, Grace, as well as Captain Tony Sanderson, an engineer, with his wife, Fiona.

Gaston, the chef, was waiting in the kitchen. Nicknamed *Gastro* by his devoted acolytes, the Frenchman came from Avignon and had learned his craft under the world's finest gastronomic masters. An ectomorph, he was lucky enough to be able to enjoy the products of his kitchen with impunity, indulging his gastronomic whims without gaining a single kilo.

In space flames were spherical and behaved quite unlike earthbound fire. All this was used to their advantage as flames and cooking juices clung to and surrounded the meat as it cooked. Naturally, he was master of microwaves in cooking. They were the logical choice for space cookery. Naked flames in a space station were normally as welcome as they were in a fireworks factory, but Gaston was trusted to use and control this potentially catastrophic element in performing his art. The kitchen was designed to his specification. After all, he was an acknowledged and leading consultant in space kitchen design.

This meant he could produce and prepare exciting and innovative meals in space to the highest culinary standards rather than rely on the processed rations in squeeze bags and tubes that were the normal space fare.

He had taken delivery of six brace of pheasant a couple of days ago, and after he hung them in a slow centrifuge, he was keen to serve them. He had roasted four of them with fresh vegetables from his experimental zero-G hydroponic garden. He was also considered one of the leading zero-G gardeners, a master in this relatively new science.

Max and Ann chatted with the others, exchanging news about the workings of the station for what was happening on Earth and details of their vacation.

"Wonderful, wonderful," enthused Grace and Fiona as the ladies gathered to hear Ann's stories of their sailing in the Emirates and Omani waters.

"How romantic and exciting. You two are so brave fighting crazy savage sharks barehanded," said Fiona on hearing of the shark and dolphin carnage. (She was apt to dramatize and was prone to hyperbole.) "It would scare me to death to jump into shark-infested waters like that. Weren't you worried they might bite?"

"It wasn't really that dangerous," replied Ann modestly "I was armed with a speargun. Also, Max and I had prods if they became too frisky."

"Even so, you must have been scared?"

"Cautious is more exact. We weighed up the situation and had our backs to the sea wall so they couldn't sneak up behind us."

"Well, I think you were very brave, and you wouldn't catch me doing that in a million years."

Ann smiled.

"I like the sound of the 'Green Flash,'" said Grace. "I've never seen or heard of that."

"Now *that* did give me a scare at first," admitted Ann. "I was keyed up. It all happened so suddenly at a time of high confusion, what with the dolphin the sharks and screaming birds. It gave me a bit of a turn."

"I bet it did! You poor thing!" sympathized Fiona, thrilled with the thought of the drama. "I would have been terrified! And with the air full of flying fish, sardines, dolphins, and sharks!"

Ann laughed. "I was for a moment until Max explained the phenomenon." She could imagine how the story would pass along through Fiona's social circle. There would also be blood raining down from a stormy sky, high seas, thunder and lightning, general mayhem and danger. Courtesy of Fiona's overfertile imagination and gift for narration, it would make a fine story to pass around. It would improve with each telling.

Grace gave Ann a knowing smile and rolled her eyes. Ann smiled.

Grace, tall and slim, was Ethiopian by origin with the natural poise of the people of that region. She had met Alsa while in London when training as a doctor. She had specialized as a general surgeon with anesthesiology as a secondary professional skill.

Her physique had allowed her to be a top tennis player and an excellent athlete. Modest by nature, she was perceptive and witty. Ann liked and respected her. The fact that Grace's husband was the L2 station chief meant she, as resident surgeon and wife of the station L1, was highly regarded. Ann trusted her judgment and would have had no qualms if she ever had to go under her knife.

By contrast, while a sweet, funny, and caring person at 155 centimeters tall, Fiona lacked Grace's athletic prowess, although she was a good gymnast. Her small stature and blonde hair contrasted with Grace, who at 185 centimeters was almost as tall as her husband.

Fiona was, however, an extremely talented chemist. The process of converting raw seawater to its component parts, extracting the salts, and refining them for chemical use was a science in itself. Fiona was meticulous and thorough. She headed up the purification and extraction plant.

Her husband, Tony, Alsa's second-in-command, a trained pilot, astronaut, and engineer, was in charge of the day-to-day running of Luna2. A keen amateur geologist, he and Fiona liked nothing more than to set off in a four-by-four with two microlight aircraft on the roof and go exploring hills, ridges, and canyons. He and Fiona had had some pretty wild times in the Rockies.

His knowledge of rocks and their formations was impressive. And as a chemist, Fiona was aware of the chemical properties of the rocks that her husband could recognize and classify. Max had joked that if they wanted, they could become precious mineral prospectors and make a healthy living.

Tony, a Californian, could only smile wryly at this notion. He held a family secret.

In fact, Tony was able to trace his roots through his paternal grandfather. His family was actually descended from a gold prospector who had come to California during the rush of 1848. He had been one of the first to the Sutter's Mill area, the birth of the Great California Gold Rush. Prospecting was in Tony's blood for sure, and there was no doubt he would make a success of any such venture if he chose to pursue it. He thought Max was unaware of this fact, but Max chose his men carefully and made it his business to research their pedigree. Max planned to admit this knowledge and beg forgiveness for his good-natured jest at Tony's expense.

"*Mesdames et Messieurs, bonsoir et beinvenu!*" announced Gaston. "The hors d'oeuvres are ready, *a vos plaisir.*" He proudly motioned to the table. "*Bon appétit!*"

The diners grouped at either side a magnetic table where dishes were heated and stuck, slivers of steel in their bases. A gentle air curtain from each side of the table kept the hors d'oeuvres from drifting. In practice, the absence of drafts meant food usually stayed in place.

The aperitifs wobbled as small spheres over the dishes a row of slow air vortices kept them from drifting far. Drinking could be performed by sucking at the spheres of liquid, but it was considered polite to use a straw.

The edge of the table had a deep edge which had a Velcro type fabric to which the patches on their clothing could be stuck, and so anchor oneself. Novices could use padded clamps on flexy arms that lightly gripped a diner around the waist. This was formal dining in space. A whole new etiquette for eating in zero G had evolved.

Normally, the daily need for nutritional intake was treated as a necessary chore and delivered by an assortment of boxes, bags, and tubes with a variety of methods of conveying nutrition without mishap or spillage. Any spillage of fluids or solids was a nuisance since they eventually ended up in the room's exhaust filter and had to be cleaned out during the regular daily chores.

The mark of one's etiquette was the absence of food particles floating where you had eaten.

They sipped their aperitifs and nibbled an assortment of Gaston's amuse-bouches that included canapes of Pate-de-foie, Beluga caviar, scrambled quail's eggs on biscotti, Parma ham, and stuffed olives, all of which were served in bite-sized portions.

Max, Alsa, and Tony briefly discussed the business of L2. Max was pressed to tell of his vacation while the ladies chatted, catching up with Ann. Most of the conversation was social chat as L2 station business was known to all. L2 was a close-knit community with senior personnel connected to each other by their electronic devices and an integrated communications network. This meant most people were fully aware of all happenings at all times.

Gaston announced the main course and offered roasted pheasant and quail with his special chestnut stuffing and truffle sauce. This was all brought into the dining room and served in the magnetic dishes by the acolytes.

Meanwhile, Gaston, now acting as sommelier, came back from his *cave* with three chilled bottles of Chateau Haut-Brion white wine and decanted one into a curious glass vessel of Max's design. Based on a type of retort, with a spout and a one-way valve, it replaced a normal wine glass, allowing the wine to give up its bouquet but preventing it from floating around unrestrained. Gaston offered it to Max to taste for approval.

"Very good, Gaston. A good choice. Pour away." Gaston glowed with pleasure and carefully decanted to the other retort glasses and retired to let his guests enjoy his creation with another bow and murmured bon appétit.

The diners ate, drank, and chatted and later sent their compliments to the chef. With the typical Gallic modesty of his profession, Gaston came out of his kitchen, thanked them with a flourish, and gave a deep bow.

He then presented sorbet and a choice of cheeses (French, of course) with coffee, Cognac, and mints to finish.

They chatted for another hour about general L2 topics, and Max was left with a feeling that the problems with the station were few and that the operation was running smoothly under his team's management. Having said their good nights, they retired at 1100 mid-Pacific Earth/L2 time.

Their quarters welcomed them with soft music. The walls glowed softly, and Max asked Jeeves to put on an underwater scene. A seaweed strewn seabed of sand with a coral cliff teeming with multicolored fish came into view, making their room seem like a transparent underwater bubble.

Tired from the long flight from Earth, they climbed into a sleep net and were soon asleep, floating in the underwater seascape.

6

E ight hours later they were gently woken by dancing, dappled sunlight streaming down through to the seascape floor, flashing off the flanks of the swirling schools of fish. Sensing movement, Jeeves greeted them and took their breakfast order.

Max replied, "Full Monty for me. Thanks, Jeeves." Otherwise known as "cardiac arrest on a plate," it was named after the WWII General's favorite breakfast. Max had modified the meal by stipulating all to be grilled, not fried, with the addition of tomatoes, mushrooms, orange juice, and coffee instead of tea.

"Museli, mushroom omelet, fruit, OJ, and coffee for me, please," Ann said.

They climbed out of the sleep net and floated to the shower cubicle and attended to their ablutions while Gaston's kitchen prepared their breakfast.

Half an hour later, the chief and his partner were eating their breakfast. They were now dressed in the L2 uniform white jumpsuits with Aqua4 logo, reflective chevrons and epaulettes for safety, and sticky boots. They were now back at work.

Having eaten, they went to the control center to oversee the operations. The new solar pumps had arrived the day before, and in the sunlight outside, they could see via CCTV the installation crews at work under Alsa and Tony's supervision.

"Good morning, Alsa, Tony," greeted Max.

"*Jambo, jambo mbwana,*" replied Alsa. In the background Tony waved his greeting. He was in discussion with some of the crew members moving the solar-powered pumps into position. Regular machines came with their own array of solar panels that tracked the Sun as L2 moved around its daily orbit. Therefore, these were stand-alone units that could be placed anywhere and ran on the Sun's rays. As powerful as the panels were, they were subject to the Sun's direct rays unobstructed by atmosphere.

Other teams were pumping purified seawater on a sector-by-sector basis. Now that L2 had its own mild gravity, the recondensed water settled as a crystalline fog on the surface. The slight gravity and the covering of Polyal film kept the sublimated water vapor on the surface and preventing it floating into space.

The early days of the formation of L2 were the hardest. The water crystals were hard to keep together and had to be contained by using an electrostatic charge that made the ionized vapor stick to the body of the nascent ice moon. Now there was a daily cycle of sublimation under the Sun's rays and a nightly condensation. "Two days to our next seeding, isn't it?" inquired Max.

"Yes, Mbwana," replied Alsa. "We are setting up in sector B right now. Do you want to have a look?"

"Not yet, Alsa. I will have a look at the PolyAl film canopy today. I noticed we had a new delivery."

"Very good, sir. Yes, we did. Want me to meet you there?"

"Yes, please. Can you meet me in forty-five?"

"Will do, sir."

Turning to Ann, he asked if she wanted to come out to the shield. She shook her head.

"No, boss," she said and grinned. "I have to see Grace and Fiona and see how their operations are going."

Max nodded. "Okay, see you at dinner," he said and went to put on his spacesuit and find a pod to take him to the canopy shield on Sun side. As the lift cable ran through L2's equator, the personnel had naturally adopted the terms Earth side and Sun side. He kitted up in his suit and took one of the pod buggies and set off for the surface. During the journey to the surface, he chatted to the various team leaders and get updated on the status of the works around L2. By the time he had reached the surface, Max was satisfied all was well and L2 had been running normally in his absence.

Coming out into sunshine at the surface, Max flipped on his gold-plated visor sun shield and guided the pod to the canopy shield over the current work area. There was an ongoing project to shade work areas from the worst effects of the Sun and to close off the surface as work progressed.

The shield was made up of PolyAl plastic sheet stretched out as a canopy over work areas, which made working on the surface less subject to the extremes of temperature and light, direct sunlight being extremely hot and bright and the shade being extremely cold and dark. The area under the canopy was bathed in a milky glow that made working more agreeable as well as easier on the eyes and their spacesuit's cooling system and also reduced the amount of sublimation of the precious water.

Max met Alsa, and they did a tour of inspection to view the new PolyAl film sheets being added to the edge of the canopy by welding along the edges. Looking down to L2 from the canopy, they could see men and women working in the glow of the shade twenty meters below them.

Satisfied all was well with the canopy, they returned to the surface and inspected the progress of the water spraying underneath them. Reciprocating snow cannons sprayed plumes of water vapor that instantly turned to ice crystals and drifted to the surface as a fog. Each successive layer served to gently compact the previous layers under the microgravity. The density of the ice increased as one approached the core.

Therefore, the surface of L2 was not a definable compacted surface but the cloud-like texture of frozen fog becoming a fine powder snow to hoar frost. As the daily water crystals warmed, melted, and froze into larger crystals, they drifted toward the core and slowly compacted. When a new area had been seeded with new vapor the canopy was allowed to drift down and cover the area with a reflective, gas-proof layer over the surface. This minimized the vapor lost to space.

Happy with the progress, Max and Alsa went to eat at the canteen, where all the surface personnel ate. This facility and the work area was protected from radiation by an artificial magnetic field that created a local shield a kilometer wide that could be moved around to protect the work area.

There were about thirty persons, and Max, of course, knew them all. He nodded and greeted them all by name, exchanging a word here and there. The kitchen was an annex of Gaston's, and he had overseen the preparation of all food sent to the surface.

The canteen structure was a geodesic sphere tethered to the lift cable's Sun-side station. Here there were no loose floating meals or drinks. Food was consumed in the normal space fashion from squeeze bags and tubes.

The afternoon was spent in further inspections, discussing progress schedules, and planning future progress. They decided to visit Earth side the next morning to oversee preparations for seeding.

This *seeding* was a monthly process whereby freshwater was reintroduced to Earth's atmosphere at precise locations in an attempt to rectify the worst effects of changing world weather patterns. The ice *bombs* were mined from the core of L2 and catapulted at precise times and trajectories toward the surface of Earth. They would lose their protective biodegradable sabots in the reentry burnout and explode at predetermined heights and locations, creating rainfall in arid zones.

An enthusiastic group of followers would track these incoming *bombs* and illuminate them with lasers to create a spectacular light show visible for thousands of kilometers. The sunsets and dawns were always a sight to appreciate in their own right in the aftermath of a seeding.

The natural migration of purified seawater toward the core of Luna2 meant the ice removed for seeding was replaced by the ice moving toward the core. This seeding ice naturally went to the Earth side. The freshwater ice destined for the Moon stations went to the Sun side.

Max returned to the core base, and later he was joined by Ann in their quarters while he was on a computer going through L2 business.

"Hello, Max, darling, did you have a good day?" she said and smiled.

"Yes, thanks, and yours?"

"Yes, good. I don't think we are needed anymore. The place runs itself. We could probably have sailed around for the rest of the year."

"Maybe so. But I would soon get bored, and there would be no new developments or innovation. My baby needs me."

"Me too." She snuggled up to him.

They kissed, undressed, and made love in the shower.

Jeeves kept a respectful silence.

CHAPTER 7

Dinner that evening was more modest at Max's request as they returned to normal working routine. Gaston would serve gourmet meals every night if not kept grounded. He was given free rein at weekends when the senior personnel were off duty as much as one could be on a space station, which by necessity ran 24-7. Saturdays and Sundays made the nominal weekends.

There were, however, recreational pursuits for those who enjoyed space watching. From the Earth-side station, one had a spectacular view of Earth. The Earth-side and Sun-side stations each had an observatory with a powerful astronomical telescope to allow personnel to study the Earth or the heavens as they wished. The Earth-side one only gave a view of the Pacific Ocean, but there was a group who loved it. The islands, the ships, the Pacstation were all a changing tableau. Also visible was the western seaboard of North and South America, New Zealand and Eastern

Australia, the western Pacific Rim islands, and Japan. From the Sun-side station, a whole constellation of the cosmos was available, and the Moon and Sun were the favorite subjects. And the sky was always clear! Understandably, this was the more popular viewing platform and had more telescopes.

There was an exercise room that Grace was keen everyone should use at least twice a week to offset the muscle degradation from living in microgravity. She had devised special workout routines designed for space dwellers. She also acted as personal trainer for all personnel and expected all to follow her regime. Devised on an individual basis, most people complied, realizing the benefit of her health plan. Only Gaston was rebellious on occasion, claiming it interfered with his digestion.

Photography and naturally astrophotography, chess, music, reading, Web surfing, and art were all popular. Max had his own airless hundred-meter shooting range where he practiced with a rifle, pistol, bow, and crossbow. These worked well in space with no air resistance and the absence of gravity, all combining to give a very flat trajectory. A projectile here would continue indefinitely unless acted upon by another force, according to Newton's second law of the conservation of energy. Max had mused upon a hypothetical coroner's verdict. "Yes, Your Honor, I return a verdict of accidental death. He was killed by an arrow shot at a range of approximately 3,000,760 meters. No question, I believe, of homicidal intent by the archer."

One Sunday evening after dining early together, Max and Ann retired to their quarters. Max went to the control touch pad, and the walls gave a real-time view of the outside of Luna2. He saw the Sun, the Moon, and the stars with Earth on the Pacific Ocean side looming large below them. They romped around naked, fooling about acrobatically in the microgravity. The effect was that of floating naked in space, not something one often enjoyed. Pushing off from any of the wall, floor, or ceiling surfaces, they would glide around the room, floating freely in space. Having played around like kids for half an hour, they climbed into their sleeping net and were soon asleep.

Max woke early, and as Ann was still sleeping, he went to his office and did some more calculations for his ongoing scheme for the Moon seeding project. This entailed sending chunks of ice to the Moon, where they were captured. The water was used in the geodesic domes where vertical hydroponic farms grew vegetables, fruit, and medicinal plants. These lunar farms were also scientific establishments to search for suitable strains of plants to genetically engineer and use in space. This was done to provide a food source for the developing colony on the Moon and the small colony on Mars. New techniques of space farming were constantly being developed. A useful natural spinoff of farming was the oxygen production and carbon dioxide scrubbing, which all helped to maintain the dome's atmospheric quality and gas balance.

These domes were getting larger as the Moon was being increasingly populated. The water found at the poles of the Moon was mixed with dust and rock, and it had to be processed. There was never enough. Wherever possible, existing lunar geological features were used to house people and farms. Caves provided ready-made structures below the lunar surface. These had the advantage of protection from the worst effects of the intense heat and cold of direct sunshine and shadow. Another benefit of being below ground was protection from the solar and cosmic radiation, a protection provided on Earth by its magnetic field and atmosphere but lacking on the Moon.

Aqua4's ice packets were fired at the Moon from a rail gun mounted on Luna2. Solar-powered, the guns were able to accurately shoot each ice packet or bomb, as they were popularly known—a task made easier because of the lack of atmospheric drag, gravity, wind, and humidity. Furthermore, each packet was fitted with a radio beacon to simplify location and interception. At the Moon end, the packets were tracked, and a space tug was used to capture the speeding packets and deflect them into Lunar orbit, guiding them down toward the Moon surface where they were they fell under the one-sixth Lunar gravity to collection areas.

These packets were added to the reservoirs in the terra-atmosphere of the geodesic domes and excavated tunnels. Some of the water was split into hydrogen and oxygen with electricity generated by surface-based solar panels and also integral into 75 percent of the geodesic skin. These technologies were used to provide experimental knowledge as part of the design development program.

Power was also provided by solar furnaces on the surface. Hectares of synchronized mirrors that lined the crucible of one of the many meteoric impact craters whose forms made for easy reforming into parabolic profiles. The intense heat was used to heat synthetic oil, the circulating heat transfer medium, in order to create a closed circuit system that could drive electrical turbines. A low-key and relatively low-power output plant, it worked for small installations, generating only about twenty-five megawatts.

In addition, there were square kilometers of photovoltaic solar panels in geostationary Moon orbit, and their power was beamed to the lunar surface.

Max had developed this ice packet delivery system as a natural extension of his Luna2 project. There was a huge demand for pure ice both on Earth and the Moon. Max's new project was to set up a similar system to supply the pioneering station on Mars.

While Mars had water, it was mainly concentrated at the poles, where there was minimal sunshine for solar capture. There was a need for a planetary supply of freshwater. Doubtless, there would be a time when the pioneers were more established and the polar ice would be exploited, however there was an immediate stopgap need for freshwater in this colony. A project to kick-start the pioneers had never been implemented, leaving the pioneers mining what water they could find in the subsurface rocks.

There was no shortage of water in the solar system. The asteroid belt between Mars and Jupiter had water. Jupiter's moon, Europa, had more water than Earth. It was made up of a thick crust of ice over an ocean at least a hundred kilometers deep.

Vast quantities of water had been discovered in Saturn's rings and its sixty-two moons, Enceladus being the most promising as a ready source, but at present it was not economically viable to mine at such a distance. The attraction of mining Saturn's rings and moons was that they were effectively free floating in space, and thus, to move the ice or minerals, one was not obliged to escape the main planetary gravitational pull. The objects needed a relatively small force to move them out of their orbit around their mother planet.

All of this was of little help to the Mars pioneers, but Max had a plan to rectify this.

However, the time was not long away when it would be possible to collect ice and minerals from within the solar system. This was what occupied Max's thoughts of late. He was working on a system using a plasma motor that would gently nudge space icebergs and minerals toward Earth, the Moon, and Mars.

Mars was the focus of Max's thoughts. It was the new frontier, and it was ripe to become populated. In the meantime, he was in the process of negotiating a scheme for sending chunks of ice to Mars by the more conventional tried and tested method used to supply the lunar stations. Unlike the Moon, which was locked into Earth's orbit, Mars was an independent planet with its own orbit, a moving target. He was busy calculating the volumes of ice he could send, the speed of transit, the frequency of the packets, and the energy required to send them on their trajectory. This entailed calculating Earth's relative position with Mars throughout their respective orbits around the Sun.

Fortunately, Max didn't have to reinvent the wheel. The relative orbits of Earth and Mars were well known, and much of the computation was now established mathematics. There were software algorithms designed for just that problem, having been created for previous Mars missions. Max had employed computer programmers, mathematicians, and astroscientists to modify established programs to meet his particular need. This meant that he was able to play around with theoretical cargo sizes and other variables according to the planetary orbital cycles to establish the necessary force, trajectory, and timing of various supply packets.

The object of the system was to send a regular delivery of *spaceberg* packets in a steady stream to Earth, the Moon, and Mars until the Earth's sea levels were reduced to an internationally agreed upon level. This in itself was a complex problem that was governed by multiple factors.

First, there was the fact that man's activity had triggered the global warming problem in the first place, creating the current rise in sea levels. It was still unclear what *was* the *normal* level for the oceans. The more it was understood, the more this was difficult to define. Through millennia, sea levels had changed with the ice ages as a result of solar and volcanic activity. In effect, there *was* no *normal* sea level.

Scientists were still unsure of the current status in respect of ongoing planetary warming. The effectiveness of the stringent measures to curb the level of emission of greenhouse gasses could not be appreciated immediately as it took time for these measures to take effect and be measured. Furthermore, there were so many variables involved. The burning of fossil fuels was long established as a major cause, but they could not be eliminated overnight. And while nuclear fuel, geothermal, wind, wave, tidal, and solar power all strove to fill the energy gap, the rising need for power had outstripped supply.

The global warming situation on Earth was under intense and constant evaluation, but the efficacy of all remedial measures was still unknown. Global air and sea temperatures were monitored and conclusions drawn, which were then overturned when new variables at play were understood. Vast computer modeling programs to predict outcomes of given variables were only as good as the quality and relevance of the input data. "Rubbish in, rubbish out," as they said in computing circles.

In addition to the physical variables, there was the seemingly insurmountable hurdle of the nations agreeing upon a policy on gas emissions and the ability to police those agreements. Some countries not immediately affected by global warming or indeed benefiting in the short term were reluctant to comply with gas emission regulations. Poorer countries simply could do little other than try to survive.

The net result was that as Earth entered the last two decades of the twenty-first century, the destiny of mankind as the dominant species—indeed, its very existence—was far from certain. The prospect of runaway global warming was still a very real threat. Mankind could go the way of the dinosaurs and give way to the insects, reptiles, and fish. As many conjectured, however, the era of the mammals would be over.

And what of mankind's existence on Earth, known as the Anthropocene? Its existence, a mere four million years, was the equivalent of maybe one nanosecond in a year.

One thing *was* sure. Earth would continue to spin on its axis and its orbit around the Sun and in a mere thousand years or so would largely repair itself. There would be little trace mankind ever existed.

CHAPTER

8

As Earth rotated, the Pacific side of the planet came into sunlight, and with it, Luna2 experienced its own dawn. The cameras creating the scene in their apartment recorded the approach of dawn, and Ann, still naked, stirred from her sleep. Noting Max was up, she climbed out of the sleep net and did some morning exercises to stretch and loosen her body and stimulate circulation. Jeeves sensed the movement and made a low beep to receive any instructions. Ann noted it and asked for a warm shower. She entered the shower room cubicle and spent fifteen minutes on her ablutions.

Max arrived from his office and entered the cubicle. They embraced and kissed good morning. Ann left Max to his shower and went to dress in a light tan jumpsuit and cream boots. She intended to do a round of the station to see how Grace and Fiona's departments were doing.

Max emerged and dressed in his commander's black jumpsuit and boots. The boots they wore were not for walking, of course. They were a fabric with micro loops that stuck to areas of the walls, floor, and ceiling, which all had a matching micro hook fabric, using a once patented fabric called Velcro. When a person needed to be anchored to a specific spot or to afford some leverage, they merely pushed onto a surface to *stick* to it. Work jumpsuits usually had integral sticky fabric patches at knees, hips, and elbows for adhering to surfaces.

When dressed, they went to the communal mess room and had fruit, cereal, eggs, fruit juice, and coffee. This was supplemented by one of Grace's special pills. This was a composition pill that Grace had devised to ensure all staff members were fully supplied with essential minerals, vitamins, oils, and any medication the individual was being prescribed at the time. Each tablet was individually made by Grace in response to a person's blood sample taken every seven days. The result was that no ailment was allowed to persist on Luna2. Also integrated was a new formula that had been devised to combat radiation, an inescapable hazard in space. It could not stop radiation. It merely assisted the body to rapidly repair the damage.

They were joined by Alsa, Tony, Grace, and Fiona. They chatted about the operations and the agenda for the day. They finished breakfast and headed off in groups to the various parts of Luna2.

Taking a shuttle pod to the surface, Max discussed his plans for sending packets to Mars with Alsa and Tony. They discussed the practicalities and what supplies would be needed. There was the decision whether to create a separate delivery launcher or to upgrade the existing Moon launcher. Max made the strategic decision to create a new launcher base dedicated for Mars.

He reasoned the Moon launcher's program could not be compromised. And he didn't want to interrupt the supply by modification work. He also reckoned that the demand from Mars would be such that, once operational, the separate launcher would be fully employed serving Mars. Therefore, they considered the logistics and material requirements needed to achieve a new launch station and the selection of a suitable location. The technical guys had established that the Sun side gave the widest sweep of the solar system and so could track Mars's orbit.

Arriving at the surface, they turned the shuttle to the proposed new launch area and had a closer look at the site. They had a long discussion on the location's suitability and practicality. The decision finalized, they contacted Commander Jackson with a preliminary procurement schedule. Commander Jackson would source the required materials and components and arrange delivery by cargo drone from ground base to Pacstation. All the logistics, material requirements, and methodology would be evaluated in detail by Tony's department on Luna2 in conjunction with ground base.

Having made their plan, the three men did a tour of some of the active areas of operation on the surface and later returned to the operations center in the core of Luna2. Over lunch they met up with the ladies and exchanged notes and information on their respective operations.

Ann had spent most of the morning with Fiona going over the water purification and pumping plant. She had witnessed via CCTV the sending of a packet of sea salt to the *graveyard* holding area in space from where it was redirected to wherever it was needed for reclamation of minerals. The new solar pumps were being installed and would soon be online for increasing the flow from Earth.

That afternoon Max talked with Alsa and Tony on an encrypted video conference with ground base, going over the plans to supply Mars and the required supplies from Earth. By evening they had drawn up a more refined plan of action, and duties had been shared and allocated to the various departments of Max's organization. Having created and installed the Luna2 base and station, they were old hands at the logistics of setting up space installations. They broke off at 1900 Luna2 time and went across to the living area to clean up for dinner.

Max found Ann in their office working on some spreadsheets that revealed the projected increased water purification figures. She had taken note of Max's plans for Mars and had made an analysis of the water volume they could send there. She smiled when she saw Max float into the office, and she floated into his arms to greet him with hugs and kisses. Exhibitions of affection were reserved for private moments. In public they showed their affection by a relatively chaste peck on the cheek as a greeting. Everyone knew, however, of their deeply passionate and devoted relationship.

Ann quickly showed Max her projection of available pure ice for Mars, and running over the figures, he was impressed by her grasp of the operation and their potential ability to meet the anticipated demand.

"Well, you certainly have done a good analysis. We seem to be initially able to send about 450 tons per week, going up to … whatever we can send on this end. The demand will be literally planet-sized. It makes one wonder if Mother Earth has enough water for itself, the Moon, *and* Mars."

"Yes, food for thought. You will have to develop your plans for mining the asteroid belt, Europa, or Saturn's rings as you were telling me. Can't anything be done in that direction?"

"Not sure. I was rather hoping that one of the big organizations would make some advances in exploration of those areas. There is also the matter of moving the stuff when you find it. At the moment we have enough water on Earth, too much at the moment and of the wrong sort.

"But that is the short-term view. There may be a time when sea levels are stabilized and we cannot afford to remove anymore."

"Yes, I have been pondering that. It is calculated that if all the water on Earth was formed into a sphere it would have a seven-hundred-kilometer diameter. Luna2 is now about five hundred kilometers in diameter, but it's snow on the surface in the process of becoming ice. There is another factor in the equation. The more we reduce the load on the Earth's crust by removing all that water, the more we destabilize the continental plates. In turn, we become prone to tectonic plate disruption. As a consequence, volcanic and seismic activity would probably increase. If we don't watch out, we could trigger an ice age. Sea levels would drop even further with resultant more crust activity and so on—a doomsday cycle of global proportions. We just don't know."

Ann pondered this. "That is a very sobering thought. How do we know when water extraction is too much?"

"We don't," replied Max. "The only thing we can do for now is to fight the battle against rising seas. We are, in a way, winning that one. If there is another pandemic like the Ebola or another virulent pathogen equal or worse, we may be in no position to care."

Ann shivered. "Not a happy thought, but we can only soldier on, combating the present threats as they occur."

"Quite so. In any case, any warnings we get that we have removed too much water will probably come too late for us to suddenly reverse the situation. The outcome of the cause and effect of our actions can take decades or longer to become apparent. We can only monitor the planet as closely as possible and be prepared to rethink our strategy at any time. And yes, if we have large amounts of water in the solar system at our disposal, we could replenish Earth's seas if we need."

"I think my Max is the only one who can save the world!"

Max laughed. "Not without you as my partner."

Ann giggled. "Listen to us. We are like a couple of lovesick teenagers."

With that, almost as proof of her last comment, they romped around their quarters, playing tag in the starlight and the glow from the Moon, the Pacific Ocean below them. They made love, showered, and dressed for dinner.

Dinner that evening was a buzz of conversation about the new developments regarding Mars. They all explored the idea, but there was nothing seemingly to delay the project. Luna2 was now of sufficient size to be a workable entity, and it was the world's first stable space platform from which to explore space. It was now of a size to allow the launch and landing of all types of space cargos on their way to and from destinations in the solar system.

The next morning Max along with Alsa, Tony, and Fiona had a video conference with Commander Jackson, and together, they drew up the program, timeline, allocation of duties, and a preliminary materials list for the implementation of the Mars plan. As this exercise had already been done for the Earth and Moon launch platforms, they were familiar with the overall requirements for the Mars launcher.

The job of estimating the demand for extra

equipment needed for the supply to Mars was allocated to Tony and his department. The logistics of material procurement and delivery naturally fell to Commander Jackson on Earth base. The bulk of these materials would be supplied via the spacelift, having arrived by ship and been sourced globally. The details of the design of the launch station fell to Tony's design and logistics department, which had already constructed the other two launchers and thus had the established expertise. Responsibility for ensuring supply of the added quantity of water packets fell to Alsa, the overall station manager, and Fiona. Together, they were responsible for the overall supply of purified water.

The meeting was not adjourned for lunch, but they managed to have sandwiches and drinks as the discussion progressed. They talked and planned until 1800 when Max summed up and set the follow-up meeting for three days later when they would again convene to evaluate progress and plan further in response to the developing situation. Therefore, they broke up after a ten-hour meeting, largely resolving all anticipated problems and drawing up a plan of action and timeline. Each member knew their respective duties in the plan.

Retiring to his quarters, he found Ann in their office checking over the available stocks of materials already on Luna2 and noting which ones would need replenishing when the Mars plan launched.

"Wow, that was a marathon, honey!" Ann greeted him with a kiss.

"Yes, but very productive, and as we kept at it, we were able to resolve the bulk of the plan and set up a formula for executing the project. Long sessions are productive as long as you can stay focused. They are also useful as participants can build the whole picture of the project and break it down to its logical components and priorities to formulate the plan of action based on the critical path."

"Woah, big boy! *Me no unnerstan'. You talk execcyspeak*," Ann said.

"Ha-ha. I guess I do lapse into business jargon after a session like that. Sorry."

"So *Operation Mars* is on its way I take it."

"Yes, I should say so. No real obstacles."

"Great. The whole idea is a winner, it's obvious. There's a big demand to be supplied."

"Yes, now it's just the nuts and bolts of arranging the supply."

"You've done it before. Your system is there. The packets will just take a bit longer to arrive."

"All true enough. It could be set up quite quickly."

"Good. Now dinner. Have you ordered anything?"

"Nothing specific. Gaston knows the meeting is over, and I guess he has something prepared, especially as we only had sandwiches at lunch."

"I'll give him a call and ask to eat at 2000."

"Good. Thanks. I'm going to shower and change."

"I'll talk to Gaston and tell the others about dinner if they want to join us. Join you in a minute."

With that arranged, Max went into the bedroom and stripped for his shower. He asked Jeeves to set a cold shower and projected an aerial view of Mars on the wall. He showered and came out as Ann was coming into the bedroom.

"I see you're really getting into the Martian thing," she said, eyeing the screen.

"Yes, I'm quite excited by the notion. As you say, it's a big project, a big demand to be filled."

"Okay, dinner is at 2000. I'll be ready in twenty. We can have a look at Mars right here while we wait for dinner. Would you like that?"

"Yes, I would."

Ann pressed a few keys on the console and a real-time picture of a Mars landscape came into view on the walls, giving an immersive 3-D view, placing the viewer into the landscape. Taking a controller from the wall, she manipulated the joysticks, and they flew across the landscape. She stripped and went into the bathroom cubicle. Climbing to an elevation of eight hundred meters, the image on the screen showed a flight southward, and rising over the lip of an old meteor crater, Max could see the land-based solar furnace that supplied the pioneer colony with their electricity. The bowl of the crater was lined with mirrors made of a silvered plastic film stretched over frames, casting their reflection of the Sun onto a black tower.

In a minute or two, Ann reappeared in her glorious

nudity and shining skin. Max's heart skipped a beat as he watched her glide over to the dressing area.

"Ah yes, I see our new PolyAI material is being put to good use. That's sector 24N39W station. I can see from the coordinate readout. They installed that very quickly. We only sent the film to them oh, about three months ago," Max observed, tearing his eyes away from her and looking back to the screen.

"Extreme need is a wonderful motivation," Ann said. Max nodded.

A flash from behind made them turn around. They saw the Sun glinting off a cargo ship making a pass overhead and disappearing into an adjoining crater. Max automatically guided their viewpoint into the crater, and they were able to see the ship landing and people disappearing into a geodome.

"More supplies coming in. They are really getting into gear out there. They will need lots of water. The sooner, the better."

"Mmmmm," agreed Ann.

"We will soon be ready to start sending ice packets to them. They will need to select locations and devise a capture system. I must get Tony to look into the technicalities of the design and supply of a system for Mars. We have an established system for the Moon, but Mars will have a different set of requirements. We will have to resolve any problems if the delivery system is to work efficiently."

"It seems Tony and the people in his department are taking on the lion's share of this new project. Are you sure they can resolve all the technicalities quickly enough?" asked Ann.

"Good point. Out of loyalty, he has naturally accepted all the jobs, which normally were part of his remit without complaint. In view of our desire to make this a fast-track project, I will discuss with him the manpower situation. I don't want the project to suffer through lack of staff. The problem is that our business is so specialized we cannot easily find suitable people."

"Maybe he has contacts in America we could draw on," Ann suggested.

"Yes, that's possible. I won't mention it at dinner tonight unless he does, but I will have a quiet chat with him tomorrow evening when he has had a chance to discuss the whole project with his department and has gotten feedback from them as to how they will manage. I think he will be more preoccupied with the supply from this end. The capture end has been partly left to the recipients, who have a vested interest in making their end work. On this project I feel the technical obstacles are going to be tougher, and it will be in our interests to resolve them as far as we can from here."

As if on cue, one of the dust storms came swirling around the planet at hundreds of kilometers per hour. It could last for days, months even. Mars could be a savage planet. The relative lack of atmosphere did not help. It was too early for terra and atmospheric forming to have begun as Man's efforts to settle on Mars was still in its infancy.

Max watched the dust storm developing with a pensive look on his face. His face brightened.

"Hey, look at that storm. Hmmmm … maybe, just maybe we could use those storms to help slow down those ice packets. The problem is the thin atmosphere, not much resistance." He mused, remembering the technical problems they had had with the Moon capture system. "Those high-speed storms could help. We must be able to harness that power somehow, deploy chutes or something. I'll mention it to Tony and see what he thinks.

"The problem is the atmosphere is so thin the wind has no real power," Max mused.

Ann pondered. "As far as I know, at the moment they just duck when those storms blow up. The solar furnaces are so efficient they don't even bother trying to harness them for power generation. They're too unpredictable. But yes, they may be useful for our purposes."

And so with these thoughts, they went to dine and joined the others. Gaston, who was aware of the long meeting and the lack of a proper lunch, had prepared one of his more gourmet creations to compensate.

"Mesdames, messieurs, I offer you a simple creation of my own that I trust will please." He bowed, and the acolytes brought in bisque as an entrée for a salmon dish served with a variety of vegetables from his garden.

Max gave Ann a gentle nudge, winked, and then murmured, "*Poisson*, Madame?"

Ann grinned. "I thought we had left fish in the UAE."

"Ah, but wild scotch salmon is a bit different to the fish we've been eating."

"Yes, and I'm sure Gaston has done us proud."

So the evening passed pleasantly without mention of the Mars project. The consensus was obviously enough had been discussed on that topic today.

They all retired early as they were tired by the mental exertions of the day.

Max and Ann went to their quarters and chatted for an hour while playing a magnetic board game that was not too mentally taxing. Then they climbed into the sleep net, leaving the walls set to a dim glow. They fell asleep almost immediately.

Next morning with renewed interest, they chatted in general terms about the Mars project. Max mentioned his thoughts on the ice packet capture on Mars, and the idea was considered a real possibility.

"I'll have my department have a good look at the idea," Tony said after he heard Max's proposal.

"It will have to be checked out by out physicists, mathematicians, and engineers but it seems to be a possibility. The system could be tried out on the Moon. The problem is the absence of atmosphere. So any chute won't work, but we could play around with packet speeds to correct for this and arrive at an ideal capture speed. I will ask them if we could use storms in some way."

Later that afternoon Max broached the question of additional staff requirements. Tony had been at a departmental discussion all day, assessing the Mars project.

"I don't think so, Max. There will obviously be a very busy initial period, but once we get a grip on the problem, I think we will cope. It will be difficult to get the right people anyway. May we leave our options open while we break down the problem. It may turn out that we may need some extra people to handle the logistics and people on the ground during construction of the launch station as I want to fast-track this project."

"Sure, Tony. Just give me the word if you need staff or anything, anything at all. I suggest however, you might like to put out some feelers in advance. You never know. There may be some unique talent out there that's useful to us. You know I am always looking for the best." He grinned. "That's how I found you."

Tony smiled modestly. "I will put the word out and see who turns up."

"Thanks, Tony. Don't try to take on too much."

"Thanks, Max."

And so the matter of extra personnel was left for the time being. Max made a mental note to monitor the situation. God forbid he worked his pivotal staff too hard and make them sick and overstressed, not to mention all the dangers that would bring. Max knew the whole enterprise utterly depended on the health and welfare of his personnel, especially departmental leaders.

Satisfied Tony would not be shy to ask for extra

personnel, Max put his mind at rest regarding the matter.

He made a visit to Grace's department and discussed the extra pressure the new project would put on everyone and asked her to be vigilant about signs of stress and any suggestions to avoid overtaxing the personnel.

"I will keep an eye on the working hours they keep as well as signs of tiredness through lack of sleep, and you can do the same and look for any indicators of stress, such as irritability, lack of appetite, and obsessive behavior. I see everyone every three days, so I can monitor them, including you."

"Yes, ma'am," said Max with a smile. Knowing she was right, he was equally prone to obsessive overwork once he had a new project to occupy him.

"I will be extra aware of signs of stress and counsel anyone who seems to be under strain."

"Thanks, Grace. Would you please check me over as I have not had your tests since my vacation? I hope I have not picked up anything in the Gulf of Oman."

"The blood samples you gave at launch base came up normal for both you and Ann, so I doubt you have anything serious."

Grace gave Max a full examination and pronounced him in peak health.

"Just make sure you take the capsules I prepare for you, sleep, eat well, and exercise in the gym, and you'll be fine."

"Thank, Grace. Will do." And so with a clean bill

of health, he went to see Fiona. She had been at yesterday's meeting and was up to speed with the proposed plan to increase ice output.

"Well, Fiona, we can't deliver on the Mars project without desalinated ice. Do you think we can increase output as we discussed?"

"Well, Max, I have had a good look at the figures and the spreadsheet Ann kindly produced this morning, and we can keep up with 82 percent of demand at the present output rate by running the present system at 100 percent. If you want to maintain L2's mass as constant, I would need more pumps and condensers to keep up with delivery. If, however, you aim to increase projected delivery over what was projected yesterday, we would need yet more pumping and condensing capacity. If you foresee an increase above those figures, we would have to look at installing more risers from the sea base."

"Mmmm, okay, I suspected as much and have come to the conclusion that between the Moon, Mars, and Earth, our customers would probably take as much as we can supply. Therefore, I propose we think ahead and plan for the highest output we can manage. I propose you draw up a shopping list of all you will need to, say, triple our current output."

Fiona's eyes widened. "Wow, Max, that's really is ambitious!"

"Yes and no. I am sure the demand will be there. Certain, in fact. What worries me is that you and your somewhat small department are responsible for the smooth running of the supply of our sole product of high value. The extracted salts are also valuable and may become more so, but at present it is the pure water that is our gold. What I would like to know is with this proposed threefold output, I need you to tell me what extra personnel you'll be needing."

Fiona frowned.

"Ahem, I'm not sure straight away. It's true a lot of the donkey work is the checking of water quality and monitoring the flow through the system. Checking water purity could be increasingly automated, but the whole process needs to be overseen. I will have to have a think about that and discuss it with my staff. They are all highly qualified chemists and technicians, and I need them to ensure a quality product. Whew! A *threefold* increase in output!"

"Yes, Fiona, it's a tall order. You are the first person I have mentioned this output increase to. I only decided on this while coming to see you. The question of demand and supply had been at the back of my mind unresolved since I decided to go ahead with the project. I am sure the increase will be justified. Please have a good think about what you will need to achieve that increase while maintaining the excellent quality you always do."

Fiona blushed. "Thank you, Max. I will give it my most careful consideration and will work out what we'll need in materials, equipment, and personnel. I'll draw up a schedule for the meeting in two days."

"Thanks, Fiona. I know I can rely on you." Max smiled reassuringly and left a somewhat stunned Fiona.

Whoooo! she thought to herself. *Max is really serious about this one!* And then she set to thinking about the effect on her operation and the changes it would involve.

Max went to see Alsa and explained what he had discussed with Tony and Fiona and the proposed threefold increase in output.

"I'm sorry. I would have discussed this with you earlier, but I only decided on that output on my way to see Fiona."

"That's okay, Max." Alsa was grateful for his chief's sensitivity.

Alsa, who knew the business as well as anyone, was in total agreement with the increase and was as sure as Max that there was a ready market for as much water as they could produce. As number one of Luna2, Alsa was in charge. Max explained his concerns about personnel levels and asked Alsa whether he needed any staff of his own.

"My requirements are only my personal administration staff, and there would only be the extra staff required to run the Mars operation. Say another four or five people. The main staff requirements will be for Tony's department, his design department, and the crew for construction of the new Mars launcher station."

"Tony said as much himself. Have a good think about the knock-on effects of a threefold increase in production and its implications on Luna2 as a whole. You more than anyone know this moon and how it operates. Your input and overall knowledge is essential."

"Thanks, Max. I will see if there are any hidden problems associated with this change in our operation. Luckily, what we already have here on Luna2 is a fully functioning distillation and delivery system. We have the know-how, experience, and equipment to efficiently deliver purified water. The template is here. With a commensurate increase in equipment and personnel, that model can be expanded to meet the new delivery quota."

"I agree. Thanks, Alsa. We will discuss all this in detail in two days when we have all prepared our reports and schedules of material and personnel requirements. I will need you to go through all this after the next meeting and give me a synthesis and your own recommendations."

"Yes, sir. I will do that."

Having seen all of the departmental heads, Max suited up and took a shuttle car to the surface, where he spent the rest of the day flying to the various work areas. He ate at the surface canteen with the snow-spraying technicians. To refresh and update his mental image of progress at the surface, he observed all the operations with the mental image of a threefold increase in his mind and envisaged the new level of activity.

One thing kept nagging at the back of his mind,

and he was not able to pinpoint its source until he was watching a snow-spraying operation sometime later in the afternoon. *If we increase the rate of snow spraying at the surface, would there be a threefold increase in the rate of compaction to for the density and strength of ice required to form the packets for delivery.*

Theoretically, the more the load at the surface, the more the rate of compaction below. The lack of gravity was undoubtedly a hindrance to the rate of compaction, and he wondered if to achieve the projected rate of delivery, they would need to artificially compact the ice or invent some new system whereby their condensate would be formed directly into solid ice—a proactive rather than the passive system they had used so far.

He was tempted to go directly to the experts and put the proposal to them. He had a dim recollection there had been a discussion on this very matter some time ago, but at the time it was rejected. New circumstances now brought new priorities, and the subject needed reevaluation. He resisted broaching the matter immediately. The various departments needed time to absorb his new directive before suggesting an overhaul to the whole methodology of ice production. He would bring it up at the meeting. Meanwhile, it was something for him to chew over.

He made his way back to the central command station deep in thought, and more than once he wondered whether he was trying to push his team too hard. They were all highly skilled, motivated, and dedicated. They would certainly make every effort to accomplish the goal, but he did not want to abuse his position and push them too far or too fast.

The mood that evening was one of suppressed excitement at the prospect of major changes, mixed with thoughts of how things would affect the structure of the operation as a whole. The conversation was therefore somewhat muted with pauses while each contributed their own thoughts. By common consensus, they retired early, each with their own resolutions for their part in the new project.

Thus forewarned and primed by Max in his usual attentive manner, the group reconvened, and they were able to each lay out their respective strategies and requirements for materials, equipment, and personnel in a clear and reasoned proposal. Max was happy to endorse their respective strategies, and he complimented and thanked them for their efforts.

They were unanimous in their backing of the project and excited by the promise of being a part of a new phase in the development of Luna2 as the major facilitator of not only the battle against climatic disaster on Earth but also the supplier of water to those who badly needed it and the facilitator of the exploration of their solar system.

The meeting was over by 1430, and Max proposed a week cool-off period to consolidate their ideas. He proposed a holiday trip to the Pacific Ocean station for a few days of relaxation on his yacht, which was moored there, starting tomorrow. Those who were to stay on the station were to have a week's vacation with only a skeleton staff to monitor the essential systems.

This proposal was greeted with smiles all around. All had been on Max's yacht before, and the thought of a week aboard away from the regime on Luna2 was welcomed. Max also knew that Grace would also approve as a return to Earth's gravity would benefit everyone's health. There was going to be an intense work schedule in the weeks ahead.

"All agreed? Good," Max said and smiled. "Try to attend to those items that need to be done to start the project. As you all know, there is space and clothing for all aboard the boat, so pack the minimum. Any incidental preliminary management tasks you are not able to attend to today can be done from the yacht. As you know, we have an excellent communications facility aboard."

All murmured in approval, and the meeting closed in a festive mood.

That night he commissioned the construction of new spaceship with similar specifications as the well tested *Titan*. It would not be ready for some months. He had asked Ann what to call her.

"SS *Phoebe*?" she suggested immediately, not really knowing why. So Phoebe it was.

The next morning the entire senior echelon and many scientists, technicians, and general staff joined the party on the spacelift to the Pacific Ocean base. Then they boarded Max's yacht *Gravity Waves*, a fifty-five-meter sailing cruiser with auxiliary electric impeller motors capable of twenty knots under power and unknown speed under sail. When quizzed about this, Max merely shrugged, claiming that he had yet to find her top speed under sail. He would say, "I don't really know yet. The maximum I have taken her to 42.5 knots with hydrofoils deployed. I was worried I was going to break something, and as I only had Ann aboard as crew at the time, I backed off from driving her any harder." He would smile in embarrassment.

The hardened *yachties* would suck their teeth and shake the heads. Their reactions were mixed and predictable. Some would say they would have driven her "till something broke" just to see. Others proclaimed outright disbelief. Yet others said that in Max's place they would never have the exquisite interior fit out, motors and anything not essential for a racing yacht, completely missing the point of the design.

The design itself was truly unique while retaining some old-school specifications. The hull was that of a modern racer in profile with a wide flat run abaft to encourage the hull to *plane*. There were retractable twin keels with spent uranium teardrop counterweights to give stiffness and stability. Independent twin hydrofoils would bodily lift the hull clear of the water and thus minimized drag when wave height permitted their use and maximum speed was wanted. The masts were of the latest carbon nanotube material, and a hollow adjustable aerofoil profile housed the roller reef sails to reduce weight aloft and keep the center of gravity as low as possible. All sails could be automatically controlled by computer to achieve a given speed, or they could also be manually overridden.

True to Max's principles, the decks were solar panels. Together with the wind generators and batteries, they gave the yacht an ocean-wide cruising range. In practice Max would cut the near silent electric motors in favor of the easier movement through the water under sail. There was emergency buoyancy which could be deployed from below the gunnels by the system Max had perfected on the catamaran in the UAE. The motors were mostly used for calms and to maneuver in port to pick up moorings. Max preferred to helm when under sail rather than leave it to the sophisticated autopilot. He just loved the joy of it.

Once all were aboard, Max set a course for the location of the now submerged Bunker Island, knowing it was now a coral reef and a haven for a myriad of fish. Excellent diving and fishing could be found there, and it was easy sailing to reach from the Pacstation.

Therefore, Max trimmed enough sail to achieve a sedate six knots, took the helm for a while, and then switched to autopilot. He joined Ann on deck. She was out getting her dose of vitamin D as were most of the others. The weather at the equator was modified by a breeze that cooled the intense sunshine. There were shower and changing rooms to take a cooling shower when needed. There was plenty of fruit and drinks with buckets of ice.

So they spent a week mostly moored at the submerged Kiribati Island, fishing, snorkeling, scuba diving, and learning to sail in the two pleasure sail dinghies aboard the yacht. The redundant buildings on pylons had had their pylons cut by explosives, sinking these temporary buildings below the water and starting an artificial reef over what was once the island's dry land. This well-known method of creating new reefs was an established and successful procedure. The existing reef fauna around the former island was quick to adopt this new seabed and rapidly became established to create an extensive new reef with all the marine life flourishing.

They spent the last afternoon at the ocean station. Looking at the operation there, they were aware that their new supplies would be coming up to them via the ships unloading at the dock before taking the ride into space. This prompted insights into the level of equipment passing through the station and the effect of the proposed increased throughput from the station.

Max, who knew the station intimately, skipped the tour and instead went to see the station boss. The commander, Albert Tongi, who had been born on Kiribati and who lived aboard with his large family, had been alerted by internal mail of the proposed increase in traffic he could expect in the coming months. He was doing his own assessment of his station's preparedness to manage the load. He was quite confident that he would be able to cope, but Max decided to order another four cargo cars to be constructed. He reasoned that should the vital link with the surface be compromised by the breakdown of one of the cargo lifts, the whole project would be delayed. Two of the new lifts would be pressed into service immediately, with the others could be kept on standby in the event of breakdown.

Later that evening they took a car to Luna2 and sat down to dine at 2000. There was a relaxed mood of merriment as they dined and chatted about their exploits on the *Gravity Waves*. Max noted this and felt content that his cadre were rested and benefitted from the break. They would need all their energy to implement the new project in the months to come.

CHAPTER

9

So began a new phase of Luna2's development. The next few weeks saw the planning, ordering, and transportation of goods to the site of the new Mars launcher. A new dedicated tunnel was cored through Luna2 to the new Mars launch site.

By March the problem of the rate of snow compaction was reevaluated, and with his scientists and engineers, Max designed a new ice-processing plant that was now being constructed in Japan and due for delivery in a matter of weeks. The new processor was able to take the purified condensate and form standardized blocks of pure ice that were much easier to handle and prepare as packets of varying size to feed into the transportation launchers. The delivery end of things seemed to be largely resolved. No doubt there would be teething problems at first. But Max was confident the science was sound, and it was just the practical application that might initially cause problems.

Far more intractable was capture at the Mars end. Luckily, as they were dealing with just cargo rather than a human payload, the speed of transit to Mars was not critical. If there were living cargo, be it human or another mammal, bird, fish, or insect, the amount of time in transit brought penalties.

With a live payload, the size of vessel had to be much larger as a complete life support system had to be incorporated in the transport vessel, and the longer the passage, the larger that would have to be, even though the living cargo could be put into a controlled hibernation. Part of that equation called for higher transit speed, which meant that greater speed had to be reduced at arrival to allow controlled landing on the Martian surface.

Martian atmosphere now came into play as a constraint. Mars is about half the diameter of the Earth but has only 38 percent of the gravity. However, the atmosphere is only 1 percent of Earth and composed mainly of carbon dioxide.

This thin atmosphere and low gravity meant it was difficult to use them to capture a speeding object into planetary orbit and slow it by using atmospheric friction as was possible on Earth. That traditionally meant the use of thrusters with all the associated fuel and rocket motors and control equipment, which added to the payload and size of the craft and demanded a larger rocket and more fuel to lift the weight to leave Earth.

This conundrum had dramatically slowed the rate of colonization of space and Mars. Mars missions launched from earth were increasingly uneconomic, but the advent of the spacelift meant that missions could be launched from Earth's orbit or the Moon after spacecrafts were assembled in space.

Max and his scientists had mulled over the problems associated with landing on Mars but had yet to solve the problem of landing large payloads gently and safely. This had taxed Max's inventiveness. If only Mars had more of either gravity or atmosphere ... or both.

Max had explored the idea of creating an atmosphere that many thought had once been present on Mars. Unless the colonization of Mars was to be restricted to man-made enclosed structures, an atmosphere complete with oxygen was essential for a habitable planet. The temperature on the planet could be made to rise from the average ambient of minus 63 degree Celsius with the benefit of an insulating gas layer. Ideally and ironically, Mars needed a global warming atmosphere.

This could theoretically be achieved by increasing the quantity of gasses, making for a thicker, denser atmosphere ideally composed of some greenhouse gasses, such as those which were presently the scourge of Earth's atmosphere.

If such gasses were available on Mars, locked into rocks or below ground, there was a chance that with technology they could be released. If carbon dioxide was found on the planet in sufficient quantities and there was a possibility of releasing it to form a gas cloak over the surface, that would be a start. If there was water, oxygen could be generated. The pioneer colony that had a shaky toehold on the planet was struggling to stay functional as all supplies had to come via the Moon from Earth. The progress was slow, especially because of the problem of landing on the surface. They were also limited in the amount of time and equipment they could devote to exploration. They were hampered by limited resources, and their primary occupation revolved around the day-to-day fight for existence and improving their tenuous grip on survival.

Therefore, there were preconditions and interlocking and intractable problems that seemed to defy resolution at the current state of progress, knowledge, and technology.

There was evidence of the existence at some period in the history of the planet of running water, which presupposed some form of atmosphere. There was a decades old debate about what had happened to the water and atmosphere, if they had existed at all, and that was still unresolved.

It had been established that there *was* water ice and carbon dioxide in the form of dry ice present at the poles, which waxed and waned with the seasons, Mars having an axial tilt similar to Earth. The amount of water ice was sufficient to create a sea if melted, and there was enough dry ice sufficient for an atmosphere. This liquid and gas were usually locked up at the poles because of the ambient freezing temperature. Max also noted that the loss of the atmosphere and water had taken hundreds of thousands if not millions of years to be scrubbed away by solar bombardment. If the atmosphere and water could be replaced, Max could accept that sort of timescale for it to be lost again. In any case, lost air and gasses could be replaced from sources in the solar system on an ongoing basis.

There was the tantalizing vision of a habitable, potentially luxuriant new planet, ripe for terraforming, populated with selected flora and fauna imported from Earth. This vision coupled with the all too real knowledge of the fragility of life on Earth and man's questionable management of his home planet added impetus to the quest to create a new Earthlike planet.

Mars was seen in some circles as a second chance for mankind. Clichés to "get things right this time" and "learn from our mistakes" abounded. There was a new sense of optimism, a determination to put our environment first and not to allow commercial expediency at the cost of nature govern progress and development. There was a realization that the huge diversity of animals and plants were our planet's heritage, our air, food, and pharmacy. It was our life support and our only real wealth.

It was also seen that what ailed Earth could benefit Mars. If only we could magically take the greenhouse gasses and put them on Mars ... and make them stay there. The only feasible method at present was to create very large domes. Some domes had been made, and as they only had to contend with one-third of Earth's gravity, they could be correspondingly larger. To date these domes had been rigid geodesic structures transported at great expense and heavy losses because of the difficulty of landing them safely. They were fragile, closely machined components that did not always withstand the sometimes rough landings.

Max had already proposed sending the raw materials to create polymer skin domes that would be self-supporting when a pressurized, breathable atmosphere was released inside them. He had domes that were kilometers in diameter. The bigger, the better, he reasoned. Twice the diameter would give four times the volume. If they also created a microclimate, that would be better for plant and animal life. He dreamed of a planet-sized skin to contain the atmosphere but accepted that was unrealistic.

While Luna2 geared up for launching ice to Mars, Max was increasingly pondering the problems of colonizing the new planet and how to overcome them. He became increasingly absorbed in the technicalities of the engineering and scientific obstacles they were trying to overcome. He was already doing as much to remedy Earth's problems as his ingenuity, finances, and world politics would allow.

His vision had led him to found Aqua4 and execute the Luna2 project, which was now operational. This left him without a major project to occupy his inventive mind. He had naturally gravitated toward this new problem, which was so closely allied to his core business. He was frustrated that little Mars was proving to be such a difficult problem to resolve.

He was reasonably sure that a location and capture system for his ice packets could be developed. There were no live passengers, so the G-forces involved to capture the packets could be high. He was sure these problems could be overcome with ingenuity. The problem was how to get large, heavy, and fragile payloads safely from interplanetary travel velocity to a safe landing speed at their destination.

He sat in front of the screens in his quarters for hours at a time, using the drone camera on Mars that relayed the almost real-time images from the planet. He studied the regular cargo ship that was able to land with reasonable reliability, although at great cost and a small payload. He had watched them at length with no inspiration for how to land the large fragile payloads he envisaged would ultimately be needed on the surface.

He switched from the drone to study the growing database of photographic surveys of the planet and looked at the geology and topography of the surface. He studied the stunning variations of topography and pondered the possibilities.

Mars was in possession of two moons—Phobos at a diameter of eleven kilometers and nine thousand kilometers and little Deimos at six kilometers and twenty-three thousand kilometers distance. Max carefully pondered both moons. Phobos could possibly be an outpost, a staging post, a landing point. At nine thousand kilometers it was close enough to serve any of these functions. But to what end? If you could land on Phobos, you still had to move cargos to the surface of Mars. There seemed no real benefit. The same argument applied to Deimos, which was even smaller and more distant. Max could not see any immediate use for the moons, so he returned his attention to Mars itself.

He studied photographic images displayed on his office wall and took virtual tours of the Martian topography from the archive database. He looked at Olympus Mons, a truly gargantuan feature, the largest known volcanic mountain in our entire solar system. At 21,230 meters high, it sat on a 550 kilometers wide base plinth that was itself three thousand meters above the surrounding land. It was about three times the height of Mt. Everest and at times was obscured by orographic clouds that could quickly appear and dissipate in the thin atmosphere. The main volcanic crater mouth is seventy-five kilometers across from rim to rim. Try as he might, Max could not see in it any potential to solve his problems.

From the extreme high of Olympus Mons, he turned his attention to the other major topographical feature of the Martian surface, the Valles Marineris. This vast valley system complete with many massive side canyons was equivalent to the Earth's East African Great Rift Valley or the Gulf of California. At four thousand kilometers long and up to two hundred kilometers wide, it is considered to be the result of ancient tectonic movement with possible modification by water. This vast scar on the surface of the planet is up to seven kilometers deep, making it a truly monumental feature, dwarfing the American Grand Canyon.

Max pondered the enormity of this geological formation. The Tharsis Bulge region formed the western edge of the various chasms, each of which looked like a Grand Canyon, branching off to the sides. The main canyon ran east until it opened out onto the *Eos Chaos* basin. This system of canyons inspired Max and stimulated his ideas. Given his already proven capture system for the lunar ice packets, he wondered if there could be a capture array of tensile webs strung across one or more of these canyons. "Mmmmm," Max mused aloud. "Just maybe. Maybe."

"Maybe?" echoed Ann.

Max turned to see Ann hanging in the portal to his office and peering at the walls.

"Thinking of doing some hiking?" Ann asked with one eyebrow raised.

"Not really. Not just yet." Max smiled and explained he had a germ of an idea and explained his thoughts.

Ann's eyes widened. "Wow! Never any half measures with you!"

"Grand plans call for grand solutions. It's no big deal really. Just a lot of string and sealing wax." He grinned.

"Ha! Can you get all that string and sealing wax down there?"

"Don't see why not. It's hardly fragile cargo. I'm not claiming it would be easy."

"Hmmm. Yes, it's possible. Bounce it off the technical and logistics guys."

"Of course. I don't have the time to do all the detail work. I just want to know if the basic concept works. It will probably come down to cost and what I am prepared to outlay to deliver the payload, not to mention how much the pioneer governments can afford. The ice packets are not fragile. It's the fragile, expensive stuff I am concerned about. Now if we can capture those, you see?"

"Ah, yes! I can see where you are going."

"Precisely."

"Mmmmm." Ann was looking thoughtfully at the adjacent wall. She opened he eyes wide and pointed.

"What's that?"

"What? What's what?" Max was bemused.

"There. That thingy there." Ann glided over to the wall and put her finger on a strange formation on the surface just to the west of the Elysium Planitia. "What on Earth— Sorry, I mean what on Mars is that?"

Max zoomed the view to where she was pointing and an almost perfectly rectangular area of land came into view to fill the wall. Even stranger was that the area was filled with perfectly straight parallel lines.

Max, too, stared in silence and glided toward the wall beside Ann.

"Umm, I don't know. I give in. Ann, please tell me."

"You mean you don't know? Why that's Washboard Plain!" Ann hid her faint grin.

Max furrowed his brow and then grinned.

"You nearly got me there. Washboard Plain, indeed. Very funny, although a good description. I really don't know. Very strange though, isn't it?"

Max switched on the scale grid so they could see distances. The area covered by the gridlines was about twenty to twenty-five kilometers wide, and it covered an area extending about seventy-five kilometers east to west.

Judging from the scale grid that lightly overlaid the image, they could see that the mysterious lines appeared to be perfectly straight dunes running almost exactly north to south. At the eastern end of this formation were two craters, both 5.5 kilometers wide, one on each side of the area, also on a north-south axis. Adding to this curious arrangement was a 4.5-kilometer-wide sloping furrow starting just south of the north crater and ending at the floor of the south.

The couple stared at all this in silence for a few minutes.

"What do you make of it?" Ann broke the silence.

"Don't know." Max was baffled. "I really don't know. You know how much that sort of thing bugs me."

"Yes." Ann knew all right. She knew him well enough to know that he probably wouldn't rest until he had satisfied his curiosity.

Max frowned, stroked his chin, and knotted his brow. "Most unusual. It is quite remarkable. Composed of such straight lines, it hard to imagine it was formed by nature." It was this that intrigued him.

"Nothing the pioneers have been up to?" suggested Ann.

"Definitely not. A project of that size, twenty by seventy-five kilometers, is not something you do overnight, and for what purpose? What would this be used for?" Max was irked by the conundrum.

"Maybe you will want to go hiking after all?" Ann teased.

"Well it's just the sort of thing to get me going." Max smiled. He didn't mind Ann's good-natured digs. He knew his obsessions could bring inconvenience or hardship to Ann, who, far from complaining, would accept his passions and was usually happy to join in his exploits.

"Checked the federation database?" Ann suggested.

"I will." And with that, Max went over to a keyboard to put in the passwords for the space federation's database. Once connected, the voice recognition could be used.

An hour later he rejoined Ann in the dining room taking coffee with Grace and Fiona.

Max shrugged in response to Ann's inquiring look. He knew she would not have said anything to her fellow girls. Even as friends, she respected Max's private business and would wait for him to broach the subject if and when he was ready. He did not see any need for discretion and outlined the oddity of the Washboard Plain to the other two. He finished by saying there was nothing about it on the SF's database and there was no record of pioneer activity in the region.

Ann could see he was frustrated by the apparent lack of information. She mentally prepared herself for him to be absorbed for as long as it took him to resolve his problem. Furthermore, she was willing to imagine Max going to Mars to solve the riddle of Washboard Plain himself if necessary.

That night Max explained his futile effort to solve the riddle. The very fact he had again raised the issue, Ann knew, meant it was intriguing him, and he was peeved he was not able to find out what was going on out there.

"You should contact the Mars pioneers themselves. Even if they are doing no work there, they may have explored the area. It's a strange enough phenomenon. I wonder if it is some secret federation installation."

"Yes, I'll be talking with the pioneers anyway. A far as the federation, they wouldn't confirm any secret installation. Besides, it's in plain sight and is not new. I checked old Google Earth database images going back to the turn of the twenty-first century. No conclusions."

Ann shrugged. "Seems like just the thing you like investigating." She was unsure how Max was feeling about the case beyond his natural curiosity.

"I am certainly keen for an explanation. However, the main issue at the moment is resolving the packet capture system."

And so they turned in that night with no further progress on either matter.

CHAPTER

10

Next day's search of other databases proved fruitless. There was no recorded activity in the area. Washboard Plain, as it was now called between Ann and Max, was an enigma. Max left the matter to be resolved at a later date. He was more immediately preoccupied by his packet capture system and had briefed a team of astrodynamicists and other specialists drawn from various departments within Aqua4. He left them to carry out the feasibility study and report when they had some firm recommendations.

What *was* clear in his mind was the need for a spacelift on Mars. Now that the technology was established here on Earth and the Moon, the project for Mars was far simpler. The gravity at 38 percent of Earth's was in this case a bonus. The success of completing a spacelift lay in getting some of the materials to the Mars surface, which depended on a safe capture system. The whole development of Mars hinged on this. So a solution had to be found. Other materials for the geostationary terminus at the top of the spacelift could be landed on Phobos, and the components could be assembled there.

Unable to pace around the room in thought, he went to his range and immersed himself in the art of archery. He took up a traditional longbow followed by a crossbow and moved on to handguns and rifles. Two hours later, having destroyed the bull's-eye of several targets, he had the germ of a solution.

He needed to go to Mars.

He knew Ann would almost certainly want to go too. He was sure that in fact she would relish the idea as this was new territory for both of them and she loved adventure. Before dinner that evening while they dressed, he broached the subject of his wish to go to Mars.

Max explained his need to have a look at Mars for himself and invited Ann. She had immediately agreed, knowing she would be sick with worry if he left without her. She could not imagine being parted from him for long.

"If you're going to kill yourself, I want to watch!" she said with heavy irony. Max would have felt guilty leaving her behind. Neither of them had been to Mars, so this was a serious exploit. It would be a serious pioneering mission.

He needed to choose other crew members to go with him to help with what was essentially a reconnaissance and feasibility study.

He did not have to think long. His old and trusted friend Joe Barnes was a natural choice. He was Max's buddy and fellow adventurer from their youth.

Judgment, intuition, and plain horse sense were the qualities Max knew that Joe possessed in spades, and he was a person Max could trust with his ideas, not to mention his life. He made a mental note to contact him in South America at his ranch and see if he was up for a trip to Mars. Joe was easygoing, which gave no indication of the adventurous wild man he had been in his younger days. He was now happy with his lovely wife, Marlena, and his eight-year-old twin boys, living his new life as a rancher. Could he be tempted by a trip to Mars? Max wondered if his friend was still the adventurer he always had been. Would he want to come? Max thought so.

If Joe could come, that was all he needed for this exploratory trip. The other things to do were to book passage on the SS *Titan*, the only regular method of getting to Mars. The *Titan* was Mars's lifeline with Earth and was relied on to ferry personnel, equipment, and essential goods to the pioneer community.

The *Titan* made the round trip to Mars as a regular shuttle service on a four-month cycle—roughly one month out, one month on Mars, one month back, and one month maintenance and provisioning on Earth. He knew the timetable by heart and that gave him fifteen days before the next outbound flight. He might have to pull a few strings to get on board. He had a lot of favors he could call in if necessary. His enterprise was so pivotal to Earth's rescue that he could call upon national governments.

"Joe, how the devil are you?"

"*Hey, Max!* Good to hear from you. What's up? Ann, okay?"

"Joe, Ann's just fine. Thanks. All's fine. How are Marlena and the boys?"

"All good here too. They are at school, and Marlena and I run the ranch. It's a bit quiet. Not much to do. I get a bit bored to be honest. What's up?"

"Got a new scheme. Just a little trip to Mars. Wanna come?" Max came straight to the point with his old buddy.

There was a moment of silence.

"Max, that's the most bat-shit crazy idea from you in a long time. How soon do we go?"

"Fifteen days. Will Marlena and the kids do without you for at least three months?"

"Hmmm, ranch is ticking over easy enough here. No problem there. She will want to chatter on the vidcom a lot, but she'll be able to easily cope with the ranch. The manager does most of the day-to-day running of the spread. She's good like that. The kids will be the same. It'll be okay."

"Great. I can have someone meet you at Pacstation."

"Don't bother. I know my way by now. *Titan* will be passing by I take it?"

"Of course. She now picks up all her water here for herself and as much free capacity as she can manage for Mars. It saves hauling it up from the surface. Heavy stuff, water."

"Expect me in about a week. I'll just sort things out here. Can't wait."

"Bye then. Look forward to seeing you. Bring some knitting for the journey."

"Ha-ha. Will do. Bye."

Fourteen days later they were boarding the spaceship as it was taking on ice for the schedule run. *Titan* hung fifty meters from the Sun side station. The elevator cable carried on into space and was tethered to the counterweight. Two elevator cars were being unloaded and goods transferred to Titan.

The last packets of ice blocks were stored in the spaceship's cargo hold in a special sector for ice. These packets were not like those sent to the Moon or used for seeding the Earth. For the Mars trip, they were loading one meter cubes of clear bluish ice, not wrapped but with separator panels that could be electrically heated to facilitate removal at their destination. Once the ice was loaded, the compartment was injected with water that immediately froze, so avoiding the load moving during transit.

Four crew members made up the regular members of the *Titan*. Patrick Hogan was the captain, an Irish American with ten years of experience with a variety of craft. He had once been a test pilot. Brian Meadows, a Brit from Manchester, was the copilot. Chris Williams, a Canadian from Montreal, was the engineer. And Amy Moss from London was the navigator. The passenger members included Max's longtime buddy Joe Barnes, who was an engineer, inventor, and maverick adventurer, along with Max and Ann making up the Aqua4 expeditionary team.

CHAPTER

11

The journey from Luna2 had taken them seventeen days Earth time thanks to their latest version of a thorium power plant feeding a plasma drive. The shortest recorded time from Earth to Mars stood at sixty-one hours for an empty craft, but speed was not the critical issue on this regular shuttle. They talked to the captain, Patrick Hogan, and his flight engineer, Chris Williams, who had made numerous trips to Mars and had a certain amount of local knowledge. It turned out that Chris had started as a civil engineer and surveyor. Brian Meadows and Amy Moss were new and so had little information.

Apart from general cargo and ice to serve the small pioneer community, there were only four new pioneers coming out to join the colony. The pioneer colony was a small group of about twenty-five persons, mainly scientists who were not self-sufficient and relied on regular supplies from Earth for the essentials of food, water, and air. This was provided by their governments.

They would land at the pioneer base and offload cargo and the new pioneers. When these duties were completed, Max arranged that the *Titan* would be at their disposal for two weeks. The next morning with unloading complete, they took off and headed to Max's chosen destination.

Olympus Mons drifted past the viewport as Max discussed his destination and arranged to bring the ship into an orbital trajectory bearing southeast to take them over the Valles Marineris, the region Max was considering as potentially suitable for his plan. They were orbiting counterclockwise eastward from Olympus Mons. They were 4,600 kilometers from their target landing zone in the Ius Chasma region at the head of the Valles.

The Valles Marineris, the gash in the planet from the foot of the extinct volcano, Oudemans, to the Eos Chaos in the east was ripe with potential for Max's scheme.

Captain Patrick studied the screen in front of his seat and occasionally tapped in commands.

"We will shortly be approaching your destination. There are two pods fueled up and at your disposal. You can take them to the surface in about thirty-five minutes," Captain Patrick announced. On the voyage Max and Joe had both been shown the controls of the pods and been assured they virtually flew themselves. One merely pointed the machine where one wanted to go, and the avionics did the rest. If photographic and video recordings were needed, they were available at the touch of a button. One could also record imagery via eye tracking built into their helmets.

"Thanks, Patrick," acknowledged Max. "Okay, Joe?"

"Sure thing, Max. Let's get suited up."

As already planned in the days of relative inactivity on the flight, they had decided that Max and Joe would go down first to make a recce to look out for a suitable location to act as a nominal base. This would act as a RV pickup point if anything happened.

They were to set up a base camp with an emergency unit. This RV self-inflated from its hard case and could sustain four people for a week. It was equipped with all life support needs—air, oxygen, medical equipment, food, water, and an all-frequency radio. The unit had a homing beacon and pulsing strobe light for ease of location. Once a grid reference was radioed, these RV units could be ejected by the mother ship to land in a matter of minutes. It was standard procedure to use one as a RV marker.

By the time Max and Joe were suited up and in their pod, the ship had slowed sufficiently to give an operational release speed, and they were to free-glide to an altitude of a thousand meters before needing to deploy retro jets and the landing gear. The pods were capable of VTOL, but normal landing and takeoff could be performed on any relatively smooth surface to save fuel.

The pods had a duration time of about ninety minutes under full power and were used to carry out reconnaissance and light lifting jobs. Flight in the thin atmosphere meant there was little air resistance, but at the same time, there was little lift for wings. A bonus was the gravitational force at 38 percent of Earth's meant less to resist. This set of conditions meant there were completely different flight parameters compared to Earth. Anyone who had used pods on the Moon was used to these flight characteristics and could quickly adapt.

They released from *Titan* at sixty-five thousand meters and had almost half an orbit to reach the propose RV area on the plain just south of Ius Chasm. They kept the pod to a flat glide with wings fully extended and flaps full out to scrub off as much speed as they descended. More than a hundred kilometers out from proposed RV location, they were down to five thousand meters at two hundred knots, too low and too fast. Max had been fooled by the thin atmosphere, so they were obliged to fire up the retro rocket to correct their trajectory.

"I should have left it to the autopilot." He grinned sheepishly at Joe.

"You haven't changed," Joe said and laughed. "Always wanting to be hands on, no worries."

With a few corrections, they made an approach to the RV on the plain above the valley called Louros Chasm. Max had switched on the high-resolution video camera. This video was simultaneously uploaded to the ship as she came into range while orbiting overhead.

They landed on the plain two kilometers to the south of the Louros Valles and sat in silence for a few minutes as the motors wound down to silence and the dust cleared, drifting away in a light Martian breeze.

"Well, Max," Joe said and broke the silence with a low whistle. "We've been some amazing places, but this sure is the best one yet!"

"You're right there, Joe." They shook hands and stepped out onto the surface of the planet. They stood for a few long minutes, gazing around at the topography. They switched on their helmet cameras, which stored and uploaded video to the ship via the pod.

The plain they had selected was almost flat and featureless. They could see to the horizon in the crystal clear thin air. Their business lay in the chasm to the north of them, and they set off to cover the two kilometers to the rim. Weighing so much less in the 38 percent gravity, they were able to reach the rim easily. The ground dropped away to a huge chasm that steepened as it went down, ending in an almost sheer drop to the bottom. They looked along the chasm for tens of kilometers in each direction. The chasm deepened and narrowed to the right to a depth of 1,500 meters according to their range finders. Max pointed an instrument across to the far side of the chasm.

"Seventy clicks," Max said.

"Doesn't look it," Joe observed "This clear air is deceptive. It looks only like five. Maybe ten."

Max nodded, deep in thought. They did not venture down into the chasm but moved along the rim to the right to see into the deepest part of the chasm. Looking left, due West from the chasm, there was Calydon Fossa, which was about three hundred kilometers long and eight hundred meters deep, a long, straight furrow leading straight into the canyon. Max nodded to himself in satisfaction. It was much as he had seen on the database maps, he thought now, *Just what I need.*

They came to a vantage point where they could see hundreds of kilometers down the canyon to what their helmet HUD told them was the Valles Marineris proper some 750 kilometers away, disappearing with the curvature of the planet. This main canyon was what Max had been studying on Luna2 and on the flight during the last days of travel. Now he stood four hundred kilometers from the foot of the *Oudemans*, the extinct volcano to the northwest end of the Valles and knew that they extended at least farther 3,500 kilometers to the southeast, ending in the aptly named Eos Chaos, where they ended in a jumble of broken landscape. The immensity was bewildering. The sheer enormity defied the senses. That with the absolute clarity of the atmosphere made an Earth mind reel as it tried to absorb the majesty of what lay before it.

The two men looked at each other and bumped helmets in a silent salute, each appreciating the poignancy of the moment. They indulged themselves for a while to savor the moment and absorb the view and surroundings. Half an hour later, they found themselves on the way back to the pod.

The Martian evening was approaching as the Sun

hung low in the sky. The evening light had a bluish glow as dust devils started to skitter around them.

"Bad sign," muttered Max. "This could blow up in less than a minute to a two-hundred-kilometer dust storm." He took a bearing of the strobe on the pod a kilometer away to ensure they could find it if visibility was lost. A sudden storm could reduce the visibility to meters in seconds and last for days. Because the thin atmosphere did not have the weight of wind of Earth storms and they also lacked visibility with the terrain being so featureless, that meant one could quickly get lost in the storms. Running out of air while lost only a few meters from safety would be a bleak demise.

Fortunately, no storm blew up. The devils had served as a timely reminder of what could happen at a moment's notice. The two novice Martian explorers made it back to the ship without incident. Max was reminded of the tricky flying conditions, and he left the autopilot to do its job.

They were greeted by Ann, who was exited to hear their news of the excursion. She was now the only one aboard who had not been on the surface, the regular crew having made several journeys to the planet. She was thrilled by the images and video that had been streamed from the pod and their helmets. She was able to play them back via a VR headset that effectively placed her on the surface.

"That was *terrific*, you guys!" she said and hugged them. "I was *completely blown away. Never seen anything like that.* I was so *jealous.* I *must* go next time. *When* are we going down again? May I go next?"

"Whoa, steady, girl. Yes, of course you can go. As you know, it's planned. But things can get rough down there very fast, so we have to play safe if we want to come out in one piece."

"Yes, I saw those dust devils. We have been watching those training videos for weeks. I was in your camera, Max, the whole time. Well, when we could receive streamed footage. I was *stunned* by how *huge* the chasms were."

So Ann chattered away as excited as if she had personally been there.

"As you know, we are going tomorrow, and you can come with me while Joe comes down with Chris. In the meantime, I have to go through the footage of the Ius Chasm and Louros Valles Chasma. I need to pull out some specific images and overlay some design sketches and send them off to Luna2 to the team working on the packet capture system. I want to show them how I intend to bring in our ice and get some water into this place."

With that, he disappeared and was not seen for several hours. He finally joined Ann to get some sleep at about 3.30 a.m. next morning. Mars had an equivalent length of day as Earth. They kept a twenty-four-hour clock on board.

"Mmmnnn, you been brainstorming?" she asked sleepily.

"Mostly a sweat storm. Scanning through hundreds of images of the topography down there."

"See anything you like?"

"Yes, we'll have a look tomorrow ... or today. Whenever I've had some sleep."

With that, he climbed into the sleep net with her and was asleep in seconds.

They rose at 1000 and breakfasted on space food, consisting of packets of porridge, bacon and egg omelets, orange juice, and coffee.

"After weeks of these sachets, I am missing Gastron's cooking," said Ann.

"Me too," agreed Max. "Imagine being a pioneer here. I know they grow their own vegetables, but we know their cuisine leaves much to be desired."

Joe nodded. He was used to Marlena serving fresh produce from the ranch and her kitchen garden.

By 1100, they were flying up the Calydon Fossa.

As they flew, Max explained his plan to Ann.

"The idea is to guide the nonfragile packets along this valley. You see that canyon ahead? That is the Louros Chasma. I plan to string a net across the mouth of the canyon to catch the packets. They'll then fall to the bottom, where they would become a reservoir of fresh water for the planet."

Ann gazed at the approaching entry to the canyon.

"Wow, that's a huge net."

"Yes, it has to be. We cannot guarantee being able to guide all the packets with pinpoint accuracy. If some are a bit wide of the mark, they will be contained by the canyon walls and find their way to the net. The choice of net material is important. There need to be a certain elasticity in the strands to accommodate the shock of impact. Any packets that break through will hit and probably smash against the walls of the canyon but eventually find their way to the bottom."

Max paused and gazed down. "It may be quite spectacular." He grinned.

"And the fragile packets?" inquired Ann.

"Ah, those will come later when we have perfected the net and the guidance system. The location need not necessarily be here. You saw all those side canyons? There may be other more suitable ones for fragile packets."

Ann nodded. "I'm not an engineer, but you will have to tie down the net to the walls of the canyon."

"Yes and no. We would have to drive anchor points on each side and have cables strung across the top of the mouth of the canyon. The net would hang from these, and maybe it would be anchored at the bottom."

"The packets would then fall to the valley below," added Ann.

"That's the idea. The materials for the net and anchors are all pretty robust and could be simply dropped into the Calydon Fossa and on the plain either side."

Ann asked, "You think it will work?"

"I'm not sure. The advantage is that it is crude and simple. The devil is in the detail. I am just exploring the idea and gathering as much information about the terrain and topography as possible and sending it back to our think tank back on Luna2 for their evaluation. If all the physics and math works out, the logistics can be assessed. We have the ability to send construction packets for the net almost immediately if all is realistically achievable."

"Are you going to send ice?"

"Yes, water is going to be a priority. You saw all the ice at the polar caps? There is a lot of water at the poles. The problem is it has to be transported and purified. Same as the ground permafrost, it has to be extracted and processed. That is a lot of work. We can get pure ice here ready to use if we get the capture system right.

"We'll need nitrogen as well to make an Earthlike atmosphere and to make ammonia, fertilizers, and explosives," he added.

"How do we stop all this nitrogen from escaping into space? Didn't you tell me that was a problem because of the low gravity?"

"Yes, until we can create gravity, we will have to build large biospheres to contain it. We need to get lots of things here. In short, we need our capture system. However when we create a new atmosphere, it will last for hundreds if not thousands of years. It's thought it took millions for the old one to be blown away by the solar winds."

"Okay, but create gravity?" Ann's eyes widened.

Max laughed. "Yes, who knows what can be done in the next few hundred years."

"Always the optimist." Ann smiled.

"Why not? Look, two centuries ago mankind was convinced flight was physically impossible and people would suffocate if trains went faster than forty kilometers per hour!"

"Hmmmm, yes, I suppose so," Ann conceded.

Still flying east, Max dropped the pod lower and flew along the Ius Chasma and into the Melas Chasma, which widened out to about 150 kilometers.

Ann sighed. "This is amazing. Look at that ahead!" she exclaimed.

"Fantastic isn't it. That's the Valles Marineris, thousands of kilometers long and hundreds wide. Truly spectacular. The Valles Marineris is the largest canyon known in the entire solar system. It's ten times longer than the Grand Canyon and much deeper. And as for the Olympus Mons we flew over, that is the biggest volcano known in the solar system. It's twenty-seven kilometers high. That's three times higher than Mount Everest."

She looked at him, wide-eyed.

"This is a serious little planet," she observed. He nodded.

"We'll go the poles tomorrow."

They flew the length of the Valles, marveling at the enormity and majesty of the landscape.

They gazed at the rugged scenery as they dropped and flew along a matter of two hundred meters off the floor of the valley. They were now indulging in sightseeing. Climbing to five thousand meters, they banked over the Eos Chaos and retraced their path to absorb the immensity of the region.

Max eyed their fuel reserve readout and realized they were due to return to the *Titan*. They made rendezvous with the ship twenty minutes later. They met up with Bob and Chris, who returned two hours later. They hadn't been burning fuel just sightseeing but had been setting off charges to get deep echo reading of the underlying rock formations around the Louros Canyon.

These readings would augment those taken by the *Titan* with its ground-penetrating radar to give a 3D map of the canyon for the boffins back at Luna2 to evaluate. These readings were downloaded to the onboard supercomputer for Max to play with his ideas.

The bundle of data was relayed to Luna2. Max could expect feedback in a matter of hours.

He returned to his quarters and continued going through the image and the seismic readings Joe and Chris had obtained. His ideas became clearer as he evaluated the terrain.

The next morning the ship's intercom came through with a message that the pods were refueled, and they headed to suit up again for another reconnaissance flight. He found the others already suited up, and they launched two pods as before. Max had already given his brief to Bob and Chris. From the *Titan's* altitude and speed, they could reach almost anywhere on the hemisphere. Their destination, Olympus Mons, was as much sightseeing as serious reconnaissance, Max admitted, but he thought it worthwhile. There were no complaints. Everyone was keen to see this wonder of the solar system.

Their destination was unmistakable. An ancient volcano that reared up twenty-seven kilometers from the surface of the planet, sitting on its 550-kilometer-wide plinth, it was truly impressive, especially when seen from a lower altitude rather than looking down from space. At about a thousand kilometers north of the equator, it was an easy glide down from their launch position, and swooping down, they were easily able to find a landing site in the sixty-five-kilometer-wide bowl of extinct crater. The thought that this immense crucible was once a seething bowl of erupting lava was awe-inspiring.

"I hope the ground doesn't tremble," Anne commented with a grim smile.

"No, dear, this volcano has been extinct for millennia," reassured Max.

They landed on the floor in an impact crater in the northeast quadrant of the main bowl, which in itself was four hundred meters deep and twenty kilometers across. Staring around at the two-thousand-meter-high sheer walls to the rims of the craters, the immensity of the landscape was vividly brought home to them. Nothing about this place was small.

This was Ann's first walk on the surface, and she slowly turned around and around, open-mouthed, letting out soft gasps of thrilled amazement.

"My God, Max, it's incredible!"

"Yes, I must say I have never felt so overwhelmed by a landscape. Austere but magnificent isn't it?" Max was equally impressed.

Joe and Chris were standing fifty meters away, just looking around but saying nothing.

Joe stooped and examined the ground and scratched the dust, curious. As a rancher and farmer, he was inspecting the regolith, assessing its potential for plant growth. He said nothing, so Max assumed he was unimpressed. Max was under no delusions concerning the regolith. He knew the chemical breakdown because he had had it tested. Creating an Earthlike soil would take time.

The four of them met up and chatted for a while, pointing while identifying features of the landscape around them. Their head cameras recorded the images they turned to. The two pods were also active, taking images and readings of temperature, pressure, altitude, wind speed, gravity, solar and galactic cosmic radiation, magnetic field, and air composition. All was recorded and uploaded to the *Titan.*

"Okay, folks, next stop," Max announced after forty-five minutes, and they climbed back into their respective pods and took off. They had to climb up and over the rim of the gargantuan crater. They set course for a southeast heading to Pavonis Mons. At a mere 13,500 meters, this next volcano was half as high but still higher than the normal cruising height of airliners on Earth. The crucible of this volcano was a more manageable thirty-five kilometers across and again offered an easy landing area.

"I've been studying this next crater. One thing that interests me about this volcano but is not immediately obvious is the fact that it lies directly on the Mars's equator." Max paused.

"And so?" Ann looked quizzically at him.

"And so it is the perfect location for a lift."

"A spacelift!" cried Ann excitedly. "You mean to put a spacelift on Mars?"

"Precisely, of course."

Ann pondered this. She was aware that Max had the technology. Had he not created the Luna2 system and four on the Moon? But Mars was a much taller order. The logistics were a quantum leap into the unknown.

"Do you think it's possible? It's a long way from home."

"I'm not saying it would be easy. In the dispatch I sent to Luna2, there was a scheme I outlined for a spacelift for Mars. As you know, the prime site for a spacelift is on the equator. The location of this volcano is also one of the best sites. It is the closest to the Louros Chasm we looked at yesterday, which is my best choice to locate the capture net."

Ann absorbed all this.

"It is about seventeen hundred clicks to the Louros Chasm, downhill all the way.

They landed in the center of the Mons Pavonis crater. The crucible bowl was an almost perfect circle, thirty-five kilometers across and 4,300 meters from the flat floor to the rim. As they all looked around, Joe's voice came over the intercom, "Max, are you thinking what I'm thinking?"

"Maybe. Tell me."

"I bet you are thinking of a dome over this bowl!" Joe grinned wolfishly.

"Have you been reading my mind again? Yes, that is exactly what I was thinking. I saw this bowl as a very likely candidate for the fragile stuff to come in via a spacelift. It is bang on the equator. The rim of the bowl would protect the inside from the worst effects of Martian weather. The lack of overall atmosphere means the altitude is little different from the lower land and hopefully would keep out of the thick of the dust storms. We would make our own atmosphere in here anyway."

"I knew it! You're mad, Max!" Joe crowed in a mixture of admiration and mirth.

"How big is this?"

"Thirty-five clicks rim to rim."

Joe paused and whistled. "That's some mother of a dome."

"Sure is. However with gravity at 38 percent, an air supported polymer material is probably a realistic solution if the materials could be brought in. Fortunately, all those new discoveries of fossil oil we can't burn on Earth can be used to manufacture this polymer sheet. It could incorporate a level of radiation shielding and will also stop loss of our manufactured atmosphere. To match Earth's air pressure, we need one bar, which I believe will hold up the dome."

"Manufactured atmosphere? How do you aim to do that?"

"I was just discussing that with Ann. Although Mars is not short of carbon dioxide—in fact, we may have too much of the stuff sequestered as dry ice at the poles—some of that could be sent here. Nitrogen could also be transported in liquid form. It would be necessary for an Earthlike atmosphere. With liquid oxygen, we would have the three main components of Earth's air, which would allow us to breathe and plants to photosynthesize.

They all fell silent in thought. Chris, the quiet engineer who was not very vocal at the best of times, just nodded his head.

Down in the bowl of the crater, the shadow of the rim was moving toward them as a reminder that evening was drawing in. On the equator, total night would fall instantly as the Sun dropped below the horizon. The thin atmosphere did not provide any twilight.

"Let's get back to the ship," Ann suggested, sensing the situation.

Max nodded. "No panic, but yes. I have some sums to do and schemes to scheme."

With that, they mounted their pods and headed back to the *Titan.*

On the way Max broke their pensive silenc. "There is also a smaller candidate for this plan. At about

twenty clicks wide, it is as yet unnamed. It's at S22'
W99 degrees 45', a mere four hundred kilometers away
from the Ius Chasma."

"Mmmm." Ann furrowed her forehead.

"So if I read your scheming, you plan to lower the
fragile stuff from geostationary orbit?"

"You've got it." Max smiled. She followed his logic.

"I have sent another plan to Luna2."

"Oh? Another?"

"Yes, I'm waiting for the guys back at Luna2 to
evaluate it. Tomorrow we go to the south pole."

CHAPTER 12

They were standing on an ice dune at the south pole. The top ten centimeters of dry ice had a crunchy texture underfoot and then got progressively firmer with depth.

On the flight here, they had seen the landscape below them. The topography was made up of a sea of ovoid depressions surrounded by ice dunes in all directions, flowing in mosaic patterns to the horizon.

"This is mostly carbon dioxide," Max stated. "It forms those clouds overhead, not particularly interesting to us in its present form, suffocating in fact without oxygen. It is, however, interesting to plant life, which through photosynthesis gives us our food and oxygen. Therefore, it is as important a resource to us as oxygen."

"When you say *mostly*, what else is it?" Ann asked.

"Ah, I glad you asked. The rest is water ice. I would also add that the south pole ice cap alone has enough water locked up in it to cover this entire planet to a depth of 12 meters if we could access it. The problem is that Mars is a cold place because of the lack of atmosphere. Our mission is to find a way to unlock that water and create an atmosphere to replace the one that is lost."

"How can we unlock that water?" Chris's engineering mind was at work.

"I was going to discuss that with you. I had this notion of using the Sun. If we put some mirrors in the sky at the north and south poles, we could use the Sun. The advantage of this method is that it would be controllable. By some method to be discussed, we could use more or less of the Sun's heat. Apart from the setup cost, it would be free energy." Max let that all sink in.

"That's my boy. He's done it again!" exclaimed Joe with pleasure. Ann glowed.

"Thanks for the vote of confidence, Joe, but there's a long way to go yet. There are a few hurdles to overcome. Here are some facts. The *average* temperature here is -60 degrees Celsius, which admittedly is not unheard of on Earth in the Antarctic, but it goes down to a brain-numbing -140 degrees Celsius at the poles in winter. As you maybe all know by now, Mars tilts on its axis by 25 degrees. That's similar to Earth, which is tilted by 23.5 degrees and thus gives us the seasons. However, as the Martian year is 687 days, the seasons are almost twice as long. It can, however, reach an impressive 30 degrees Celsius in summer at the equator."

Max paused to let them consider this when

suddenly the ground gave a tremble, and looking fearfully around, they could see a fountain of ice, sand, and rocks spewing hundreds of meters into the air. In contrast to the brilliant white of the snow, this was a spectacular yet unnerving sight.

"Blimey," exclaimed Joe. "What the heck is that?"

Ann jumped back and grabbed Max.

"Do they have geysers here too?" She looked at him, amazed.

"Yes, sort of. They normally come out of the same place but are unpredictable. You can see the holes in the ice, and the debris on the snow is a telltale sign. However, fresh snow covers them. We had better keep our wits about us."

"What if one of those was to erupt nearby?"

"Pray, and move away fast," Max advised dryly.

"What causes them?" asked Ann.

"Because of the very low melting or sublimation point in the case carbon dioxide, through the Sun or geothermal heat the dry ice evaporates to gas, sublimates, omitting the liquid state, and comes out under pressure through fissures in the rock. It also blows out all that debris you see around. Needless to say the falling rocks could be dangerous."

"I'd hate to have my visor smashed," observed Ann.

"Not recommended," advised Joe.

Chris made a futile motion to scratch his head and looked up.

"They seem to be found on the Sun-facing slopes, but I am sure there are no hard rules here," Max added.

"How deep is this stuff?" asked Chris.

"It depends on the location, but according to my reading of the available data, it's about two kilometers thick here."

"Calculating the volume of dry ice at the south pole has led to the estimation that, if thawed, it would create an atmospheric pressure of one third Earth's atmosphere, equal to being at the top of Everest. It would be unbreathable, of course, but it would eliminate the need for a pressure suit."

"How do you melt all this stuff then?" quizzed Ann, getting interested at the prospect.

"Elementary, my dear," Max said and smiled. "It's all done by mirrors."

Ann pondered. "You mean land mirrors or sky mirrors?" she replied, warming to the game.

"Why, *sky mirrors*, of course," he replied nonchalantly.

"*Why, of course.* So easy. Why didn't I think of that?" Her eyes widened in mock surprise.

"Because you're not barking mad like him," Joe cut in, grinning like a chimpanzee.

"I'm used to him." She smiled, indulging them.

Max laughed. "Well, I try to be rational, but I suppose I come across a bit crazy at times."

They all just smiled. As crazy as his notions appeared sometimes, this man had given them the spacelift and Luna2.

"Okay. I think the pod has finished up its

topographical survey now. We had better get back to the *Titan* to refuel and get to the north pole."

"All in one day!" Ann marveled. "I suppose that's the advantage of a world half the size of Earth."

"Well, yes, it also allows for close monitoring of the planet. We also need the data from the pod's equipment."

Returning to the *Titan*, they did a low-level circuit of the ice cap, the ship mapping and taking multiple readings to be stored in the database and relayed to Luna2.

Having returned to the ship, they took the opportunity to take lunch while the pods were being refueled and checked over.

Over lunch they discussed the morning excursion.

"Tell me about your mirror trick," Ann said.

"A *statite.* You all know about them. It's a stationary satellite, a bit like Luna2, that we install over the north and south poles to reflect the Sun's rays onto the ice cap. The process can be speeded up or slowed at will by shifting the mirrors or with the use of a black dust, carbon for example. The size and number of mirrors is a matter of calculation, and there will probably be a certain measure of trial and error."

"It sounds too easy," Ann said.

"Theoretically, yes, but we would still have to install them after getting the materials here, assembling them, positioning them precisely, and then keeping them in position."

"But it would have a good cost-benefit ratio?" queried Ann, who rarely spoke like an accountant.

Max raised one eyebrow at this. "Yes, you could say that. More bang for your buck."

"Well?"

"Well, yes, I guess the accountants will have the final say on that, but I think it is hard to put a value on these things. It finally comes down to the most practical solution and going with it."

Meanwhile, they took their lunch while the pods were being fueled and checked over.

When the pods were ready later they resumed their expedition and were soon gliding down to the north pole where the *Titan* had moved during their break.

"This pole is quite different from the south. Firstly, it is lower at 2,600 meters above datum whereas the south pole is at 3,700 meters above. This north plateau is a hundred to two hundred kilometers wide, descending in a series of terraces to the floor of what is believed to have been the old ocean bed that covered most of the northern hemisphere. The north pole would probably have been an ice-capped island much as Antarctica is on Earth," Max explained.

"These terraces are generally fifty to sixty kilometers broad and dropping a few hundred meters to the next level down a steep scarp. The whole of the polar high ground being about 1,500 kilometers across, it was still unknown how much of it used to be underwater.

"While there is subsurface ice at both poles, the

north pole differs from the south pole. Mars has an almost exactly similar tilted axis as Earth and therefore has seasons. The long Mars year gives a long summer that burns off much of the dry ice, which has a lower freezing point. It also sublimes. In the process, the temperature, especially on Sun-facing slopes, can give rise to liquid water, which can flow until it either freezes when it gets into shade or evaporates in the sunlight.

"The ice at the warmer north pole is therefore mainly water, and as we get established, we can progressively use its water to split into hydrogen for fuel and oxygen by using solar power," he continued.

"But for now we don't have to worry about water. After all, we're in that business. It rather looks like we may be getting into general long haul provision. I have mentally tagged ammonia as a must-have."

"Oh?" Ann looked surprised.

"Yes, ammonia, NH3. We need it for a number of reasons as a basis or on its own as fertilizer, also for the nitrogen to get an Earthlike atmospheric balance, and the hydrogen as fuel. Hydrogen when burnt with oxygen gives water. Ammonia is also an ingredient for explosives for use in mining and land forming. Also, ammonia in itself is a powerful greenhouse gas."

"Are we going to import ammonia, or can we make it here?"

"I guess it's simplest to bring it in from Earth in anhydrous form. After all, we are planning sending all sorts of materials, so why not ammonia? We'll also need methane or a similar hydrocarbon. That'll have to come from Earth unless—"

"Unless?"

"Unless we bring it in from our ship's namesake."

"Namesake? You mean Titan? That's Saturn's biggest moon! It's beyond the asteroid belt, even beyond Jupiter!" Ann's jaw dropped.

"Well done. You've done your solar system homework. Yes, it's between 750 million and 1.2 billion kilometers, depending on the point in its orbit, give or take a few hundred thousand," he clarified with a grin.

Joe and Chris were now fully attentive.

"You serious, boss?" Joe was used to Max, but he was having trouble here.

Chris said nothing, just stared wide-eyed, clearly dumbfounded.

"I'm not sure," admitted Max with a shrug. "I haven't fully weighed it up yet. I heard the atmosphere is mainly nitrogen and the seas are liquid ethane and methane. The newest versions of the plasma drive are very fast, and there is always the *SolMin* group. They have one of the new drives. They should be able to do a round trip in a few months. If they could tow a few hundred thousand tons, it would have to be looked at."

"SolMin!" exclaimed Chris, making one of his few comments. "I know those guys. They pulled off a really big find snooping around the asteroid belt. They found about two hundred tons of 24 percent pure californium-252 bearing ore, a cosmic freak just floating around the asteroid belt! Built themselves a fancy new ship. Offered me a job, but it sounded way too risky. They're real daredevils." That was one of Chris's longest speeches in quite a while. All were impressed. Max had a huge grin.

"Yes, I heard about that. They're a pretty wild bunch. *Intrepid* is a polite description. They have something of a reputation as being modern-day swashbucklers, but I respect their guts to go out and look for opportunities. I am sure they sometimes take incredible risks, so they earn the rewards. I don't begrudge their successes. However, I have had some bad dealings with them in the past and would rather do without them."

"So is there anything else on your shopping list?" Ann was enjoying this. It made for interesting times ahead.

"Well, I'd like to make an ozone layer, a magnetosphere, and a Ionosphere. Unfortunately, those are more difficult to come by. They will develop in time if we can provide the atmospheric balance of gasses. They will help to protect us. Earth's atmosphere took millions of years to evolve, but it can be quickly changed as we are painfully aware."

Everyone nodded soberly.

"We will also need plant life, *flora*. That fortunately is easier. They can be transported easily in seed and spores and would probably be the lightest and most rugged of all our cargos. Fortunately, the bio-conservationists had the foresight to create the Svalbard Global Seed Vault, which with other similar facilities have preserved a huge collection of diverse seed species so that they would not become extinct. At one time farming was restricted to a very few strains of plant types, so there was extensive monoculture. This left crops prey to natural disasters, pests, and fungal attacks. Recent biological developments have engineered strains of resilient plants to use natural Martian soil elements."

"So it seems that water ice is going to be a small part of our shipments?" Ann observed.

"Yes, I think diversification is the challenge here. And it will be a challenge. Each of these shipments needs to have its own transport protocol according to its properties and handling requirements."

"The other abundant resource here is perchlorate, one atom of chlorine and four of oxygen," added Max. "It's as much a curse as a blessing. As a powerful oxidant, it was a primary source of chemical rocket propellant in the old days and is useful to make explosives. It's awful stuff, a fine, colorless, soluble, and corrosive dust that gets everywhere, including your lungs. The effect on the thyroid is not pleasant, so keep taking Grace's pills, which contain an ingredient to help the body combat the ill effects. We will have to be very careful to filter our air supplies to remove this stuff. Most important, however, is that it absorbs water like crazy and gives it up easily, so it can be used for collecting water. Also there are the four molecules of oxygen. Need I say more?"

They then went on a short hike to get the feel of the terrain. They stood on the edge of the first scarp and looked down the sequence of terraces to the distant plain that was thought once to have been Mars's ocean.

"Imagine looking out over a blue ocean under a blue sky with green on these terraces," Ann ventured wistfully with a sweep of her arm.

"Yes, worth working for," Max agreed.

As time was running short, they spent the remaining available time making a video recording of the surroundings.

An hour later they started back for the *Titan*.

"One thing surprises me, Max," Ann commented as they were high over the pole, heading for the ship.

"Oh yes, what?

"The Washboard Plain. You seem to have forgotten about it."

"You're quite right. Thank you for reminding me. I must admit with all the other things on my mind, I had quite overlooked that little conundrum."

"Well?"

"Well, I guess we ought to make time to go see."

"Good. It's been nagging at me too. I really would like to know what it is all about. You don't think it is some sort of mapping glitch?"

"Don't think so. We rely on the accuracy of our databases, so I'm sure it really is like that. Strange as it may seem."

"But those dunes or whatever they are so *straight* and *regular* and cover such a large area."

"Yes, I know. We really must get to the bottom of

that. It's worth making time for. Your reminding me has aroused my curiosity again."

"Oh yes? That's good. I'm itching to see the place. I wonder if just looking will explain it?"

"Can't tell, but it will do no harm to have a look. It may be more obvious when we are close up."

"That's settled then." Ann wanted to make it a firm resolution. "Promise?"

"Yes, of course, dear. I'm keen too."

Ann settled back into her copilot seat, satisfied.

Max mused over the mystery for a while, becoming ever more intrigued.

"I will quiz Captain Hogan about it. He has been coming to Mars often enough. Maybe he can shed some light."

"No, don't do that!" exclaimed Ann.

"Huh? Why not?" He stared at her curiously.

"Just don't. It's our secret place."

"Okay, I won't say a word." Max left it at that, pondering nonetheless her strange quirkiness.

Arriving at the ship, they were greeted by Patrick Hogan. Max could feel Ann stiffen with unease. Surely, she didn't think he would break her trust. She must be very keen to keep their "secret place" secret. Although Max did not fully understand why she was so secretive, he would not dream of breaking his vow.

"Hi, Patrick, everything okay?"

"Hi, Max. Fine. Thanks. You have a coded dispatch that came in from Luna2."

"Oh, great! That was quick. I wonder what conclusions they've come to."

Max went to his office and opened his mailbox and tapped in his code to run his decryption software. The dispatch opened to give page after page of files with headings for all the items Max had requested to be researched together with files on various topics of background interest, ranging from prices of materials to solar flare activity. There were some files with the findings and proposals for the location, deceleration, guidance, and capture and landing of various materials and provisions. There was also the physical, mathematical, chemical, and engineering reports and a cost-benefit analysis.

Max came to dinner in a pensive mood.

"Good news?" Ann inquired. She was voicing everyone's thoughts. They were happy to leave it to her to broach a subject.

"So far, so good. There is a lot of stuff to go through, but there doesn't seem to be any major objections. I haven't seen how much it's going to cost me. No worries. What's a good price for a habitable planet?"

"Well, would you negotiate for cost sharing?"

"With whom? The pioneers are dependent on their governments to fund their activities. The International Space Federation will put in about 60 percent, I would say. I guess I will have to find the rest."

"Hmmm. I guess for now we will be creating our own terradomes as it will be for our own benefit. It's the new pioneering situation. First to come has the pick of the land. The rules of land acquisition are internationally agreed upon. There aren't many players anyway," observed Ann.

"Quite so," agreed Max "I have a lot of information to go through. It's going to be a long night. Please excuse me." Max left dinner to return to his office.

Ann let him go. She knew he would be buried in his work and would call her if he needed. She would remind him of the hour at about 0230 if he had not reappeared. He tended to lose track of time when absorbed in a project. She chatted with the others, going over the day's events and discussing the possibilities of life on Mars.

Chris was unusually talkative and animated, obviously inspired. He showed unexpected enthusiasm for the prospects, and as an engineer, he seemed to think Max's scheme was workable.

"From what I can see from the readings, there are suitable strata around the canyons to find stable anchor points for the net structure," he said. He had obviously busied himself with the practicalities of realizing the structure.

"It's a matter of getting the right materials in the right place. Fabrication could be kept to a minimum by the design of the structure. Once the anchor points were installed, it would be a matter of bolting and weaving it all together," he added.

"As Max pointed out, the components for the net structure are pretty robust and could withstand pretty much anything we throw them. They could be landed at points where it would roll along the surface, coming to rest against a suitable scarp wall to be collected at will. I don't see a problem there," he concluded.

Joe had been listening carefully. He was in broad agreement with Chris's analysis. "Yes, I agree. That all seems straightforward enough. My concern is the assembly. I foresee we will need some machinery to do the heavy lifting. The mere tensioning of the support cable may need some hydraulic pullers."

"Yes and no, Joe. I envisage using the suspension bridge technique of building up multiple thin wires strung back and forth until the desired cable size is built up. No critical tensioning required in this case as we are not trying to have a precisely aligned road or rail. We just want a strong net with a certain elasticity to *give* enough under impact. Trial and error with impact velocity will tell us the best method," he concluded.

"Furthermore, as Max pointed out, the foot of the net may not need to be anchored because the net's own weight may be enough. It needs calculation. Or as Max suggests, trial and error." Added Chris

"Go on," encouraged Joe, who liked the logic.

"Well, the idea originally was to send ice here, but now the brief has widened to encompass all sorts of materials. I propose we line the floor of the valley under the net with PolyAi sheet to avoid water loss by absorption into the ground and to maintain purity. The idea is to create a soft platform with airbags. The ice packages may well shatter, but this is no problem as we want to melt them anyway. This would probably need one of Max's mirrors to keep it liquid. Any local water could be added. Once we have the lake, it would provide a soft splashdown for the more fragile cargoes."

"Yes, that all sounds reasonable." Joe was beginning to like this quiet engineer. He had no doubt that Max would only have the best men on this project. He felt proud Max had asked *him* and resolved to be proactive to justify his friend's trust. However, he knew Max had probably not asked him along as a working member but as a longtime friend and fellow adventurer.

He was grateful to be on what he considered a terrific adventure at a stage in his life when he had all but given up notions of such exploits years ago. He was a happy man. Although he liked his farm and was content with Marlena and kids, he missed the excitement he had known with Max on all their various wild projects.

Max did indeed lose track of time. He was deeply buried in the dispatch with all its facts, figures, and report findings from his think tank back at L2. There was much to go through, but as he studied the reports, he had yet to see anything to discourage him as to the viability of the various plans he intended to implement. He had to weigh the natural urge of his men to please him. He knew them well enough to know they were not simply yes-men and would not falsify the hard facts just to please him. They were a professional team. Max relied upon them to make shrewd, unbiased evaluations and draw measured conclusions.

The conclusions (with provisos) indicated that his

proposed schemes were sufficiently practical. There were no doubt other possible methods to deliver all the materials he needed. They all called for more sophisticated equipment, special lander vehicles, among other things, but they would also need time to put in place and considerable capital. He knew his proposal was a rough and ready solution. He did not see that as necessarily a weakness. Given the distance from Earth, the inherently hostile environment, the lack of infrastructure, and the physical challenge of construction in an alien environment, he considered simplicity a bonus.

"Hey, boss, you tired yet?"

"Oh, hi, what time is it?"

"It's 0240. If you want to have an early start tomorrow—"

"Mmmm, not *that* early. If we are on the surface by 1000, that'll be fine."

"You want to join me? I'm going to get some sleep."

"Yes, I have gone through most of this stuff, and I see no reason why we can't start straight away and start sending the components for the capture net."

"Oh, good! I'm glad. I was listening to Chris and Joe discussing it since you left. Chris seems to have done a lot of homework too. He has considered the engineering practicalities and seems to think the problems are not too severe. Joe heard him out. They discussed various technicalities but decided it was 'doable,' as they put it."

"Did they? I'm glad to hear they are putting their minds to it. So they also think we are good to go."

"Yes, so it seems. I am sure your instincts are right, Max. You know I have the utmost faith in you."

"Thanks, sweetie. I cherish your support. It makes me strong."

Ann's eyes glistened. She closed them and offered up her lips to him. He gently accepted.

A few seconds later, he said, "Excuse me one moment." He turned to the communication console and tapped out, "Expedite all. ASAP," and then he hit the send button.

"I think concludes that. Let's go."

There was only one conclusion to this situation, so they floated to the sleeping net and undressed each other.

Some while later they fell asleep, entwined in space, in love.

CHAPTER 13

Next morning found them over the extinct cauldron of Pavonis Mons. At this altitude they could see the summit of Olympus Mons about 1,200 kilometers to the northwest, the bulk of the volcano hidden by the planet's curvature.

"Are we landing in there?" asked Ann, peering down at the thirty-five-kilometer-wide basin. "Let me guess. You want to investigate putting a dome in it?"

"Not today. We are going armchair spelunking."

"Spelunking? Caving? Are there caves to explore? Oh, dear!"

"Yes and yes. Mars has many caves, fissures, lava tubes, and such formations. Because of the lack of water erosion, these are largely undisturbed. While water creates many caves on Earth, especially in limestone rock regions, water has been absent here for millions of years. It is mainly old volcanic and tectonic activity here."

"Don't we need equipment for that?" she asked anxiously.

"I don't plan on squeezing down into any tight spaces or hanging off any ropes."

"Oh good!" Ann was visibly relieved.

"At breakfast I didn't imagine I would be doing anything like that today."

"Why? If you had, would you have put on your caving gear?" Max teased.

"No, silly. I might just have backed out of the trip altogether. You know I'm a bit claustrophobic."

"That's why I didn't tell you."

"Rotter! I hope you're not going to scare me."

"I doubt it. I don't intend on taking any risks. There is little backup here if things go pear-shaped."

"Thank you. My tummy is not very brave today."

"Oh?" Max looked at her inquisitively "Oh! Does that mean?"

"Too early to tell yet. I could find out if I do a test."

"I'll leave it to you. Do what you have to do."

Ann pondered. She was not sure what her tummy was telling her. Although they had considered having kids, she was not sure if this was the right time to start a family. Then again they didn't use any protection. Maybe it was just her cycle. She did a mental calculation and realized she was a few days overdue. This was no big deal, she thought, as space flight wasn't particularly conducive to regular cycles.

"This trip may have just upset my cycle. It's probably nothing."

"You know I wouldn't mind. We've discussed it." Max was quietly excited by the prospect.

"Like I said, it's probably nothing but space travel."

"I'll leave it to you. You know I'm behind you whatever the case, darling."

"Thank you, my love. Thanks."

They were quiet as Max scanned the flanks of Pavonis Mons, peering around.

"There! Look!" He pointed to a circular feature that could at first glance be one of the innumerable impact craters that dotted the planet's surface.

By now they were able to see right into the feature and could see there was a hole where the floor of an impact crater would normally be. The opening was some fifty meters across. Max guided the pod into the opening, and the other pod with Joe and Chris aboard followed. They dropped slowly into the opening with the walls of the inverted conical depression closing in on them as they descended.

Ann's hand tightened on Max's arm, but she said nothing. Although apprehensive, she trusted his judgment.

Closer and closer the walls enclosed them until there was only a few meters clearance from the pod. The direct sunlight was gone. They were now in intense shadow with only the reflected light from the rim. Their eyes struggled to adjust to the sudden change in light intensity. Ann tried to penetrate the gloom. The walls suddenly disappeared, and they were surrounded by total blackness. The front lamp disappeared into the gloom where its light was unable to penetrate.

"Here, use the joystick," Max suggested, indicating a small knob on the dashboard and flipping a switch. A powerful searchlight shot into the gloom.

She soon got the hang of the lever and swept the light beam around to explore the vast cavern where they now found themselves. Max moved the pod forward into the gloom by using the headlights and avionics. They were followed by Chris and Bob in the other pod. Max flipped on the intercom.

"Hey, guys, you okay? I'm just going to spin my pod to have a look around. Stand by. Copy?"

"Copy. All okay," came the reply.

Max could see the screen showing the view below. It showed the floor sloping away from the opening to the surface. He spun the pod slowly around while Ann played the searchlight beam until the situation slowly became clear.

Under the entrance opening was the spoil from the crater above. Through the swirling cloud of dust, it was now clear they were in a vast underground tunnel. They had just entered through a section of the tunnel roof that had collapsed to the floor in a conical mound below the opening, leaving about thirty meters clearance above the mound to the opening.

"Whooooo!" Ann trembled slightly. "What now? This place is spooky."

"Well, I want to have a look around. I'm looking for a home."

"*A home*? Not very cozy." She gave a moue. "I'm not sure I'd trust that roof."

Max smiled "I wouldn't either. If we were to use one of these tunnels, which are actually lava tubes, we may have to do some stabilization work. It would be worth it. The rock above us will protect us from long-term solar and galactic radiation."

"Us? Are you planning to live in a hole in the ground on a strange planet?"

"Well, not *forever*. Just until we can build some decent terradomes."

"Give me terradomes any day." She shivered.

"Don't worry, love. I have no intention of living 'in a hole in the ground,' as you so eloquently put it." He grinned.

"I should hope not. I wouldn't want to bring up kids down here."

Max gave her a sympathetic look. "I wouldn't either, although they wouldn't know any difference."

"True, but why would we if we had the choice?" she insisted.

"I would also like us to end our days under a blue sky with clean, clear air and my toes in the sand of a beautiful beach with clean, clear water and fish in the sea," he trailed off wistfully.

Coming back from his reverie, he maneuvered the pod along the tunnel as the pod took readings of the space, building up a 3-D profile of its shape and size. The readings showed that the tube was roughly ninety-five meters wide and eighty meters high.

"Well, this is the sort of place we are looking for. I will call this Tube1 for reference while we look around for other contenders." He communicated with Joe and Chris and gave instructions for a detailed exploration of the Mons for other suitable locations sites for habitation.

"Have you forgotten your promise?" Ann was worried they would spend the day exploring holes in the ground.

"Not at all. We're going there now," he replied.

Ann relaxed. "Oh, good! I am not happy in this place. I keep thinking of all the rock above."

Max carefully guided the pod up and out of the entry opening in the roof and set course to return to the ship. They left Chris and Joe to their survey work. Washboard Plain was some 5,600 kilometers due west on the equator, which meant it was out of range for the pod, so they were obliged to hitch a ride and refuel for an afternoon excursion.

On arrival at the *Titan*, they we greeted with the news that a new dispatch had arrived.

"I hope you are not going into your office for the day." Ann looked at him reproachfully. She feared the trip to Washboard Plain would be canceled.

"No, dear. I guess it is a progress update." He went and logged on to his secure computer.

"All progressing well. Shipment 1 of equipment departed 0230. ETA 10.6 days. Shipment 2 in twenty days and shipment 3 in thirty days." The message was short, to the point, and for Max, very good news.

"Those boys have really done their stuff." He told Ann, and as they had ninety minutes to their destination, they went for some lunch. This consisted of more sachets of convenience space food and drink; however, these were made up by Gaston for them, so they consisted of French onion soup, Pate Ardennes, "bake in the bag" baguette, Roquefort cheese, and coffee.

"That *Gastron* really is a wizard with his sachets. I actually look forward to see what his meals are just to see what he has dreamed up next. He really has mastered the art," Ann said.

Max nodded agreement while munching on fresh baguette and cheese.

The intercom announced the approach of their destination. They went back to the refueled pod and set off to the surface. While they could be closely tracked by the *Titan*, Max had made no special mention of their purpose in that location. Captain Hogan for his part was at Max's disposal and was not unduly concerned by his client's business. He did not question the entrepreneur's intentions.

Ann was pleased their secret place was not mentioned. She had no idea why she felt so secretive about this place or why she felt any attachment to it at all. She was as puzzled as Max probably was, she thought. Maybe she *was* pregnant? She shrugged and settled down for the ride to the surface.

Gliding down over Wafra crater (seemingly 1,500 meter deep) to the south of Cerebus Palus, they lined up on their destination. They flew east over the Washboard Plain, the pod taking topographic and electromagnetic measurements.

"That's seventy-four clicks long by ... twenty-three from north to south. That crater on the northeast corner is six clicks wide and eight hundred meters deep. The corresponding crater is the same size but only three hundred meters deep, they are joined by a sloping furrow of the same width." Max looked from the readings to the ground two thousand meters below and knitted his brow in puzzlement.

"A very strange formation. That plain is almost flat. There is a fall from north to south of generally sixteen to a maximum of forty meters over the twenty-three kilometer width. The north and south boundaries do not vary more than forty meters over the whole seventy-four kilometers. Compared to Mars in general, this is a billiard table."

"Yes! *And I didn't see a single crater on the whole plain!*" Ann was excited.

Max stared at her. She was right, he realized. He had seen no impact craters either, which was very odd. They were silent while Max landed on the north edge of the plain, fifty meters from the rim of the northeast crater. Therefore, they could look at both features from the ground.

Looking out over the plain while the pod hummed behind them taking measurements, they could only see out about ten kilometers because of the natural horizon of the small planet. As far as they could see, there was a series of shallow ripples over the plain, each generally no more than two meters high, each running perfectly straight from north to south. They stared in puzzlement.

"What on Earth— Sorry, what on Mars is this all about?" Ann asked.

"Beats me." Max was equally puzzled. "Whoever said nature has no straight lines should have a look at this! I have no explanation. I really don't know what to say. Let's have a look at those two craters." They went to the rim and looked into the bowl of the impact crater. From the south rim, they looked down the gently sloping furrow, which sank deeper until they knew it came to a stop in another crater of exactly the same size on the southern edge of the plain.

"I can't make this out either," Max admitted. "Did some object strike the north crater at the north edge of the plain, and some or all of it skim along the surface and make the other crater exactly the same size on the exact south edge of the plain and following the exact north-south pattern of the plain's ridges? What on Mars is going on here?"

"Dunno." Ann shrugged and made a helpless gesture. "It's very strange. There must be some explanation. It doesn't look natural to me. Could the pioneers have done this?"

"No chance. They haven't the equipment to form a plain of this size. Also they haven't had the time. They are too busy trying to stay alive and getting a foothold here with the stuff they get from Earth. Not possible."

"Well, who then?"

Max stared at her. He pondered. He had realized what she was tacitly implying.

"What do you mean who? Are you suggesting—"

"I'm not suggesting anything. Just asking."

"I think it's a bit soon to mention the Drake equation or the Fermi paradox."

"*You* just did!"

Max grimaced and spread his hands. He considered himself a logical, rational person. This situation made him troubled, uneasy.

"I have to admit I'm grasping at straws at the moment. I haven't seen any LGMs around, have you?" he said, trying to be lighthearted.

Ann looked at him with a knowing grin. She seldom saw him confounded. He was normally so self-assured and commanding.

Max shrugged helplessly. "I really am baffled. Let's not jump to wild conclusions here. It needs to be investigated. What I am wondering is if we can use this feature in some way."

"Well, yes, it needs further investigation. Just be careful you're not trespassing on sacred ground," she said with a huge grin. She could not help playing on his discomfort.

"I said you're evil. Just look what you did to that poor lobster." He grinned, again resorted to levity to hide his uncertainty and unease.

"Maybe it would be a good landing zone or drop zone for incoming goods ... or something." She felt remorse for teasing him, so she was now trying to be helpful.

"Yes, that's possible," he said, distracted. Although what she had suggested was possibly a good use, it did not explain the *reason* for the plain, how it was formed, *why* it was so geometrical. It troubled him. He hated this sort of unresolved conundrum and decided to start asking some questions. He was also troubled by the fact that their secret place may come under the spotlight of close scrutiny. How would she feel about that? Why did she feel so attached to the place anyway? He had more questions. He would have to discuss it with her before doing anything.

They took off and made a slow tour around the whole plain, taking high-resolution video and images as well as the usual topographic readings. They flew back to the *Titan* in silence, each pondering what they had seen in their secret place.

Dinner that evening with Joe and Chris brought news that they had found a number of similar lava tubes and some caves. One cave in particular had attracted Joe.

"The advantage of this cave is that it is more accessible, the floor being roughly at the same level as the surrounding land. Vehicles could drive in and out." He was satisfied with the find.

"Oh, good! I prefer the sound of that already." Ann really didn't like Tube 1 at all.

"Sounds promising. As long as it's stable and big enough," added Max.

"That would depend on a seismic survey," Chris observed. "I agree with Joe. The ease of access is a plus point. It would make moving materials and equipment and construction much easier. I'm not sure why, but my gut feeling is that a cave is inherently more stable than a lava tube."

"The lava tubes tend to be closer to the surface and thus generally offer less radiation protection than caves. However, the walls of the tubes seem quite smooth and sealed by the liquid rock that flowed through." Max weighed the pros and cons. "Get a detailed physical and seismic survey done for each type so we can make an informed comparison."

"Okay, boss. We've already done a certain amount of survey of the inside thanks to the pod's scanning systems, but we need to have a seismic survey to determine stability." Joe was happy to be involved. Although they had ground penetration radar, the old method of echo sounding through the use of detonations was a low-tech but tested and reliable indicator. Joe also liked the detonations part.

Later that night Max discussed the question of the Washboard Plain with Ann. "I think we will have to investigate what it is all about," he said. "I can't see how we can keep so large and curious a feature a secret for long." He need not have worried.

"Well, of course not, silly. It's only a secret place *between us,* you see? Because we found it and explored it." She wondered why men didn't really understand such romantic notions. "Of course people will come and maybe use it, but it will always be *our* secret place."

"Oh, I see." Max vaguely understood but was pleased she was sufficiently pragmatic to realize her secret would not remain undiscovered. If that was it? Was it? He felt slightly out of his depth. Ann—and women in general—were still sometimes a puzzle to him.

"Is it all right then if I get some second opinions on this?"

"Of course. We need to understand what it is."

Max shook his head, relieved but still confused.

"Good. I hate things I can't explain."

"Yes, I know, dear." She smiled and kissed him. She was herself unsure of her emotions. Maybe she would take that test.

They spent a couple of hours at the terminal going through the images they had amassed during the day of exploring tube1 and the plain.

Max had a hologram conference with the pioneers and updated them about his activities. He tentatively mentioned the question of the plain. He had to give a grid reference. They were clearly unaware of the region and confirmed they had no activity there and had not explored it since they were so preoccupied with their area. They had gone through some tough times and were desperate for a powerful friend like Max to help them out. Max reassured them and arranged to meet with them as soon as he had a moment in his program, and he promised he would be sending various provisions.

Together with all the other readings from the pod, there was a wealth of physical information but nothing to answer the basic questions Max had about the plain. He sent as much data as he thought relevant back to Luna2 for the scientists to speculate over.

With no further information from the pioneers, he had done all he could. He sent a reply dispatch to Luna2 with further instructions of provisions and equipment to send. He also sent images of the Washboard Plain to various experts without being too specific as to its exact location, and he made inquiries about their explanation for such a formation.

Having done all he could, he called it a day and retired for the night.

There followed an intensive week of survey and exploration. *Triton* was also due to return to Earth as part of its regular shuttle schedule. The temporary living quarters needed to be established, and all provisions were offloaded to supply them while they awaited the delivery ship due in fourteen days.

They had landed the *Triton* just south of the Louros Valles Canyons near the site of the proposed net trap. They had to set up their living pod with all the support systems. Also unloaded were cylinders of liquid oxygen and hydrogen, water and food for four people for a month. This gave them a two-week safety margin should there be any delays.

"You don't have to stay on site here, you know. You

could stay as a guest of the pioneers," suggested Max. "Or even go back to Luna2 if you want. It may not be much fun here."

"Nonsense. I wouldn't miss the camping for the world! I used to go camping with Ma and Pa when I was little and used to love it!"

Max gave her a sidelong look. "That's maybe because it *was* in the world. It may not be such fun here."

"Yes, I know. Just joking. I didn't come just for fun. You know that. I don't mind roughing it for a while until the cargo ship arrives. We have a lot to do, and you'll need my help."

"True, I will. Just making sure you are prepared for the regime. All space food. At least we will be in gravity for a change, even if it's a third of Earth's."

So the living quarters were set up. The dome and solar panels had come in two packs, each a cube of three meters. The dome system was an inflatable structure of fifty-centimeter tubular ribs, which thanks to the thin atmosphere and low gravity needed little pressure to erect them. It was, however, pressurized internally to make it habitable without space suits, thus making it inflated from the internal pressure alone. The inflated ribs being sufficient to maintain integrity without internal pressure.

In the absence of a magnetosphere as found on Earth to protect the planet, it was necessary to provide radiation protection normally enjoyed when in the pods or aboard the *Triton*. To partially achieve this, the skin of the dome was a double layer with a cellular structure. The polyethylene material used included hydrogenated boron nitride nanotubes (known as hydrogenated BNNTs), which were self-healing if punctured. A variant of this material was also used for their suits. The 300-millimeter gap between the four layers provided insulation from the extremes of temperature, and the aluminized BNNT reflected the sun's direct rays.

In addition to the structure of the dome, the radiation protection was supplemented by an artificial magnetic shield that replaced the magnetosphere and provided a protective bubble or force field around the dome up to a range of seventy-five meters.

Electrical power was essential and was provided by solar panels on an inflatable structure that was quickly erected and rose twenty-five meters high. In addition, heating and cooling were supplemented by using generators, burning the hydrogen and oxygen as fuel.

Communications were going to suffer. Messages were normally relayed via the *Titan*. Even the pioneers could only be contacted through the ship. The lack of an ionosphere on Mars meant radio waves could not be bounced around the planet as on Earth, and so until communication satellites were installed, communication relied on line-of-sight radio waves. Therefore, communication with spaceships, Luna2, or Earth relied on the time when Mars's rotation meant they faced Earth. As radio messages took four and a half minutes to reach Earth and a similar time for a reply, it ruled out any meaningful conversation and tended to me more exchanges of information.

The pioneers could therefore not be contacted from the dome once the *Titan* had stopped orbiting and was returning to Earth. As their base had been set up near the north pole to make use the water ice, there was no communication from ground level unless relayed by the returning *Titan* when she was reachable. They could only be contacted by the pod when it was in flight and had a direct line of sight.

As they watched the mother ship arcing into space to return to Earth, a deep sense of isolation overcame them. Ann could not help but feel the conversation at dinner that evening was overly cheerful and belied a certain sense of foreboding that she, for one, was feeling. This isolation would only be broken on arrival of the *Phoebe* with their provisions, the construction crews, and materials in about thirteen days. That night as they lay in their bunk, she cuddled Max extra close, burying her face on his chest.

The one-third gravity was a novelty and also a welcome sleeping partner.

C H A P T E R

14

The next two weeks gave little time to consider their isolation as the four members of the advance party were occupied preparing for the arrival of the construction crew with the first consignment of materials. The first few days were taken up with extensive mapping and planning of the capture zone. As Max had observed, the Calydon Fossa made an arrow straight alignment with the proposed site of the capture net at the western mouth of the Louros Valle Canyon. The team surveyed the ground on either side of the canyon by using ground penetration radar and more conventional explosive charges to verify the rock structure, which would become the anchoring points of the tensile cable suspending the net.

Having identified the optimum sites for anchoring the cable they found sites either side for landing the materials. All of this data together with images were relayed in a daily basis to the approaching ship so that the plan of operation could be finessed aboard during flight. These messages were also copied to Luna2, so there was a daily three-way conversation whereby the plan was updated and Luna2 was able to accordingly modify the successive supply cargoes.

Phoebe, the supply ship, arrived as scheduled, and there followed an intense daily period while it went through successive orbits to finish slowing down from its interplanetary velocity and to align themselves with the drop zone. From the surface they could see the craft as it flew overhead, the sunlight sparkling off its flanks and the plume of ion particles from the thrusters as it slowed. Each pass was marked by rapid radio conversations as both side updated each other.

Tension peaked as the ship came in for its first drop, still out of sight of the waiting surface party. Their first glimpse of the packet was the braking chute lit up in the morning sunshine as it flew overhead in its final orbit. Despite the thin atmosphere, there was a loud whoosh as it passed overhead. In anticipation they counted down the minutes until finally the cargo came in down the Calydon Fossa, and with a very close pass of their observation point, its chute billowing taut behind, it struck a sloping side of the fossa and bounced for a few kilometers. It bounced off the walls of the fossa until it came to rest in a cloud of dust some ten kilometers away.

All gave a shout and danced around for joy. Max was shouting congratulations to the crew of the supply ship, Captain Keane, and his fellow Irishman Sean Ryan as first officer.

"Bang on target! Brilliant timing, you guys. Perfect. Send the rest just like that. Maybe a whisker to port!"

There followed several more passes with mixed success. Their luck didn't last. Two packets completely missed the fossa. Bouncing off the plain, they disappeared behind dunes on the horizon, maybe to be lost for some time. These losses were anticipated, and there was redundancy built into the consignment, any essential components were duplicated in separate packets. The surface of the planet was so pristine that any new traces were clearly observable, so Max reckoned the missing packets would soon be found.

By the end of the day, there were about forty packets strewn along the floor of the fossa. As the sun was falling to the horizon, the supply ship landed a kilometer away amid its scattered cargo. When Max and his fellow crew arrived, the loading bay doors were open with vehicles, and the provisions that were too fragile to drop were being offloaded. Some men and women were setting up two domes.

There were two squads of ten, men and women, and their leaders came immediately to report to Max. They were soon joined by the captain, first officer, and crew of the ship. Congratulations were exchanged. All were in a celebratory mood as the mission was considered a success. Losses were minimal and would not hinder their progress.

Max and the construction crew went to work to prepare for the next day's tasks. That evening in the relative comfort of the ship, there was a lengthy discussion over dinner to finalize the planning. All retired at 2100 in anticipation of a long day with an early start.

Before sunrise the construction crews were off chasing down the scattered packets and moving them to preplanned locations for later use. All day the rovers could be seen moving around with their loads stirring up plumes of dust that drifted away in the light Martian breeze.

Two more pods were aboard that were used to take particular packets to either rim at the mouth of the Louros Canyon. They slung the packets below them and were able to drop them at the points that Joe and Chris had selected as the anchor point locations for the main suspension cable.

Overall, it took three days to transport the packets to their allocated positions. One of the stray packets was found twenty-four kilometers away and returned. The other was given up as lost for the time being. It was identified as one of the many rope bundles and was nonessential since it was a duplicate item.

Chris and Joe with the construction crews had been working at the anchor sites for the main net support cable. Shaped chemical charges had been used to form multiple 130-meter-deep vertical tubes into the rock. Liquid PSP had been poured into the tubes and backfilled with rock, the liquid set to form anchor points for the anchor cables which fanned out weblike onto the desert to multiple anchor tubes.

The primary cable and net were all to be made from

a standard ten-millimeter-thick rope made from a high tensile but elastic synthetic compound derived from synthetic spider silk. First, a single rope was strung across the mouth of the gorge, carried across by one of the pods. That was followed by a dolly that ran back and forth, roving additional ropes, building up multiple strands to form the final cable. This process would continue nearly automatically for days until the final cable was completed. The net was then formed by the warp ropes let down from the main cable, while a robot ran back and forth across the main cable forming the weft.

Ten days later as scheduled, the second incoming shipment was tracked on its way in. While still fourteen million kilometers out from Mars, it was met by the *Phoebe*, whose task was to capture, slow down, and maneuver it into a trajectory where it could be broken down to individual packets to be landed and captured by the net.

The capture and deceleration procedure would take time before they came into orbit. They had time to finish the net. It was not crucial now as the packages could be released to the surface when they were good and ready. They were ready when the *Phoebe* was still twenty hours away, and so they were able to have a small net completion ceremony on site and an evening party at the construction crew's main dome.

The second shipment was made up of different types of cargo, some not destined for the surface as they were to form Statite mirrors that would beam sunlight into the Louros Canyon to light and heat the area. The ready purified ice could be melted when the sunlight was available.

The shipment also consisted of large amounts of heavy-gauge reinforced polythene sheeting to line the floor of the canyon under the net to form an impermeable barrier to contain the ice and keep it uncontaminated. These packets were relatively light and robust, so some were going to be used to test the net.

Once the whole shipment was brought under control and orbiting the planet, the various packets were to be separated using manipulator arms on the pods to move them either to Phobos, to the Statite location, or into the landing trajectory.

Two days after arrival, *Phoebe* radioed they had split the shipment and were ready to launch the first PolyAl packets. The crew, having already made forty drops along the Calydon Fossa, had established the optimum approach speed, height, and trajectory for success. However, this did not calm anyone's nerves as they made their final release orbit. There were now thirty-three persons who formed the spectator ground party. They congregated on the rim of the fossa overlooking the capture net to witness the packets' arrival.

Once again they witnessed the first packet rushing overhead, trailing its supersonic chute on its final approach. Coming in for what was supposed to be its capture at the net, it was clear it was on the right orientation but too high. The packet and chute flew over the net by at least three hundred meters and disappeared over the horizon to the east.

This was immediately relayed to the *Phoebe*. With their apologies, a second package was released. Unfortunately, this was now too low and came down on the floor of the fossa twenty kilometers short of the target, bouncing high into the air along the valley. Approaching the net in long bounds, it finally came to rest two kilometers short.

Again, the result was communicated to the ship, and again, they received an apologetic reply. This inaccuracy was put down to the considerably lighter mass of the PolyAl packets. The third drop was immediately seen to be on target as it shot past below them down the valley where it hit the net at about two hundred kilometers per hour. The bottom of the net rose from the floor and enveloped the packet, and in what appeared almost as slow motion, the net tightened, strained, and swung back. The foot of the net fell away and neatly deposited the package on the valley floor.

A cheer went up from the ground crew, and the good news was relayed to the ship with orders to standby while the net was checked for damage. Two hours later after the net was found to be none the worse and undamaged, the delivery passes were continued until there were thirty-four packages at the foot of the net. The sun was now dropping, and it was decided to halt the drops until first light. They wanted to give the net another examination for damage while the light lasted.

That night there was a debriefing followed by another celebration as the project had been a success. Max felt vindicated. He was pleased his design worked with such a simple and quickly implemented system. It also required the minimum of materials and infrastructure. Its possible weakness was that it was not yet known if it would be suitable for the more fragile deliveries. The inclusion of accelerometers in the packets would give them a clearer idea of the forces undergone when they were retrieved the next day.

The video footage of the impacts on the net were run and rerun to study its behavior. The difference of gravity, atmospheric friction, temperature, mass, speed, and elasticity had all been modeled mathematically, but the speed of the program had precluded exhaustive testing. It had been reasoned the relative low value and rugged nature of the goods allowed the first materials to be dropped with minimal risk. The testing was therefore being done in the field, and lessons were being learned.

There was a debate as to whether a weighted or restrained foot for the net would be needed for heavier packets. It was decided to proceed with caution, testing the net with heavier loads and evaluating as they went. Max liked the way the foot served to wrap the packets when it rose after impact. He could imagine a packet bouncing back from a taut net fixed at the foot, so for now they left the foot loose.

Before dawn the construction crews were already corralling the packets and unpacking. There was communication with the orbiting *Phoebe* when all personnel and vehicles were clear of the drop zone and the deliveries were restarted. With the coordinates from the successful drops logged into the guidance system, the accuracy was almost 100 percent perfect. By nightfall there was another 423 packets stacked up on the floor of the valley. Each drop had seen a rover collect the two-ton packet and move it to the collection area. The system was being honed into an efficient machine.

The net was beginning to show signs of wear, but there were no real problems. When the occasional parcel slipped through, it had sufficiently slowed and simply came to rest a bit farther down the canyon. Repairs to broken ropes were a simple exercise remedied within an hour.

Max was increasingly satisfied his net system was working, crude though it was. Having repeatedly played the video footage of the impacts, he could see the system could be improved by minor modifications; however, they would keep the present design until it was beyond reasonable working life. He derived much satisfaction from the fact that most of the materials he had transported here for the domes, net, and mirrors were all largely made from plastics that had once been clogging and polluting the Pacific Ocean only a matter of weeks ago.

Another week went by as all the packets were sent down in a steady stream and were stockpiled on the valley floor and surrounding rims. Sections of the net needed repairs as the constant impacts took their toll. The very nature of a net made this a relatively simple procedure as more strands could be woven in to repair damaged sections. It was not rocket science. The parachutes were reused three times and then retired to be reused as shelters over working areas to give addition protection from sunshine, storms, and dust.

They were fortunate the *Phoebe* was in orbit as they were forewarned of approaching dust storms. They had planned this exercise to avoid the storm season but were not able to avoid all bad weather. The storms were more of an inconvenience than a real threat to them, the wind carrying little weight despite its speed. It was the dust particles which got everywhere and were a constant annoyance and a maintenance chore. Because of the low gravity, they also took longer to settle. When a dust storm did blow in, they retreated to their domes and waited them out. These periods were used to catch up with inside chores, perform maintenance tasks, and discuss plans. They were seldom idle.

Past the net, the Louros Chasma canyon drops down 2,400 meters to the Ius Chasma. This canyon was a natural low point that formed an ideal place for a habitat. It was largely protected by virtue of the surrounding walls, which minimized direct radiation. Being close to the equator, the greatest risk was from the sun passing overhead, which could be shielded by overhead canopies.

To clad these canopies, recycled Pacific Sargasso

plastic tiles were used for their radiation-shielding qualities. The plastic to make these was literally fished out from the Pacific Ocean and made into tiles and taken up the elevator to Luna2. They were the cheapest of materials, needing no special storage. All types of polythene, which was too costly to reprocess, was simply heat-formed into molded tiles. They were comparatively light and extremely durable, which meant tons of them could be unceremoniously dumped onto the canyon floor without fear of damage. This durability also protected people from meteorites that did not burn up in the thin Martian air as they would on Earth.

That evening the *Phoebe* reported the two pods had completed assembly of six square kilometers of mirror to reflect light into the canyon, and the array could be positioned the next day. This was good news. It meant the self-opening mirror system was working as planned. All that remained to do was to add the other thirteen square kilometers and for the pods to gently fine-tune it by nudging the completed mirror into position. Max was pleased this was working well because it served as a practice run for the main mirrors planned for the poles.

Ten days passed since the last shipment. That night they had warning from the electronic tracking devices that the next shipment would soon be arriving, so the *Phoebe* was completely unloaded and set off to locate and capture the third consignment. This was again a mixed cargo of goods, light, heavy, robust, and fragile. The ship would again capture and guide it into orbit. This was a much larger consignment than the first two and was equipped with its own thrusters, which had boosted it from Luna2 and were to assist in deceleration.

Once the consignment was slowed to approximately the rotation speed of the planet, it could be left in geostationary position while various packets were delivered. They would sort the component parts to be delivered to the surface or kept for use in orbit. The thrusters were to be left in orbit where they would be used later.

Chris and Joe had struck up quite a friendship during their work together and had been away almost every day, exploring and surveying the area. They had found a cave they both agreed would make very useful accommodation space. They said it was further east down the Louros Canyon and went about five hundred meters deep into the wall of the canyon with a mouth thirty-five meters high by sixty meters wide. They reckoned vehicles could drive in and out to access building equipment and material storage. It was sufficiently deep that living quarters could be installed and be completely shielded. If mirrors were installed across the canyon, natural sunlight could be reflected into the deepest parts.

That afternoon Max and Ann went with them to have a look. It turned out that the cave was eight kilometers away on the south wall of the canyon, and they entered by a plinth ten meters above the valley floor. It was protected from any overshooting packets by the convolutions of the canyon. They spent two hours looking around. It was indeed a very good proposition, and the survey showed the roof to be stable. Some areas of loose ceiling would need to be removed, but the basic structure was stable. The great benefit of this cave was its proximity to the center of operations. Reassured, Max was enthusiastic about the find, and they continued the discussion back at camp with the other engineers from the construction crew. All were seated while Chris gave a presentation of the images, video, and survey data. The whole presentation, including all data, was streamed to the *Phoebe*, which in turn beamed it back to Luna2 to be evaluated.

The next morning a plan of action with a list of materials needed to be dropped from the orbiting shipment was received from the logistics department on Luna2. Max gave it immediate approval, and a working party was assigned to prepare Cave1. By night that evening, the materials were assembled at the mouth of the cave and a site dome inflated. The cave renovation crew was installed, and all their vehicles and equipment were at the mouth, ready to start work the next day. At the drop zone, there were twelve hectares of valley with plastic liner over the leveled and smoothed ground under the net.

It was planned by some of the engineers to make a double-skin pillow by using some of the PolyAl material, weld the edges, and inflate it to a thirty-meter-high air mattress under the net to take some of the more fragile cargo. Thanks to the crew of the *Phoebe*, who were now very accurate through repeated practice, they reckoned this was another way of landing fragile goods. They intended to have such an airbag made in two days and proposed testing it with nonfragile packets with accelerometers attached. Max was all too keen to give it a try. If his net system could be adapted and used to deliver fragile goods, he was delighted.

The engineers got to work immediately. It was a simple project to make. They refined the bag design so that it now had cellular compartments. They thought these would perform better and make the design more resistant to deflation in the event of puncture. True to their word, they proudly presented their bag on time. This plan had been discussed with the *Phoebe* crew from inception. They were now confident of their accuracy and prepared to do a few tests runs.

Meanwhile, the net had been given a thorough inspection, and a few additional strands had been added at points showing greatest strain. All considered they were optimistic and well pleased with their progress. They were keen to test out their new improvements when the next shipment arrived.

That night they had a party in the big construction dome. The men and women were now a tight-knit crew, bonded by shared experience, remoteness from Earth, and common purpose. There was music, food, dancing, and a certain amount of good beer and wine. While alcohol was not normal in space, this was not space, and their situation was not *normal*. In any event, all personnel were highly qualified and educated professionals who were mature and responsible for their own actions.

The party was noisy and boisterous. The music was loud, and the dancing was sometimes wild.

CHAPTER
15

By common consent, the next day was a rest day. People slept late and recovered from the festivities of the previous night. The last of the partygoers had turned in at about 0430.

The *Phoebe* had rendezvoused with the third consignment, and the *Titan* was due back the next day with 240 personnel who had been accommodated in her cargo hold in a set of living quarters designed for the ship as part of its function as a colony support vehicle.

Although warned, the *Phoebe* crew were overwhelmed by the size of the third consignment. It was an assemblage of packets locked together and spanning more than five kilometers by a kilometer wide. They claimed they had been running the shipment's thrusters at full power for the last two days, adding her own thrusters in their effort to slow it to orbit speed. This had been planned by Luna2 logistics, which had provided extra fuel for this purpose. They were still calculating their arrival velocity and making corrections to avoid overshooting Mars's gravitational field.

Max spoke to the crew at 0915 to thank them for their efforts and to raise their spirits. They were obviously rattled by the ordeal and had spent two nerve-racking days as they kept up a twenty-four-hour vigil to monitor "the Beast," as they had come to call their load. They were aware the *Titan* was behind them, and Max reassured them it would be sent to assist them if they got into trouble. "Just don't crash into the planet. Aim to miss! It doesn't matter if you overshoot. We'll bring you back!" He had made light of the situation, reassuring them, and so he defused their tension.

Max and Ann took breakfast at 1030 and decided to go on a tour of the area. They took one of the pods, and rising to three hundred meters, they flew slowly down the canyon. They passed over the Cave1 site, waving at two of the cave work crewmen enjoying their day off and relaxing outside the mouth of the cave. They flew on farther and eventually came out of the gloom of the canyon at the head of the Valles Marineris and into the morning sunshine.

They flew east toward the Sun. The dunes, valley walls, and rocky outcrops facing them were in deep shadow. A blanket of fog created by ice crystals lay in the valley of the canyon, making flying over it eerily similar to flying over clouds on Earth. Ann suddenly pointed ahead to the right.

"Look. What's that bright patch over there?"

Max followed her pointing to an area a few kilometers ahead where a number of dunes and mounds were not in shadow but brightly lit. He frowned and knitted his brow until realization made him smile, wide-eyed.

"Of course! The mirror! Remember, the *Phoebe* had to leave to meet the shipment? They were saying they were set to move it into position the next day! They left the mirror as it was when they had to leave on their capture mission. We have not been showing them enough appreciation. They've been working so hard. We didn't even give them time to finish one job before sending them on the capture mission. They even missed out on the party. I must give them some time off when they are done."

Ann nodded. "Yes, we should do something for them when they get back."

Max steered the pod to the bright patch. As they broke into the double illumination, they were effectively under two suns. The heating system got quieter as it reacted to the increase temperature. He noted the pod's indicator, which read 22 degrees Celsius externally.

"That's shirt and shorts weather," he said, nodding at the gauge. "And only 1030 in the morning! Come spend your vacation on sunny Mars!"

The area lit up by the mirror was an oval shape of about fifty by thirty kilometers. The combined sunshine was making a warm local microclimate.

"I'm looking forward to seeing what that mirror

does down in the canyon." Ann was imagining how it would light and heat the darkness of the bottom of the canyon. The sun did penetrate the canyon during the midday, but direct sun radiation was to be avoided. Hence, Max's choice of location.

"Yes, we can add mirrors to achieve the ideal conditions," he suggested. "Our first steps at terraforming."

They pondered the possibilities. Max was brooding. Ann could sense it. She looked at him and inquired, "And?"

"Just thinking." He paused "Ironic, isn't it?"

"Ironic? I think it's wonderful. I think we can make some real progress here. The more we can protect areas from radiation with domes and shields, magnetic field technology, and stuff—"

"I don't mean our work here. I mean it's ironic we're using the garbage from our overheated, abused planet as the means to warm up this one. Do you see?"

Ann pondered this seriously. "Yes, it's symbolic. Our damage to one planet helps another to live."

They laughed at the irony and went home to the base for lunch feeling they were doing something meaningful that just might save humanity from itself.

Having enjoyed a hot shower, they met Joe and Chris at the main dome and went to eat together. Inside the dome the artificial atmosphere and temperature meant they could dress normally. The self-appointed cook was able to produce a very reasonable meal, only slightly hindered by the low gravity. They had by now become used to the weight of everything, including themselves. Restrained movement was the key. It was all too easy to overestimate the muscular requirement for every action.

Therein lay the danger of muscular wasting. The body would reduce muscle to adapt to the level it was used to. Grace had warned them and set up an exercise regime for them to combat this. Few had yet followed this so far, so Ann mentioned it on behalf of her friend, pointing out it was in their best interests to look after their health. They all made a resolution to do their prescribed training. However, as Chris and Joe pointed out, in their capacity as surveyors, they were obliged to cover many kilometers and remained pretty active in the course of their jobs. Ann smiled and agreed their activity was healthy but explained that Grace's program nonetheless called for a more thorough exercise regimen.

An observer watching the four of them chatting, eating, and sipping wine would find it difficult to imagine they were sitting in a tent 225 million kilometers from home.

That afternoon they forced themselves to relax. That wasn't so easy when they had been working seven days a week for so long. To Max, life was work. He worked as he played, and play was work. There was no real dividing line. His position as his own boss meant he was naturally self-motivated, and he would work any hours while he felt something needed to be done. He could not be idle and sometimes felt even mere conversation, which to some was a primary occupation, was time when he could be *doing something.*

Ann was herself an athlete and reveled in her physical health, but she was content to spend that afternoon chatting, reading, or listening to or playing music. She had been an accomplished cellist until she fractured her left hand while skiing once. She still played, but she was no longer of professional orchestral standard. Instead she now played the guitar and composed songs.

Max became fidgety after a while and went to his work area and checked up on the *Phoebe* and the *Titan.* The *Phoebe* was fast approaching orbit while the *Titan,* unencumbered by a large shipment of cargo, had overtaken *Phoebe* and was on standby to assist her. Speaking to the *Phoebe,* he realized she was indeed in a borderline situation. The next few hours would be critical. It would be pretty serious if she overshot because it would be no mean feat to stop and restart the monster back to Mars with all the recalculation of velocity and trajectory, allowing for gravitational effects with the available thrust at their disposal. The crew was doing some serious number crunching. There was no time for the *Titan* to land and offload. They had to assume they might be needed and were obliged to stand by to assist if *Phoebe* was in trouble.

After another hour of tension, they could see that the *Titan,* while not strictly necessary, would be a welcome help and would make the delicate maneuvering into orbit that much easier. Therefore, they agreed the *Titan* would assist the the Beast before landing. The minutes ticked away as the two ships used their thrusters to slow and maneuver the huge deadweight.

Ann came in, and sensing the tension, she stood quietly by, listening to the occasional comments from the two ships and Max. She quickly picked up on the situation. Another thirty-five minutes, and it became clear they were safely on the correct trajectory and their speed was now under control. There was no definable point when they could relax. It was more a growing relief and shedding of tension as the situation developed minute by minute.

Finally, a prolonged silence was broken by Shane Keane, the *Phoebe's* Captain, saying, "Well, thanks, guys. I think we are in the clear now. I appreciate the help, Patrick. And Max, thanks for your support."

"Call it the luck of the Irish." Max laughed "You didn't need my help."

"Ah, but you called in that ex-Dubliner," Shane replied, referring to Captain Hogan. "He'd probably have let me sweat a while before coming in."

"True, very true," Patrick said and laughed.

The crisis over, all was good humor and bonhomie among the Irish crewmen. They now had time to chat for a while and catch up with their news. The space crews were a close-knit fraternity, and all knew one another well. They finally said their farewells and went their separate ways. The *Titan* went to land the contingent of new pioneers on the plain to the south of the fossa, and the *Phoebe* went to stay in orbit until she had secured the Beast in orbit and handed it over to the tugs, which would break it up and distribute the containers to Phobos, stationary orbit for sending down to the net, or either of the polar mirrors under construction.

To thank the crew of *Phoebe* for their efforts and to recognize they had enjoyed little rest for days, they were given a week to rest while a stand-in crew watched over the ship and shipment. They were there to monitor the alarms and could call on the resting crew should something happen. Meanwhile, the four available pods were busy breaking up the shipment.

A special section of the shipment was destined for Phobos, Mars's larger and closer moon that was six thousand kilometers away, a rock eleven kilometers wide. This was destined to be a fabrication and assembly base with just enough gravity so goods would stay where placed but remain virtually weightless. Its real advantage was that it was atmosphere-free, which meant that large pieces of equipment could be fabricated using cold fusion, otherwise known as cold welding. This was a phenomenon whereby two similar materials that were oxide-free were brought into contact at low temperature and would fuse together as one. A feature of material behavior normally impractical on Earth as normal welding was cheaper than creating the correct conditions for cold fusion. Phobos was also seen a convenient staging point for missions to be able to deliver cargo destined for Mars without the need to land on the planet. It was decided it would be the stockyard and fabrication area for materials destined for the Mars spacelift.

Deimos, the other moon, was half the size at 6.5 kilometers and was twenty-three thousand kilometers from Mars. Max had no plans for it at present, but he would bear it in mind, always open to possibilities.

For the present, however, the major priority was to establish a sustainable foothold on the surface, and all efforts were focused to that end. Phobos proved a useful staging post for cargo storage and redistribution and fabrication of statite components.

The next day the huge consignment was shunted around in orbit, and packets were sent down to the capture net. There were inevitably some spectacular misses because of the sheer number of passes. All four pods were in use for this task, using their manipulator arms to place the packets. Some of the pilots were not used to the procedure. They were given ice packets to practice with. The inflatable mattress was kept for the fragile loads when accuracy was established. An overshoot from an ice packet would end up crashing into the walls of the canyon in an explosion, a rainbow of sparkling ice shards falling hundreds of meters to the chasm floor. They landed on a plastic lined, pre-formed shallow bowl under the net. Some ice, however, was just lost.

Soon there was an efficient routine with a packet coming in every twenty minutes or so. People got used to the regular whoosh and thud as the deliveries flew along the fossa, collided with the net, and dropped to the valley floor. At night the whole area was lit while mechanical rovers collected stray packets and moved them to their destination. The ice packets were left under the net to form the ice store, and the others were taken to depot points to be unpacked and distributed to their destination.

CHAPTER 16

Ten months saw vast changes to the new settlement. Max had arranged that the ships would arrive in rotation every six weeks. When a shipment arrived, the loads were delivered to the surface at twenty-minute intervals. The statite mirror bathed the net and the chasm floor with sunlight twelve hours a day, which combined with direct sunlight melted the ice, forming the ice store under the net. The air mattress awaiting fragile goods. When a batch of fragile loads was programmed for the day, the mattress was moved out under the net to give a softer landing.

An array of 3-D printers had been landed in pieces and assembled in various locations. A dedicated machine was building components to supplement the primary girders, tubes, channels, and boards of all sizes that had come preformed. The principal material was PSP (Pacific Sargasso Plastic). Some of this PSP came as solid blocks. When treated, these made the raw material for the printers. There were numerous other 3-D printers producing specialized products and components.

Outside the cave, cables strung across the canyon supported a net tent structure whose ropes were used to fix the plastic tiles. These tiles were eight by four meters and of varying thickness and colors according to the radiation protection requirements.

The cave roof and walls had been stabilized by removing loose rock. Next was a liquid plastic (PSP-derived) sprayed onto all surfaces and partially absorbed by the rock. It cured to a hard, thick skin. A set of large mirrors had been installed to bounce sunlight across the canyon illuminating the valley floor under the canopy and deep into the cave, thus providing light and heat.

The construction crew was now joined by 210 personnel of all functions who had come out on the *Titan*.

On the ground there were now five main sectors— the accommodation domes, the net with maintenance crew on the rim of the canyon, the depot with mechanical rovers, the cave installation crew, and the tent construction crew. All had their own domes for living and support. Radio beacons were erected to establish contact with all zones. Standard multi-tube pipes were laid to carry water, hydrogen, oxygen, electricity, and communications. Sewage water was processed for fertilizer and used for the plant greenhouses.

In orbit there were now two mirrors installed. The north

pole mirror was started first to melt the polar water ice. Streams now occasionally flowed and froze regularly. This added to atmospheric water vapor, which was in itself a greenhouse gas. The south pole mirror was at work sublimating the dry ice and was now adding carbon dioxide, a greenhouse gas, to the atmosphere. Some of the dry ice had simply been moved in its solid form to supply the greenhouses for plant respiration and to build a normal air balance in the habitation areas.

It was found that the only way the water ice at the poles was usable was to mine the surface ice before it melted into the ground. The permafrost ice in the ground was too saline for human consumption and would have to be purified by reverse osmosis. They experimented with salt-resistant plants, but the greenhouses mostly used hydroponic methods with Earth-supplied water. Anhydrous ammonia had formed a sizeable part of the shipments for its many potential uses, primarily for a basis for fertilizer and a source of hydrogen and nitrogen. Liquid nitrogen was needed in planetary quantities to make up the 78 percent atmospheric mix as found on Earth. For now nitrogen was brought in as a liquid from Earth. But it was a heavy item in the quantities needed, and there was eventually a limit to what Earth could afford. Liquid oxygen was brought from Earth to supply the domes and suits and to burn hydrogen.

There was a problem that had vexed Max. To achieve the 78 percent nitrogen to 21 percent oxygen planetary atmospheric balance necessary for human respiration, he needed nitrogen, a lot of nitrogen, which acted as a neutral mixer for oxygen as well as a element for radiation protection. This was the problem: Where to find in the quantities required for a planet? How much was locked up in the Mars rocks?

The answer, he knew, probably lay on Titan, Saturn's largest moon, which was known to have a thick atmosphere of nitrogen and liquid methane and ethane on its surface in abundance. The task of merely visiting Saturn was a lengthy process. To do so in a sufficiently large craft to mine and return to Mars with methane and nitrogen in a suitable containment system was a complex undertaking.

He did not yet have the wherewithal in his organization to carry out such a mission. This was an endeavor for a multinational conglomerate unless Aqua4 made the investment. He knew of only one other solution, but he didn't even want to think about that option. It involved the group SolMin, those of the californium fame … or infamy, depending how well you knew them.

There was no doubt that their new ship, the *Eridanus*, was up to the job. There was no finer ship in the solar system. The problem was not the ship but the group called SolMin. Max had reason to be cautious of their captain, "Tea-leaf" Charles Mason, and his first officer, Arthur Dixon. These two were a right pair of rogues together with their navigator, Eddy Horton. Max thought grimly of his past dealings with them. He was not sure whether he wanted to get involved with them again. They had tried to swindle Max, who had managed to foil their scheme. They had left their last deal wiser and more cautious of Max and his Aqua4 organization. They were unlikely to do him any favors. Their presence and snooping in his business was a problem that he knew he may have to deal with later.

To avoid dealing with SolMin, he realized he had to make the investment to commission a special exploratory and mining ship. This had been ordered and was being completed at Luna2 and due to join them soon at Mars. This ship would have the capability of reaching and mining the asteroid belt and possibly getting nitrogen and methane from Saturn's moon Titan. Her trial journey to Mars would act as a test flight to measure her capabilities and suitability for long-haul flights to the outer solar system.

Meanwhile, Phobos was being prepared as an orbital docking station and supply base to serve her. This eliminated the need for the ship to land on the surface, allowing it to haul much greater loads. It was essentially an interplanetary equivalent of a super-container ship with proportions to match.

Luna2 was now populated by 2,400 ship construction workers. The whole construction project was based around the spacelift since it was the terminus for all the materials and equipment coming from suppliers all over Earth. In addition, there were all the backup administration and logistics personnel, scientists, engineers, and designers required for the fast-track project.

The advantage of construction in space outweighed the inconvenience courtesy of cold fusion. This process could take place in the extreme cold of space and the absence of oxidation and was employed to advantage for rapid construction.

For now they would use the liquid nitrogen and ice imported from Earth, expensive though it was. It just meant that life on Mars without breathing equipment would be confined to artificial atmospheres in domes. "We will need some big domes," he thought aloud.

"Excuse me?" Ann looked up. Max looked startled. He was not aware he had said anything. She must be reading his thoughts.

"I was thinking about big domes, my dear."

"Big domes, dear?" She smiled sweetly. "Or big, big domes? Or big, big, *big* domes? *My dear.*"

Max eyed her warily. "I do believe, *my dear*, you are making fun of me."

"Moi?" She effected wide-eyed innocence, giggling.

He laughed. He hadn't been paying her enough attention while he was brooding over his plans.

"Come here, you." He grabbed her around the waist. "I should spank your evil little ass, you cheeky minx!"

She squealed, bursting into laughter. "Oh, yes, please, *master!*"

There was only one way this sexually charged

foreplay would end. They went to their quarters and were not seen again that night.

Anne opened her eyes. She stretched. "Mmmm ... morning, superman." Max gave no reply. He was still fast asleep. Early morning sun filtered into their sleeping room, bounced from the statite mirror and into Cave1 by using strategically place mirrors across the canyon. She gently peeled back the coverlet and padded lightly to the bathroom. If last night didn't make her pregnant, nothing would, she mused. Since the last time she had thought about pregnancy, there had been no sign she was expecting a child. She was not sure if she was ready for that yet. She was not using any birth control, letting nature take its course. She did wonder, however, why she had not become pregnant yet. She put it down to the rigors of her new life on a strange planet. Maybe they would have to go back to Earth for her to conceive. Maybe she was unable to have children. Maybe she was—she didn't want to form the word—barren! Such an ugly word. She made a mental note to talk to Grace.

This decided, she stepped into the shower cubicle and let out a soft sigh as the hot needle spray hit the skin of her breasts and belly. She pumped the soap dispenser and was lathering herself when she heard Max's voice in the sleeping chamber. A few minutes later, he came into the bathroom and joined her.

"The new ship has arrived," he announced. "They fast-tracked its completion at Luna2, and it is due into orbit at 1230. That's in a couple of hours. They'd mentioned they were ahead of schedule in the last dispatch. They've done well."

"What's she called?"

"Only a project number as yet—SSM1 for 'Space Ship Miner 1.' It's my privilege to name her."

"Do you have a name?"

"No, I thought I'd leave that to you, sweetie."

"Oh, thank you. I'll have to give it some thought." She felt a sudden irrational rage boil up. She was to name a *bloody spaceship* rather than a baby. She suddenly felt sick and wretched. *Why* did that bother her? She had no idea, but she felt a strange emptiness.

"You okay, hon?"

She gave a shrug. "I think I must be getting broody, naming spaceships and not babies." She admitted honestly, surprising herself by voicing her innermost troubles, this one inexplicable even to herself.

Max paused and looked at her, concerned. He gently lifted her chin, and looking into her eyes, he lightly kissed her lips. He was about to say something consoling when her bottom lip started to tremble and her eyes filled with tears that then rolled down her cheeks, mingling with the shower water.

"Oh, my poor darling!" Max wrapped her in his arms while she gently sobbed into his chest. The shower hissed over them, unable to wash away her confusion and misery.

They dressed in silence. Max was worried. He understood the broody part but didn't really understand the depth of her emotions or their cause.

He had been preoccupied with the Mars project, he knew, but she was there with him, participating in it all. Why should she be so unhappy so suddenly? Their love was as strong as ever. He was sure of that. They shared and did everything together. Why the sudden *baby* business? He shook his head.

"Listen, honey. Do you think we need a break from all this? We haven't had a vacation for a year. How about we go back to Earth for a while?" He looked at her earnestly. She paused, looking at the floor.

"Oh, Max, darling! I'm sorry, making all this fuss. The truth is I don't really know why I'm so emotional. Maybe it's just this place. No, I'm excited about Mars. That's not it. Oh, Max! I really don't know." Her telltale bottom lip trembled, and her reddened eyes again started to glisten.

"Oh, damn it! Here I go again! I will talk to Grace. It's a girly thing. I don't expect you to understand." She sat on the bed while Max looked on, confused. *What's to do? If she doesn't know, how can I help?* he thought.

He paused a moment, looking at his love sitting miserably with tears in her eyes. He felt helpless, a feeling he was not used to. This sort of thing could not be resolved by the sort of actions to which he was accustomed.

Max had to greet the new ship and insisted she didn't have to go with him if she wasn't up to it. She really didn't want to be in public with her red and swollen eyes, and she gladly excused herself. (God only knew what people would think Max had done to her!)

Max went off to greet the new ship, uneasy, but she promised she would be all right.

Ann put in a long video message to Grace on Luna2, signing off, checking the time. *It's 1205, so Grace won't get it for twenty-one minutes, say 1230, and she would then have to read it and send back a message. I can't expect a return message before 1330 at the earliest,* she thought, missing a face-to-face chat. She sat, hands clasped together on her lap, head bowed, not really knowing what to do with herself, feeling desperately miserable. What was she doing here? On this barren planet! *Barren, barren. Ha-ha! Barren!* What a sick irony! What sort of life had her love for Max brought her to? *A barren woman who's barren on a barren planet,* she thought. She tortured herself with this bitter irony. *Ha! Oh, God, am I going crazy?* She threw herself on the bed and sobbed her heart out, alone and wretched.

Later she rose and wandered around the bedroom. She was at a loss, wishing Grace was there to comfort her. Dear Grace would understand. She went to the bathroom to wash her tearstained face. She looked into the mirror of the drug cabinet. She paused and thought, *Is there something I can take to cheer me up?* Dear Grace had always provided all the medication they needed. Surely, she would have provided something for her present condition? Gently, she opened the cabinet. A sunbeam reflected off the mirror, momentarily flashing across her tearstained face. With trembling fingers, she began to go through the various drug containers. She went through the regular medicines with growing desperation.

"Damn it! There *must* be something *strong* here!" She started tossing the rejected capsules into the basin.

"*Bloody hell!* What are all these stupid drugs *for* anyway!" she yelled in sudden fury, hurling a bottle at the wall, and then she collapsed to the floor, sobbing again. Slowly, she composed herself. In a daze she rose and mechanically splashed water on her face. She sighed and dabbed her face dry with a towel. The drug cabinet door stood open. She gazed at the contents. Her eyesight was still blurred, but she recognized something—her pregnancy test kit. She numbly looked at it. Was this some cruel joke? Ha! What did a *barren* woman need with a *fucking pregnancy test kit?* She swallowed a sob. Mechanically, she took the tester and squatted to give herself a test. She counted, and withdrawing the probe, she squinted at the readout.

Positive.

She rubbed her swollen eyes.

Positive.

Stunned, she rocked back on her heels and landed on her bottom on the bathroom floor. She sat, mouth agape, staring into the distance and back to the readout.

"Oh. My. God! I'm pregnant! *I'm pregnant?* I. Am. Pregnant!"

She rose to her feet, catching sight of herself in the mirror. She took a low bow to herself, and with a sweep of her arm, she did a little pantomime.

"Madame, forgive me. May I inquire if you pregnant?"

"Why, yes, kind lady, I am indeed pregnant!"

She did a pirouette and sang, "I'm pregnant, pregnant. I'm pregnant. I'm pregnant, pregnant. Pregnant!"

"Okay, okay, I heard you first time!" Max's voice came from the doorway. He stood there, leaning against the doorjamb with a wry grin.

Ann stopped in the middle of a twirl and spun round. Her mouth dropped open, and with a shriek, she flew into his arms.

"Oh, Max! Max! Max! Oh, God, Max, I'm pregnant! I'm pregnant." She was trembling, clinging to him, alternately kissing and telling him between laughs and sobs of relief. "I thought I was going crazy!"

Max swung her off her feet and took her to the bed and gently put her down.

"Max, love me. Love me now. *Love me now!*" He did. *They* did.

Later that afternoon a soft chirrup came from the communication console. Ann correctly predicted it was a return message from Grace. Ann played back the message. Grace's face came up on the screen.

"My dear, you poor thing, you sound in a terrible state. Very emotional. You sounded ..." Graces face looked serious and then suspicious, and with a frown, she continued, "Is there something you're not telling me? Have you taken a pregnancy test lately?"

Ann screamed and collapsed in peals of joyous

laughter. "Oh, my dear Grace, you are a treasure!" Tears welled, and she sat down to compose a long reply.

Max had gone to witness the arrival of the unnamed SM1. He had reluctantly left Ann in a bad state. He felt guilty, leaving her like that, but she wanted to skip the ceremony. He made his presence as short as decently possible, and excusing himself, he returned to witness Ann's pantomime. He was overcome with relief and happiness at the spectacle of his love, unaware of his return, dancing for joy and ranting to herself. He had to chuckle to himself. He was relieved there was a reason for what had seemed a worrying development in Ann's mental state. He sighed. So he was to be a father. He was pleased.

He went to finish some arrangements concerning the still unnamed MS1 and came back to wash and dress for dinner. He found Ann already showered, dressed, and sweet smelling. She was radiant, smiling, relaxed. He stared at the change in her demeanor. She was bewitching and utterly adorable. He felt a lump in his throat. God, he loved her!

"*Ganymede*, name the ship *Ganymede*," She whispered to him.

The events since the night before had not gone unnoticed by Joe, who had noted his friend's mood. He had gone from amusement at their manner of departure the night before to concern for Max at the MS1 ceremony to bemusement when seeing the couple come to dine in party dress like lovers.

"Well, my dear, you look ravishing tonight." He embraced Ann. "You smell wonderful too!"

Ann smiled. Her faint blush was hidden by her already heightened complexion.

"Why, thank you, Joe. You look pretty dapper yourself." She admired his well-cut tuxedo.

He nodded quizzically at Max, who simply smiled back.

There was a general air of festivity as many people had come to see the new ship's arrival. A banquet was organized on as part of the celebrations. That night the couple dined as lovers in their own world.

The dinner passed as a dream to Ann, the conversation floated by her. She was on a shimmering cloud of cotton softness, her reverie unassailable. They stayed until such time as they could politely leave.

Max gave a short speech and asked Ann to say a few words. She apologized for her lack of attendance that day and explained the reason to much enthusiastic applause and congratulations. She announced the new ship would be christened the next day.

Returning to their quarters, they retired immediately to bed, happy and contented the storm of emotions was over.

That night Ann slept like a baby.

C H A P T E R

17

The new ship, the *Ganymede*, was clearly visible as it orbited overhead every few minutes. It was indeed a planetary-class ship in every respect, an interplanetary mining ship using the latest technology. To an engineer, it had its beauty. The structure and bulkhead plate work was largely made of liquid metal or metallic glass, an alloy of titanium, steel, and aluminum. The natural finish glowed in iridescent colors. The hardness of the material was valued for its resistance to puncture by meteors. Its light weight, although not a factor in zero gravity, did matter when one had to overcome inertia to accelerate or decelerate or indeed overcome the local gravity to land and take off from a planet.

Notoriously difficult to work with, the jointing technique of cold fusion requiring extremely low temperature made assembly in space much easier to achieve. Therefore, fabrication and assembly of the ship made the Luna2 station a logical and convenient choice of location. Some large or complex preassembled components were fabricated on Earth and transported to Luna2 on the spacelift.

Having a series of holds, it was able to land and take off vertically from planetary bodies up to six times Earth's gravity. Such extreme maneuvers were to be avoided if possible because of the fuel penalty. It could accommodate several million cubic meters of internal cargo as well as acting as a space tug to guide, accelerate, brake, and maneuver external cargo loads from interplanetary space and guide them into planetary orbit.

Powered by different motors according to the situation and available fuel, its primary thrust was a thorium-powered core. Thorium was the natural choice because of its stability, low toxicity, and abundance. The core generated huge amounts of electricity that could be stepped up using a variant of the Tesla coil to ultra high voltage to create a plasma thrust. Because of its abundance, liquid hydrogen/oxygen fuel was reliable, and it was easy to make and use. So it was a faithful low-tech fuel, which made it a natural choice for the thrusters and many other old-school applications. Its lack of radioactivity and ease of storage made it a perennial favorite fuel. Water, the sole raw ingredient of the fuel, was abundant in the solar system, and for Aqua4, it was the stock in trade. The arguments for this basic fuel were unassailable. Hence, its common adoption. These two gasses would provide a conventional rocket-type thrust that could be used alone or in combination with the main motor. Hydrogen and oxygen were continuously produced when the thorium core was active.

The ultra high voltages were also used to drive the ship's magnetic radiation shield, which was essential for protection from the solar and cosmic radiation.

The *Ganymede* was a new class of modular design, which meant its configuration was open-ended in that it was made up of units that could be added and subtracted according to the mission. Additional thrust-power modules, cargo bays, living accommodations, hospitals, workshops, and laboratories could be attached at will. External cargo similarly could be added, albeit at the expense of speed of acceleration, deceleration, and maneuverability.

At present the ship was occupied with arranging the huge external cargo it had brought so that specific containers could be sent to the surface. A swarm of its own tugs and pods busied themselves around the cargo-releasing containers and sorting them according to type and destination. These tugs, also used by the *Titan* and *Phoebe*, were larger and more powerful than the pods, the smaller personnel carriers.

Ganymede would later go to Phobos to unload its internal cargo of the more delicate and high value items, not unlike ship at container seaports on Earth, but choreographed in zero gravity here. Little Phobos was now gaining massive amounts of equipment and materials destined for the surface. The complexity of Phobos's orbit created logistical problems and made the building of the geostationary Martian space elevator a matter of urgency as it would offer a more stable platform to deliver goods to the surface. At present a fleet of tugs ferried packets from Phobos and guided them into their landing trajectory. Two extra nets had been installed along the Calydon Fossa to make it easier to capture inaccurately aimed loads, reducing the number of lost packets to be retrieved. Three more nets had been erected at various locations around the planet to facilitate the landing of goods at points identified for their natural minerals and other resources. There were more planned.

At headquarters in the deepest parts of the Louros Valles canyon in the caves and under the tent, filtered Martian carbon dioxide was mixed with nitrogen and oxygen and released into all living areas, greenhouses, and workshops. People could now walk around freely without breathing equipment such was the level of air production. There was a positive pressure in the tent, and the numerous doors were protected only by loose curtains. Air was allowed to naturally bleed out as a controlled process to create the new atmosphere. In the canyons the air pressure rose with the newly evaporating polar carbon dioxide and water vapor. People were able to move outside in designated "air zones." Electronic signs giving real-time air pressure and quality were affixed over all doorways and in every space. A variety of backpacks or belts with emergency breathing units would give twenty-minute supplies while people walked to the next air zone. Recharge oxygen points were everywhere to fill the canisters.

"Marts are smart" was a slogan to raise awareness to any signs of respiratory problems. Everyone was trained to recognize the symptoms and give whatever respiratory assistance was needed. The code for sharing air was the way as it was among scuba divers. Hyperbaric chambers were stationed at strategic points for serious cases of oxygen deprivation or carbon dioxide poisoning.

Radiation shielding was effective under the PSP tents. Magnetic shielding and the plastic roof together gave good protection. Areas that were not covered were protected with portable magnetic shield generators placed at strategic intervals. These could be moved around at will to protect new areas and keep up with the ever-changing installations and work areas until permanent shelters could be built.

The other less persistent hazards were the storms that whipped up the fine dust at a moment's notice and could last for days. If it were not for the thinness of the atmosphere, these storms would be more of a hazard. However, they were abating, becoming less frequent as the polar warming and melting process continued. They were now more of a nuisance and a maintenance problem. They also tended to be confined to the higher altitudes and blew over the deep canyons where there was the main concentration of development activity.

Under the protective tent, new caves were being excavated into the walls of the canyon. There was a lake fed by a stream under the capture net at the top of the canyon. Plants of all types had been introduced.

Fish arrived from Earth as frozen ova and served as a growing stock of food to groom the lake. The PSP tent was expanded along the canyon as the lake grew longer. Plants and trees were progressively introduced as the habitable areas grew.

The plants were grown from the seeds of selected strains from the Svalbard facility and other specialist seed banks. They had also been genetically modified to flourish with low gravity, low barometric pressure, and high temperature fluctuations. They were germinated and seedlings nurtured in greenhouses at one-tenth atmospheric pressure. The growing medium was either hydroponic or artificial soil, the Martian dust containing too many salts. There was no soil as such. On Earth, it is a complex mix of mineral, salts, and a variety of chemicals, bacteria, and rotting vegetable matter, all of which were nutrients for plant growth with water. The naturally occurring flowing water, once it mixed with the Martian dust, became saline, totally unsuitable for plant growth. Some strains of plants were being tested to grow in these conditions with mixed success.

As a controlled ongoing experiment, various insects and animals had been introduced, first tested in special incubation, breeding, and acclimatization areas and then released to adapt in the ever-growing habitable areas. Strains of honeybees were carefully bred since they were such valuable pollinators for all food crops, fruit trees, and shrubs, not to mention the honey and pharmaceutical products they produced.

On Earth, bees had been almost driven to extinction

through use of pseudo-nicotine-based pesticides commonly known as Neonics. America had lost all of its original bee colonies early on. Unlike Europe, they were slow to react to bee colony collapse disorder (BCCD), the collapsing colonies succumbing to the ravages of modern pesticides. Also the stress of nomadic commercial beekeeping practices combined with the use of bees to pollinate monoculture crops on a year-round cycle made the colonies weak and susceptible to BCCD.

Up on the plains above the canyon, hectares of solar collectors and several solar furnaces where constructed to meet the growing need for power. A fusion reactor was in the process of construction. The population was now approaching twenty-five thousand. Man had truly established a sustainable colony on the planet.

As the months passed, one of Max's schemes was taking shape. From the outset he had this plan to use one of the volcanic craters as a location for a huge dome to act as the base for the Mars space elevator. The net as a capture system had been adequate for the sort of goods they had been landing up to now, mainly robust building materials and ice. More delicate items had to be landed by the ship, or if something was small and light enough, one of the tug pods could deliver it. It had become clear there was a need to have a regular and stable method of landing large, relatively fragile cargo. This was Max's specialty. He was the spacelift maestro.

To locate his Mars spacelift, Max had set his sights on Pavonis Mons for three main reasons. It was on the equator, which was the ideal location for a space elevator. The fact that it was at an altitude of 9,500 meters was a bonus, and lastly, it was an almost perfectly circular forty-five-kilometer crucible with the rim some six hundred meters above an unobstructed, level floor. This would make a fine ground base for his Mars Spacelift 1.

Max also had visions of gravity assisted railcars freewheeling with their loads to their destinations in all directions, generating enough power to bring the empty cars back up to the base. The Martian spacelift, unlike its Earth counterpart, would mainly bring loads down under gravity and would therefore also generate its own power.

There had already been multiple drops of the raw materials for the dome project. Large quantities of PSP panels and pellets for 3-D printers were simply dumped onto the floor of the crater to come to rest at the wall of the bowl. The *Ganymede* had to make some expensive landings to offload special equipment, 3-D printers of all sizes and types, and other multifunctional machinery in component forms, ready to be assembled in temporary work domes. These machines would turn out a continuous stream of tensile rope and PSP fabric. This fabric was interwoven with a special synthetic spider silk rope to give added tensile and rip-stop properties.

As with the capture net, the cables forming the

dome's main support cables were roved by robots that ran back and forth, building up the required thickness. A net structure was built up with a design inspired by spiderwebs. Robotic spiders moved around repetitively bonding the junctions of the net with sonic welding. The web net in its completed state hung down into the bowl of the crater as an inverted dome under its own weight. This was covered with the rip-stop fabric, which was then bonded to the web.

Next came Max's toy, or as many called it, "Jumbo." It was a bubble blower. It blew bubbles to make any child happy. Indeed, footage of the machine in action intended as a promotional video for Aqua4 together with a predictable theme tune (much to Max's wry amusement) quickly went viral.

The tracked vehicle in reality, like many of Max's schemes, was essentially a simple idea. It was after all just a bubble blower. Or as Ann would say, "A big, big, *big* bubble blower!" It moved, computer-controlled, on its tracks across the floor of the crater and simply blew bubbles. It had tanks for the liquid ingredients and gasses, and it had a long, telescopic, bell-ended snout that blew the bubbles. Hence, "Jumbo."

The bubbles were hot, liquid, PSP-derived plastic filled with heated nitrogen gas for its radiation and insulation protective properties. The hot, wet sticky bubbles would be blown from the machine's skyward snout to a diameter of about three meters. Once inflated, they were shot up to the underside of the net with a last blast of nitrogen so that they would rise, wobbling their way skyward whereupon they would stick to the underside of the net and fabric. Then they would rapidly set in the freezing atmosphere. That was it. The bubble blower would relentlessly move under the net, blowing bubbles. There was no particular need for extreme accuracy, one just kept adding bubbles until there was a ceiling of bubbles.

The bubbles stuck to the net and to one another, which made for a flexible roof. Once the inverted dome was filled with a layer of bubbles fifteen to twenty meters thick, the crater bowl could be progressively filled with atmospheric gasses. As the gas pressure built up under the dome, it would rise and assume its finished shape in its own good time. To be a usable space, there was no urgent need for the dome to be a *dome* as long as the air inside was a breathable pressure. Any punctures or leaks were largely self-sealing by the press of adjacent bubbles and fabric overlay, but these could also be sealed simply by blowing more bubbles at the problem area.

After initial trials and improvements to the prototype, a fleet of twelve Jumbos were manufactured largely using 3-D printed components since they were mainly plastic and deployed on the floor of the crater.

The whole process of lining the dome was completed in eight months because of its simplicity and little need of equipment or manpower. Max's toys just needed to be supplied with four things—liquid PSP, hydrogen and oxygen as fuel to drive the machines and heat the ingredients, and liquid nitrogen to be heated and fill the bubbles. Roving supply trucks followed the herd of Jumbos around automatically, supplying the four essentials twenty-four hours a day with minimum supervision.

Once the pressure had reached 0.6 bars inside the crater, the dome spontaneously inverted itself to take up its designed shape. The extra volume dropped the pressure to 0.5 bars, but people could breathe without an artificial supply. The twenty meters of nitrogen bubble insulation meant the inside could maintain a stable temperature. The combination of a Stellarator compact fusion reactor, solar panels, and the greenhouse effect of the roof meant the internal temperature could be maintained at a tolerable average of 10 degrees Celsius in winter and 24 degrees Celsius in summer with minimal energy input.

Tunnels from the crater floor were easily bored through the soft pumice to give access to the inside and allow goods to be sent out by the gravity railway. The Pavonis crater had rapidly become a new operational hub with living quarters, workshops, warehouses, and a variety of support, housing, and recreation facilities.

Meanwhile, as the centerpiece, the original raison d'être for the Pavonis base, the spacelift itself was being fabricated overhead. The storage and assembly work for this had mostly been done based on Phobos and by a geostationary base centered over Pavonis Mons. This was established technology for Max and his Aqua4 technical teams. The engineers at Luna2 were able to modify the Earth and Moon spacelifts to suit the conditions on Mars. They had been working on the design and sourcing materials since Max had left for Mars, and they had produced a ready-built system to transport, assemble, and deploy on location. The task was made easier because of its smaller, simpler system, which did not need all the seawater tubes and associated equipment as Earth's Luna2 system did. The low Martian gravity as on the Moon was an added bonus that made the whole design much lighter and less complex.

From the geostationary station Phobina, as it was affectionately named, the daughter born of Phobos, the elevator umbilical support tape was fabricated and continuously fed down to the surface and vertically up into space. The tape was the same carbon nanotube as used on Earth. At first, it was a modest six millimeters thick, but the thread widened the longer it became. The more weight it assumed, the more the planet's gravity pulled it taut. Because of the lesser load, the tape needed to be only forty-five centimeters wide. At the space end, a counterweight was gradually enlarged to keep the top end taut. This process was continued round the clock until the foot of the tape was anchored to the ground base. The preassembled lift cars were then attached to the support guide tape. Once installed, the tape was then electrified to power the cars. The elevator system was finished in five months to coincide with the dome's completion.

Twice a month there would be a new shipment of cargo with more and more personnel to grow the population of Martians, which was how they now identified themselves. Many were here to stay with no intention of returning to Earth. They were the new pioneers. They brought with them the same pioneering spirit of adventure and ambition that drove the early settlers of the American west of centuries earlier.

Once the spacelift was operational, development grew exponentially. Highly expensive precision equipment and finely machined manufactured goods could be safely taken to the surface without the spaceships having to land, unload, and get back into orbit, a costly and time-consuming activity.

While the last stages of the dome project were being completed, Max had addressed the question of generating an atmosphere for Mars. The filling of the dome was easily completed with their existing stock of gasses, but a planet's worth of gasses was another matter.

The original Mars atmosphere was approximately one hundredth that of Earth and composed mainly of carbon dioxide, which was fine for plant growth but poisonous to humans, so Max knew that to create a friendly atmosphere, there was a massive task ahead. Many had thought about solutions for replacing what was thought to be Mars's missing air. This wasn't just about breathing. At present they had to wear pressure suits to create the one atmosphere their bodies were used to. Also there was the question of radiation because of the lack of a magnetosphere and the protective shield it offered. The need of an atmosphere to provide some shield was all the more important. It was known that nitrogen in any form had good shielding properties and was also the major component of an Earthlike atmosphere.

The carbon dioxide component was easily found. He merely had to melt the dry ice found in abundance at the poles. He had implemented that part of the solution by the installation of the statite mirrors, and they had raised the atmospheric pressure to 0.23 bar. This was a start, but it had been clear from the beginning that the missing gasses would have to be imported.

The polar caps would quickly melt under the effect of the solar mirrors, and that caused the outgassing of the carbon dioxide. As the temperature of the planet rose under the greenhouse gas effect of the carbon dioxide, this would lead to the defrosting of the polar ice and ground water. These would then in turn evaporate to create water vapor in the air with clouds and rain. The effect of this thickened air would create more warming until there was a tolerable, warmer atmosphere.

To accelerate this process, a potent greenhouse gas was needed. The presence of methane in small quantities on Mars needed supplementing. It was for this purpose the SSM1, or the *Ganymede* as she was named, was built.

Her main mission was now ready to be undertaken. She was to fulfill her designed role as the original SSM1 designation indicated. She was to assist in the search and mining of all resources needed for the new planet.

Her first mission in that role was to visit Titan to mine for the gasses and liquids found there—methane, ethane, and nitrogen, all of which it had been established were present in abundance on Saturn's largest moon.

Max was under no delusion about the magnitude of the task. It was a pioneering project without precedent and the technical challenges had taxed the project development department's best scientists, engineers, logicians, and mathematicians. Now that the *Ganymede* was here and had efficiently completed the journey to Mars with a full consignment of supplies, she had effectively completed her space trials and was now commissioned and considered ready to undertake the mission.

The last two months had been spent in preparing her for the mission.

CHAPTER 18

The successful completion of the dome was in no small part due to the efforts of Joe Barnes, who, not being a spaceman or pilot, was more of a land man. With his practical mind, he came into his own on the surface, acting as a project manager for the work on the dome. He was in his element and swore he felt younger every month despite the long hours he devoted to the project. This was all well and good, but there was a downside to this.

Joe had wanted to go with the *Ganymede*. He had become so involved with the happenings on Mars that he had all but forgotten to visit his wife and kids. He found the work he was doing for Max far more interesting than his ranch back home. It also fulfilled his need for adventure. True, he had sent video messages and news of his work to Malena and the kids on a regular basis.

But Max was now feeling guilty and responsible for his friend. The tempting prospect of adventure had attracted Joe. When it was clear Joe now wanted to join the crew of the *Ganymede*, Max felt this was going too far and knew he had to reason with him, dissuade him, and get him home. He had to suggest that maybe he should spend a little time with his family. This had further been brought home to him by news from Luna2 concerning the well-being of Marlena, Joe's wife back on the ranch.

Max had had Joe's family protected by his HR department. Without being overbearing, a lady from HR would come every month and chat with Marlena to see that she and the family were all well. Joe's salary was paid into their joint bank account, and so she was comfortably well off. Joe was able to talk with her and the kids regularly, but this was not the same as him being around. The HR lady, Mrs. June Bliss, indicated that Marlena and the kids were showing signs of missing Joe.

"Nothing dramatic, Max," she had insisted. "She's a resourceful woman. But I heard from the gardener that the boys were getting a bit wild at school. And although Marlena didn't complain outright, she did ask when his 'contract would allow him a home visit.'"

"Hmmm, I see. I will have a word with him. He hasn't been home yet since we came out, has he?"

Mrs. Bliss shook her head. "No, he hasn't."

"As you know, June, Joe isn't under any contract. He is free to come and go as he pleases. You yourself have known him as my friend for years. It's a mutual arrangement." Mrs. Bliss nodded and smiled wistfully.

She had been with Max from the early years. She felt a motherly sense of protection, and she had seen the two young men come and go on their adventures. She was a constant, a part of the company.

"I know Marlena talks to him regularly and would not want to drag him away from this Jumbo thing he is doing for you. She probably hasn't said anything to him. She has put on a brave face, so to speak. Maybe you could have a word with him?"

"Sure thing, June. You're quite right. I should have thought of it myself. We have all been working pretty hard. He should take a break and see his family. I'll mention it to him."

"Thanks, Max. I'm sure it would do them all good." Mrs. Bliss smiled.

They had said their good-byes, and Max thought about the length of time they had been away and realized it was getting on three years now, a long time to be away no matter how often one could communicate via video messages. The problem with this form of communication was there was always the time lag. The messages were restricted to the speed of light. Therefore, they weren't really conducive to a chatty conversation. The new telepathy booths had not fully come online yet.

With June's conversation in mind, he decided the best way to broach to Joe the subject of home visit was for them to be away from the job. To that end he briefed Ann that evening and proposed the three of them go explore the Washboard Plain. Ann thought it a good idea. If she still had any possessive feeling about the place, she probably felt Joe was the only other person she was most comfortable sharing it, Max thought.

Joe was predictably delighted at the prospect of going exploring with his old partner and was even more pleased when Max suggested they take a cruiser.

"We'll need it because our destination is more than seven thousand kilometers, so we need the range. We'll take a couple of pods on it in case we want to look around in places too tight for the cruiser."

Ann gave him a wary glance. She was quick to pick up on the "too tight" bit. She didn't have to say anything. Max knew what she was thinking.

"Sounds great. Where are we going?" Joe inquired. Max looked at Ann.

"We call it Washboard Plain," Ann replied. "I don't know if it has an official name. I don't think so."

Max said nothing. Ann continued, "We—or should I say Max ... well, both of us really—found it on the maps when we were still on Luna2, and it became a mystery. We discovered nobody else has seen it close up."

"I see," said Joe, cautious now. He knew Ann well and his antennae were working. "So it's a sort of *secluded place* ...er, a not too well publicized sort of place?"

"Quite so." Ann left it at that, so did Joe. Max said nothing.

"How's Marlena? You haven't mentioned her for a while," Max ventured.

"Spoke to her last week. She's okay and sends her regards," Joe said. Max looked at him closely. He knew Marlene was missing Joe by now and doubted she would be sending him her regards. After all, he had taken her husband away. It was this sense of guilt that led Max to feel he should not encourage Joe to stay away from home any longer.

"Look, Joe. I know you want to go on the *Ganymede*. But I have a team of specialists, and there is no room for supernumeraries, tourists if you like. Second, the *Ganymede* is going on a first-time exploratory mission that, quite seriously, will be hazardous. The crew knows that but are willing to go. And third, no matter how brave a face she puts on it, I'm sure Marlena and the kids are missing you." At the mention of Marlena, Joe looked embarrassed.

"Even if there was a position for you on the *Ganymede*, I would not let you go. I don't want to lose you, and I couldn't face Marlena if you were lost. You must understand that."

Joe looked at the floor somewhat sheepishly. He was torn between his sense of obligation and his love of adventure.

"You're right, of course," he admitted. "I was hoping that both of us could go to Titan. It'd be the trip of a lifetime! Just like the old days … you and me!" He looked up at Max, grinning, eyes sparkling. Max smiled at his old buddy.

"Joe, you old rogue, we're not in our twenties now, you know. We have obligations. And yes, I would have also liked to go. But there is too much to do here, and I'm sure Ann would also be extremely reluctant to let me go." He shrugged. Ann nodded.

Joe thought for a moment. "I wonder. If I could interest Marlena to come out here, would you agree?"

"Why, of course. We need as many pioneers like her as possible to populate this new world. With any luck, the *Ganymede* will have a successful run and pave the way for future mining on Titan. I'm sure there will be future voyages you could join, but make your peace with Marlena first, okay?"

"Okay, Max, you know best. I'll send her a message tonight saying I'm coming home on the next ship. When I'm home, I'll put the proposal to her and see if I can persuade her to come out. I know the boys would be mad keen."

"If they're anything like you, they'll climb on your back to come!" Max said and laughed.

"I guess so. No problem with them. I'm not so sure about Marlena. I'll have to see."

"The Titan is due for her return run to Earth in ten days. Be a good dad and go find out what's up at the ranch. Just go and see your family and bring them out here if they want. They can give it a go. Don't sell up the ranch until you're sure they'll want to stay. Keep your options open. Don't burn bridges."

"Good idea. I'll pitch it to Marlena as a sort of vacation! The poor thing won't know what's hit her.

She'll be blown away! The boys will be knocked out."
Joe was warming to the idea. Max had pricked his
conscience. He was now keen to get back to his ranch
and bring out the family.

"Good man. I'm sure you will feel better when that
little issue is sorted out."

Max was quietly relieved he had steered Joe away
from chasing around the solar system, leaving Max to
worry about him and feeling responsible for his family.
Joe's boyish enthusiasm and his wilder side needed to
be restrained at times for his and his family's sake. It
wasn't the first time Max had to restrain Joe's crazier
side.

"I suppose so," Joe agreed with some reluctance.
"Just don't go anywhere exiting without me!"

"I won't unless I can't help it." Max grinned.

"You're a bad as me." Joe accused.

"Probably, but as a peace offering, I can propose
you can come on this interesting little trip here on
Mars. This has been nagging at me since we arrived,
and we can investigate further before you go back to
Earth."

"Investigate *further*?"

"Yes, investigate further." Max was unapologetic.
"It's, ah, what can I say, a conundrum?"

That worked. He had Joe's full attention. The mere
mention of a conundrum was guaranteed to fire him
up. He was immediately aroused, sensing adventure.

Max was relieved he had broken the news they
were not going to Titan on what Joe saw as some sort

of new adventure spree. He knew his friend too well
and was concerned he was neglecting his family back
home. He had discussed the problem with Ann, and
they agreed that they would go on a little exploration
trip together before Joe went back. It was she who
had suggested, somewhat to Max's surprise, to go
and have a closer look at Washboard Plain. They had
been so busy with the pioneering organization, Ann's
pregnancy, and bringing up the baby in her first few
months, the issue of the plain had been postponed.

"You don't mind showing Joe our secret place?"
he had asked.

"No, I don't mind at all. I realize now I was being a
bit silly about it. I think I was either getting very broody
or already pregnant. I can't remember. Those early
days are all a bit of a blur to me now. I think I went a
bit crazy. The baby has settled everything for me now."
She blushed.

Max hugged her. "I love you," he said simply.

She trembled and kissed him. "And me you."

Next morning with a cruiser serviced and fueled
overnight, they rose out of Louros Chasma and climbed
vertically between the wall of the canyon until they
could fly through the valley at the top and out into
the sky high over the Calydon Fossa. The Sun was just
rising over the horizon behind them, throwing the
dunes below into sharp relief, bathing the landscape
in a deep red with a spellbinding glow. They took in the
view for a few moments.

Max punched in a bearing of 271.6 degrees and a

speed of two hundred kilometers per hour and was given an ETA of 1930. That made for a fairly long flight.

"We may well speed up later if we stop to look at anything on the way," Max proposed. "I don't particularly want to arrive in the dark, not that that matters. The autopilot would set us down okay."

"Didn't you boys want to get in your pods and go into tight places?" Ann inquired in a deadpan tone.

Max grinned at Joe.

"I think she's mocking us. Don't you want to come too, darling?"

"No, thanks, *darling*. I'll keep ship and pull you boys out of trouble later," Ann nonchalantly countered.

"Touché," Max said and grinned. She was a match for him any day.

They flew slowly as there was no rush to arrive and they could afford the time to study the landscape.

"You look as though you are looking for something." Ann knew her partner.

"Well, yes, actually. I was studying the survey photos, and I spotted something interesting and worth a look. I'm afraid it might just remind you of a day when we went spelunking."

"Oh no! Not that again! I knew it! You know how I feel about those holes."

"Yes, I know, love. But I'm sure you're not as fragile as you were then." He looked at her, and she nodded silently. "This, I believe, is a much better hole in the ground. You never know. You might actually like it." He tried to reassure her. She was unconvinced but was not intending to spoil the expedition. They flew on until Ann with her sharp eyes pointed ahead to starboard.

"There! Is that it?" She was pointing to a black spot on what was a gently sloping and featureless plain on the northeast slopes of Arsia Mons. As the craft came up to the feature, it became clear there was an almost perfectly circular opening. It was not an impact crater as there was no impact ejection material surrounding it. It was just a neat circular hole in the ground. Furthermore, looking down, they could see no floor to the hole. Joe grinned to himself. He was caught by Ann's sidelong glance.

"I think you like scaring me."

Max gave an exasperated shrug. "Honest, love, just inquisitive. Look at that! Doesn't that arouse your curiosity?"

"It arouses mine," Joe ventured.

"Now Joe Barnes, we are bringing you out on an expedition for a treat before you go home, so *you behave*, and don't encourage *him* to do anything stupid," she jokingly scolded him.

"No, ma'am! *How* could I ever lead *him* astray?" Joe pleaded. Max grinned wolfishly at him.

"Okay, you two, just don't go scaring me or *killing us all!*"

Max patted her knee and noted the digital compass—5 degrees 05'S, 118 degrees 40'W. He tapped the memory button to fix the location. He tapped the dimension icon after putting the cursor on each rim. The screen gave out the reading.

"Hmm, 150 meters. Think we'll fit in *there*, Joe?"

"*Oh, yes, boss!*" Joe affirmed.

Ann shrugged and sighed. "Okay, boys, have your bit of fun."

Out of respect for Ann, Max very carefully lowered the craft into the hole, although it was quite plain there was ample clearance.

This time there were no walls closing in on them as they descended. There was little in the way of walls at all. The hole opened out almost immediately. There was no spoil heap under the opening, no swirling cloud of dust, just darkness. Knowing the routine, Ann flipped on the searchlights and was quick to take charge of the control joystick.

It became clear this hole was another order of magnitude compared to the Tube1 of their first excursion. This also probably led from the Arsia Mons volcano some 175 kilometers to the south southeast. Arsia Mons had other well-known tubes on its northern slopes, but this was big.

Even at this distance from the volcano, it was about one hundred meters in diameter. The powerful searchlights just disappeared into the gloom when pointing down the tube. There was no sense of claustrophobia for Ann, there was no sense of being enclosed. One was simply flying in the dark. Max slowly moved away from the oculus and toward where the laser range finder indicated a wall about fifty meters away. The beam of the floodlight gave little idea of what they were looking at. As they approached the wall, the reason for that became clear. The walls, and presumably the ceiling and floor were composed of a black vitrified, glassy rock, probably obsidian or some sort of igneous rock.

Joe whistled. "Wow, what a beauty. A ready-made radiation shelter and it's huge. You have a city-sized hole here, boss."

Max was impressed, and so was Ann. Ann was so struck by the size and the smoothness of the interior surfaces she felt no fear. There were no loose bits to fall down, and it was big enough to excite wonder and awe rather than claustrophobia, Ann was calm. Max noticed and smiled reassuringly.

"You like this one? I'm rather pleased we found this. I'm sure we can use it, not necessarily to live in," Max said.

Ann nodded in agreement. "Yes, love, I'm quite happy with this one, no threats. You should hire me as your feng shui decorator."

Max laughed. He was happy she was not afraid.

"Joe? How's your feng shui indicator?" Max smiled at Ann.

"My gut says it's okay, boss," he replied simply.

"Good enough for me." Max frowned and consulted the screen, brought up a map of the area, and tapped a few times. "Hmm, 470 clicks from Pavonis Mons with a 5,800-meter drop to the saddle and then a rise of 2,440 meters to here. Not too bad. Let's survey this right away."

"You have any idea what he's talking about?" Ann eyed Joe.

"He's talking about comparative levels," Joe replied.

"Quite right, Joe. With comparative levels, gravity is our friend," Max confirmed. "Okay, let's go to the real purpose of our expedition. We'll get the survey boys out here to go over the structural integrity of this place. I trust the lady. I have good feelings about this place."

With little more to see at that time, they left what they decided to call the "Glass Tube" and flew out of the oculus into sunshine again. Having spent some of their travelling time on this diversion, Max tapped 3 degrees 30'N, 151 degrees 30'E, 1,000 m, and he upped the travel speed to 1,300 kilometers per hour into the autopilot. The craft rotated, rose to the specified cruising altitude, and set off at the inputted speed. Their destination was 5,270 kilometers to the west, about a quarter circumference of this little planet.

Flying on their bearing, they could see Olympus Mons to the north, its massive bulk just clear of the horizon. Being now more pressed for time and facing a long flight at their current speed, Max upped the speed to a more realistic 1,800 kilometers per hour, cutting their travel time. They now had a flight of two hours and fifty minutes. This made their ETA around 1500.

They settled down to eat an in-flight midday meal courtesy of Gastron's culinary genius. Once again they toasted the chef's ability to produce presentable, delicious food in the most exacting conditions. The menu was Pâté d'Ardennes with his space baguette recipe, a vacuum-sealed barbecue chicken with fresh tomatoes and salads from their own Martian greenhouses with cheese or sorbet to finish. They also had Ann's favorite green tea or Earth water to drink.

"Here's to Gaston's skill and Earth water!"

They arrived at Washboard Plain at 1456 and brought the craft down at the designated reference. They transferred to two pods to explore the plain. An hour later they had little to report. The plain was much as they had seen before—kilometers of parallel low dunes running perfectly north-south, regular as a ploughed field, a field that measured seventy-five by twenty kilometers. They chatted over the radio, comparing notes.

During the flight Joe was intrigued.

"What the hell?" Joe observed, eloquent to a fault. "Can't make this out at all. A conundrum indeed. Can't be natural. It's too regular and flat, not a single impact crater. Weird!" he decided.

He was as bemused as Max and Ann had been on their visit. They returned to the tug to have a rest and compare notes over green tea. Max tapped away at the console, taking various readings—atmospheric pressure, wind speed, altitude, temperature, light level, radiation, magnetism. Magnetism! The readings were abnormally high.

"What is ..." Max frowned and leaned closer. "Hey,

you guys, have a look at this. Magnetism is way, way up here!" Ann and Joe joined him at the console.

"And so?" Ann quizzed.

"And so I would guess there is a high metallic content to the ground around here, maybe iron ore, or there is a local anomaly, a local magnetic field. Pretty unusual. Maybe an ordinary explanation."

"Why would you think it would be anything other than ordinary?" Ann's antennae were switched on.

"Don't know. Just a hunch. Man's intuition." He grinned mischievously. Ann ignored the jibe.

"Well, I can believe there is something spooky here." Joe was uneasy with things he didn't understand. "I can't figure this place out. It ain't natural."

"It's certainly hard to believe this formation *is* natural." Max agreed.

Ann looked puzzled. "I wonder why I was so silly about this place. It's weirder than anything." She lapsed into thought. Max studied her. He had a genuine faith in her *feelings* despite his teasing. He let her intuitive juices work.

"Joe, can you think of any other tests I could run to understand this place?" Max looked to his friend.

"Uh, I dunno. I'm not too good at all this fancy electronic stuff. I believe in boots on the ground."

"Okay, what do you want to do? Go outside and kick some dirt?"

"Can't do any harm. Yes, let's have a look outside. I haven't had breath of fresh air all day!"

Max grinned. "Very droll. Let's have a look. I'm

going to take one of these new californium-powered detectors. Let's see what they say."

They suited up, leaving Ann in the tug. She declined the excursion, absorbed in her thoughts.

The two of them walked along the crest of one of the low dunes, and having discovered nothing of interest, they moved down into the parallel troughs and followed it south. Max was sweeping the head of the detector before him, getting a solid indication of something magnetic in the ground.

"Mmmm, looks like there is a high iron content here," he observed.

"So? This is the red planet after all. High iron," Joe countered.

"Yes, but these readings are very high."

"Rich iron seam? A good source for mining?" Joe was ever practical.

"Yes, maybe." Max was frowning. He stooped and scooped up a handful of the reddish gray sand. He straightened up and let the sand trickle through his fingers. He kicked the ground and pondered.

"Let's dig," he announced.

Joe looked at him. "Dig? How deep? For what?"

"I dunno. Let's dig."

Joe shrugged. "Okay, boss." They trudged back to the tug and found a folding shovel in the tool cupboard and set about to dig in one of the troughs. They took turns digging the hole. Joe was bemused. He was not sure what his friend was up to, but he resisted asking if he had found Australia yet. Joe was digging when he hit something solid. He straightened.

"Don't think we can go deeper than that." He was standing in their hole up to his waist. "Want to take some soil samples out of this hole?"

"What's at the bottom? What's the hard stuff?"

"Dunno." He crouched and scraped with the shovel. He brushed away the dust and scraped some more. Max was sitting on the dune, watching as Joe took his turn on the shovel. They had to pace themselves to avoid overheating in their bulky suits. A few moments later Joe straightened.

"Max, what do you make of this?"

Max came over to the hole and peered in. Joe had cleared the bottom of the hole. It was a hard rock surface that could not be dug up with a simple shovel. Max thought for a moment.

"Looks like basalt," he decided. "Can we break out a chunk as a sample?"

"Don't think so. Not with a shovel. I'll see if there is a hammer and chisel ... or a little explosive." He added slyly, looking at Max expectantly. Max grinned.

"You crazy redneck, you'll kill us all yet! Let's go see what there is." Max knew exactly what equipment was on board. After all, he had been involved from the outset in the specifications of his craft.

"You'll find some *plastic* in the explosives box. Make a shaped charge, and don't go mad!"

Joe went off to find his beloved plastic explosive. Max knew that given the choice, Joe would not even look for a hammer and chisel. *Well, let him have his fun*, he thought. He dropped into the hole a squatted down and brushed the surface of the rock with his glove. It was certainly hard and smooth. He struck it with the edge if the shovel, no impression.

Joe returned triumphantly with half of a kilo of plastic. Max eyed the sticks of explosive.

"Jaysus Joe, what are you up to? You want to flatten the place?" they looked at each other. Joe and Max both laughed then.

"Yes! Yes! Make a really nice big bang. Blast a good hole. See how thick the basalt is!" Joe suggested.

"I guess so. We'll need to know that. Let's see what's down there."

Like a pair of mischievous schoolboys, they went back to the ship and raided the explosives store. A ten-kilo case of explosive and a remote control detonator were carried back to the hole. Max stood back and let Joe do the business. Yes, Joe was an expert. Max had no worries on that score. Joe laid the shaped charge in the hole. Then they backfilled the hole with half a meter of dirt and retired to a safe distance. (As it usually says in the instructions when playing with this kind of thing).

It was a big bang. It was a very big bang. It was, not to put too fine a point, a huge bang. It knocked them flat. Stunned, they lay on their backs as debris rained down for a good minute while Ann's voice was crying in their ears.

"What's that? What's that? Max, Max, Joe, anyone

hear me? Max? Max? Max?" Her voice ended in a sob and whimper.

Max forced himself to come to his senses, realizing he was in for a chastising from Ann when the dust had settled on this particular piece of mischief. He winced at the thought and answered her.

"Okay, all okay. Don't worry, love. We're just doing a little bit of surveying," he offered meekly.

"Surveying! *Surveying?* Are you two bloody idiots *completely insane.*" She had gone from being frightened and afraid to getting mad, very mad. It didn't look good.

"Sorry, love. We should have warned you." He offered weakly, knowing he was in trouble.

"*Warned me! You're joking. Did you warn God you were coming early?*" She was yelling now. That was a bad sign. Things were getting worse. All went quiet, which was an even worse sign. Max looked at Joe. He was sitting there with an inane grin on his face. He saw Max watching him. He started laughing and was soon rolling around in the dirt, helpless in fits of laughter. The access door of the ship flew open, and suddenly fully suited in record time, Ann was stomping her way over to them. That was a very, very bad sign. Max winced. He knew he was in for it. He was sure the sight of Joe rolling around in the dirt and laughing his head off was not going to help. He shook his head helplessly. He could only wait to hear the music.

He watched Ann's approach, quickly trying to think about how he was going to calm her. She was *really* upset. She was as much frightened as angry. He hoped she would calm down when she realized they weren't hurt. She stopped, arms straight by her side, fists clenched inside her gloves. He waited. She didn't move. He waited more. She still didn't move. This was surreal. He turned around to look at Joe behind him. Joe had stopped laughing, and he was staring at the blast crater they had made. The hole was bigger, no surprise. More than that, the floor of the hole was gone. There was no floor, just a gaping hole. The three of them slowly approached the rim and peered down into a huge underground cavern.

"Maybe a tad too much plastic," Max suggested lightly.

Joe nodded. "Yes. boss, but how were we to *know how thick it was*?" He appealed with wide-eyed innocence.

"True, true." Max nodded gravely.

Ann's mouth dropped open. She looked from one grave face to the other and squinted. The two fools were poker-faced. Unfortunately, *she* was not fooled.

She started very quietly and slowly. "I ... should ... shoot ... the pair of you two *bloody imbeciles!*" With that, she spun on her heel and stomped back to the ship and slammed the hatch. Not good.

Duly castigated, the two imbeciles sheepishly looked at each other. Then the reality of their discovery sunk home, and they looked at their handiwork. There was, admittedly not due to any precision on their part, a fairly neat, large round hole. It was after all a shaped charge, just a rather *large* charge to obtain a rock sample.

Rock samples were forgotten in the face of this new development despite their abundance scattered around them. They were after all merely something to show for their fruitless digging.

They looked in wonder at their hole.

"How big do you reckon?" Joe wondered.

"The hole, the cavern, or the bang?" Max inquired with a quiet laugh.

"All I suppose." Joe laughed louder.

"*I can still hear you two bloody jokers!*" Ann said loudly over their headsets. They jumped in unison. They were truly caught off guard. They were left wondering how much of the entire exploit's conversation had been overheard and what they had said. That was a sobering thought. The intercom traffic went suspiciously quiet from then on.

CHAPTER

19

M ax and Anne's little girl was called Marsia. She was now eighteen months, and the image of her mother, happily toddling and chatting, a slender and precocious little darling. Being the only child in the community and the firstborn on the planet, she was more than a novelty. She was special, a legend. The center of attention wherever she went, she easily won people's hearts. There had been other pregnancies among the pioneers who were already there when Max and Ann first arrived, but sadly, mainly because of their arduous, basic lifestyle and the medical staff being unequipped for maternity patients, none had come to term.

Ann was ecstatic, and Max was deeply happy for the gift of the child. He was especially happy for Ann, who had bloomed in motherhood. Ann had decided to give birth on Mars as it was considered equally risky to attempt the journey back to Earth and possibly have a miscarriage en route.

Under Grace's guidance during her pregnancy and subsequent postnatal care, Ann had paid particular attention to Marsia's physical development. To combat the low gravity, the toddler was given progressively more strenuous *games* to play. Ann used gymnastic games, which disguised Marsia's physical training as play, so that she was less likely lose interest. Consequently, she worked harder than she would have if she had been made to exercise. In the low gravity, she would perform the jumps, vaults, and summersaults like a true little gymnast.

Initially, Grace was keen for her to be sent to Earth to grow up in a normal environment, but Ann didn't want to be parted from Max. Anyway, the little one had responded so well to Grace's physical regimen and diet that she grew supple and strong, so Ann had no worries on that score.

Grace had briefly come out to Mars for two months to give a month's prenatal attention and deliver the baby. She stayed a further month after the birth to attend to mother and baby's welfare. She had since provided Ann with postnatal advice from Luna2.

Anne's only regret was the lack of other little playmates for Marsha. She did as much as possible with the virtual reality facilities and video contact with other kids on the SpaceWeb, but she accepted this was no substitute for real companions. *I'll have to provide her with a little brother or sister,* she thought wistfully.

Since they had come back from the Washboard Plain excursion, both Max and Joe had been busy. Joe had to hand over his projects to his assistant, and Max was overseeing the preparations and outfitting of the *Ganymede* for her pioneering voyage to Saturn. This task seemed endless as more and more contingencies were considered, which required more planning and equipment.

The Titan had returned with a massive supply train of containers that stretched some twenty kilometers and taxed the combined thrusters of the *Titan* and the *Ganymede* to slow and bring it into orbit. The logicians at the Luna2 worked out the combined power of the two ships exactly, leaving little room for error. Max voiced his reservations, but the two captains countered, making light of the risk, "What's the worst that could happen, short of running into Mars, which is a one in a gazillion chance? We overrun and have to drag it all back?"

Joe had made himself busy with scheduling the breakdown of the load, and he was on his return trip home to his family aboard the returning *Titan* within the week. They had a farewell party for him, and while he was sad to leave, he was hopeful that he'd return with the whole family.

A week later they could delay the departure of the *Ganymede* no longer. The respective orbits of Mars, Jupiter, and Saturn were calculated to be at their most favorable for the mission, and they could not delay further.

Max, Ann, and Marsia had watched the *Ganymede* disappear into the blackness on its mission far out into the solar system. It was an ambitious plan to mine nitrogen and ethane from Titan. The environmental cost of robbing Earth of her resources was no longer viable. Achieving a tolerable atmosphere here on Mars meant they had to look to the solar system to find the gasses they needed. After much thought, the *Ganymede* was equipped with as many insulated tank container units she could reasonably manage. When all the tanks were clamped together, she resembled a sea container ship, the poor *Ganymede* dwarfed by her load. She would act as a tug and engine combined. Her pods together with four of the large tugs from Phobos would assist with maneuvering the tanks and ship.

This was literally a leap in the dark for the *Ganymede*. Max had appointed Captain Patrick Hogan to head this pathfinding mission. It was a first for him, for all of them. No one had attempted to mine resources so far out in the solar system. There were unknown dangers, untested systems. It was a feat of daring, a daunting venture.

Max pondered the glowing light diminishing into the starry sky with a certain sense of apprehension. There was a lot riding on the success of that ship's journey into the unknown. He had wanted to go, but there was so much to do on Mars. And for the first time, Ann had flatly refused to go with him if he decided to go. Her motherly instincts forbade it. The little one could not be expected to be exposed to the confines of the ship on a long voyage, not to mention the dangers. Ann didn't want to be separated from Max. She didn't want him to go either. The adventurer in Max struggled with the responsibilities of his position as head of his enterprise and as a father. He could not leave Ann and Marsia. He had decided to stay.

Patrick, he reasoned, was the best captain and could be relied upon to make the right decisions. Max's presence would be superfluous to the mission, and he would only be there for the experience of exploration, a joyride he could no longer justify.

"Bye, bye," Marsia's soft voice came to him. Her little hand waved at the retreating ship. "Bye, bye, Gan-ee-eed!"

CHAPTER 20

The *Ganymede* had already completed the journey to Mars from Earth. The crew was now seasoned and familiar with her capabilities. The latest design of the main propulsion system installed in her meant that near light speed was a theoretic possibility with a clear intergalactic trajectory. Within the confines of the solar system, it was a case of continuous acceleration followed by maximum deceleration. For the next few days they accelerated toward the asteroid belt on the first leg of their journey. They had the daily round of checks to perform to ensure the smooth running of the ship, navigation, and scientific readings to be taken. The crew settled into the routine.

Patrick Hogan was captain. Chris Williams was elected to stay with his captain as his first officer. They were joined by Deborah Moore as second officer, and Dave Brooks was the navigator and engineer. They were joined by a staff crew of five made up of technical and scientific specialists to run the ship, take data, and ensure safety of the all-important pressurized cargo after they filled the empty tanks that they towed in a huge train behind them.

In its position in the solar system, Mars was close to the inner edge of the asteroid belt which presented the major obstacle to be negotiated before getting into the unobstructed space of the outer solar system.

This belt was a zone of space between Mars and Jupiter with no hard boundaries. It was a loosely defined ring around the Sun and thought to be the possible remnants left over from the formation of the solar system. It is a zone very sparsely populated by all sizes of objects made up of a variety of materials—carbonaceous, silicaceous, or metallic ranging from dust particles to truck-sized chunks of rock, metal, ice, or a mixture of all. There was even the dwarf planet Ceres with a diameter of 950 kilometers followed by the proto planet Vesta at 525 kilometers.

Ceres alone accounted for more than a quarter of the entire mass of the belt. Vesta was about 20 percent followed by Pallas and Hygiea. The rest of the mass was made up of smaller rocks scattered around the Sun in a band roughly 375 million kilometers wide or one and a half times the distance from Earth to the Sun, known as astronomical units (AUs). The total number of significant bodies numbered approximately thirty-five thousand.

To counter this, the Ganymede was equipped with sensors that, coupled with an automatic avoidance system, allowed the crew to negotiate the major hazards. These were backed up with two other systems. The first was an array of lasers that could vaporize small objects, and the second was explosive reactive armor designed to deal with larger objects. This was similar to that developed for use by old battle tanks in the twentieth century.

While numerous, these objects were spread over a wide band and present in a low density, but nonetheless, they were real hazards when considering the speed of the spacecraft passing through. An object the size of a football was sufficient size to cripple a ship.

The use of Jupiter as a slingshot to achieve greater velocity was an often used tactic to reach the outer solar system faster and conserve fuel, but with all the varying orbits of the planets, timing was all important.

In a truly historic stroke of serendipity, the planets of Jupiter and Saturn were about to be in alignment with the Sun in 2118–19. It was early 2116 now, which meant they were at a nearly perfect time to use the planetary alignment.

Mars's orbit of 687 Earth days was such that they could use the relative planetary positions and thus use the slingshot to their advantage. A close examination of the relative orbits of Mars, Jupiter, and Saturn had been computed to evaluate the slingshot assisted trajectory, and they found there was an almost perfect conjunction. The planets were approaching an almost perfect alignment. The optimum was found to occur in mid-2118. The next such alignment of Jupiter and Saturn would not come until August 2139. In short,

2116–2118 were the best years for a long time. Hence, the urgency to depart when they did. This was a truly historic coincidence at a time when the journey to Saturn's moon Titan was critical to obtaining the gasses they needed.

The *Ganymede* was able to continuously accelerate through the asteroid belt, relying on the object avoidance system to either alter course to avoid collision or to zap small objects before hitting them. In two weeks they were into Jupiter's gravitational sphere and accelerating toward the giant gas planet.

The asteroid belt marks the transition from the inner to outer solar system, and the farther they left the asteroid belt, the more the influence of Jupiter was apparent. They closely watched the instruments constantly monitoring the highly turbulent planet with its red spot, a twenty-thousand-kilometers-wide hurricane that has swept around the planet for at least the last five hundred years—that was since man was able to study the planet in any detail. As with everything else on this torrid planet, the radiation was intense. Constant and careful attention had to be kept up to balance the maximum speed with the minimum radiation.

As the largest and most massive planet in the solar system with the highest gravitational field, Jupiter has consequently collected more than sixty moons, and therefore, it also has a very powerful slingshot effect. The fortuitous alignment of planets gave the *Ganymede* the opportunity of making possible the fastest possible journey to Saturn. Also, as long as their stay at Saturn was not long, they would enjoy the same free boost on the way back. Otherwise, the next free ride was not for another twenty-three years. This free ride however, had to be won.

Jupiter is extremely hostile in that it has a huge lethal radiaition field that traps electrons and electrically charged particles in a belt hundreds of thousands of kilometers deep. The on-board magnetic shielding would be run at its maximum to provide adequate protection. It was a careful tradeoff between the speed gained and the radiation endured. The closer they approached, the more speed but the more radiation endured too. Should their calculations be incorrect, their approach too close, the magnetic shield fail, or any one of numerous possibilities occur, they would be at the mercy of the giant.

They would find themselves in short supply of mercy. Jupiter has 70 percent the mass of the entire planetary solar system. Scientists consider Jupiter a proto star with the same composition as the Sun. Many say that with a little more mass, Jupiter would have become a star. It is as big as a gas giant planet can be without spontaneous stellar ignition. The Jovian atmosphere, like the Sun, is made up mostly of hydrogen and helium under a huge atmospheric pressure so dense it liquefies and rains *metallic* hydrogen. Despite its huge size, being one thousand times the volume of the Earth, it rotates so fast that a day is less than ten hours. This gives rise to constant storms with hydrogen, ammonia, and sulfur winds of hundreds of kilometers per hour.

With the help of the data gained from past outer solar system missions, an extensive database of the Jovian environment had been assembled, and this was used to evaluate the optimum trajectory for the fly-round. With their own instruments monitoring the planet, they would also add to that database of knowledge. The parameters were uploaded, and the navigation algorithm gave the optimum approach trajectory and speed. Once the *Ganymede* was on this course, it was up to the autopilot systems to maintain it, automatically correcting for fluctuations.

With that done, the crew members were free to either watch the show or try to studiously ignore the maelstrom outside and bury themselves in some other distraction. As it turned out, with curiosity roused by the chatter from the spectators, everyone was eventually drawn to watch the spectacle of the gargantuan storms raging below them and join the collective thrill. Nonetheless, they were all grateful that they were safe aboard a good ship.

By the time they had made a full circuit of the planet, they recorded with satisfaction a speed of about five million kilometers per hour. With a clear run, this would theoretically get them to Saturn in a little more than five days; however, they had to eventually slow down to a stop to land on Titan. Two days out they had to employ full braking thrust to slow down to achieve an orbital and then entry speed for Titan.

The whole process of maneuvering to a landing site on Titan would take three days in itself. Titan orbits Saturn about every sixteen days, so an approach to intercept it has to be calculated to optimize speed and trajectory.

The plan was that the bulk of the pressure tanks to transport the methane, ethane, and nitrogen would be left in orbit around Titan while the ship would land with two tanks as a test run. The next two weeks were a period of constant and feverish activity. The deceleration process had to be constantly monitored, and the interception trajectory for Titan constantly updated as their trajectory was refined.

Tomorrow would be their descent to the surface, marking the successful completion of the outward journey. There was an elated but fatigued mood among the crew. They felt a deep sense of achievement in having made their longest and farthest journey into the solar system.

CHAPTER 21

A gasp from Samantha, one of the scientific crew, brought them to the large observation window. They had gotten used to looking out at just stars, but now the view they saw silenced them immediately. The sense of being so far out in the solar system came forcefully home to them. Saturn loomed so large ahead, filling nearly half the sky, casting a pale reflected light over the rings surrounding it, their sparkling ice crystals presenting a breathtaking vision of beauty. The crew stood in a tight group at the window. Open-mouthed, they stared for several minutes in silence, helpless, dumbstruck by the otherworldliness of it all. The majesty of the scene stunned them with amazement, wonder, and awe.

"What's that?" asked Samantha, pointing to a perfect hexagonal formation in the swirling gas clouds near the north pole of the planet.

"It's thought to be a circular storm with an uprising

at one point. No one really knows. It's one of the mysteries of this beautiful planet," Patrick explained.

"It's amazing. This whole planet is amazing. Look at the speed of those clouds." She pointed down to the swirling cloud formations now below them. They were so reminiscent of Jupiter.

"Yes, it's a special, beautiful planet. It has no less than sixty-two moons. It is the second largest planet of the solar system, and like Jupiter, it is also gas giant. Do you see that moon in the ring ahead? That's Enceladus. It's five hundred kilometers wide and constantly spews water crystals from a hundred ice geysers that feed the rings. It is a water planet, a bit like Jupiter's Europa."

"Beautiful." Samantha gazed down at the moon streaming plumes of ice crystals glittering in the sunshine. This was one of the wonders of the solar system's most spectacular planet.

"Titan, our destination, is quite special too. Besides being the second in size in the solar system to our ship's namesake, Jupiter's Ganymede, it's the only moon in the solar system with a dense atmosphere—95 percent nitrogen and 5 percent methane. It's also thought to have a lot of water below the surface."

The *Ganymede* gently moved high over Titan's north pole, searching for their objective, the Ligeia Mare, a lake of liquid methane and ethane, which slowly came into view. Carefully monitoring the land below using the surface- and ground-penetration radar instruments, they surveyed the moon's surface and substrata, searching for a suitable landing point. The ability to fly over this moon was made easier as it had less gravitational pull than Earth's Moon. The landing point would have to be close to the lake so the liquid could easily be sucked up into the ship's insulated storage tanks. The crew studied the screen showing the surface below, their faces lit by the glow of the instruments. They identified a suitable area that the scanners indicated was solid ground at the lake's shore. They cautiously brought the ship down to land on a rocky slab bordering the lake they had just passed over.

Settling on the surface, they slowly shut down the thrusters while checking for any indication of the ship sinking into the ground. Reassured, they finally shut down all thrust and waited, ready at a moment's notice to boost. After so long a flight, the ship made strange clicking noises with occasional creaks and groans as the hull flexed and motors cooled. There was heart-stopping jolt as one of the landing feet crushed a section of rock and the ship settled. All seemed stable now. After a minute while no one moved and with a sense of relief, they switched the main reactor to standby. All that remained was the faint hum of the auxiliary motors providing power for the ship's systems.

This marked the end of the longest journey they had ever undertaken. They had traveled from their home station at Mars and reached out across the solar system to Saturn, a journey of more than a billion kilometers. The journey from Earth to Mars seemed like a mere hop. The Sun, which plays such a major part in the climate of the inner planets, was now so far that it merely appeared as an extremely bright star, giving more light than warmth.

Having overcome the initial amazement of their location, they took stock of their situation. The ship gently vibrated to the pumps as they collected materials. The ship's compressors were sucking in the 98 percent nitrogen from the atmosphere. That was one and a half times denser than Earth's, and they were compressing it all to liquid. The Ligeia Mare liquid methane and ethane was being taken on board from the lake, sucked into a separate tank. The lake's hydrocarbon mix was being tested for its purity and was found to be usable in its raw form as the scientists had predicted. From millions of years of evaporation and condensation, it was free of sediment since the liquid was so much lighter than the silt. These two resources, nitrogen and ethane/methane were key resources and their sole reason for being on Titan.

There was little for them to do outside the ship once the harvesting process was running. The temperature outside was -280 degrees Celsius. They did a visual inspection of the craft to identify any small defects or damage that the sensors had not recorded. They moved awkwardly and carefully in their thick suits, which protected them from the intense cold of the moon. The hull showed signs of abrasion by dust and microparticles, probably incurred during their passage through the asteroid belt, but it was otherwise free of damage. There was a limit to the self-healing properties the skin of the craft could withstand and repair. Their outside duties completed, it was now left to the ship to fill itself with its cargo of liquids and gasses.

After two hours outside, they returned to the ship and shed their suits. They showered and gathered to eat in the in the common room.

"Well, so far so good." Captain Patrick Hogan was relieved. He had been appointed captain of the pioneering mission because of his caution and wealth of experience.

"Nearly halfway through the mission and the worst has been the anxiety of the asteroid belt," added Deborah.

"And the boredom," added Sean.

"Let's hope boredom is our only enemy from now on," Hogan said. He was always suspicious when things went smoothly. His constant attention and vigilance mixed with pragmatism made him an ideal captain.

"Don't court misfortune," Deborah warned.

"Not the courting type. I have a pretty wife at home." He grinned. "Chris, you should get yourself married too."

"Not me. I like my freedom. I'm too young to be tied down." His first officer laughed, continuing their long-standing banter on the matter.

"No decent woman would want him." Deborah remarked with a cheeky grin. "She would never know where he'd been."

She had a bit of a *thing* for Chris and wished he would recognize her cheekiness for what it was—a thinly veiled desire. Chris, a seasoned bachelor, was in fact well aware of her but pretended otherwise. He had yet to yield to her unquestionable allure. He was after all a mere mortal, and after so long a voyage, he found it increasingly difficult to resist her. If it wasn't for Sally—*Smokin' Sally*, as he privately thought of her—one of the ship's scientists, he would probably have succumbed to Deborah long ago. The heavenly Sally was, however, as difficult to impress as Chris was for Deborah.

The ship was not without its sexual dynamics. It was both a flaw and an asset to the well-being and cohesion of the crew.

Chris adopted a wounded expression, "But my ma says I'm an angel."

There were catcalls, hoots, and cackles from all within earshot. The tensions of the journey and safe landing were now released in good-natured nonsense. And so the idle chatter went on.

The life aboard on long voyages was often difficult to fill with meaningful occupations, so there were periods of boredom interspersed with moments of abject terror in the face of imminent oblivion. There was every effort made to provide amusement in a dedicated VR room. The virtual reality environment could be programmed to create almost any scenario. There was also an interactive facility with an assortment of single or multiplayer VR games.

At that moment Saturn blocked their ability to radio Mars and Luna2. They could only record a message signaling their arrival and the fact that they had started pumping their gas cargos. Like Earth's Moon, one face of Titan always faced its mother planet. They had two days before their message would be automatically sent when radio contact was established. Even then the signal traveling at the speed of light took more than an hour to reach its destination.

They now had a new shift routine monitoring the smooth and uninterrupted pumping of gas and liquid. As most was automated, this amounted to being available to rectify any faults or stoppage of pumps. Most of the time, there was nothing to do. A totally automated robotic ship had been considered when the *Ganymede* was designed, but considering the cost of the ship, it was felt that a small supervisory crew was more flexible and needed to be able to react to any unforeseen problems.

A case in point was when the liquid ethane pumps started to run hotter than usual. The source of the problem was discovered to be outside at the inflow to three of the hoses that sucked up the liquid. This involved working outside in suits to fix the problem. It was found that although the pipes had intake heads that floated on the surface to avoid sucking up silt and rocky material from the lake bottom, they found the intake heads were being clogged by partially frozen, slushy, and icy chunks of ethane obstructing the flow. This had not been foreseen and needed an ad-hoc fix. The solution was to fabricate metal mesh baskets. They designed these and then printed them out on one of the 3-D printers. They were heated by passing a current through embedded wires. These were quickly fabricated aboard and installed fourteen hours later. Thereafter, pumping continued without a hitch.

In reality, it was not the pumping of liquid ethane that was the major undertaking. It was compressing and liquefying the gaseous nitrogen that proved the most time-consuming task.

Twelve days pumping saw their tanks full, and they returned to geostationary orbit, where they found the other seven hundred of their double storage tanks. They had only taken one hundred of the eight hundred tanks on the first landing to save fuel and stay as maneuverable as possible for a first landing on a strange moon. They considered taking the remaining tanks down but decided on caution and took another one hundred tanks to be filled, leaving one hundred full and six hundred empty tanks in orbit. They exercised caution on Captain Hogan's orders based on his pragmatism. He had also observed that their landing place would not comfortably take seven hundred more of the tanks. Furthermore, there were only six suction pumps so there was little advantage to be gained.

Another two months of continuous pumping found them with all tanks full and on their return to Mars. The ship was now little more than a space tug. It had to move 118,400 times the weight of the *Ganymede*. This was a time when monitoring the pumps was replaced by monitoring the ship's thrusters. She was running at full thrust, building up speed for the following three and a half weeks.

Back at Mars their progress with the gas harvesting and return journey was keenly followed by Max and the backup team on Luna2. Their flight path was closely monitored and compared with the ship's own computations, and any necessary flight corrections were made. Radio waves traveling at light speed were still taking about fifty-five minutes to reach Mars.

A few days brought them into the realm of Jupiter's rings. While these were not as pronounced as Saturn's, they were apparent in space when approaching the planet. As on the journey out, they calculated a slingshot orbit. Their position and trajectory calculations were passed on to Mars and Luna2 for verification. Minor corrections were made, and they were on their corrected approach to Jupiter. To maximize the slingshot effect in light of the latest readings they had taken on the way out, they were able to predict the optimum trajectory to use the planet's gravitational pull to its maximum, which also meant making as close a pass of Jupiter without entering its atmosphere.

Jupiter's largest moon, Ganymede, after which the ship was named, was the largest in the solar system. It had large amounts of water ice and a thin oxygen atmosphere, and it's the only one with a magnetosphere. This is followed by Callisto, Europa, and Io. Europa has ice and a subsurface ocean, making it a contender as a source of water. Callisto has a similar composition as Ganymede—water ice and rock. The closest to Jupiter is Io. It has a high level of tidal friction from the planet's and the other moons gravity, causing internal heating that results in high volcanic activity, ejecting sulfurous eruptions five hundred kilometers beyond a thin sulfur dioxide atmosphere. Unsurprisingly, Io was not considered a suitable place to colonize.

By contrast, Europa is more hospitable, but it's made up of a crust of ice floating on more than a hundred-kilometer-deep ocean with no land, which means it's barely habitable despite a very thin oxygen atmosphere. Ganymede has a firm surface and water ice so had potential for habitation, but with mankind's attention firmly focused on Mars and the considerable extra distance, the possibilities of Europa, Ganymede, and Jupiter's sixty-five other moons had yet to be fully explored. For the present Jupiter and her moons were the object of robotic missions, and of course, its gravitational pull was valued to boost interplanetary travel speeds.

The *Ganymede's* approach velocity to Jupiter rose as is came under the influence of the giant planet's pull. They continued at maximum thrust to make full use of the slingshot effect. The on-board navigational system, which used stellar location to fix its position and speed, logged the rise in ever faster increments. The sense of speed totally lacking in space was now apparent with the planet so close. The massive planet grew in the viewports until it filled their field of view. The turbulent atmosphere of Jupiter with its huge red Earth-sized storm broiled ahead of them.

The rotation of the planet gave a ten-hour day,

which for a planet of that size meant a rotational speed of 43,500 kilometers per hour, all of which exaggerated the sense of movement. There were no reference points for the eye to fix on. There was no way of seeing how far away the clouds were and no means to mentally orient oneself. Into this all-consuming, disorientating maelstrom they were plunging, all senses were null. They could only rely on their instruments, which they consulted more often than necessary.

Hours passed as their speed climbed under the planet's influence, and with their huge cargo, they had considerably larger mass for the gravity to attract. The viewports showed the constant stormy hydrogen clouds. The crew members were tempted after a while to blank out the viewports so they could forget the stormy planet below. The attraction of the view on the way out held less fascination on the return trip. There was nothing for them to do. They were passengers locked onto their course. They could only trust the system as usual, the avionics and computers to guide them. It was just that at times like this in the close presence of the giant planet, they felt their frailty. They were subject to enormous forces. They could only trust in precise mathematics and their good ship to evade gravitational extinction.

The slingshot sent them on their trajectory to Mars with a greatly enhanced velocity, perceptible only by consulting the computer systems that recorded the diminishing distance to Mars on a big readout over the main screen. The crew settled to the routine of observation and communication. Their next round trip was already being planned.

"I suppose one could get used to this after the first run," suggested Deborah.

"Not sure I'd want to," Patrick replied. "Things would get too workaday."

"I suppose so. It's just the lows between the highs that are tedious. I'm sure half the routine of ship monitoring is designed to give us something to do."

"It is. The shrinks prescribe it. Gives us a sense of purpose. In a few years, we will become redundant, and the whole thing will be robotic." Patrick gave a shrug.

Deborah knew this, of course. They all did, but she felt there was always going to be a need for crews for spaceships. There was only so much a machine could do. Complex intuitive decisions were still the domain of humans. Besides, the higher objective was humankind's exploration and colonization of new domains, and humans had to eventually be there to do that.

"No bad thing. It would leave the interesting stuff to humans," she suggested.

Patrick nodded. He thought the same. He was increasingly feeling redundant in his present role. There was little real piloting anymore. He had learned his skills as a test pilot, flying machines a pilot actually controlled. He had more fun flying the pods than a ship. At least you had some direct *feel* and feedback from the machine. These new spaceships were so big that all sense of actually controlling the things was lost. It was all buttons and keyboards. The vessel was a moving city. Maneuvering was all in slow motion, no thrills. He sighed. Maybe he should retire back to Earth and go back to gliding … or stunt piloting. Before he was too old.

"Penny for them."

"Uh? Oh, nothing. Just dreaming of the good old days."

Deborah smiled. "Okay, grandpa, shall I fetch your slippers and cocoa?"

"Very funny. Actually, I was thinking of stunt flying."

"Like in the good old days?"

"You read my mind, and yes. Don't knock it. I was weaned on it."

"You mean them things with a fan on the front?"

"Yes, ma'am. You wouldn't know, but those fans gave a real kick when you opened them up. Not like a jet that builds up speed slowly."

"That so? So that's more fun? Being kicked, I mean." She looked mischievous.

"Of course it is. That's part of the thrill—the g-forces, the quick maneuvers, and stuff. More feel, more … alive." He ignored her teasing.

"I might try it."

"You should. That's *real* flying."

The tranquility of the bridge was disturbed by a strange alarm. They looked at each other, each wondering the same thing.

"What the hell is that?" Deborah gasped, not immediately recognizing the meaning.

"*That is the proximity alarm.*" Patrick looked concerned and puzzled. "*I don't like it.*"

He grabbed a handhold and flew to a console closely followed by Deborah, who had recognized the alarm a second later. It had taken her off guard since it was the first time it had sounded this trip.

They studied the console. An object was approaching them from behind. The ship was automatically moving over to let the object pass harmlessly. There was a pause, and the thrusters fired. Then there was another pause, and the thrusters fired again.

"What. The. Hell!" Captain Patrick Hogan was now very serious, his brow knitted, his eyes fixed on the console's screen. "Why's the ship taking evasive actions?"

Deborah had no idea. She had gone quite pale. She was thinking furiously.

The thrusters fired again, paused, fired again, paused, and then fired again. They looked at each other in concern.

"Why does she keep firing like that? Surely, there should be a continuous burn until there is sufficient momentum to avoid the object?" Deborah remembered the avoidance maneuver on the simulator.

"You're damn right. It's not a normal evasive thruster pattern. Maybe there is a problem with the thrusters. Sound the general alarm. All hands, this could get nasty." She sprang over and hit the alarm button.

"What a bloody time for the thrusters to fail! With

a blasted rock coming up our butt!" He was thinking out an emergency reaction. The thought of having to go outside to repair a thruster or two still red hot as it had just been firing did not amuse him. With a rock fast approaching, it amused him even less. How close was the bloody thing anyway? He scanned the console.

Deborah was studying the console, deathly pale now. She squinted and peered closer.

"Hang on! I'm getting a readout here, and a visual is getting clearer. It's coming up quite fast!"

Patrick peered at the printout, shrugged, and squinted at the screen. "Looks like a ..." he started and then paused. "That looks like a roundish rock we have there. It's too far to make it out clearly. How long have we got?"

Deborah consulted another part of the console. "About three hours and forty minutes at current velocity."

"We can't go any faster. It wouldn't do us any good if we can't get out of its way," Patrick observed grimly. "Out of all the space in the solar system, why does the bloody thing want to ram us up the butt?"

They were quickly joined by Chris, Sean, and Sally. The six others came in within the minute. Patrick swiftly briefed them while running a check routine on the thrusters. They flew to their designated positions and performed emergency checks. The more the tests checked out, the more Patrick became puzzled. Each engine was reporting normal while firing at intervals.

One after another gave the same story, all functioning normally.

"Damn it. Damn it. What the hell?" He was thinking furiously. If the ship was continuing to make evasive maneuvers, maybe there was a fault in the tracking system. Maybe it was unable to sense when it was out of the way of the incoming rock? He thought about how to check that and ran a diagnostic. This took an agonizing seven minutes to run. That left three hours and twenty six minutes on the countdown Deborah had set running. This countdown was now very much the center of everyone's attention.

"Captain, shall we suit up?" Chris asked.

"Yes, good idea. Don't know what's wrong yet." He scratched his head. "It might save time. Let's hope you won't be needed. I'm running more diagnostics now."

Patrick continued to run the diagnostics, which took another twenty minutes. No faults. He frowned. The timer showed about three hours left. He looked over to Chris and Deborah. The timer now read two hours and fifty-five minutes.

"What is the distance reading now?"

Deborah flashed him a quizzical look. "Oh! *Distance!* Yes! Um, forty thousand clicks."

Patrick frowned. "But I got a reading of thirty-six thousand a few minutes ago. Therefore, it can't be on the same course as us. It must be on a different course."

Deborah studied the readout. "No, this says it is in exactly the same position."

"Hmmm. Very strange. If the range finder is correct, it implies the thing has slowed down."

"No definitive way of telling at this point. We'll just have to trust the rangefinder. It is giving a steady reading now for what that's worth."

"Just keep an eye on it and yell if there is any change."

"Will do, Captain" Formal address had returned with the serious business.

"Right. Let's sum up. We have a rock that appears to be closing on us on our course. A few minutes ago it was, we think, thirty-six thousand clicks away. Now it *seems* to have slowed and is now forty thousand behind on the same course. That, therefore, is one very strange rock, or our instruments are fooling us. Although the immediate danger seems to be over, we are left with a lot of unknowns. A bad situation. It defies explanation."

No one stirred. No one had any suggestions either.

"Okay, I want an immediate status report sent off to Max and Luna2. Rerun all the diagnostics. Keep a close watch on the object. Unless anyone has any bright ideas, I think that's all we can do for the moment."

Messages were sent via a focused beam. Messages of this sensitive nature were kept short. They were strongly encoded and sent as microbursts in a millisecond. Only someone tuned to a matching frequency with the correct decoding algorithms could receive or recognize it. Such messages mingled with the white noise of space.

They were all busy running every test they could and were failing to find any defects in the systems. The automatic avoidance system had shut itself down when the immediate threat from behind had ceased.

The message reply from Max came in an hour and a half later. It consisted of five words; two questions, and an order.

Eridanus? Any change? Stand by.

Patrick scanned it, eyes wide. He slapped his forehead. "My God! Is it possible?" All eyes were on him. All waited for some revelation. He looked down again at the message as if to extract some further meaning from it. He looked at them all.

"This could explain everything if correct. Max suggests our rock could be the *Eridanus*—you know, the *Eridanus* of the SolMin fame?"

"Or infamy." Chris was quick to add. Patrick nodded for him to elaborate. "Our friends the three pirateers—Captain Charles Tea-leaf Mason and his sidekicks, First Officer Arthur Dixon and Navigator Eddie Horton—are a very choice trio. They struck lucky in the asteroid belt, made a fortune, and have a fancy new pirate ship that outclasses anything in the solar system. They tool around looking for opportunities to make a quick buck in their flying whorehouse/gin palace." He made a derisory gesture.

Patrick grimaced sourly. "Indeed, Max has had some bad dealing with them in the past. If that *is* the *Eridanus* back there and it's apparently tailing us, it's not a good omen. Their ability to find us, catch up with us, and stay outside of our scanning range indicates they know our systems' capabilities and highlights the superiority of their craft. Furthermore, we are burdened by all our full tanks and lack maneuverability. In short, we are a fat sitting duck. Also, it doesn't look healthy the way they sneak up unannounced and seem to be dogging us without attempting to communicate. I don't like it at all."

There was a long silence while they absorbed the implications.

"Typical old pirate tactics to psyche us out," muttered Chris.

Patrick stared at him and nodded grimly.

"Okay, let's get an updated status off to Max and confirm receipt of his message. Can we prepare all the readouts from the diagnostics we've been running? They may tell the eggheads something. Max also said to stand by, so we can expect another dispatch from either him or Luna2. Send the status readouts as soon as they are ready."

They jumped to their tasks, and in ten minutes they sent all the relevant information they could muster. After ten more minutes, there came an overlapping dispatch from Max with a readout of all known activities of the *Eridanus*, a full set of drawings of the ship, and a complete technical specification that detailed performance and equipment, including a sinister addendum titled "Armaments."

"Armaments! *Armaments!*" Patrick exploded. "What the *hell* do they want with *armaments!*"

"For *self-protection*, of course." Chris smiled sweetly, feigning wide-eyed innocence.

Patrick snorted. "*Who* are they going to protect themselves *from*?"

"*Pirates, of course!*" replied Chris triumphantly.

Patrick had to smile at this twisted logic. "Okay, Chris, you win. I can see why they offered *you* a job. With your devious logic, I'm glad you're on our side."

"*Touché*. It's easy. You just have to adopt their mind-set. Rogues are always paranoid. They assume everyone is as crooked as they are. I rest my case."

"Quite so," Patrick conceded. "Now let's get to work studying their ship. Chris, this is your forte. Can we all, everyone, go over these plans and specifications and see what we're up against?"

The crew congregated, and the images were put into the VR system. Chris started with his explanation of the drawings when they all had put on VR headsets. The computer gave them a space-by-space tour of the *Eridanus* as if they were present on the ship. Meanwhile, there was a voice-over giving the technical specification of the ship and its equipment.

Lastly, there was an addendum put together by part of the security department that dealt with counterespionage, surveillance, and electronic firewalls. These guys were often recruited from the ethical hacker fraternity, and they seemed able to check anything out. They had apparently gotten wind of the armaments installed on the *Eridanus* and were able to give a detailed specification of the "self-defense" measures the pirates had discreetly fitted to the Eridanus. It made alarming reading, and the manufacturer's promotional videos were chilling. The Eridanus was like a flying aircraft carrier. Multiple zones of protective and offensive capability were covered by a daunting array of weapons to cover different targets.

Chris wrapped up the briefing. They took off their VR headsets and looked at one another. There was a tense and sober atmosphere. Nobody spoke.

"Okay, everyone," Patrick broke the silence. "I know it sounds grim, but look at it this way. If that ship is so hot, they may have picked up the fact we are communicating with base. They don't dare harm us. After all, they need to visit Earth to resupply. Even if their motors are nuclear and can run for years, they need to take on food and water at some point. I doubt they could decrypt the messages, but even if they could, they'll know we've rumbled them. Anyway, there is a slim chance it's not them." He looked around. They were not convinced by his last statement. That was clear. As for the rest, they wondered how many hiding places there were where desperados with a lot of money could get their supplies. There were still high-ranking officials in marginal countries on Earth who could be bought. Sixty-nine minutes later, a new dispatch came in from Max.

We confirm tail is Eridanus. Have had communication. Don't approach or attempt to communicate. Maintain code-red alert. Carry on. Stand by.

Patrick read it twice. Then read it out to the others. It was accepted with mixed reactions. The message confirmed it was not a rock back there. What had Max meant when he said he had communicated with them? What would the *Eridanus's* next move be? What should they do?

There were too many questions.

Patrick broke into speculation. "There's no point trying to second-guess these guys. We can't predict their intentions or actions. As Max says, we just carry on as normal and maintain a sharp watch. Any evasive actions would be futile and send a message of weakness. Stand by for further messages. He may be firing them off to us every ten minutes for all we know, so stay sharp and be ready to react quickly if needs be."

That ended the idle guesswork and theories. They kept their stations and set up a watch routine so no one spent more than half an hour at a screen. Twenty minutes later a new dispatch came in.

CHAPTER

22

The communications terminal gave a low chirrup. Patrick jumped to retrieve the message. Max again had an update. This time the message was not so cryptic. He obviously realized they were worried, unsure of what was happening next and needed some clarification.

Solmin trying to sell nitrogen from unknown source. Inflated price. Rebuffed. Probably vengeful and stuck with cargo. May attempt sabotage. Extreme caution and alertness required. Deploy pods on sentry. Stand by.

Although this was not exactly good news, at least they knew why the *Eridanus* was shadowing them. What *was* clear was that SolMin had been watching Max's progress on Mars and had made the easy assumption that nitrogen would be a valuable commodity and were keen to capitalize on that. If SolMin *had* obtained a load of nitrogen from somewhere and were trying to make a killing offering it at an inflated price only to be turned down, they would have no market for their cargo. They would have been frustrated and enraged the deal was rejected by Max. They would probably have found out about the *Ganymede's* mining expedition and put two and two together.

It was anyone's guess how a bunch of rogues like them would react to being outsmarted by Max ... *again!* One thing was for sure. They'd be mad as hell their gambit had backfired. What those guys would do when angry, vengeful, and in possession of the most powerful spaceship in the solar system was a dreadful unknown.

Patrick felt a convulsive shudder. *Caution. Alertness. Deploy pods.* The message was clear. *Max, buddy, you're not kidding,* he thought. He realized everyone was staring at him expectantly, keen for the news.

"Uh! Sorry. I was just thinking," he explained. Knowledge was better than ignorance, he reasoned, so he read out the message. The message wasn't exactly met with cheers of approval. There were solemn, thoughtful faces all around. Deciding inaction would only feed on their nerves, he broke the silence.

"Well, you heard Max's orders. Let's get going. Chris, set up a round-the-clock armed patrol outside. The pods are to patrol 24-7. Also carry your usual personal weapons. No one else around but them bogeys, so if anyone is snooping around, they are the enemy. Don't ask questions. Shoot."

So for the first time during the entire mission, they got out their personal weapons and checked them over.

"Oh, and full suits in the pods in case you have to get out fast," he added.

The activity focused the mind and left little room for anxiety. The reassuring feel of their personal weapons steadied their nerves. They were pilots, scientists, and technicians, not fighting people, so they were not comfortable in their new role as armed guards. They were by necessity skillful and resourceful people. Furthermore, their own self-preservation was at stake. They applied themselves with determination.

An hour later three of the pods were inspecting the train of clustered storage tanks, slowly making their way to the rear of the shipment. Fortunately, there were few hiding places, so the pods had a good visual command of the ship and cargo. It was more difficult to find and remove any mines that may have been attached. Such a tactic, as Patrick had advised at the preoperational briefing, was possible. Chris had pointed out to him that an inexplicable explosion would be hard to prove as sabotage, and so that could be a likely tactic. It was the most likely action open to the enemy, he argued.

"Maybe, Chris. However, I'm not sure they care about subtlety out here. They probably feel they are beyond the reach of the law. This is the new Wild West, and I feel we could be hijacked at any time or simply torpedoed out of existence," the captain replied grimly. "We must be ready and prepared to cut loose and jettison our hard-won cargo at any time. We have to be flexible enough to respond quickly to any situation."

Therefore, the patrolling pods had a clear idea about what to look for. With a clear brief and operation objective, they could apply themselves effectively. They were being monitored by the ship's CCTV systems, so they were rarely out of sight, a small comfort.

This cat-and-mouse scenario continued for the next six days. As they approached the asteroid belt and the distance to Mars shortened, the communications improved. It now took only twelve minutes for a signal to travel one way. Messages were being exchanged at all hours as much for moral support as an exchange of information, Patrick suspected. He was glad for it. The relentless regime of twenty-four-hour patrolling and constant vigilance was taking a toll on everyone. There was little of the usual joking and laughter. The constant threat, broken sleep, and tension affected their spirits and made people quiet and thoughtful. Patrick did his best to raise morale. He discussed the problem with Max. Diversions and luxuries were devised but did little to brighten their situation. There was nothing to do other than knuckle down, maintain vigilance, and grind the journey out.

A few days later, the proximity warnings sounded again. The first alarm saw Sally leap with fright clear across the bridge in the zero gravity. A flurry of activity followed until they realized the source was ahead of them, the first of the obstacles in the asteroid belt. This was followed by more frequent alarms as they progressed through this rock-strewn zone. *Perfect time for a surprise attack*, Patrick mused sourly. Under the cover of these objects all around them, the *Eridanus* could maybe sneak up unobserved.

Max was holding back. He felt he could not fully communicate with Patrick as he was unsure of SolMin's decryption capabilities. He could not speak freely for fear of showing his hand. On matters of tactics he had to maintain radio silence. He had a plan but could not communicate it to Patrick. It had to work without any action on Patrick's part. Max was sure that by now the *Eridanus* probably knew he was in contact with Patrick and may or may not know the content of the messages. All he could do was to keep up normal communications activity and let the situation unfold. To a certain extent, it was a waiting strategy, a moving of pieces in this deadly game of strategy. This waiting game frustrated Patrick and wore at everyone nerves. It is extremely difficult to maintain a high state of alertness for long periods.

Still, there was no sign of action from the Eridanus. Whatever game they were playing, they were playing it close. Patrick was trying to guess their next move if any. He could not even get a fix on them. There was too much clutter from other objects. When he tried certain topics with Max, he got evasive answers. So he had guessed correctly. Max was being cautious on the radio. All he could do was follow his flight path unless Max indicated otherwise.

Patrick was obliged to change course several times over the next few days to avoid asteroids, and he assumed his follower, if it was still there, would have to do the same. He considered doing some sort of evasive maneuver when leaving the asteroid belt but quickly rejected the idea. It was probably futile against a superior vessel and would show weakness, and quite simply, Max had given no new orders. No indication any action was expected from him. As frustrating as it was, he had no other course of action open to him as far as he could see. So on they went with the last long leg back to Mars.

The crew was now reduced to mechanically going about their routine, punishing as it was. They realized the relative boredom of the outward journey was infinitely preferable to the drudge of this return trip. The hours of security patrol found them dreaming of sun-kissed beaches and palm trees. This caused some amusement when they discovered they all had much the same daydreams. It gave a new twist to feeling homesick, a natural emotion astronauts had to suppress for fear of being considered "temperamentally unsuited" for any extended missions. Predictably, it was one of the most popular choices on the VR simulator.

An alarm signaled on the console. Sally, who was on duty, consulted one of the screens. It was a locator beacon, very faint on the port bow quarter. She looked at it thoughtfully. "Hey, Chris, what d'you make of this?" Chris went to her side and peered at the screen. He looked carefully and made some adjustment to the visual image. "Dunno, Sally. It seems that it's a location beacon, a faint one, but what is it doing out here in the asteroid belt? I can't explain that." It pained him not to be able to give Sally a positive answer. He was keen to appear to her as infallible. He marked the position of the beacon and tagged it.

"You don't think it is a cry for help? An SOS?"

"No, I can't imagine that. If someone, God knows who, is out here in trouble, why is it not signaling SOS? All these beacons have a variety of messages they can send. It's a simple matter to send SOS if you are in trouble."

Sally nodded thoughtfully, wondering if someone was in such trouble they had no time to set the alarm correctly or if there was a malfunction. Later they consulted Patrick who looked over the facts and ran the screen image and associated readings.

"You were right to tag this. It's a puzzle. Who or why there is a beacon out there is a mystery. The fact it's set as just a locator rather than an SOS relieves us of any obligation to check it out. Judging from the readings, it is some way out. Send off a report to Mars to see if they know of anything that may be out here. Meanwhile, Sally, keep it under observation."

The inquiry was duly dispatched, and the message returned. *We have no record of activity in that quadrant. Do not—repeat—do not investigate. Keep watching. Maintain high alert status. Report change.*

So none the wiser and ordered to keep up their constant vigilance and remain on course, they continued with a growing sense of foreboding.

"No news, in this case, is bad news," observed Patrick grimly.

C H A P T E R

23

On Mars, with the *Ganymede* getting progressively nearer, messages could be exchanged with increasing rapidity. The news of the mysterious tail had put the communications center on high alert. It was now being manned twenty-four hours. Max had made it clear he was available at all times, night or day, to be updated with any communications from the ship. As the days rolled by, the concern grew with each report of the continued threat.

SolMin had made contact four days after the *Ganymede* had left Titan. Out of the blue, there came a message for Max offering a "deal of interest to him." Max looked at the brief message with skepticism. He was all too wary of Charles Mason and his offer of a deal, which probably meant it was only of interest to SolMin. Their story was suspicious, a barely credible coincidence.

In essence, the claim was that the *Eridanus* was "on an exploratory journey in the outer regions of the solar system" when they heard of Max's requirement for nitrogen, and in the interests of repairing past relations, they were offering to bring back a load of liquid nitrogen and sell it at a "reasonable" price. There followed an extended series of dispatches between the two parties.

Max, ever suspicious of Mason and his merry band, firstly wondered where Mason had *heard* of Max's need for nitrogen or whether it was a calculated guess. To be safe, it called for a complete review of communication codes. Second, Max wondered about the source of their nitrogen. On this subject Mason was evasive, which led Max to suspect its pedigree.

Had Mason been tracking the *Ganymede* from the get-go and shadowing her movements while collecting nitrogen himself from Titan? Max found this hard to believe. It sounded like too much hard work for a speculative deal. They surely would have agreed to some price before undertaking such a mission. Maybe they had stumbled on a source of easily mined nitrogen somewhere. That somewhere, Max thought dryly, could well have been Earth, which was in violation of the strict internationally agreed-upon extraction quotas, not that Mason would care about those. The origin of the nitrogen was therefore unknown and probably suspect.

Furthermore, the supposedly reasonable price offered was three times the cost of his *Ganymede* mining venture. In short, the whole deal stank. The fact that the *Eridanus* was almost certainly tailing the

Ganymede gave the whole situation a sinister twist. It would be all too convenient for an *accident* to befall his ship. He was concerned. The poor communications made it difficult to establish the situation and left Max with an awful sense of impotence. Max, a man used to action, could only fret and advise. His ship could be sabotaged or completely destroyed, and he would be powerless to respond. He hated the situation. He had acted.

"Firepower! I must have firepower!" He had appealed to the major international powers with whom he was busy in negotiations. He had been briefing them on the situation as it unfolded, but there was the agreed international treaty governing heavy armaments in space. It had been agreed that space would be an armaments-free zone. Most of the world's nations were signatories to the International Space Armaments Limitation Treaty (INSALT). Max's appeal would be in clear contravention. It would not be easy to arm himself. Even his claim that the *Eridanus* was heavily armed did little to help. Because there were so many parties involved and so many signatories, it would be painfully slow to procure armaments legally.

This all put Max and the *Ganymede* in a helpless position. He felt powerless, unable to protect or give aid to his ship, a feeling that was unfamiliar to him. He fretted and racked his brain for a solution. The *Triton* was unloading at Phobos, and the *Phoebe* was busy installing more mirrors over the South Pole. He pondered. After a particularly disturbed night of sleep, he had come to a resolution. Every instinct in his makeup, every fiber screamed that he act. He now had a plan. He did not dare communicate any part of his strategy with the *Ganymede* for fear of possible interception of his communications. It had to rely on the *Ganymede* continuing as if all was normal.

That night he called in the captains and had a meeting during which he briefed them on the situation and the background leading up to it. He explained the nefarious deal and the fact the *Eridanus* was now almost certainly the mystery tail behind the *Ganymede*, and then he invited observations. It was agreed that the situation was probably very delicate, but they said it would be foolish to initiate any armed action. He outlined his plan.

"We can't fire first," Max pointed out.

"Fire with what?" countered Shane Keane, *Phoebe's* captain.

"Let me arrange that. You *will* be armed, not to the firepower standard of the *Eridanus*, but armed," Max reassured him.

Nick Abbott, Patrick Hogan's replacement on the *Titan* was new to the situation and clearly skeptical.

"Look Max. I know you have unfailing loyalty from your own people, but as you know, my ship is jointly owned by a group representing several governments. I can't go breaking INSALT," he pleaded.

"You won't have to. Don't worry on that score. I have sent a complete explanation to your consortium, and they have agreed that you can use the *Triton* in this exercise. Confirmation is coming tomorrow. After all, the *Ganymede's* success is in everyone's interest.

That settled, Max continued with the briefing, and as his plan unfolded, the two captains began to warm to the idea. They were space commanders after all, and as a breed, they were natural adventurers. They talked into the night, each contributing to the scheme using their knowledge and skills. They explored various scenarios that might develop and appropriate responses. They finally adjourned at 0330, agreeing to take their ships to Phobos at 1000 for modifications and installation of equipment. They would reconvene at 2100 the next day to refine their strategies and discuss any further suggestions for improvement.

Max retired, feeling he was getting somewhere close to a resolution at last. He found mother and child fast asleep, so he threw himself into a spare cot and was able to forget everything and sleep soundly.

The next day saw a frenzy of activity as the two ships were outfitted from the workshops on Phobos. Equipment was being brought up from the surface on the spacelift and ferried to them for installation. Normal communications with the *Ganymede* were kept up to keep them reassured, exchange position computations, and give the impression of normality. Their participation in the plan was not needed. Their ignorance of the situation was seen as an asset as they would be unlikely to give any indication that anything abnormal was developing.

That evening the strategists reconvened to fine-tune

their plans. They planned for further contingencies. Again, they debated the whole situation, rerunning the various eventualities and their responses. They devised procedures and codes for the various gambits. New situations were anticipated. Responses devised and agreed upon. They explored every avenue, and finally, they had hammered out a plan of campaign. As they saw it, they had to treat it as a military operation. They had no weapons but felt they might be going to war.

Another two days saw the two ships stripped of nonessentials, modified, equipped, and fueled. The commanders had refined their plans and were clear about their roles. Nightly meetings between them and their crew briefings had seen the human element of the defense machine brought to a high pitch of preparedness.

The evening of the fourth day saw the two ships leave Mars orbit and head out into the star-filled velvet blackness of the solar system sky under the never-ending rays of the Sun.

CHAPTER 24

Aboard the *Eridanus*, life was under no such pressures. The challenge was to relieve boredom. Louise Clarke, the number one of the entertainment girls, was fond of her gin slings, and with no routine for the girls to follow, they spent most of their waking hours in a state of drunken torpor. The three men argued tactics, unclear on how best to deal with the *Ganymede*. They wanted to take control of the *Ganymede* but were unsure what resistance they would meet. They were but three, and they had no idea of the size of the *Ganymede* crew. To eliminate her out of hand would gain them nothing and incur the wrath of Max with the might of Aqua4 at his disposal. He would surely make their options for resupply on Earth almost nonexistent and chase them down without mercy. It was a tricky situation for them.

How can we make her stop? They asked themselves. *Or board and overpower the crew?* They argued for days without coming to an agreement. Their indecision made them frustrated, which led to petty bickering. Jealousies over the girls' favors did little to improve the situation. The girls for their part didn't give a damn about any of the men. They were aboard for a good time and what money they could get. They were completely unaware of the drama in which they were playing a part as the men were careful to keep the *Ganymede* business a complete secret. Not that the girls would care anyway—not unless they thought they could make money selling the men out with what they knew. The men knew that, so they kept their secret. If the girls found out too much, they would have to be permanently silenced.

So the prevarication and arguments continued. As the days passed, they became more desperate. They were aware the closer they got to Mars, the more difficult carrying out their intention would become.

After a particularly frenzied attempt to carouse with the girls one night, their drunkenness led to rashness, and Captain "Charlie Boy" fired a warning missile. "Just to let 'em know we're 'ere. Har-har," he said.

That did the trick all right. The missile was small, but it was an accurate, state-of-the-art, self-guided little piece of ordinance that had no trouble hitting the back of the *Ganymede's* cargo train.

Aboard the *Ganymede*, the reaction was instantaneous. This had been one of the events they had anticipated. Captain Hogan had ordered one of the ethane-methane tanks be partially drained and refilled with some of their oxygen reserve and an explosive charge to detonate the liquids after three seconds, a powerful infrared source was then attached to the rear of the tank. Any missile would almost certainly have an infrared sensor as one of its primary homing systems. Therefore, they anticipated any missile would unerring hit their decoy tank and its explosive mix of liquids.

When the *Eridanus's* small missile hit the decoy, the automated system immediately blew charges and jettisoned the prepared tank. The force of the charges blew the damaged tanks away behind them to erupt in an enormous growing fireball as the very cold liquids rapidly heated and swelled into a huge fireball. Furthermore, as a result of a long preprepared reaction, a constellation of flares and proximity sensitive cluster bombs made by the techies to pass the time waiting for such an attack was fired off to foil other missiles. All these were sensed by the *Eridanus's* systems.

This immediately set alarms off aboard the *Eridanus* as sensors reported multiple hazards ahead and activating avoidance maneuvers to what they perceived as a retaliatory offensive. The intensity of the *Eridanus's* reaction with demands for avoidance and requests to retaliate with more missiles took Charles by surprise. Never having actually used their impressive firepower and ordinance avoidance systems, the suddenness and ferocity of their ship's reaction bewildered Charlie.

It shocked him that the *Ganymede* was apparently so well armed. He was now furiously trying to assess the threat and his best way forward. Realizing he had acted without really planning the thing through and finding the situation almost out of his control, he froze for a few moments. In short he had shown his hand and the suddenness of the reaction had given him a bad fright. Charlie thought the Ganymede's explosives and flares were defensive missiles, so he fired off interceptor missiles. Soon the sky was filled with explosions, and they were fast flying into the shrapnel, which in turn set off more alarms. They were all busy at the controls, trying to stabilize the situation. It was some time before they got their ship under control and prevented it from unleashing an all-out missile attack and thus destroying their golden goose of a prize. It left them badly rattled. None of this was conveyed to the girls, who remained unaware of the unfolding drama, the men fobbed them off with a story they were testing systems and that all was normal.

The girls were no so easily fooled. They'd seen the men obviously unnerved and heard them snapping at each other, arguing what was happening and how to control the ship. It left them deeply suspicious and mistrustful.

The Ganymed immediately reported the attack to Mars. The Ganymede received a reply congratulating them on their foresight, and they were told to continue as normal. The news of the attack was picked up by Titan and Phoebe, which according to the agreed-upon engagement protocol were now free to return fire.

CHAPTER 25

From the outset the *Ganymede's* predicted return course had been carefully plotted and confirmed by her own readings. As she was also under orders to continue as normal unless she received directions, many knew with relative certainty what her return trajectory would be.

Since the original alarm message was reported by the *Ganymede*, Max had been planning his course of action and reaction. The responses to messages he gave had to be made on the assumption the security of their communications was compromised. Hence, his cryptic replies. Following Max's futile negotiations with the INSALT signatories his plans for defense had to be carefully prepared so as not to infringe the regulations. By the time all preparations were complete, the *Ganymede* was just entering the asteroid belt. Now the backup force of the two ships was leaving Mars. The *Ganymede* was still unaware that assistance was on its way and was following her return course as instructed.

Max's plan had been based on his confidence that Captain Hogan would follow these instructions. His confidence was not misplaced.

The time would soon come for Max to give new instruction when his two ships were in place. Now it was a tense waiting game in the hope that the *Eridanus* would not attempt to do anything aggressive before the trap was set. There was great temptation to contact the *Ganymede*, if only to reassure them that they would not be alone, but Max dared not do this. Even if the communications were secure, the exchanges could be monitored if not deciphered, and it could arouse suspicion. Communications had to be kept to a minimum and appear as normal mission exchanges. Surprise was essential. Because of the delay in arrival of messages, the whole chess game had to be played out as if in slow motion, which served only to heighten the tension.

Apart from the element of surprise, Max had one other advantage that he aimed to use to the fullest, namely the information he had received from Luna2 regarding the armament the *Eridanus* carried. As soon as the first message came through, he asked for a full inventory of those weapons. He already had a list but wanted to know their range, power, and locations on the ship—as much information as could be gleaned from the suppliers as possible. Such suppliers always had a weak point, an employee who could be bought. Funds were made available. Very soon with additional information, Max was able to fill in the blank areas on the *Eridanus's* blueprints. An analysis of those plans showed their logical location in order to be effective. Thus, a fuller picture of the Eridanus, its capability, armament, and layout was built up. It was with this knowledge that Max, the two captains, and a strategic group crafted their plan of action. It was hoped that there would not be any firepower involved as they were clearly outgunned. In such a situation, the only recourse was secrecy, surprise, and strategy. Hopefully, with no sacrifice or surrender.

According to their prearranged plan, the *Triton* and *Phoebe* were on a course to a location close to the path of the returning *Ganymede*. They had recently plotted the location of all the asteroids that the *Ganymede* had updated them about during her outbound journey as standard procedure. This proved to be extremely useful under the circumstances. What had become clear was there were numerous asteroids they could use to their advantage. In particular Vesta, an irregular body of around 450 to 550 kilometers in diameter, was in the vicinity of the *Ganymede's* return path. They knew the return path with accuracy, and as the *Eridanus* was shadowing the *Ganymede*, they could predict its location. Their tactic was to approach the area under the cover of Vesta, so if the crew of the *Eridanus* were scanning, they would be unseen.

In a tight side-by-side formation in order to bring the maximum scanning power to bear, they aligned themselves with Vesta's position. The delicate part now was to judge their speed to arrive at the rendezvous at the most effective time and velocity. The crews were hunched over their screens, constantly monitoring their position and speed, making adjustments as required. On the other decks, a group of men were making preparations for the rendezvous. They knew that timing was everything.

The next few hours were spent in a high state of vigilance and activity. Few were in any doubt that if the *Ganymede* was to return unmolested, it depended on their performance. The equipment in the two ships designed for their protection and a safe passage for the *Ganymede* was inspected, tested, and adjusted tirelessly to make sure all was in order and functioned flawlessly. All this repeated inspection and drill were as much a familiarization exercise as any doubts about the readiness of the equipment. The crew members were now so accustomed to their roles that they could stand in for each other if necessary.

The approach behind Vesta was accomplished without incident thanks to their prior knowledge of its position.

On the *Ganymede's* bridge, an alarm sounded shortly followed by an encrypted message. *Triton and Phoebe behind Vesta. Continue past Vesta for ten seconds and then break to port 20 degrees behind Vesta and continue.*

The crew of the *Ganymede* was expecting this message as twenty minutes prior they had received a cryptic message that merely said, *Stand by.*

That alert meant they were all at their stations

expecting the new message. Patrick Hogan looked at the message and smiled.

"Action stations, everyone. Prepare for a course change. Sean, ETA to Vesta?"

"Six hundred and twenty seconds," the navigator replied.

"Prepare for course change by 20 degrees to port in six hundred and *thirty* seconds."

The ship was abuzz with activity and expectation. They had no idea what was going on but were happy that *Triton* and *Phoebe* were obviously on hand and screened from view behind Vesta.

"I wonder what the plan is." Patrick voiced everyone's thoughts.

"I hope it's good," Deborah added.

"I'm sure it will be. They have had plenty of time to plan this one out. I wonder what they're up to." Patrick sounded confident nonetheless.

"Just a course change?" observed Sean. "That doesn't ask us to do much."

"Considering our load, that's quite enough."

"True."

CHAPTER 26

A board the *Eridanus*, a halfhearted sort of party was now in swing as Captain Charles Mason in his effort to placate the girls had broken out a case of champagne. Captain Charlie, thinking this had worked, was now salaciously necking with Louise Clarke. She had a glass of champagne in her hand and was obviously drunk. Arthur Dixon and Eddie Horton were likewise seeking the attentions of two of the other whores who showed little enthusiasm. They were more interested in the champagne. They had been persuaded aboard with the promise of the high life and luxury; however, the reality of long-term space travel had lost its attraction, and delusion had set in. What with all the weird happenings a while ago when all the alarms went crazy and with the men doing all sorts of things, it was fair to say that the girls were suspicious and rebellious. They wanted to go back to Earth.

"Hey, Charlie, where are we going now?" she asked.

"I told you. We are on our way back to Mars."

"How long is it going to take?"

"I told you. About two weeks."

"Another two weeks! I think space sucks! It's boring as hell, and you said we'd have a good time. Ain't that right, Betsy?"

Betsy, her eyes glazed, nodded glumly. "Sure does. I wanna go home. This ain't no fun."

Charles looked at Arthur and rolled his eyes.

"Well, you're here now, and we are on our way to Mars. I can't change that. We still have some business with the ship up ahead." Suddenly, he realized he had said too much.

"Ship? What ship? You said it was goin' to be fun. Now you want to do business instead of goin' home. This sucks!" Louise whined.

"Yeah, sucks," Betsy chimed in.

"Well, too bad for you. Do you want to get off?"

"Very funny. I might just get off at Mars."

Charles paused. He didn't like this threat. She knew too much. He would sooner shove the bitch out of the garbage chute. He glowered at her.

Eddy was busy with one of the whores. He looked over to Arthur and shook his head as if to say, "There goes Charlie opening his fat mouth."

"More trouble than they're worth," he commented with a grin only to receive a hearty slap from his girl. He gave her a ferocious backhand. That did it. All the girls started screaming and fighting, scratching the three men. They were joined by three more girls who were all part of the *amusement facility*.

Pandemonium broke out. The long months of the mission and inappropriate passengers had created hostilities and jealousies that only needed a spark to set off an emotional crisis. The situation rapidly developed into a brawl with all kicking, punching, and screaming.

Over the din a light and beeping alert was showing on the control panel. Eddy spotted it first, but it was a few moments before he could draw the others' attention to it. Finally, Charles got to the panel and rapidly took in the situation. The *Ganymede* had been lost by the tracking system, and it was giving an alarm to that effect. He registered the *Ganymede* had apparently been screened by Vesta, and quite, simply the tracking system had picked it up. No big deal. He was a bit drunk and paused, looking at the control panel. Eventually, he switched off the alarm, and he was going to reset it when they, too, got to Vesta. There was still a way to go to Mars, plenty of time. Besides, if things didn't work out, he wanted to be able to cause a spectacle in full sight of Mars. He leered to himself.

He did, however, set an alarm for when they approached within two minutes of Vesta. He then turned his attention back to dealing with the girls. Arthur and Eddy were being swamped by six screaming, biting, and scratching whores. He pitched back in to try to sort them all out. All this pantomime was taking part in zero G, so to an onlooker, it would have had a comical air despite the venomous intent of the combatants.

CHAPTER

27

"**O**n my mark. *Mark.*"

The *Ganymede* made her turn to port, and within a matter of seconds, she was behind Vesta. As the view opened up behind the asteroid, the situation became clearer. The scanners soon picked up the *Triton* and *Phoebe* about three minutes away, racing toward them. Instantly, they used their laser com, which sent data down a tight beam. They could safely use it without compromising security as it was strictly used with lines of sight. Even better, at that range it gave instant, delay-free communication.

"Good to see you, Pat. Just hang in there. We have this covered," Captain Nick Abbot's reassuring voice came from the *Titan*.

"Likewise, bud. They're right on my tail. Glad to see you," Patrick replied. "Hi, Shane!" he greeted *Phoebe's* captain.

"Hi, Pat, don't worry. We'll deal with these jokers. Just go to base, and we'll see you back."

"Copy." Captain Patrick was more than happy to see the two captains deal with the *Eridanus*. With the huge cargo he was carrying, his maneuverability was severely limited.

Almost as soon as this exchange of greetings was over, the three ships crossed paths.

Aboard the *Eridanus*, the fracas had been subdued with some violence. The women were bruised, sullen, and vengeful. They whispered among themselves, conspiring.

Captain Charles Mason was watching his control panel, studying the screen, waiting to draw up on and see around Vesta, which was rapidly getting larger on his screen.

"Hey, you two, get them women locked up in their rooms and get back to your posts."

Eddie and Art looked at each other and rolled their eyes. They resented Mason giving *them* orders. Who was *he* to be so high and mighty? Where would he be without *them*?

Anyway, who was it that had found the californium. Only me! Me! thought Eddie. *Where would they be if it wasn't for that, eh? If anyone should be the captain, it should be me, and as for that Arthur bloody Dixon, he was just a waste of space, a sponge. What did he do anyway?* Eddy was not happy. He made for the girls, intending to lock them up and give them a beating, especially that whore Minnie, who had bitten him. He was going to give *her* a really good slapping. The bitch.

Arthur could see Eddie muttering to himself,

approaching the girls. In his drunken state, he got the idea that Eddie was going to lock them up and went to help. Seeing the two men approaching with clearly malevolent intentions, the girls reacted as one and flew at them like a tribe of banshees. Minnie could see Eddie was coming directly for her. She could still taste his blood smeared on her chin. She broke a bottle on the bulkhead and flew at him again. The other girls took her cue, and the befuddled Arthur was easy prey. He disappeared in a flurry of slashing glass and blood. All hell broke loose. The prior fracas was tame in comparison.

Captain Charles was powerless to intervene. Exasperated, all he could do was futilely yell for order, all others were beyond reasoning. What the hell? Did they care if he had lost sight of that other ship? It was his own bloody business. They had some serious revenge to deal out.

Seven minutes of utter mayhem passed during which Charles gave up trying to restore order. He just left them to get on with it. He had more serious matters to attend to. Hunched over the control panel, he waited to draw past Vesta to reestablish contact with his quarry while the yelling and screaming went on abated behind him. A broken bottle flew past his head and smashed against the control panel.

He snapped, whirling around. He came face-to-face with Juno the Amazon, upon whom he had especially enjoyed satisfying his own particularly depraved and sadistic sexual fantasies. Her blood soaked erototunic and maniac eyes told all. He brought up a laser gun and blasted her dead on the spot. Turning back to the screen, he was confronted by a shimmering white screen.

"*What the hell!*" he yelled at the console, punching buttons in an attempt to get a readout. It dawned on him that there was nothing wrong with the screen. They were heading for something that was giving the scanners a very solid reflection. They were about to crash into something!

Flo, Juno's best friend, saw what Charles had done, and she chose her moment when he was distracted. Bent on revenge, she attacked him with a stiletto. She got in a quick stab that was stopped by his right shoulder blade and deflected toward his spine. He screamed, jogging the joystick hard over to port. He corrected and turned to face her while grabbing for his laser gun.

CHAPTER 28

The two Aqua4 captains shot past the *Ganymede*. Captain Shane gave a low whistle as he saw the bulk of the mining ship go past in a blur. Seeing her from that vantage point, he realized how big she was. She was enormous. She would indeed have made a fat prize.

As he followed the *Titan*, they came out from behind the cover of Vesta, and on cue, they released multiple time bombs of chaff made of shredded PolyAl from either side of the two ships. Having laid down their pattern of chaff, they took up a side-by-side formation to confront the *Eridanus*. Delay timers detonated the bombs, creating a wall of chaff tens of kilometers around, adjacent to and merging with Vesta, while they themselves were two nearly invisible dots against their own huge reflector.

Stripped down to the minimum, they were considerably lighter and more nimble. They were soon in a position to bring their armaments to bear in unison.

Armed they were, not purpose made armament, but deadly nonetheless. The weeks of preparation at Phobos with full access to all the amassed equipment meant they had at their disposal a number high-power lasers used for blasting rock to form caves. The engineers had modified them to override all safety mechanisms that were necessary when blasting rock at close range to avoid hurting the operatives. These were now able to be shot into space at full power without fear. Tests had shown they were extremely effective in space at a range of 150 kilometers. Being state-of-the-art lasers, these were as powerful as the *Eridanus's* armament, but they only lacked the sophisticated target-seeking and -locking systems their foe enjoyed.

Their advantage was surprise. There was radio silence. There were effectively invisible against their chaff screen, which merged with the 550 kilometer bulk of Vesta. To an onlooker, it would appear that Vesta had grown in size. A rapidly approaching ship would already be expecting that. The Aqua4 crews were fast closing on the *Eridanus*, which, if it did not alter course, would pass harmlessly through the chaff cloud.

Aboard the *Triton* and *Phoebe*, there was a top-level alertness at battle stations. All crew members, honed by weeks of preparation, were ready and eager to react to any situation.

By contrast, aboard the *Eridanus*, no such preparedness was in place. Flo was all over Charles like a tigress. Having drawn first blood, she had the advantage. Captain Charles, enraged with pain, a stiletto in his back, was struggling to get at his laser gun while Flo was biting and trying to gouge his eyes with her fingernails.

There was the sound of multiple concussions. Everyone stopped fighting and wondered what had happened. Alarms were going off all over the ship as sensors were triggered in response to the multiple system failures and warnings of hull damage.

The two Aqua4 ships had opened formation to about twenty kilometers either side of the approaching *Eridanus's* trajectory. Lacking the sophisticated aiming systems of the enemy, the laser cannon crews each had merely given a long crossfire burst ahead of the Eridanus, which, unaware of the threat, had obliging gone through it with the result the laser cannons had strafed both sides of the ship. At the crossing speed, it was only a matter of a fraction of a second. The *Eridanus* was badly hit, and the armaments on each side were mostly crippled.

The *Eridanus* was still a fearsome opponent in the right hands. Had she been on full alert and expecting such an attack with all systems running, there were multiple automated systems that would have reacted to a hostile act by identifying the source and bringing her own armament to bear.

While accepting the asteroid was a convenient waypoint, Captain Charles Mason had been suspicious about why the *Ganymede* had chosen to change course and go behind the asteroid. There had been no reason to activate all the armament systems and put the whole ship on battle stations. The apparent speed of reaction from Ganymede had taken him by surprise. While he was trying to discover the situation, that she-devil Juno had attacked him, the bitch. The concussions had shocked everyone into immobility. The fighting had stopped. Now Flo was coming at him. It was all too much. He shot her dead.

"Bitch! Anyone else?"

The girls cowered.

"*What are you fucking idiots standing there for?*" he yelled at Arthur and Eddie. "*Action stations!*" That galvanized them. They leaped to their stations.

Having made their devastating first pass, the two Aqua4 captains threw their ships into maximum turn to come round and chase the *Eridanus* from the rear, which was traditionally the least defended quarter. Given their previous closing speeds, this was a lengthy maneuver, and they knew if their enemy had control, they would be ready when they caught up. During this time the two captains were watching the *Eridanus* to see how she would react, looking to see how badly she was hit and how much fight she was prepared to put up.

Aboard *Eridanus*, there was a barely controlled panic. Automated systems dealt with the hull integrity and air pressure. Sections of the ship were automatically sealed. Compromised electrical systems were shut down, and fires were quenched. The alarms shut down one by one as the three worked the controls. The imminent danger over, Charles turned his attention to external threats. As to what exactly had happened, he was not sure.

"Full armament check!" he ordered. There was a pause while the status of their defense and arms were checked.

"I've got number-two and number-four bow cannon and belly missile launchers intact," answered Arthur.

"I've got the aft turret cannon and the roof missile launchers," added Eddy.

Charles suddenly froze at his console. His last look at it showed a shimmering white screen. It was unchanged. He was confounded, thinking furiously, he remembered it had been set at maximum range to track the *Ganymede*, and he quickly changed it to zoom out. The distance to Vesta showed eleven thousand kilometers. He zoomed out more, but with no change.

The chaff cloud had all the while been expanding and was still giving a reading on his sensors. While not as dense as before, it was enough to give a reflection. With his jangled nerves and the stiletto still stuck in his back, this was enough to create alarm and confusion in his tortured mind. The turn of events had taken less than five minutes.

"*Vesta!*" he screamed at the console, thinking he was about to run into the asteroid. He threw the master joystick over to port to avoid the hazard, instinctively following the way the *Ganymede* had gone. Seconds passed while the ship veered to the left, and all aboard held on in silence.

He was premature in his haste and confusion.

Had he maintained his course, he would have passed through the chaff cloud unharmed. As it turned out, two things happened.

First, the alarm he had set for his approach to Vesta went off, which gave his shattered nerves another shock. Second, the proximity alarm went off. The proximity alarm was only triggered in extreme emergency when the ship was in imminent danger of crashing into something and was intentionally very loud and strident, demanding attention. He jumped violently and threw the joystick full to port to avoid the hazard.

Three heartbeats later there was an explosion.

CHAPTER 29

The *Titan* and *Phoebe* had successfully completed their turns to take up the chase. This had involved a few thousand kilometers to execute. They were now in position whereby they were approaching the *Eridanus* from the rear rather than in her wake. Otherwise, they knew they were in danger of losing her against their own chaff cloud.

Stripped to their bare minimum, they were fast and agile. They had been built with motors to haul huge loads. They soon caught up behind the slower *Eridanus*, which had been tailing the heavily loaded, relatively slow-moving *Ganymede*.

As they closed, they fully anticipated the *Eridanus* to start shooting, but nothing happened.

"Maybe we crippled 'em," Captain Shane guessed.

"Stand by," Nick replied.

They were swooping in at full readiness only to watch in puzzlement as the *Eridanus* did a sudden veer toward Vesta, bringing it into a very close pass to starboard of the asteroid. That alerted them to expect some clever tactic. They were sure they could be seen by now. What happened next amazed them. Instead of breaking off to execute some clever maneuver, the *Eridanus* made *another* sharp veer to port, bringing them into what was a suicidal close pass of Vesta.

"Whoa, watch this. *What?*"

In an instant they were through their chaff curtain. The other side saw the *Eridanus*, which clipped some high points of the asteroid. It was now slowly tumbling end over end through the asteroid belt.

"Wow. Did you see that? They must have been in bad shape to do that. What do you think?" gasped Captain Shane.

"Dunno. Hard one to call," Nick replied.

"Should we finish them?"

"No, let them go for now. I'll report back to Mars and see what Max wants done with them. It'll take a few minutes to get an answer, so we'd better follow them for now." This involved slowing down considerably as the *Eridanus* had lost speed after its brush with Vesta. The message from the *Triton* was first picked up by the *Ganymede* on her way back to Mars, and then the signal arrived at Mars base. Aboard the *Ganymede*, the news was received with a shout of sheer joy and cheers as it brought such relief after being so long under the sinister shadow of their stalker.

On Mars, Max was more circumspect. *Is anyone aboard still alive?* he asked in his return message along with his congratulations. The two captains were unsure

as the *Eridanus* was not making any move to correct its
tumbling, but they doubted it. They were told to follow
for a while to see if the *Eridanus* recovered enough to
pose a threat. If not, they could leave well alone and
not endanger their ships. Given no time limit by Max,
they watched the stricken ship for ten hours, and with
no sign of activity, they left to return to Mars.

C H A P T E R

30

The news of the outcome of the "Battle of Vesta" quickly became known, and it was greeted with huge relief. The strain of the prolonged vigilance, both on the *Ganymede* and Mars, had put great pressure on everyone. The news had created a general feeling of unity and bonhomie. Max, who had borne the responsibility for the outcome, well aware of this mood, was indeed part of it. Ann's loving support had helped him through this intensely difficult period. Because of the nature of the prolonged standoff and secrecy, any commander in charge could identify with Max's position. His relief and elation was so great that he ordered a one week general vacation to mark the occasion. As the years passed, the date was marked with a general holiday known as Vesta Day.

The arrival of the *Ganymede* with the *Triton* and *Phoebe* in convoy marked a renewed period of consolidation and expansion. The *Ganymede's* cargo was put into orbit and progressively broken down.

Ten of the tanks of liquid nitrogen was put into geostationary orbit above the Pavaronis dome and used for its supply. Others were used for the Louros Chasma main base, the capture net base, and the other base being developed in the glass tube at Arsia Mons. The rest of the cargo was piped down to the surface using a pipeline prepared in their absence attached to the spacelift support cable.

After a month of maintenance and refit, which gave her crew time for rest and recovery, the *Ganymede* set off to make another trip to Titan to repeat her mission. This time she was free of the worry of the ominous presence of the *Eridanus*. Her mission objective this time was to pass Ceres and dispatch an exploration party with two of the larger tugs and two pods to set up a base there. This was to become a base for the exploration of the asteroid belt in the search for mining possibilities. This would not delay or hinder their outbound journey. A similar expeditionary team would also be sent to her namesake, the Jovian moon Ganymede.

All this was now possible as the fleet of tugs and pods became available as Mars was more established, and replacements were being made to be sent from Luna2. Furthermore, the installation of the spacelift meant that much of the shuttling of materials to the surface of Mars was sent that way, thus freeing the tugs for other duties. The *Titan* and *Phoebe* would return to their normal duties, making runs back to

Luna2 to bring more material, equipment, and pioneers wishing to join the Martian colony.

Stories of what was happening on Mars had been circulating on Earth, and those who had the pioneering spirit were overwhelming Aqua4's recruitment offices with applications to go to the new planet. All these people, either singles or couples, had to be carefully screened and tested to establish those who were genuinely suitable. Most had no real idea of what they would face. Others were merely dreamers. Families with young children didn't need to apply. It was too dangerous at the moment. There was always the possibility, Max had pointed out, that there may still be elements with allegiance to SolMin and who may wish to cause trouble.

Having tucked Marsia into bed, Ann quietly came in to see Max at work in his private atelier and found him at his console working on a 4-D spreadsheet. He did not register her presence since he was so totally focused on his work. She paused behind him, looking at the screen to get the gist of what he was doing. Finally, with a grunt of satisfaction, he hit the hologram key and swiveled his chair to see the holographic output at a huge table beside his workstation. At this point he noticed Ann.

"Hello, Mommy, how goes? Is she asleep? How was your day?"

"Woah, big boy, three questions without waiting for the answer to the first?"

"Sorry. I'm asking myself quite a few as well."

"I'll answer your questions in order, but I'll be brief. I'm fine but lonely. She's asleep. Busy, but as I see, not as busy as yours. I am more concerned about you. I want you to know Marsia has been asking to play with you. I want to play with you," she added with a seductive smile. "And we should take a break ourselves."

Max considered this for a moment. Ann noticed the lines of fatigue on his face.

"From a glance at your spreadsheet, I can see you are almost there."

He looked at her in surprise. He had to think a moment, thus showing his fatigue.

"Yes, I think I'm almost there with the future planning. As you see, I have just ordered a holographic image to have a good look. Shall we have a look now?"

Ann said nothing, and holding his appealing gaze slowly, deliberately, she leaned close to him, allowing her personal aroma to register and shut down the hologram and his command center.

"There, that's done. Come to bed and love me, tiger."

C H A P T E R

31

The following months saw the consolidation of the colony as the newly arrived nitrogen was piped around the various stations to boost the air mixture to something similar to an Earthlike mix. Humanity had evolved breathing Earth's air, so people were hardwired to expect a certain ratio of gasses. The entire body and brain was geared to expect that mix. The colony was now able to provide itself with a very close air match to satisfy that need in all the protected areas, and now people were able to breathe easier. No emergency breathing equipment was necessary unless one ventured outside the green zones.

From the outset, at times being forced to breathe low-pressure air supplies, many found they were short of breath. In the same way as on Earth, people who lived at sea level found breathing at, say, 3,500-meter highlands difficult, whereas the locals were acclimatized and found it normal. So it was with the new Martian residents who found they breathed deeper to compensate, and their lung capacity and metabolism adapted to meet the ambient conditions.

To add to the newfound supply of nitrogen, the plentiful supply of perchlorate chemicals (at between 0.5 to 1 percent in the easily mined Martian dust) provided oxygen. Together with the abundant carbon dioxide at the poles, they were provided the raw materials for the production of a new atmosphere.

The *Ganymede* was again on her way back to Titan for fresh supplies of ethane, methane, and nitrogen. This was now to become a regular run for the foreseeable future. There was a whole planet's atmosphere to replace.

Early that summer saw the equatorial temperature rise to 29 Celsius. Under the Chasma tent, people wore lightweight jumpsuits with only a small hip pouch for emergency oxygen. Unhampered by spacesuits, productivity shot up as people went to work with a will and were far more effective in whatever pursuit occupied them. Everyone was happy and greeted each other with a true sense of optimism. There was a new mood of camaraderie and common purpose. The colony now felt it was winning the battle for survival.

And then it rained.

Everything stopped as people stood at portals and windows, staring in wonder. Those people who were working outside with lightweight breathing equipment stopped working to marvel at this new phenomenon. The shower lasted about five minutes and then slowed to a fine drizzle for a further twenty. The ground, which had been starved of this rare substance for millennia, instantly absorbed every drop.

Needless to say there was no other topic of conversation for days. Mars Radio enthusiastically chatted over the airwaves all day. Max was called upon to comment and give his thoughts. As a man of few words, he admitted it was a momentous day, and not seeking to be overoptimistic, he thanked everyone for being diligent and conscientious participants in the Grand Plan. He welcomed the sign that the polar melt strategy seemed to be working.

He mentioned that short-lived rivulets of water had been reported at the edges of the polar ice caps. He confirmed that because of the release of carbon dioxide as a result of the overall melting, there was a welcome 12 percent rise in barometric pressure, but he reminded everyone to remain vigilant for signs of carbon dioxide asphyxiation and stressed the value of the buddy system to ensure everyone looked after one another.

Marsia, who had never seen rain before, flew fearfully into her mother's arms, tembling.

As that six-month summer season wore on, there were many more days that brought rain. This in turn brought about dramatic changes. The dust storms diminished, dampened by the increasingly frequent rain showers, which meant in turn that the potential hazard from the fine perchlorate particles was reduced. The hydroscopic perchlorate in the ground was being diluted and washed into the regolith with every rain shower.

The *Ganymede* had come back and gone away on another run to Titan with a fresh crew. The returning crew heard the news of the rainfall, and they were desperate to witness it for themselves. They eagerly pointed to the clouds, which were now common, marveling at this new development and eager to witness every rain shower. There was now a daily weather report, which in addition to the usual reports of solar activity, radiation levels, barometric pressure, wind speed, air chemistry, and likely dust storms, was now added the chance of rain.

Once the Pavonis dome and all development sites were filled with nitrogen and the reserve tanks full, the excess nitrogen was released to the atmosphere to boost the barometric pressure. This was all part of the original planned strategy. From now on, this would be the rule. They would fill the reserve tanks and then release the rest.

In the huge Pavaronis dome, once the three-meter-thick layer of perchlorate-contaminated dusty regolith was removed, the rich volcanic ash was perfect for plant growth. The methane was used to heat the air throughout the year to an optimum growing temperature while the carefully selected plants, which had already been tested in the nurseries, were now planted by the hectare. Vegetables of all varieties were planted and grew rapidly in the greenhouse conditions. Fruit and nut orchards were planted, and they thrived in the rich ash. All this superabundance of vegetation was fed by a carbon dioxide-enriched atmosphere. The thorium power station was used to create electricity to power lighting of wavelengths to supplement the reduced sunlight.

The perchlorate-laden dust mined from the floor of the crater was loaded into the railcars and went downhill under gravity to the oxygen manufacturing facility, generating kinetic energy which was converted to electricity to power their un-laden return. The facility stripped the oxygen molecules from the chlorine atom to give people valuable oxygen. The empty cars returned under their own recharged battery power.

Late summer brought the return of Joe along with his whole family. Marlena was at first cautious and somewhat overwhelmed by the turnaround in her life, but she refused to let Joe go back on his own. The two boys were agog and in a high state of suppressed excitement about this new adventure. Max observed them with amusement and saw straight away they were just like Joe, splinters off the block, and in time, they would be fine Martian pioneers.

Joe and Chris quickly resumed their friendship and would go off together on exploratory and surveying expeditions. The boys had to go through a fairly intensive education to learn how to live on Mars. Being young, they adapted easily. They felt at home on the farms in the Pavaronis dome when they weren't being schooled. However, they were too young and inexperienced to go with Chris and their dad. Marlena was also a natural on the farms as she was already an experienced kitchen gardener and understood plants.

Max reckoned they would not want to go back to Earth as they seemed happy and enjoyed the pioneering challenge of this new life. The boys thought the whole thing was cool and couldn't wait to explore the world outside the protected zones.

For the time being, Chris had given up his position as the engineer on the *Titan* to concentrate on the huge task of exploration and mineral prospecting with Joe. They made a good team, and they were building up a comprehensive map of metal, mineral, and chemical deposits for future mining.

After an extended survey expedition in the Valles Marineris, the pair came back with some exciting news. They had found something at 5050 meters below datum in the Valles at 13 degrees S by 58 degrees W. On a hunch they duly set charges and took readings, all of which proved promising. Therefore, they drilled a borehole. They drilled a mere two meters when they struck water, which sent a fountain thirty meters into the air. Furthermore, the borehole continued to gush forth, so it was obviously under steady pressure. They capped the borehole, took a grid reference, and set up a radio beacon for easy relocation. They had brought a sample of the water for analysis, and it had proved to be virtually pure with very little trace of dissolved salts.

This was indeed good news. A ready supply of pure water was as valuable a resource as could be imagined. If this proved to be a large aquifer, it would mean that they need no longer rely on packets of ice being sent from Luna2. They would be immediately self-sufficient. Plans to mine the poles for water could be shelved.

Although the well was 1,600 kilometers away, this was a minor obstacle, considering the alternatives. A suitable pumped pipeline could be laid to bring water to the Louros Canyon settlement. A railway line to Pavaronis was already under construction, so rail tankers could supply the dome and the glass tube at Arsia Mons. It all looked very promising. Max was pleased at the prospects, but before making any changes to the existing arrangements, he asked for a thorough assessment of the size of the aquifer to establish the anticipated yield.

After a general meeting held to discuss the implications of the find, Max took Joe and Chris aside to thank them for the good job they had done and how well they had handled the discovery. He then mentioned that the problem of the water supply had been occupying him and explained he had been studying the topography for potential locations of aquifers and asked them to have a look at a much closer location that he felt offered a possible location for a potential underground water source.

"I have here a couple of grid references for you. The place is between our Louros base and Pavonis. The grid references are on your handsets. The place is called Tithonium Chasma. You will need to fly all your stuff in as it five thousand meters to the bottom of the chasm. Unlike your find at five thousand below datum, the bottom of Tithonium is only 1,400 meters below grade. However, I feel it is worth having a look. I would be obliged if you could conduct a survey and drill if you think there is any chance of water there. If we find water, we may consider laying our pipeline from there direct to Pavonis, which is 1,300 kilometers away, and to here in Louros, it is only 240 kilometers."

The two explorers looked serious and nodded. It would save having to send the water uphill by rail to Pavonis, and the length of pipeline would be the same as it would be from their find. They could see the logic.

The strategy to exploit the Valles water well discovery having been discussed and the best action agreed upon, any immediate action was put on standby while the Tithonium site was explored. Joe and Chris quickly set about putting together an exploration team to survey and make a subsurface analysis of the region. Looking at the database of the aerial survey charts, they could see why Max thought it was a possible location. The high southern plateau with the Oudemans crater and highlands at 5,500 meters were to the south of the gulley, and there were plains at four thousand to the north, which in the past would all have drained into the Tithonium gulley, making it a very real candidate for an aquifer. Looking at the charts, it was easy to follow Max's thinking.

"You know something, Joe? I think Max may be sending us a message. If he is sending us there because it is a sort of sinkhole dropping to 1,400 meters below grade, he is surely aware that our very own Louros

Chasma base has its lowest point at only a little over four hundred meters, so in itself it's not a bad bet for an survey."

Joe paused, looking at the chart on the screen. After a few moments, he replied, "You may well have a point there, Chris. Max can be tangential like that sometimes. I think there is a real chance there is water in both locations. Both are low points surrounded by high plateaus, and so they would have been natural water collection points. But remember, the Valles well was 5050 meters below grade, so water may be deep. I don't think we will be lucky enough to hit water after drilling a mere two meters around here."

"Okay, we'll survey the Tithonium site and see what we get. If we hit water, we'll suggest to Max we also look in Louros on the basis that it's likely we'd find water there too."

"Agreed."

That settled, they loaded a pod with their seismographs, automatic theodolites, charges, and everything for their survey kit, and before dawn next morning, they set off on the short 240-kilometer flight to Tithonium Chasma with a team of four assistants to speed up the process.

Max was confident they would come back with a positive result in a few days. He made the strategic decision to order the supply of 1,500 kilometers of pipe and pumps in the sure knowledge it would be used no matter what option they finally adopted. This called for more supplies of PSP from the Pacific Gyre. This gave him a good feeling. He looked forward to the day when all the oceans, including the Atlantic, Indian, and Southern Ocean as well as the South China Sea and the already polluted Arctic Ocean would be free of the curse of plastic waste.

CHAPTER 32

As the long summer progressed and the rain fell with greater frequency, the mood of optimism in the colony grew. From the spacelift station high over Pavaronis Mons, the commanding view of the surface below meant the crew at the station was the first to notice the morning sun glinting off small lakes of water to the east and northeast of the equator. Surveys of the planet had established the ancient shorelines of the ocean that used to cover mainly the northern hemisphere of Mars. These were the natural lowlands. Any water table would be closest to the surface there, and that was where melt water from the ice caps would naturally collect.

Sitting and thinking in his office at his command center, Max was pleased to see the results of his planning. He was surprised at the rapidity whereby the statite mirrors brought about polar melting and was not concerned by the speed of change. If things moved too fast, the mirrors could be moved to slow or stop the process. He looked forward to seeing an ocean over the northern hemisphere as in prehistoric times. They could choose how deep to make that ocean. The calculations indicated that there was plenty of water locked up at the poles. He could envision mining the asteroid belt for water should they need to. Indeed, the exploration party on Ceres was there to search for asteroids, map their position, and record their mineral makeup. Any ice bodies would be found and noted for possible future use.

The increasingly frequent rain showers meant that other things happened fast. The spores and seeds that had been scattered in select areas had started to germinate. Max had been persuaded by his specialists to bring in a mixture of soil bacteria that was cultivated in large tanks and sprayed over the areas intended to be seeded.

There were now large areas carpeted in greenery— grasses, mosses, and sedges. These varieties had been carefully selected from the Svalbard and other seed vaults and specially modified for use on Mars using CRISPR gene modification. The resultant plants were therefore resistant to the Martian conditions, its regolith, low pressure, and prevailing weather conditions. As soon as an area received rain, the seeds germinated, and within days the first shoots would appear. The roots stabilized the surface dust and started the process of forming a soil by fixing nitrogen.

For this initial planting phase, vegetation with a dark green coloring was favored as it gave the maximum heat absorption. Max was under no delusion that the six-month winter period would be a testing time for the vegetation, which was flourishing during this summer season. He knew the plants had been selected for the low-temperature and low-pressure resistance and growth. However, the mechanics of plant growth was such that there would be a natural slowdown in the next six months. The Pavonis Mons dome had its own microclimate. So too, it was artificially lit and heated, so he had every reason to believe that plant growth would continue uninterrupted, and therefore, they would enjoy full food production.

Which brought his thoughts back to the atmospheric mix. The bulk of the cargo from the first trip to Titan had successfully boosted the nitrogen content in all the habitable zones to give breathable air. With the return of the second consignment for Titan, the balance of the first cargo was released to the atmosphere, and the third consignment would trigger the release of the second. And so it would continue with always one consignment in hand.

As far as Max was concerned, the nitrogen couldn't come fast enough. Making an atmosphere was a slow process. He resolved to build a sister ship for the *Ganymede*, and reviewing Aqua4's accounts, he realized that funds were not a problem. The water business was good. There seemed an unending demand for pure water. Unless Earth's climate could be persuaded to refreeze and restore the polar ice caps to their former condition, any further melting would merely raise sea levels even higher. He knew that another ship could be fully employed in bringing nitrogen back from Titan, and should the asteroid survey find a source of valuable materials, he would need a ship to mine it without taking the Ganymede away from her principal task. The *Phoebe* was still needed for her regular runs to and from Luna2 for all the specialist equipment they could not manufacture on Mars. In any case, the *Phoebe* was a general purpose spaceship, much smaller than the *Ganymede*, and it was not a dedicated mining vessel.

The *Titan* was not his, and it sustained the original pioneers, although Max had noticed that Aqua4 had now become the major provider for their needs and that the people had increasingly merged with his colony. He could see that he may come to an agreement with the International Space Foundation of Nations that funded the ship's activities, whereby he would buy their ship and assume all supply for Mars's colonies.

The barometric pressure now stood at 0.39 bars largely because of the release of carbon dioxide and water vapor from the melting poles. There was still a lot of nitrogen to be added. Oxygen was the next prime gas required and was now being wholly produced on Mars. New additions were being built to supplement the sole facility that was extracting oxygen from the perchlorate. There were currently seven underway with immediate plans for another seven as soon as the teams had completed the first group. In short, they were being constructed as fast as manpower and materials allowed. The one completed oxygen plant was easily able to supply the colony, and once a safety reserve had been stored, the surplus was being released to the atmosphere.

This is where the importance of the seeding of plants was such a priority. If the planet could be cultivated, including tree planting, they would naturally produce oxygen as a by-product of photosynthesis. Once the water at the poles was released to the atmosphere in the form of water vapor, the plants had a chance to grow and multiply with rainfall. Six hundred hectares of the dome had been devoted to producing plants and trees for planting and seeding strategic areas where experts figured they would thrive and populate.

All of this would take time and careful planning. The development of the correct types of vegetation was crucial to the success of the introduction of plant life to Mars. The subject of pollinating these plants occupied the botanists and entomologists. It had been considered in the selection of the plant types. Those strains that were naturally wind pollinated were favored.

It could not be ignored, however, that sooner or later insects would have to be introduced. This proved a thorny problem as researchers were cautious to recommend which species to use for fear of making an environmental blunder. The one species that had been selected from the outset without reservation was the honeybee. This species had already been introduced and a suitable variety of strains had pollinated the research gardens and was already at work in the Pavonis dome.

The other member of the animal kingdom considered an essential for inclusion on Mars was the earthworm. Its contribution to the well-being of soil was well understood, and great efforts were made to find species that could tolerate the salty Martian regolith. The common lugworm was selected among others.

And so the slow and careful process of selecting which fauna and flora would be introduced to the Martian ark progressed. Each additional plant or animal was carefully considered to assess their environmental impact. All new introductions were bred or harvested in quarantine to ensure they were defect- and parasite-free. Where necessary, their genes were modified using the CRISPR technique to eliminate imperfections.

Fish had been introduced to the lake in the Louros tent, and they proved successful. Moreover, they were a welcome addition to the sometimes monotonous diet. Fish were easier to manage as they could be restricted to a lake. Careful consideration was given to which species would be suitable for the Martian ocean when it was reformed. The question of salinity played a major part in the choice of suitable species, and again, this was the subject of rigorous investigation.

The Louros Chasm Lake was freshwater, so new lakes of varying levels of salinity were created for research. Frozen ova of various fish species where brought in to assess their suitability for this new environment. By necessity, food fish were favored, and the smaller species were all the experimental lakes could sustain.

It was realized that it was almost impossible to reproduce the complex food chain from scratch, so the fish food had to be developed from experience of fish farming on Earth. Studies were being undertaken regarding the key elements in the food chain to identify those critical food species, flora and fauna, that were best for the new Mars ocean. It was established that a mix of plankton size was necessary, ranging from the picoplankton to the nano, micro, meso, macro, and megaplankton.

All these minute organisms were seen as the basis of the food chain and provided the food for the smallest fish, which were in turn predated by larger fish and so on up the chain. Furthermore, these organisms were responsible for oxygenating the oceans to allow fish to breathe. It was decided that these microorganisms would be an essential part of the nascent ocean, and steps were taken to introduce them to the saline lakes. They were to be mixed with the ocean waters as the ocean swelled in size so that they could establish themselves from the outset.

Similarly, the different types of plankton were important—phyto, zoo, bacterio, and mycoplankton—all of which were necessary for a healthy ocean and source of food at the bottom of the food chain.

Max was advised by the top specialists in their fields as to how to build a new planetary ecosystem from what was basically a sterile desert. No one was under any delusions. This was a hugely complex problem, and the mantra was "caution and more caution." Lessons had been learned on Earth when alien species had been introduced to new environments, either intentionally or accidentally, with sometimes disastrous results—all because of a lack of due consideration concerning the impact of their introduction.

Max realized he was not and could not be an expert in all of these diverse fields, and so he had to rely on good advice from the experts. Beyond that, all he could do was rely on his gut feeling for what was right and made sense. In truth, he reasoned that no one was an expert since this had never been done before. All anyone could do was bring their experience of how things worked on Earth and learn from the mistakes that had been made. Mankind did not so far have a record of sensitive planetary management. Max hoped to change that.

The other problem occupying his thoughts was the all-pervading enemy largely generated by the life-giving Sun. The source of all energy and life in the solar system also produced the most deadly radiation that induced degeneration in living tissues. The Sun gave with one hand and took away with the other.

The Earth was protected by its magnetosphere, which was generated by its swirling molten iron core. Because of its smaller size and subsequent heat loss to space, Mars's core had cooled, and whatever magnetosphere it once had was no longer. For people to walk freely on the surface, there needed to be a level of protection. Nitrogen was known to offer some protection. This was already being provided as part of the building of the atmosphere. That nitrogen was coming from Titan, and in its raw form, it naturally contained 5 percent methane, a potent greenhouse gas. Rather than remove it, he opted to release the mix as mined for the present until the planet warmed. This level could be reduced later. Meanwhile, they needed the strong greenhouse effect the gas gave.

Max felt the only long-term solution to give radiation protection within the framework of current technology was to have local magnet shielding to protect selected areas much like they were already using but on a much larger scale.

There were rapid advances in space medicine which involved genetically modifying the human biology to give greater resistance and repair mechanisms against radiation.

The other method of radiation protection Max was increasingly employing was a by-product of the oxygen generation plants. A certain proportion of the oxygen was used to create ozone. Although produced naturally when oxygen was subjected to sunlight and lightning, the weaker Martian sunlight did not produce as much ozone as on Earth. Ozone is naturally unstable, so it needs to be replaced on an ongoing basis. Max planned to have the whole process automated to produce a deep and dense planetary ozone layer to achieve the maximize radiation protection.

The last line of defense was already being used by them all. Advances in the biomedical field had produced a medication taken daily. While this pill did not stop the energetic particle from penetrating the body, it did enable one's metabolism to rapidly repair the damage. One of the dangers of radiation in the twenty-first century was the risk of developing skin cancer in later life through prolonged exposure. Cures for the various forms of cancer had been found by the 2080s, so this was not seen as a major threat. The main danger was of the inexorable cellular degradation and the risks of DNA damage. The multiple defense measures being put in place greatly reduced the worst effects of exposure.

All these latest measures against radiation were in addition the basic good practice of getting into protective shelters during periods of solar flares and mass ejections. To this end, they relied on Luna2 and their own observations to give advance warning of solar activity typical of a precursor to a solar eruption. The original cave system headquarters deep in the Louros Chasm were still the safest protection, closely followed by the glass tube protected with a minimum of three meters of basalt and then the Pavonis Dome, which had a dedicated shelter for use when there was risk of solar activity.

The *Ganymede* was due back from Titan with her next cargo of nitrogen, ethane, and methane. This cargo of nitrogen with its 5 percent methane would be released into the atmosphere, and the ethane and methane mix would be sent with the *Phoebe* to Earth's moon as fuel, bringing in revenue for Aqua4. Max was not surprised that they didn't hear from the Eridanus, and the round trip was uneventful. The journey was now well understood and had become routine.

Fate had smiled on Max's expedition to mine Titan in that the celestial march of the planets had put Jupiter in near conjunction with Mars and Saturn during the years when the journeys to Titan were essential. The slingshot effect of Jupiter's immense gravitational field could therefore be used to best advantage, thus saving time and fuel. The full alignment would occur in June 2119, and the slingshot could be used for a few years beyond that. By that time Max wished there would be a normal, breathable atmosphere at something close to the one bar enjoyed on Earth.

Joe and Chris came back from the Tithonium site with mixed news. Yes, they thought there was water there, but they were as yet unsure how deep and what size the aquifer would be. Further investigation was necessary. Max was happy for them to spend whatever time was necessary to establish the viability of the site. If Tithonium was a viable aquifer, so much the better. It would make a more efficient source. Furthermore, it would be even better if the guys also found sweet water in the Louros Chasm, their doorstep. They had come to seek Max's blessing to drill deep and to organize the drilling equipment necessary. Max freely gave his approval, thanked them, and wished them the best of luck. They duly went about the business of organizing a deep drilling exercise.

Ann reminded him it was Marsia's birthday in a couple of days and suggested he take a break and give her some sort of treat. With Joe and Chris occupied and the *Ganymede* not due for another few days, he was happy to agree.

"What sort of treat did you have in mind?" he asked, somewhat embarrassed that he had failed to remember the approach of his daughter's birthday.

"How about an adventure trip to show her some of the planet? She doesn't get around much. Show her maybe one of the poles, the Valles Marineris, Olympus Mons. There is plenty to see. How about Washboard Plain, for example? We haven't been there for a while."

"Um, yes. We don't have time to visit all those places." He thought a moment. "How about we show her Olympus Mons and Washboard Plain? They are both west of here, so we would minimize traveling time."

"Fine. She will be happy wherever we go as long as you are with us. She misses you with your long working hours, you know."

Max felt a pang of guilt and resolved to try to spend more time with her.

"Fine. We'll do that then. Things are relatively quiet just now, so we can leave tomorrow. If we are going to Olympus, we are going to need a tug because the summit is in space. We'll also piggyback a pod as a runabout. I'll organize that if you can organize food and drink for, say, four days with a reserve of the same. We can make it a bit of an adventure for her."

"Wonderful! She doesn't realize it's her birthday yet. I haven't told her. She'll be delighted we are going on an adventure as a family."

"Fine. That's settled then. I will order a tug and a pod to be prepared with extra long-distance fuel tanks and oxygen for eight days. If you organize the food and drink, we will get them loaded overnight, and we'll leave at about 0800 in the morning."

"Great. I'll get to it now. Thanks, Max. I know she'll love it."

34

Overnight a tug and a pod were given a thorough service, and long-distance tanks were fitted and filled with liquid hydrogen and oxygen. The rig was ready fully provisioned as Max had requested, and it was waiting on the pad when the family came out from breakfast the next morning at 0730.

"Good morning, sir. All serviced and checked. Tanks fitted and fluids filled. Here is your preflight checklist," the senior engineer said to Max.

"Thanks, Martin. Good morning." Max took the proffered clipboard and carefully ran over the machines. Fairly new machines had been selected for him, so the list was short. He was briefed on some of the new features and extra capabilities.

Twenty minutes later they boarded and settled in for the three-thousand-kilometer flight to the top of the solar system's largest volcano. Taking off, they climbed vertically out of the Louros Chasma and set off on a heading of 300 degrees to take them to Olympus Mons.

By chance, the heading took them directly over the Tithonium drilling site, where Joe and Chris were setting up their borehole, and sure enough, at their altitude of five hundred meters, they could see people setting up the drilling derrick. Max resisted landing there to see the progress. He knew Ann would not approve. Marsia wouldn't care and may even be interested. Max mentally shrugged and carried on.

A further seven hundred kilometers, and Max announced that they were crossing the equator. Ahead to port and starboard, they could see the two volcanoes of Ascraeus Mons and their own Pavonis Mons another seven hundred kilometers ahead. Their direct course would take them midway between the two ancient volcanoes but asking Marsia if she wanted to see Pavonis, she enthusiastically said she did. Max duly changed course to fly over the dome.

Marsia had spent some time in the dome, running free of spacesuit and breathing equipment on the farmlands, and she had loved it. She had only really seen Pavonis from under the dome, so the opportunity to see it from the air appealed to her. Ann fully approved.

Max had been flying at a modest thousand meters, so they had to climb to fourteen thousand meters to fly over the summit. Once they were above the lip of the volcano, the Dome came into view.

"Look, Daddy. The dome! The dome!" She pointed excitedly as they cleared the summit.

There was no doubt the dome with its sheer size and beautiful symmetry was a spectacular sight compared with the often haphazard topography on Mars. Max slowed the craft to allow a good view of the dome and the surrounding walls of the crater.

Having taken in the sights of the dome, they set off for Olympus Mons. They planned to drop down to an altitude of five thousand meters to fly over the somewhat featureless highland region on the way to Olympus. Then they would approach about two thousand meters below the edge of the vast plinth on which the volcano stands.

As they flew over the plain Olympus, they had a picnic snack on the way with a variety of fresh fruits from the dome's orchards and kitchen gardens for Marisa's delight followed by milk and *Swiss chocolate!* The last item was a rare treat brought from Earth and procured by Ann. Marsia was ecstatic, and her excitement was further fueled by her sugar intake. The rest of the flight, she hugged her daddy's neck and chatted happily.

The approach to the plinth was the signal to start the climb to reach the summit at an altitude of twenty-seven kilometers, three times the height of Mount Everest. From the edge of the plinth, it was still 250 kilometers to the center on the volcano's crucible.

Forty minutes later after a hard climb to the summit with spectacular views of the flanks of the monster volcano, they flew over the lip of the crucible to look out across the bowl formed by the volcano's walls. Inside there was a main depression with three further depressions within it, each showing signs of repeated impact activity in the distant past. Two separate impact craters made up the features on the rim walls, breaking its symmetry. Max landed the craft on the top of the lip of the crater so they could look out over the vast bowl inside, and within a short walk, they could then look out over the Martian landscape on the outside. At this altitude they were well above most of the clouds, which were now a welcome—and increasing—feature of the planet's atmosphere. From this vantage point, they could see the newly formed lakes to the north and east in the lowlands, which was once the home of the Martian ocean.

They moved the tug into the crucible as evening approached, and they explored until darkness set in. Ann cooked a supper mainly centered around Marsia's favorite foods—boiled and baked haricots in spicy tomato sauce, potato chips, and chicken sausages followed by yogurt and honey with milk and fruit juice to drink. She ate every scrap and fell asleep in her bunk almost immediately.

Max and Ann quietly chatted and planned the next day's activities, finally turning in themselves at 1100.

The morning sunshine arrived on the mountain long before it came to the land below. They were effectively in space at the top of the volcano. The proximity of the horizon of the small planet and size of Olympus exaggerated this fact. Marsia was the first awake, and remembering it was her birthday, she was soon in high spirits. She jumped on her parents in their double bunk, full of questions, chatter, and general excitement. Max and Ann were soon fully awake, and all took turns in the little washroom cubicle. This was a shower, toilet, and basin formed in two plastic moldings, measuring just ninety by ninety centimeters.

Ann and Marsia squeezed in first. Max could hear Marsia's squeals of delight and Ann's laughter as they showered together. Max followed while the girls got dressed and Ann made breakfast. He joined them and found Marsia eating a huge breakfast of scrambled eggs on toast with ketchup, her favorite chicken sausages again, muesli with milk, and fruit juices. He raised one eyebrow. "Good appetite this morning, birthday girl?"

Marsia beamed while munching on a piece of sausage and nodded vigorously. Ann smiled indulgently.

Max was happy. Here he was with his beautiful wife and daughter on top of the highest mountain in the solar system, successfully forming a new planet for all of them to live. He counted his many blessings.

"Well, I'm pleased you are eating well, sweetie, because we have a longer journey today. It's more than 4,400 kilometers to Mommy and Daddy's special place. That's where we're going next."

"Will we arrive today?" she asked.

"Oh yes, we must arrive today on your birthday. You know that you have two birthdays? Because you were born at exactly midnight, your birthday is also tomorrow! I will make the ship go really fast, and we can get there for lunch today, okay?"

She thought about the logic for a moment,

wrinkled her nose, and grinned. "Lucky me. I like *two birthdayth*!" She had recently lost her two front teeth and consequently spoke with a soft lisp.

She nodded and grinned, and happily munching with cheeks full of scrambled egg and toast, she started humming a little "Happy Birthday" tune, swinging her legs dangling from her stool.

Max and Ann smiled at each other, and Max sat down to breakfast himself. Ann had prepared enough scrambled eggs and toast for them all, and as a surprise for Max, she had opened a can of Norway's finest herring rollmops. She knew this was a favorite of his. Because they were canned and preserved in vinegar, they traveled well.

All had a hearty breakfast before they then took off and set a heading of 269 degrees to take them to Washboard Plain. As promised, Max set a speed of a thousand kilometers per hour, easily achievable in the thin air, not to mention the fact that they were dropping altitude. As expected, they arrived in plenty of time for lunch. Having had a hearty breakfast, they only needed open salad sandwiches with fruit cake and milk for Marsia. Ann and Max finished with cheese and coffee.

That afternoon they cruised the area around Washboard Plain, going as far as Elysium Planitia, where they found the area composed of a strange web of ridges interspersed with flat areas as if formed by fairly fresh but rapid lava flows. They explored the strange double crater at the east end of the Washboard

Plain and again unsuccessfully tried to work out how they were formed. As evening was approaching, they decided to stay where they were, and so Ann made a party dinner for Marsia while she and Max played board games in the small cabin area.

The next morning they returned to continue exploring Elysium Planita and discovered the unnerving crater called Wafra, a hole about thirty kilometers across shaped like an inverted cone that was more than one thousand meters deep. It had steep sides dropping to a dark unseen floor of ten kilometers wide. Max wanted to take the tug down to look at the bottom, but Ann turned pale and flatly refused to allow him. He didn't argue. He knew that look. He would go some other time with Joe and Chris and check it out. Max was thinking of water. Anne was thinking about how the whole family was in that craft.

"That must have been a mean impact to have drilled a crater that deep," observed Max.

"Yes, I didn't like the look of those steep walls. They looked as if they would collapse anytime and bury anyone at the bottom." Ann shivered.

They left the crater and flew back to the plain. Max set the craft down close to the spot where they had stopped during their last visit. Max felt he had to explain to Ann where they were and why he had come back here. She agreed with his reasoning. She had long since forgiven him for the fright he had given her that day.

Max and Marsia went out to explore while Ann

prepared lunch. They explored the low dunes for a while. Then Max showed Marsia the large hole he and Joe had blown. He had been motivated to return to this spot as he was still intrigued by the hole and the fact there was an underground chamber below it. Last time they hadn't had time to explore it. He had no idea how big it was. He assumed it was a volcanic formation, but he was puzzled by the fact there was no volcano nearby to form lava tubes. Whatever it was, it may be useful for radiation shielding or a working area if it was big enough.

"Whath that hole?" Marsia asked. Max remembered with some embarrassment the occasion when he and Joe had blown the hole and how upset Ann had been.

"That's a hole Uncle Joe and Daddy made."

"Why d'you make the hole for?"

"Well, good question. We were digging this hole, and we hit rock. So we made an explosion and made the hole."

Marsia thought for a moment. "But why did you want to make the hole?"

Oh dear, like mother like daughter, Max thought. No chance of distracting his daughter either.

"Well, you see, this Washboard Plain is Mommy and Daddy's special place, and Daddy wanted to know if there was anything special in the ground. Like water or metals or chemicals that would be useful."

She thought about it and seemed satisfied that his answer made some sort of sense, so she nodded.

"Is lunch nearly ready?" the little eating machine inquired.

"Maybe. Let's go back and see."

They made their way back to the tug. Max was proud of his daughter's ability to focus on a subject and not allow herself to be distracted. *She's as sharp as Ann*, he thought proudly.

Having taken off their suits, they found Ann busy in the tiny kitchenette. Their arrival was expected. Ann had a meal ready, so they sat down to eat a birthday lunch party complete with party hats, streamers, and crackers with silly jokes. Ann had prepared a whole chicken with homegrown baked potatoes, green beans, and broccoli with delicious gravy. She had also made a cheesecake for dessert. That was a miracle from so small a cooking area. *She must have used every piece of cooking equipment*, Max thought. They opened a bottle of a beautiful fruity white wine to complete the celebration.

"Daddy thowed me the hole he and Uncle Joe made," Marsia informed her mother.

"Did he now?" Ann only had to look at Max to make him uncomfortable. "Did he say *why* he made the hole?"

"Yeth, he wath looking for water, metal, and chemicalth."

"Oh, I see. That's all right then." She avoided Max's gaze.

"Yeth." She thought a moment. "Mommy, can we go and explore down in the hole?"

Max nearly choked.

"Did Daddy say we were going to explore the hole?" Ann felt a twinge of her claustrophobia just thinking about it.

"No, but *I* want to. Pleath, Mommy. Ath a birthday treat. Pleeeath."

Ann knew she was beaten.

"All right, honey. I'll have to come to hold your hand in case you get frightened." She looked at Max, daring him to utter one word.

He didn't dare. He was proud of his daughter and relieved she showed no signs of her mother's phobia. He was more than happy with this turn of events. He had been wondering how to broach the delicate subject of going into the hole. It was a relatively small opening unlike the glass tube, for example. However, his daughter had done the groundwork for him.

All this in no way fooled Ann. She could see he was apparently not the instigator of this idea, but knowing him, she was sure that was his intention either now or later. It seemed that her daughter was either fearless or utterly trusted her dad, probably both. She would have to go with them. The thought of anything happening to them and leaving her the sole family survivor was too much to bear. She would have to go with them.

What was the matter with her anyway? She was not usually this nervous. Okay, she had some occasional claustrophobia if things were really dark and cramped, but she had no idea what was under the hole. So why the anxiety? She had a thought. Was she perhaps pregnant again? She remembered the havoc her hormones had played on her emotions when carrying Marsia. She must give herself a test as soon as they got back.

"When do you think is the best time to go?" she asked Max, realizing immediately it was a silly question. It was going to be dark down there whatever time of day.

Max perceived the torment played out on his love's face, and he gently took her hand. With the other, he cuddled Marsia, and then he said, "Marsia, Mommy doesn't like dangerous holes. They worry her. And it's also because she loves us and doesn't want anything bad to happen to you … or me. That makes her worried."

"But you will look after uth, and if Mommy cometh too, we can all look after each other!" She nodded to herself to confirm the logic of her thinking.

A teardrop escaped Ann's eye as she broke into laughter.

"*Of course we can!* Silly me. We'll all go together tomorrow morning. It will be a wonderful adventure." She discreetly brushed away the errant tear and smiled bravely.

Later as Marsia slept, Ann explained her irrational fears and her suspicion as to the cause.

"Oh, that would be wonderful if you were. I remember how upset you were last time. You remember? It was when Ganymede had just arrived," he noted.

'"How *can* I forget? It was horrible. I was a mess emotionally. You must have suffered too."

"I was concerned for you, yes, but you were the one really suffering."

They went to bed that night after they decided on a plan of action for the morning. Max recommended they take the pod since it was small and agile. He would take it out for a good test flight to ensure everything was in tip-top order before they committed to the hole. He would fly carefully and avoid any tricky maneuvers. Confident they would be reducing the risks as much as possible, Ann felt more at ease and went to sleep relieved and reassured.

CHAPTER
35

M ax was the first awake as the Sun cleared the horizon. He eased himself out of the bunk, showered, dressed, and made coffee. The activity woke Ann, and she joined him.

"I'm going out to give the pod that test flight. I'll be about forty-five minutes. Then I'll have something to eat. You and Marsia go ahead and have your breakfast."

"I'll wait until Her Ladyship wakes up. So you will probably be back, and we can breakfast together. It will be nicer. Fly carefully, and good luck."

"I will. Thanks." He kissed her forehead, suited up, and went to work.

He climbed onto the top of the tug, disconnected the umbilical, which kept the batteries charged and electronics updated, undid the fastenings, and gently placed the pod on the ground alongside the tug by using the manipulator arm. The tug's manipulator, being designed for moving large heavy containers made quick work of the lightweight pod.

Having inspected the outside, he climbed aboard and carefully ran through the preflight checks. Satisfied, he took the craft for a test flight. Martin, the chief engineer, had done a good job. All systems functioned perfectly, and the instruments and sensors were well calibrated. He performed various maneuvers—vertical ascent and descent, hover, flying backward and forward obliquely while ascending and descending. All worked perfectly under auto or manual control. Then he returned and set the craft down beside the tug. Marsia's nose was press to one of the viewports. She was laughing and waving. He returned her wave. Shedding his suit, he joined his family for breakfast. Marsia ran to him and threw her arms round his neck.

"Daddy, Daddy, we go and ecthplore the hole today?"

"Yes, if Mommy says so." Then mainly for Ann's benefit, he added, "The pod flew perfectly, so there are no worries there."

"We go then?" Marsia was forcing the pace.

Max looked at Ann. She smiled, letting him know she felt reassured by his test flight.

"Yes, we go," she agreed.

"A two-birthday adventure," Marsia declared happily and beamed with a huge smile.

They ate breakfast. Marsia once again surprising them with her appetite, she polished off oatmeal porridge with dried fruit, chicken, and salad in pita bread with hummus, two pancakes with honey, and a half liter of milk. Max had a similar meal and felt quite full. Ann omitted the pancakes but took coffee with Max.

Thus fed, they suited up and climbed aboard the pod.

Max patted Ann's knee.

"All good?"

"All good," she said and smiled. She had obviously come to terms with her misgivings overnight, feeling more confident in the bright morning sunshine.

Max took things slowly. The hole was only about a kilometer away, so there was no need to hurry. He kept the pod low at about twenty meters altitude and slowly moved across the low dunes to the site. The opening appeared. He brought the pod gently to a hover.

"Here we are. Are we all ready to explore?"

"Yeth, yeth!" Marsia immediately piped up from the dickey seat behind them.

Max looked at Ann, who squeezed his knee and smiled, but she kept her hand there as if she could guide the pod through his knee. He placed the pod directly over the hole, and it was clear to Ann there was plenty of room all round. Max knew this, having planned this operation since the day he and Joe had blown the hole. At the time he had measured the opening and knew a pod would enter easily. This was the reason they had brought a pod. Ann had suspected as much.

Max turned on all the lights, spot lamps, and the searchlights before entering the hole to minimize the sudden transition to darkness. He slowly descended.

Max knew there was a short period of being enclosed by the walls of the hole as the roof of the cavern was only about four meters thick. Then they were in the cavern. It seemed vast. The reading to the floor showed it to be forty-five meters below. They were now ten meters below the ceiling. The laser range finder showed the cavern to be eighteen kilometers wide by sixty-five kilometers long. There were readings indicating wide pillars of rock that stabilized the roof.

Marsia was agog. She was wide-eyed and silent, not missing a thing. Ann was similarly impressed by the size of the cavern. Keeping ten meters below the ceiling, Max slowly moved around, went to the nearest wall, and noted it to be fairly even and straight. They encountered one of the rock pillars and flew around past it. Then they encountered another about 150 meters away. Max turned his attention to the floor and noted there were lumps in a fairly regular pattern much like the dunes were on the plain above them. *Maybe the winds blow the sand through here too. Maybe there is an open end*, Max thought.

He decided to land and take a look around outside the pod. He slowly descended and chose to land the pod in a valley between the lumpy dunes. As they descended, the thrusters blew up a thick cloud of fine dust, which soon reduced visibility to about two meters. Thus, Max had to rely on his instruments to gauge his height above the floor. The pod landed with a bump. Max cut the thrusters immediately, and the pod's motors wound down to silence. The three occupants stared out at the dust cloud illuminated by the pod's lights.

As the fine dust slowly settled, the pod's lights were able to pierce the gloom into an ever-widening view of the vast cavern. At last they were able to see for a few hundred meters. It became clear they were looking out over regular serried ranks of similar shapes. They stared, puzzled, trying to comprehend what they were actually looking at. Ann stretched out her arm and took the joystick controlling the powerful searchlight. She swung the beam to one of the closer shapes. Their entry had blown away much of the accumulated dust from that area. She stared. Her face ran through a sequence of expressions—puzzlement, astonishment, wonder, realization, and ... nothing. With the realization of what she was looking at, her face drained of all color and letting out a low 'Ohhhhhh!'. Her brain, seeking to protect the unborn child she carried from stress, shut down her conscious mind. She fainted.

There was silence then. A long silence while Max was experiencing his own mixture of similar emotions.

Marsia had been keenly watching all this, and she tugged his tunic earnestly.

"Daddy, why'th Mommy thleeping? Wha'th thoth?" Ever curious, Marsia pointed at the looming shapes.

"Mommy's having a little nap. What do they look like to you, sweetie?" Max gently asked his daughter.

She wrinkled her nose, paused, smiled, and

finally announced in her soft slightly lisping speech, "Thpacethhipth, loth of duthty old thpacethipth." She giggled and said, "And thomeone thould clean them!"

END

About the Author

J ohn Ashcroft-Jones is an Architectural Consultant working internationally. He lists sailing, sub-aqua, two wheeled transport and photography among his interests. This book is the first of a trilogy.

Printed in the United States
By Bookmasters